i am you, you are me

Sabrina Dinucci

I Am You. You Are Me © 2023 by Sabrina Dinucci

All rights reserved. No part of this book may be reproduced or transmitted in any form or by any means, electronic or mechanical, including photocopying, recording, or by any information storage and retrieval system, without permission in writing from the publisher.
The characters and events portrayed in this book are fictitious. Any similarity to real persons, living or dead, or events is coincidental and not intended by the author.

Cover by Cynthia De Gregorio

ISBN 978-1-7387748-0-7

Gratitude and Blessings

There are so many people who have motivated and supported me through the years during this project. I want to share my gratitude with each and every one of you.

Readers, Clients & Followers—Thank you for opening your hearts to receive my soul story.

Vanessa—You continue to be my inspiration at a soul level. I love you always and forever.

Mom—It doesn't matter how long you have been gone; your light is forever present.

Shalom—The moment I read you one of the many drafts, you jumped into full beast mode. There were times when I didn't have the courage to go back and finish it. But you were a constant voice of encouragement, and for that, I will forever be grateful to you.

Nancy—You've been with this book from the very beginning. You've listened to countless versions without ever rolling your eyes. I thank you and appreciate your unwavering friendship.

Cynthia—How many times can you change a book cover? Thank you for your dedication to my book and your soulful insight.

Christina Strigas—Thank you for being my lighthouse in the finishing stages.

Dad & Felicia—my forever friends and (parents). Your unconditional love has been my constant.

ART OF LOVE

WHO AM I?

The mirror seems to know who I am
But do I know who I am?

My family seems to know who I am
But do I know who I am?

My friends seem to know who I am
But do I know who I am?

My lover seems to know who I am
But do I know who I am?

How can I ever find the other half of my soul
When I don't know who I am?

1

Rewind. Pause. Click. Done. Having just edited her YouTube video on "Discovering our God inside" for the umpteenth time, Sofia pushed back her swivel chair from the table. She twirled round and round, drinking in each lyric and vibrational wave pouring out of the speakers. After seven years of producing videos, she had morphed from daily motivations into exploring duality; our soul calling, divine symbolism, and the new energy. The content was controversial, but it propelled her to research further into this planet's "past, present, and future." She relied on her soul tribe here on earth for support and her higher self for guidance. Sofia was not for "everybody," but she was "something" for over 100K loyal subscribers.

Eyes shut, her mind drifted to her "happy place"—a cliffside home set atop a lush carpet of green; dotted with age-old trees. The aquamarine sea below spilled over to each side, with only the waves as her companion. Before she could dive deeper into her Neverland, the chair wheels snagged the silk threads in the hand-woven carpet she bought at a retreat in the mountainside of Medellin and, just like that, was jolted back into reality.

Drifting off into her thoughts had become a refuge since she remembered where she came from. A gentle knock at the door snapped her out of this momentary pause. The glare from the sun made it difficult to grasp who it was. She rolled the chair toward the street front and caught sight of wisps of blonde hair bobbing in the glass pane. Donned with cat-eye sunglasses, Emma rocked from side to side, waving her hand. She lost track of time and forgot that she was meeting the girls for coffee before heading to New York City for the weekend.

Sofia looked out the window and said, "Go ahead, and I'll meet you there."

Emma rolled her eyes and gently murmured, "Don't be too late, Sofia."

Fortunately, she had the foresight to pack her carry-on the night before. She cleared the notepads and pens from the table, stored all the video equipment in a drawer, and fluffed the throw pillows on the sofa. It was a habit picked up from her Italian family. *"You never know when someone is going to show up."*

Right before calling on her guides to cocoon her loft in a bubble of white light, she said goodbye to the crystal collection set atop her sacred altar. Passing the mirror by the door, she noticed a patch of gray hair right by her ear.

It serves me right to choose the ambiance of candles over proper lighting.

Typically, she would cover it up with dark brown henna, but the advantage of having wavy hair was just that. So she bent her head and tousled it up to hide the sneaky grays. She further inspected her face. Sofia had stopped wearing makeup when she did an exposé about all the toxins and inhumane ingredients in cosmetics and skin creams on the market. She remembered receiving a negative backlash, but it never weakened her stance. Sofia amassed so many loyal followers because she never backed down, no matter the fury.

Scurrying to her favorite café a few doors down, she passed Emma & Lola's Interior Design Studio. Although rushed, she still stopped to admire the mesmerizing window display with dark green foliage drooped over the antique gold frame. The vibrant peonies caught her eye, but even they couldn't deter her from the silhouette in the window. And when she turned to look, there was no one and nothing there. Sofia often sensed presences around her or flashes of light from the corner of her eye. She scanned the area again, composed herself, and made a beeline to the café.

Lola & Emma were sitting in their usual spot, the high table right by the window. Lola knocked on the window when she passed them, covertly pointing her finger to the door. Sofia could not distinguish what Lola was gesturing about between her friend's bright orange dress and the glow of the blinding sun. She only made sense of it as soon as she swung the door open and crashed right into someone, and as a result, she heard a loud clanking of ceramic hit the floor. Claps and cheers from her friends, the owner of the café, and the regular patrons, echoed out onto the street.

Amidst the warm welcome, the person she erroneously knocked off his feet yelled, "*Merde* (Shit). Watch where you're going!"

She recognized the voice. It was Jude, her longtime crush.

She didn't have time to apologize because he received a string of text messages that momentarily distracted him. For one split second, their eyes met, and a rush of heat engulfed her body. It seemed like he was going to say something to her, but his phone rang, and that was the end of that.

They were never officially introduced, even though they saw each other almost every day at the same time for the past few years. There was no time to scrutinize. She exchanged pleasantries with the staff, ordered her usual to-go, and rushed to the girls.

"We have no time for chit-chat," Lola said, getting up. "You're late. We have to leave now!"

Oh, Lola. As assertive as you try to be, you inherently are filled with too much 'love and light' to allude us.

Without further ado, Sofia grabbed her cappuccino with a double shot of espresso, and they were off to the city that never slept.

As they turned the corner, she again came face to face with Jude, who was still on the phone. His usually sea-green eyes were as dark as a forest. Gone was his usual cool, debonair composure. Furiously smoking a cigarette, he momentarily stopped talking when he saw her. He almost eked out a smile, but it was soon replaced with ire. He flicked his cigarette away and bellowed an endless dictionary of hateful words in English and French, consequently launching his phone against the side of the heritage building. Her higher self kicked in and advised her to walk away for now.

As Lola stood at the door ushering her friends into the fiery red vintage BMW, she instantly switched the mood from gloom to boom! Dressed in her tangerine dress, floral runners, extra-large gold hoops, and her signature silk scarf wrapped around her jet-black curls—she managed to divert Sofia's attention away from Jude. As they piled into the car, Emma diligently prepared the vehicle for travel: she lined up their top-of-the-line water bottles in the console, laid out the snacks she organized in collapsible containers, and ensured the wipes were handy.

As soon as they hit the road, they plunged into their love lives or lack thereof. Of course, the first topic of conversation was Jude. They were superb at diving deep into topics and analyzing every detail. Sofia had been single for way too many years. Every courtship had ended so dramatically, she made it a point to never attach herself to another man again.

Lola eyed her in the rear-view mirror. "I know how you feel about dating again," she said, "but I'm sure you felt that chemistry between the two of you. I mean, it's undeniable!"

Emma jumped in. "Right? When you bumped into him, the whole café gawked at you, not because it was funny—which it was—but because something happened, like a spark or glint of light. It was strange."

Sofia didn't believe in strange—that word was no longer part of her vocabulary. To avoid the conversation from ensuing, she cleverly veered the spotlight onto Lola, which she graciously accepted and regaled them with tales of her many trysts from her latest buying trips to Columbia, Bolivia, and Brazil. As the buyer, she often traveled to exotic locations. Sofia joined her on many of her expeditions. Still, the one to Peru they went on years ago was the beginning of Sofia's spiritual awakening. The power of the Incas and their magical history was too powerful to ignore. They reminisced about their Ayahuasca adventure deep into the Amazon jungle with the Shamanic healer who spoke neither English nor Spanish.

Meanwhile, clearly annoyed by their tale, Emma returned her gaze to the road and wallowed in self-pity. Lola caught Sofia's attention in the rear-view mirror and rolled her eyes. So once again, Sofia steered their train of thought to a memory that included Emma.

For the next hour or so, they reflected on why Emma was still single and why her quest to find the "one" always seemed to fail. Fail was a big word. They were all essentially in the same place—single and alone. Their journey into the dating scene took them deeper into the abyss of modern romance. While Lola and Emma chattered away, Sofia rested her eyes and returned to her "Happy Place." And Jude conveniently popped up in her thoughts. Ever since she could remember setting up this happy place—there always was a man's presence (never a clear image of one) and a boy.

As they inched closer to the city, a wave of nausea engulfed her. Out of nowhere, a stabbing pain sliced through her head. She breathed in deeply a few times and found her center. Perhaps this was a sign she needed to pay attention to. Regardless, she was there with an open mind and heart—ready for whatever New York City offered her.

2

Sofia was instantly struck by an overwhelming sense of familiarity even though she had never stayed in that hotel. Lola and Emma breezed right by her as she stumbled onto the neon-lit escalators, amusing the valet staff. It took all of thirty seconds before tripping off the escalators and bumping into a dapper man sporting a cashmere tweed blazer. With a folded newspaper in one hand and a Prada briefcase in the other, he turned his back and stoically glided across the room. All eyes on Sofia, the concierge disdainfully leered at her, as expected in the bustling City of New York. After veering off the path of "shoulds" and "rules," nothing fazed her anymore. Life became a steady stream of clichés as friends and family dwindled.

When they finally approached the desk in the "cool hunter" approved lobby, the uptight concierge took a second look at Sofia and her passport.

Grinning from ear to ear, he asked, "Are you Divine Sofia from YouTube?" He then went on for a few minutes, raving about her content. "I make a point to watch your videos as soon as they're posted. You're so brave to be airing that information. How do you navigate around censorship?"

Sofia shrugged and repeated the same reply she so often did with many of her subscribers. "I have become less mindful and more heart-centered with expressing myself. I'm sure you've noticed how differently the words resonate in your soul."

He nervously bobbed his head up and down, outright giddy. And at that moment, Sofia received the confirmation—humanity was clicking in. He confirmed their reservation at Tao later that evening.

Winking at her, he whispered, "I asked them to seat you by the Buddha."

"I guess there are some perks to being your friend," Lola teased.

Sofia felt compelled to look toward the escalator as the girls headed to the elevators. It felt like someone other than the concierge was staring at her. There was a huddle of girls clamoring around someone, snapping selfies and such. Everyone else seemed to be going about their business. She couldn't shake off that same negative feeling from earlier today. Instead of listening to her inner voice to pay attention, she pushed it aside and ignored it for the sake of the "girl's weekend."

The impressive lobby left them feeling less than impressed with their actual room. The room was literally a square box with wood-paneled walls resembling a cruise ship. Two mirrors on either end created the illusion of being more spacious than it was.

Lola and Sofia jumped on the beds while Emma rolled her eyes and promptly set up her little corner with bathroom and makeup essentials. She snapped, "You realize germs are all over that bedspread, right?"

They ignored her, as they often did. She finally made her way over to them but sat at the edge of the bed and just listened while they went through the weekend plans. There was a time when Emma was more carefree, but Sofia feared that time had hardened her. Perhaps it was because of her last relationship. Rodrigo was self-absorbed, never allowing her room to speak freely and openly. Even though Emma did finally muster up the courage to leave him, she was never the same again.

Lola grabbed Emma by the arm and pulled her down on the bed. "Emma! Wipe that frown off your face. How many times do we get time away from our clients? How many times do the three of us get to travel together?"

Finally, Emma eked out a smile. "You're right. I guess New York always makes me think of Rodrigo."

And there it was. "Okay, ladies," Sofia tried distracting her, "from now until the end of the weekend, no talk about boys, no men, period. Let's make it a girls' weekend. Deal?" They piled their hands one on the other and swore to liberate their minds from men just for the weekend.

3

They spent the entire nine-minute cab ride to the restaurant listening to Lola chat it up with the driver. She asked all the questions. He hardly listened, but that didn't stop her. It was a delight to watch her in her element and to observe Emma at her heels, apologizing to him for any missteps on Lola's part. Drivers in the countries Lola had visited always engaged with her. But Manhattan was a different story.

They arrived right on time. Of course, their table was not ready; it was part of their pretentious M.O. As the hostess guided them to the sardine-packed waiting area, it was easy to fall under the spell of the hard thumping and meditative beats coming from the DJ booth. Low leather benches lined the wall, but they opted for the bar. Lola took the lead, coiled her way around the pack of 'good-looking' people, and snagged them a stool. The night began with their usual; one gin martini semi-dirty with three olives for Lola, one gin and tonic for Emma, and one water with cucumber. Sofia stopped drinking after doing a segment on how alcohol lowered the vibration. It was not an easy transition. She was once the queen of late-night drinking but had turned the corner.

Only a few minutes in, two men dressed in head-to-toe designer-fitted suits wormed their way to their side of the bar. One of them apologetically leaned in between Lola and Emma, placing an order with the bartender. Lola couldn't help herself and began the first act of flirtation.

After what seemed like hours of waiting, they were finally seated at the table by the 16ft Buddha. Michael and Pedro joined them too.

"When in New York," Lola beamed.

As the ladies settled with their newfound friends, Sofia quietly took in the joyful Ascended Master, and then her higher self kicked in and urged her to go back to the bar. Meanwhile, the louder voice in her head—a.k.a. the ego—told her to stay put. So, she excused herself and headed back.

Crammed with people playing out their roles in the Matrix—it was a tough barrier to crack. She was about to turn around when she caught a glimpse of him. Jude was sitting at the far end of the bar. She pinched herself to see if she was making this all up in her mind, but it was as real as the pain she felt at that moment. And still, the pitter-pattering of her heart reverberated in her ear even after all the events of that morning. Then everything went blank, and all she heard was Lamb's ethereal and haunting voice flowing from the speakers—pulsating in her heart.

Sofia tried hard to turn away, but her feet felt cemented into the tiling. His eyes were fixated on the square ice cube he swirled round and round in his drink. The supple fabric of his jacket traced every muscle in his arm. He looked up at that moment, right at Sofia. When their eyes met, he seemed just as dumbfounded as she did. She only snapped out of this mesmerizing stupor when realizing she was standing in someone's way. When the patron raised his voice for her to move, Jude jumped in and expertly navigated the situation. When he intertwined his fingers into hers, shyness and her seventeen-year-old self made an appearance. Heat rushed to her head, and she felt faint. When he tugged at her arm to weasel them out of the pack, his movement caught her off guard, and she half-stumbled into his chest. Having him so close feverishly aroused her.

He chuckled and whispered in her ear, "You seem to misstep every time you see me."

Inches apart, he smelled of Cognac and soap. Sofia could barely look at him. But she was not alone in this. His tightened grip weakened as droplets of sweat settled into their palms. She climbed back down to earth and stepped back.

He leaned in toward her and asked, "I was just about to go outside for a walk. Would you like to join me?"

His face turned multiple shades of red. It was a side of him she had never witnessed back in Montreal. He always seemed so stoic and cool-headed. Even this morning's incident was out of nature for him. Meanwhile, the butterflies in her stomach performed front flips, back flips, and handstands, if that was even possible. She hadn't eaten yet, but this was an opportunity she couldn't pass up. She calmly nodded. He released the grip only once he started to walk away from her.

"*Donnez-moi une seconde* (Gimme a sec)," he said. "I need to tell my friends."

Sofia did the same. She was neither here nor there as she headed back to the table. Her mind was a blur. She kneeled between Lola's and Emma's seats.

Both pairs of eyes were on her. She said, "Sooooo, about that deal we made earlier?"

Jude then appeared behind Sofia. Both Lola and Emma's heads lifted upward.

Lola squeezed her shoulder and whispered, "Hello. We are not holding up our end either!" She pointed to Michael and Pedro. "Do what you need to do, girlfriend. Work your magic."

Emma winked at her and politely nodded at Jude. She then grabbed a napkin from the table, nestled some appetizers in the base of the fabric, and handed it to her friend. When Sofia got to her feet, Jude gently laid his hand on her shoulder. It took only one simple gesture for her butterflies to come back.

They snaked their way through the crowd and out onto the pavement. He quickly pulled out a cigarette, offering her one. She shook her head.

As he lit up, he apologetically said, "I'm trying to stop. Really, I am."

She mused he felt the need to explain himself to her. And then she left the earth plane for a few seconds to imagine a world with him and her, as a couple. Going off into fantasyland while wearing heels was not the wisest decision.

Jude swept her up in his arms. "Let me hold you close to me in case you stumble again."

Awkward moment number three of the day. His face was dangerously close to hers. His scent inundated her senses like a meditative walk in the forest. It was the perfect moment for a kiss, but nothing happened because he received a slew of notifications on his phone. He walked away in a somewhat agitated state.

In the meantime, Sofia unfolded the napkin and feasted on the spring rolls. She momentarily lost sight of Jude but could soon follow the sound of his voice. She finally spotted him. He was at a fair distance, and he was texting.

He was leaning against the tree with one foot resting on the trunk. His white shirt was half tucked into his navy blue fitted pants, and his charcoal jacket was neatly draped over his shoulder. Even as he frantically texted with the cigarette dangling from his lips, he looked elegant and poised.

Sofia quickly snapped out of her daze when he whipped his head around and caught sight of her. Her butterflies came back in full force, but she remained steadfast in her line of vision. For a moment, he paused and boyishly smiled at her.

Then she heard his voice in her head. *She's so beautiful.*

She looked to her right and then to the left, but no one was there. And when she looked back, he was rapidly punching in words.

Sofia pondered. I *am seriously losing my mind.*

It was common for her to feel "crazy" since she began this awakening journey. She twisted her body and looked toward the seedy bar nearby to deviate from what had happened.

Having recently learned that the 440 Hz frequency in mainstream music was used to program avid listeners, she switched her preferences to 432Hz and 528Hz frequency music. It was a hard lesson to digest since music was her salvation, and she spent most of her life listening to all genres. And the heavy metal sounds thundering out of the bar were no exception. Her mind drifted slowly into Neverland until an electrical surge zipped through her body. Jude had placed his hand at the base of her back. It seemed he experienced a similar jolt, witnessing him flick back his hand.

And then she fell into his mind again. *Why does this only happen with her?*

Sofia pivoted her head to see who he was talking to. No one. She remained silent, not revealing her new spiritual gift, hoping not to scare him off.

They crossed the congested street filled with marathon-paced locals, slow ambling tourists, and an army of honking cars and ended up at Columbus Circle. That one entrance to Central Park was a splendor with its roundabout of low wooden benches set against a backdrop of cascading water fountains. Skyscrapers, heritage buildings, neon-lit signs, and a shiny silver globe lined the circle, creating a 3D postcard feel. He pulled out another cigarette to mask the awkward silence and fidgeted with the cuffs of his shirt. Sofia was instantly drawn to his perfectly manicured fingers; each inked with symbolic tattoos.

Why hadn't I noticed the symbology before?

The designs were the exact ones she had been discussing in her recent video segments. A shrill alarm sound snapped her out of the dream state. It was coming from inside his jacket.

He muttered, "*Putain* (Fuck)," and speedily shut off his phone.

His eyes turned black as coal, his posture changed, and his head slyly rotated from right to left. He inadvertently yanked Sofia behind him in a protective stance. He masked the discomfort by swiveling around and taking her in his arms. His heart pounding a million miles a minute, he held on to her for a few seconds.

Again, she picked up on the conversation in his head. *This girl is going to leave me before I even ask her out. Why does Gabrielle have to get in the way of everything?* Luckily, Sofia's face was buried against his chest; he didn't have to see her expression turn from elation to worry in a matter of seconds.

Thoughts swirled in her mind. *Who is Gabrielle? Should I be worried? He's going to ask me out, like, on a date?* Her seventeen-year-old self was alive and well.

A few feet away from them was a gypsy traveling band plucking away at their guitars. Many years back, she had visited a medium and was told that she had lived a life as a gypsy back in the early 1500s. She was determined to enjoy this weekend like the free-spirited gypsy she once was—no drama whatsoever. The first step was not allowing a mystery girl to ruin her night.

Stepping back from Jude's grip, she entwined her fingers into his and headed toward the music. Jude's hand molded into hers. The connection she felt with him was too familiar. A circle formed around the lively band. Jude made his way in front of her, moved stealthily past the crowd, and surprised her by twirling her in his arms. He pressed his body against her and moved to the rhythm. The band members encouraged them by crying out in their native tongue. Jude took command of the pavement and her body. His hand traveled down the length of her dress. It was just Sofia and Jude and the tongue-clacking, hand-clapping, and clicking of wooden spoons from the trio of musicians. Their chemistry was undeniable as their bodies curved into each other with every step. Her breath and heartbeat synchronized with his every touch. Once the music and singing ended, they slinked away from the thunderous claps and cheers from the crowd.

Jude pirouetted Sofia around and around as they made their way along the iron gates of the park. The moment was jovial. She tried hard not to fall for him because she often did that in her past. This was a new leaf for her; she was determined not to return to that old self.

They reveled in each other's company for a little longer until silence surrounded them. They stood a few feet apart, hand in hand, staring into each other's eyes. A tingling sensation coursed through her body. She usually felt the same goosebumps when her spirit guides were around her. She couldn't seem to unlink her hands from his.

There's something different about him. And then she asked her higher self, *Am I right? Yes*, was the answer.

Jude lovingly gazed into her eyes and asked, "Shall we head to my hotel?"

Sofia arched her eyebrow and laughed. "Well, you work fast."

He blushed. "N-no…"

"No?" She smiled.

He chuckled but got serious, "Yes, but no…."

Sofia placed a finger on his lips. "I'm just teasing you."

His shoulders relaxed, and when his lips puckered and kissed her finger, she melted instantly.

He composed himself and asked again, "Would you like to join me for a drink at my hotel rooftop bar?"

Sofia curved her lips into another smile and obliged.

****

After a few short blocks, the taxi came to a stop.

Puzzled, she stepped out of the cab. "Is this where you're staying?"

He nodded. "Why?"

"Me too." *What a coincidence.*

His eyes widened, and he instantly smiled from ear to ear.

Let's just call it destiny for now.

She stepped onto the escalator, firmly gripping the handrail. Once they made it safely to the lobby area, Jude stepped away to talk to the night concierge. The lobby was bustling with über-stylish people. As Sofia eyed everyone and everything, she fell upon Jude's gaze. His eyes burrowed into hers. And her legs turned into liquid jelly. Feeling the earth move under her feet, a hearty pat on the back distracted her.

"Excuse me." When Sofia twisted her head, her eyes fell upon a striking girl—her brass-colored skin matched her brassy personality. She peered into Sofia's eyes and raised her voice, "I know you!" She wildly talked to herself until she exclaimed, "Yes, yes! You're the girl with the channel about everything-spirituality!"

The girl didn't give any room for response—she dove into one of Sofia's latest videos. "I couldn't believe my ears when you talked about how the masculine energy was rising. What do you mean, girl? What happened to the divine feminine ruling the world?" She rotated her head from left to right, seeking approval from the passersby.

"If I may," Sofia capitalized on the momentary pause.

"Please do!" She eyed Sofia—one hand on her hip, the other flailing.

"Every human is an incarnation of both divine feminine and masculine energies. If we came into this lifetime as feminine, our higher self is masculine. We are not one or the other; we are both—it's just another distraction for us to live in separation."

Before she could continue, Sofia felt an intense energy swirl around her. Jude nudged her and teased, "Please go on. This sounds most riveting."

Enamored with the Divine Masculine before her—eyelashes fluttering like dragonfly wings—the girl extended her hand to Jude and coquettishly introduced herself, "My name is Trinity."

Jude politely shook her hand. She wasn't done swooning over him. "Mmm…mmm…mm, you are fine!" She raked her bejeweled fingernail along his arm. "Are you together? Because if not…."

The girl's candor caught Sofia off guard. She could feel her cheeks heating, her palms sweating.

Jude was quick to reply, "Not yet."

Who knew that two words could cause an eruption of heat to blaze throughout Sofia's body? While she regained her composure, Trinity didn't care for his answer and unwaveringly flirted with him.

Jude was courteous at first. But then, Sofia heard the thunderous rumblings in his mind. She glanced over at him and noticed a shadowy energy enshroud him. The gentle, light-hearted man she had spent the past few hours with switched into what she always imagined black tourmaline to look like in human form.

He sighed heavily and lashed out, "What happened to the Divine Feminine ruling the world? It didn't take much time to give your power away to the masculine." He barely looked at Sofia, "*Je me casse* (I'm out of here)." And he stormed off.

Unfazed by his ire, Trinity still made lewd comments about his appearance. While she went on, Sofia fell into his mind.

C'est quoi ce bordel? (What the hell). *I'm tired of all these games. C'est tellement chiante* (It's so annoying). *Why can't I enjoy one night without staving off the vultures? One night without drama is all I ask.*

The goings-on in his mind intrigued Sofia. She didn't have time to explore further as she had to do damage control by semi-apologizing for Jude's warranted reply. Then she tactfully ended the discussion by leaving Trinity with one last insight. "Remember, your divine masculine energy is rising within you. The masculine needs us more than ever. It's our turn to help them rise."

Trinity regaled Sofia with a warm hug. "Thank you, girrrl." She pointed at Jude. "Oh, and…if you put him on your channel, you'd certainly get more views."

Is this girl for real?

Then, Trinity audaciously waved at Jude, clicking her heels and sashaying towards the bar. As Sofia watched the sassy girl walk away, secretly, she admired her spunk and forthrightness.

When Sofia turned back to look at Jude, he was nowhere to be found. She quieted her mind and tried to listen in—perhaps, she could telepathically find him. Success. He was smoking in the courtyard adjacent to the lobby. She took the time to observe him—his movements were manic, shifting from frantic to mellow in seconds—almost Gemini-like.

The moment his eyes landed on her, a swoosh of energy enveloped her. He continued to stare at Sofia, rendering her muddle-headed. *Why does he make me feel so flustered? Where is that Sofia-spunk that lures even the unsuspecting?*

Jude made his way back to her. He bent his head and whispered in her ear, "Are you ready to continue our night together..."—and rested his lips on her earlobe— "without drama?"

She would be lying if his closeness didn't render her speechless. As they walked to the elevator, neither brought up the encounter nor his response. He changed the subject altogether, telling her that the concierge warned him that the rooftop bar might close early due to rain.

It seemed like no one else cared much for the weather forecast, as the place was jam-packed. As they waited for a seat, Sofia couldn't help but notice, at the corner of her eye, a group of slim model-type girls waving at Jude.

It didn't matter how in tune she was with the Universe; Sofia's pangs of jealousy were still alive and well—first Trinity, then these Goddesses. *The tests are never-ending, it seems.* They magnified when the hostess made a beeline toward Jude—turning a blind eye to Sofia; she guided them to a table.

They passed a party of young elitists decked out in designer labels, eating and drinking the best of the best. Their boisterous nature was off-putting in the dreamy setting. And when one of the girls shouted, "Hey, Jude."

He smirked and whispered to Sofia, "Family friend. I know her father." He nodded and tugged on Sofia's arm to move quicker. He pointed to a more intimate nook at the far end, away from the herd. The hostess snapped her fingers at the busboy to clear the table.

As soon as they settled on the wrought iron framed couch directly facing the skyline, Jude instructed the hostess, "Send us a server, please." She fervently obliged. In less than a few seconds, a server appeared.

Apparently, it was a rule that they all had to flirt with him. The waitress bent over, exposing her very ample bosom. He rolled his eyes at her.

"I'll have an old-fashioned with Elijah Craig Small Batch" He turned to Sofia. "And you?"

She ordered still water with lemon and mint. When the waitress rolled her eyes at Sofia, Jude stepped in."You have a problem with that?"

The server immediately excused herself. Jude then ordered veggies, dips, artisanal bread, cheeses, and fig treats as if he knew the menu by heart.

What is it with these women fawning over him and fearing him at the same time?

Sofia took in the galaxy of neon lights. In the quest to quiet her mind, she lowered her eyelids and attempted to drift off to her "happy place" but was soon brought back down with the feathering of his fingertips along the palm of her hand. She couldn't help but laugh inwardly at her preposterous giddiness.

She opened her eyes only to fall on Jude's intent gaze.

"You were good with Trinity. It speaks volumes about how your parents raised you. My mother was not a good role model."

By the way Jude spoke, Sofia learned more about him than she knew about her last boyfriend of seven years. Silence ensued for a few minutes as they stared into the bright lights. The stillness was a comfortable one.

Sofia asked, "So, what brings you to New York?"

"I can ask the same of you. If I didn't know better, I could think you were stalking me."

Sofia wasn't sure if he was joking because he seemed too serious about it. "Why are you here in the city?"

"I'm here for work."

And that was that. For a man of few words, he was most expressive. Or she was most intuitive and picked up on his nuances.

When the food arrived, they devoured the charcuterie board. Usually, Sofia would not be so bold to ravenously eat in front of a "stranger." But since her awakening, she had cared less and less about what people thought of her. And it seemed Jude was on the same wavelength. When they finally finished eating, they chuckled at their master clean-up of the wooden board.

When the server returned to clean up the plates, she said, "Well, you have a ravenous appetite," and gave him a wink like a sly kitten.

Jude fake-smiled and rolled his eyes.

Most men would welcome all this flirtation. Hmmm…why the distaste? Where are the girls when I need them?

A prolonged silence followed.

Jude said, "I'm also here searching for some rare books for my dad." He paused. "I know a book dealer in lower Manhattan that may have some interesting finds. And I was wondering…"

Before he could continue, his phone rang. He mumbled something under his breath and quickly shut it off. It rang again. Again. And again. At that point, he jumped to his feet, apologized to her, and ran to the other end of the rooftop. Her higher self reassured her that all was well and she had nothing to worry about. Sofia listened.

It took years before she even believed her inner voice was always right. Most humans never really listened to their inner knowing. She recorded a three-part series just on that. It hit millions of views within the week. It was a topic that many loved to talk about, but they rarely genuinely believed they held such power. Pulling out her phone to type in more ideas for the next episodes, her higher self appeared, advising her to sit still and enjoy the open air. Her higher self was the only voice that had dominion over her.

Sofia nestled her back into the pillow and attempted to clear the noise around her. But Trinity popped up in her mind. *What lesson is she bringing up for me? Or perhaps, it's a trigger that needs addressing.*

Just like that, butterflies began to flutter when she felt Jude's fingers intertwined into hers; she felt the strength of his grip and the softness of his skin. He apologized again. His demeanor differed slightly, but she chose not to delve into it. She had made a mistake in the past, trying to fix other people's problems. She may have been a powerful being of light in a human body, but she was still living in the Matrix.

He fidgeted in his seat before opening up. "My life is complicated right now."

"Are you already breaking up with me?" she jokingly blurted out.

Jude grinned from ear to ear. He angled his body to face her and reached over to hold her hands. He slyly whispered, "Not yet."

Sofia's butterflies intensified.

His words chimed in her mind: *Why do I want to tell her my whole story? It's like she has a magic spell on me. I need to tread slowly.*

He broke the silence. "I am someone who believes in signs and synchronicities. There is no such thing as coincidence. Everything is written in the stars. I believe you are on the same page as me. So the fact that we met each other here in New York City means a great deal to me."

He stretched his hand over Sofia's head and threaded his quivering fingers through her mane. He wasn't done conveying his feelings to her. "I have a confession to make."

Another long pause.

I can't do it. I don't want to bring her into this mess; who knows if she's to be trusted, even though a little part of me knows she isn't like everyone else.

Sofia was now half-enjoying her newfound gift. *What secrets did Jude have that he was so afraid to share with me?* Nothing like adding a little insecurity to the mix. Yet, she still got the go-ahead from her higher self—at least that.

Another moment of stillness set upon them until they were once again interrupted by a string of texts and three consecutive phone calls. Jude shut down the phone and swore under his breath. "*Putain* (Fuck)." He slipped it back into his jacket pocket.

What's with all these calls and texts that anger him so much?

They returned to staring out into the night. She got lost in the moment, oblivious to the chatter around her. People were coming and going. It almost felt like she was in a movie, but everyone else was on fast-forward, and they were on play. When their eyes met, the chemistry was undeniable. Without delay, he leaned forward, all signs of anger completely gone, and ready to make his first move, but before she could respond, the sky cracked open, and the ice-cold rain poured down on them. They quickly scooted off the precious white couches and sheltered under the billowing canopy at the other end of the rooftop terrace. Pinning her up against the brick wall, Sofia felt his heart beating as loud as thunder. The moment their lips met, a sweet aroma of mint and Bourbon fanned her lips. His warm breath caressed her as he tenderly but eagerly kissed her. He kissed her lips. He kissed her cheeks. He kissed her jawline. She had never felt this with anyone else and wondered if he thought the same.

He stretched his arm into the rain and asked, "Are you ready to run for it?" As they surveyed the area, practically no one left except for the drunken lingerers and the servers waiting on them. They squeezed their way through the beautiful people to get to the elevator.

All the New York socialites seemed to be in the hotel's lobby. They were spilling out of both bars on the main floor. Jude caught Sofia mid-eye-roll and squeezed her hand. He touched her shoulder and led her to a private area beside the concierge's desk. They passed guests sitting in chairs carved from logs. Jude seemed to know where he was going as they journeyed around two oversized plastic palm trees and tropical flowers to a rattan day bed tucked away into a neon pink-lighted nook overflowing with pillows. "I discovered this area the last time I came here," he said. "I make sure to reserve it whenever I stay here. It's a great place to hide from others."

Sofia lounged against one end and he the other. The silence was deafening but also comforting in a we've-been-together-for-years kind of way.

He pulled out a notebook adorned with a gilt-edged dragon motif.

"I have the same book," she said.

"I know." He smiled. "I saw it on one of your videos and rushed to get it."

Why am I feeling giddy about him watching my videos? Snap out of it, Sofia. I can be such a teenage girl sometimes.

He then nonchalantly lifted his shirt, exposing his taut chest, and pointed to a dragon tattoo on the side of his torso.

She was speechless, first at the sight of his very fit body and secondly at the tattoo. She twisted her body, lifted her waves of hair, and awkwardly pointed to the phoenix tattooed at the back of her neck.

He gathered Sofia's hair away from her hands and twirled it around his hand. He then scrutinized her tattoo. As his fingertips traced the lines of the artwork, the sizzling energy was non-stop.

"You know that in Feng Shui," he whispered, "the dragon and the phoenix are considered the perfect couple."

She felt the phoenix mobilizing to rise. He went on to say, "There's a Chinese saying that says, 'When the dragon soars and the phoenix dances, the people will enjoy happiness for years, bringing peace and tranquility to all under heaven.' Did you know this?" She shook her head. His fingers now traveled along the nape of her neck, up through her hair. A spine-tingling sensation ripped through her body.

He let go of her hair in one fell swoop, propelling Sofia to turn and face him. When their eyes locked, the shyness was swiftly set aside when Jude dove into his questions. It didn't take long to distract herself from the "perfect couple" declaration as they exchanged views on the illusion playing out there and the "ancient-future" they came from.

At one point, she heard him say, *Why did I wait so long to talk to her? I've let my hang-ups come in the way for too long. She's everything I want in a woman.*

She couldn't help but smile timidly.

Jude eyed her and asked, "Why are you smiling? Why are your cheeks turning red?"

Knowing she was not a very good liar, she distracted him by scrutinizing the tattoos on his fingers. He welcomed her touch. "Did you get them after watching my segment?"

"No. I got them before."

The moment their fingers met, another surge of electricity traveled through her arm, and she let go.

"Did you feel that?"

"Darn right, I did," he said. "Okay, let's try it again, but slowly."

He enclosed Sofia's hands in his and glided closer to her. She felt more than electricity now—she felt overheated too.

"Do you know the symbolic significance of each tattoo?"

He shook his head.

"How did you discover them?"

"I dreamed about them," he replied.

Sofia couldn't believe her ears. He dreamed them, and she got them in a download.

She added, "You know, the first thing I'll do when we get back is to do more research."

He squeezed her hand. "Not alone, you won't."

Her heart swelled with bliss. *Perfectly good reason to see him again!*

They touched on their personal lives.

Jude opened up about his life. "I was born in Paris." He laughed, "My accent is a dead giveaway."

And a sexy one at that.

He continued, "My father and younger brother still live in Paris. They are the only reason I miss my city." He pointed to his phone. "Thank God for FaceTime!"

Sofia's curiosity kicked in. "And your mother?"

He lowered his gaze and mumbled, "Oh, yeah. She lives in Saint-Jean-Cap-Ferrat." His energy dipped when he spoke about her.

Sofia's higher self chimed in. *Leave it be for now. He will divulge more when he's ready.*

She eked in another question. "Why Montreal?"

His fingers tightly coiled into Sofia's. "I came to Montreal because life was a little hectic back home." He fell silent. He then cleverly veered the topic away from him and onto her. "And you? What's your story?"

Sofia regaled him with funny anecdotes about her Italian family. Then she got serious. "When my mom died at seventeen, life changed for me."

He instinctually wrapped his arms around her and whispered, "That must have been awful. I'm sorry, Sofia."

She gladly remained in his arms and continued, "My dad remarried and soon after moved to Italy." Jude stroked her hair as she talked. "My brother met his Kiwi wife in university, and they moved to her homeland, New Zealand. They now have four beautiful children."

The air was thick with reverie as they lay in the nook's stillness.

Jude broke the silence. "Interesting that both of our families live abroad. I could only assume that Lola and Emma are what Etienne is for me in Montreal."

Together in unison, they said, "Family."

He curved his lips into a broad smile and fluttered his fingers through her hair. "Just when I lost hope in humanity, you come into my life."

As she leaned in to kiss him, they saw the plastic leaves ruffling.

Jude's body language quickly changed. He sprung forward, jumping to his feet. His movements were erratic. He motioned her to stay put and investigated between the "bushes." The mood altered in a matter of seconds. The culprit was a handsome man with olive skin, dark chocolate disheveled hair, and shiny hazel eyes peeking his head between the trees.

"*Wesh* (Waz up)," said the stranger amicably.

"Etienne," Jude admonished, "you know better than to sneak up on me like that."

Etienne smirked and loosely put his hands in the air. He looked at Sofia and then at Jude, and back at her again.

Etienne stepped over the plastic trees, plopped right next to her, and said, "So, you are the elusive Sofia."

Jude shook his head and apologized for his friend. He then told them he was walking away for a few minutes.

Etienne shamelessly asked, "Has Jude mentioned me yet?"

Sofia giggled at his audacity. "Briefly."

Perplexed, he grunted. "Well, I'm Jude's best friend. We've known each other since we were teenagers." Etienne sheepishly grinned. "Wherever he goes, I go. So, if you guys pursue this, I will become your best friend, too!"

I hope I'm not blushing too hard at the mere prospect of pursuing this with Jude.

He cocked his head to the side and gave her a once-over. "You're nothing like the girls he's been with in the past."

Sofia's interest peaked. "Do tell."

He said, "Well, for one thing, you have a shape to your body."

Sofia of the past would have been irked by that comment. But, the Sofia of the present rather appreciated it. She dealt with body image issues her whole life because she never looked like the models on the cover of all the fashion magazines. When she came into her knowing that she was, in fact, a light being temporarily residing in a physical vessel that she chose, she fell in love with herself all over again.

Meanwhile, Etienne hadn't stopped talking—going on about the differences between Paris and New York City and Montreal. His demeanor was nothing like Jude's. He was more vibrant and extroverted and a delight to listen to. He reminded her of the male version of Lola.

Jude returned with bottled water and snacks to tide them over into the night. Etienne's smirk swiftly turned into a smile when Jude revealed a mini bottle of champagne from his ticket pocket and handed it to his best friend.

"*Tu gères,* frérot (You slay, bro)," Etienne swooned as he slipped it into his jacket.

"Okay, you can be on your way now." Jude shooed him away.

"But, I was just…"

Jude didn't have to say a word. Etienne understood he wanted to spend alone time with Sofia.

Etienne kissed her on both cheeks and said, "We will have plenty of time to catch up. I'll see you tomorrow, right?" He looked over at Jude and repeated, "Right?"

Jude lovingly pushed him away. "Go!"

Etienne winked and waved at both of them, and he was off.

Sofia didn't realize how late it was until she received a text from Emma asking her where she was. It was 1:26 a.m. *Have we been talking that long?*

She showed Jude the time, and he asked, "Are you tired?"

She shook her head, and he went on to talk about Etienne. "He's like a brother to me. His parents live in Dubai most of the time. They only return to Paris for business." Jude rolled his eyes."He was so often left alone that my dad eventually welcomed him into our home as one of his own."

"So, in essence, you have two brothers."

"Yes. That seems about right. Etienne has my back. And when things get crazy, he's always there for me."

****

The sound of voices and the high-pitched clinking of wheels rolling on the marble floors woke Sofia up. It took her a few seconds to decipher her whereabouts. She twisted her head to the right and noticed she had fallen asleep in Jude's arms. Once again, reverting to her seventeen-year-old self, she turned her head back toward the tropical scenery and immediately checked in with her higher self. Amidst the millions of questions filling her mind, she felt his fingers lightly caress her arm. A sense of calm befell her while she waited for his next move. He seemed content lying there beside her.

I think I'm falling for her. How will I manage all the crazy in my life? It was time she got used to erratically hearing his thoughts.

Sofia impulsively answered the question aloud.

He inched closer to her and whispered, "Were you talking to me?"

She shook her head. She learned early in life how her instinctive responses made many uncomfortable; "they" often criticized her for being "too honest." Lying to "keep the peace" actually dishonored the soul. And yet, Sofia still came up with a white lie, knowing full well she would have to pay the price with a hard lesson or two.

Getting up, she ironed her dress with the palms of her hands and looked past the trees for any semblance of a mirror, but to no avail.

He propped himself against the nook's wall and softly said, "You look beautiful."

Her cheeks flamed, but still, she mustered up the courage to face him.

When her eyes rested on his, she wondered, *Does he hear my thoughts, too?*

And then suddenly, a wave of golden light shimmered between them. The energy veiled all around them. Before Sofia could make sense of it, his phone rang. He shut it off. Then a parade of notifications chimed in. He leaped out of the nook to deal with whatever that was.

Shortly thereafter, they made their way out of the alcove and back to reality.

With a sparkle in his eyes, he clutched her hands. "Do you want to spend the day together—just the two of us?"

Her heart skipped a beat, and she blurted out, "Yes. I would love to." She immediately recanted, saying, "But I'm here with my friends, so I should check with them first."

"Let's meet at the restaurant in the lobby." He insisted.

4

A half-dressed and mascara-smudged Lola lay across the bed—the sheets rumpled in pockets of waves, covering only parts of her body. A low whistling sound melodically streamed out of her mouth.

Meanwhile, Emma already had her bed made: sheets and blanket tucked in on all sides. She was sitting upright on her bed, scrolling through her phone.

She waved her hand and whispered, "Come, come. I want to hear everything."

Sofia offered a brief rundown of the night but expertly maneuvered the conversation to their night. She wanted to keep her night with Jude untainted before foraging into their usual analysis.

Emma went on to recount their bar-hopping night with Michael and Pedro.

She pointed at Lola. "As you can see, we had a lot of fun."

She continued that the plan was to meet up with them today. "We assumed you would spend the day with Jude. But, if that's not the case, we can cancel since it's our girl's weekend."

Sofia was on the fence. A huge part of her wanted to spend the day with Jude, but another didn't want to drop her life for a man. She wouldn't want to repeat the past over again. Emma seemed delighted to spend time with Pedro, in particular. She always had a thing for Latin men. She was definitely not twisting Sofia's arm to spend it with Jude, so she agreed as long as they had dinner together.

Sofia jumped into the shower. Most of her visions came to her when immersed in water, but this morning her mind buzzed with snapshots of the night before. The butterflies were back. She thanked the water as usual but jumped out as quickly as she jumped in. Even as she rummaged through her clothes, Lola was comatose.

She told Emma she would join Jude for breakfast. "Did you want to come? It doesn't seem like Lola will make it in time."

"You're probably right," Emma said, "but I need to wake her up. You go on ahead. We'll catch up with you soon."

Sofia made her way to the breakfast area but was held back by her biggest fan, and while he went on and on with pleasantries, she felt an energetic wave come from across the room. She heard the concierge's jabbering, but the beam of light leaning against the column dominated her vision. Wearing dark jeans, the latest Adidas runners, and a golden yellow T-shirt complementing his olive complexion, Jude made his way to her.

When he laced his fingers into hers, the concierge stopped mid-speech and pointed at Jude and then at Sofia. "Are you together?" He blushed and screeched, "Of course you are. You make such a gorgeous couple." He then turned to Sofia. "Okay, you will tell me later what you need, sweetheart." He stepped away, clapping his hands, entranced in his own little world.

The breakfast area resembled a hip Ivy League cafeteria. Elaborate, majestic chairs in chocolate brown leather offset by solid oak long tables and benches took center stage. A plethora of bulbs spanned the ceiling, illuminating the room in a celestial symmetry. Etienne was there, seemingly waiting for them. He was flirting with the table of girls beside him.

But when Jude approached, he swiftly curtsied and pulled out the throne chair for Sofia and said, "Madame."

Jude shook his head and snickered.

She welcomed the attention and made her way to the head of the table. "Why, thank you. Now go fetch me some breakfast."

He eyeballed her, but she kept her serious face on.

He arched one eyebrow and asked, "Are you serious?"

"No. Just teasing." She smiled at his puzzled face.

Jude was already doing just that. He was organizing their menu with one of the servers.

Sofia turned to Etienne. "Does he always control everything?"

"It's not control; it's more nurturing. Jude likes to take care of his close friends and family. He's a doer and a lover." He winked at Sofia. She couldn't help but laugh.

But now, he stirred up her overactive imagination. *Is he a lover, i.e., a "player"?*

Thankfully, Lola and Emma showed up to take her mind away from the assumptions that she loved to come out and play every once in a while.

Etienne promptly stood up and introduced himself.

When Jude returned, he slid onto the bench closest to Sofia's throne. He reached over, swept his fingers through her hair, and gazed into her eyes, smiling. Her cheeks surely turned crimson-red, but still, she held onto his gaze.

He then graciously turned to Emma and Lola and engaged in a conversation with them. Jude was skillful in directing the conversation so that all attention was on the others. The waves of exchange seemed to animate them all, and if one could see auras as Sofia did, they would witness the room's frequency rise by the second. She sat back on her throne and silently observed the fiery energy arising between Lola and Etienne. Emma, meanwhile, sat as still as a mouse. Jude went out of his way to include her in the conversation, but still, she preferred the wallflower role. Lola asked all the right questions and revealed why Jude was in the city.

Strange that he didn't tell me the night before.

"I'm a photographer for my uncle's company—a travel and lifestyle website. We're here shooting an editorial at the hotel." He was most nonchalant about it, almost embarrassed.

He shifted the focus back to Lola. And she took the reins, as she did so well. And she sprinkled upon each event that happened the night before—just enough for Etienne to join in and do the same.

Jude slanted his head toward her and asked, "So, are you spending the day with me?"

Sofia nodded.

His eyes twinkled with delight. He looked at his phone for the time. "*Ah bon* (Oh good), we need to go."

He waved his hand at Etienne and turned to them. "Sorry, ladies, but I must steal him from you."

Etienne lifted his shoulders and said, "The master calls."

Lola and Emma darted to her end of the table and expressed their elation for Sofia.

"Relax, ladies, with the wedding plans. We just met."

Emma finally spoke up. "Really, though, Sofia? With your senses always activated, are you not feeling like he's "the one?""

She peered into Sofia's eyes. She was right, but still, Sofia didn't want to go down that road again—repeating old relationship patterns.

Fortunately, Jude and Etienne interrupted the moment. Jude slipped his arm around Sofia's shoulders, and once again, a stream of shyness cascaded around her.

Emma poked Sofia's nose and whispered, "As I was saying...." And she walked away.

Jude didn't pry, but she sensed he understood the quick exchange. There was something very elevated about Jude. She wondered what role he was to play in her life.

"So, are you ready to go?"

She had no idea where they were going, but her innate nomadic self was raring to go.

"Ready."

And they were off. Alone. Just the two of them.

5

Jude ushered Sofia into the Uber, promptly waiting for them outside. The driver didn't wait for them to settle into the car before sharing his story about the requested destination. "I remember going there as a child. From what I remember, it was dingy and dark. And the old man has become more grumpy over the years." Jude stopped him, informing the New York native that it was a surprise.

The driver nodded and then unabashedly asked, "Why not take your lovely lady to a museum or the Park for the day?"

Jude graciously smiled but didn't engage any further. The driver seemed in his own world, blabbing away throughout the ride. Sofia did not once inquire about the location, but her curiosity was high.

She heard him say, *Why must people constantly meddle in my life?*

The ride was comfortably silent between the two of them. A first for Sofia. She always wanted to fill in conversations with most people, but Jude was different. He constantly weaved his fingers into hers. She didn't complain. It felt normal.

What could have been a short ride was not to be in the city of perpetual traffic.

Sofia nodded her head listlessly and voiced her opinion to Jude. "I increasingly realize that I can no longer live in congested cities. There are too many—"

"Energies," They both said simultaneously.

He nodded. "I completely agree. There was a time when I did love this city, but as of late, it feels like evil has surfaced from the underground."

Excitement filled her that someone else aligned with her train of thought. "God, I love you." She blushed and stuttered, "I-I mean, this, I love this. " She pointed to him and then to herself. His eyes smiled as he fluttered his fingertips along her arm.

She had a hard time looking his way. They both sat back in the comfy sedan and looked out toward the city landscape as it rolled by them, frame by frame. There was a knowingness that settled around them. Her higher self fired up and nudged her to pay attention to what transpired.

The driver stopped the car in front of a dark alleyway. Jude didn't seem fazed, so Sofia rolled with the punches. He held the car door open and helped her out. As she caught his gaze, she still felt flustered from her previous declaration. Maybe he's used to women declaring their love to him. Maybe, maybe, maybe…. the ego was ablaze. She quickly shut it down for the sake of the adventure.

He wrapped his arm around hers as they inched deeper into the darkness. She welcomed the closeness and blindly followed him into the depths of New York hell. The sun was concealed by towering buildings making the short trek to the destination all the more ominous. The rumblings of tiny paws in the dumpsters and mounds of garbage bags echoed in the narrow path. Jude stopped in front of a worn-out steel door defaced with gang writings. "We're here."

Sofia was intrigued, not frightened, because when she allowed her higher self to eke through, she was given the confirmation that it was a "go." He knocked three times, and the door opened slightly.

The young teenage boy dressed in a paint-splattered hoodie and black fitted jeans cheerfully greeted Jude. "Hello, Mr. Jude. So nice to see you again."

Jude introduced Sofia to Micah. Right away, she sensed he was a new soul. As per her usual, she thanked him in her mind for coming to volunteer on the Earth plane. As Micah led them down the rickety circular stairway, a musty odor swept under her nose. By the time they reached the bottom, the teenager pointed to an older man crouched over a stack of books.

Jude patted him on the back, "Thanks. Say hi to your mom and dad."

He nodded. But, before walking away, he whispered to Sofia, "Thank you. We are here for you now. You can rest easy."

The boy disappeared into the mounds of books. She felt both dubious and joyful. It was the first time she received actual confirmation they were indeed among the "new" old souls. Enveloped in wonderment, she failed to drink in the beauty of the underground library. Books of all sizes, colors, and shapes neatly lined mahogany shelves. Everywhere she turned, her eyes caught sight of books, books, and more books. The ceiling was dome-shaped and adorned with a detailed mural of an astrological chart set in a cosmic background. Every star illuminated, bringing Sofia back in time until she was brought back to earth by the sound of a book falling.

When she glanced at the noise, she noticed she was not alone. A petite blonde-haired girl with ringlets of gold and celestial-blue eyes sat on the floor, gathering all her books in piles. Her meticulousness entranced Sofia. She propped herself against one of the columns and rested one of the more voluminous books on her thighs. Her eyes widened at every turn of the page. Sofia secretly wished she were as enthusiastic as this girl about books, who looked to be in her early twenties.

She lost sight of Jude, so she wandered about. For some reason, she felt compelled to go behind the circular staircase. Stacks of books masked the impressive wall of massive gray stones. Directed by her higher self to a specific shelf, she meandered around the towers of tomes, delicately sweeping her fingers along each book until she felt the need to pause. Sofia left her fingertips on the spine for a few seconds while she cleared her mind and breathed in and out. She cautiously pulled it out when she got confirmation that the book was the one. The front cover was slightly tattered. She was blown away by the title: "Alice in Wonderland." Sofia had been working on a 4-part series on the correlation of the book with their current reality. It was an 1898 edition, and strangely, Alice was depicted as a voluptuous young lady with wavy brown hair.

She cautiously opened the book on a random page and fell upon this passage: 'Everything was happening so oddly that she didn't feel a bit surprised at finding the Red Queen and the White Queen sitting close to her, one on each side. She would have liked very much to ask them how they came there, but she feared it would not be quite civil. However, there would be no harm in asking if the game was over.'

Sofia did not believe in happenstances, so she contemplated taking a quick pic, but her higher self popped in. *Not necessary. You have the gift of remembrance of all.* She was always on a learning curve regarding her authentic self. Before slipping it back onto the shelf, she felt a flaming light surround her. When she turned toward the center of the room, she didn't realize Jude was standing right behind her, and she yelped.

He laughed. "What are you doing, cowered behind all these books? Did you find something interesting?" He removed the book from her hands and glanced at the back. "It seems you have an eye for rare books." He pointed to the price, then surprised Sofia by offering to buy it.

That gesture rattled her. Never had any man ever offered to pay for anything pricey so quickly. It was always a long-winded discussion on whether she really needed it or why she couldn't just save the money for a rainy day, blah, blah, blah. She shook her head and said, "Ugh, no, thank you!" She got defensive and continued, "I can afford it, but it's not a priority right now."

Jude grinned and lowered his gaze. "Okay." He put it back in its place. "I didn't mean to offend you."

The old man called out to Jude, "I found it."

The man seemed like a ray of sunshine to her as he raised his arms upon their arrival. He exclaimed, "I'm so happy that he has finally brought Divine Sofia to me." He reached out his hand. "My name is Milton. I've known Jude for a good twenty years or so." He sneaked a peek at Jude. "About that, right?"

Jude nodded.

Sofia returned the handshake and asked, "You watch my videos?"

"Oh yes, indeed. Jude introduced me to your channel about one year ago. I've watched every single episode. I usually watch them with my grandson." He paused to catch his breath. "I appreciate all the research you do to create your videos. Only a bibliophile can fully comprehend the time you put into that."

His words were sincere and resonated deep in her heart.

He peered through his glasses and asked, "Why are you turning red, my dear? I have learned a lot from your findings; it has opened my world. And because of it, I have a better relationship with Micah. So thank you. You are bringing people together, and you don't even know it."

Jude interjected, "She has no idea what impact she has on people. Thank you for sharing." He nudged Sofia. "You see, it's not only me."

Sofia's cheeks flushed with embarrassment. She nodded, acknowledging the compliment from both men.

Milton handed Jude the black, tattered antiquated book with raised lettering. "You will find some of what you requested. I put the word out amongst my fellow librarians and researchers. I may be receiving a special shipment from Egypt in a few days. We're sure to find something of interest there. We shall wait and see." He winked at Sofia, then looked over at Jude. "When are you heading back?"

"I'll be here for another few days, but you can just mail it along with the rest of the order to my address in Montreal."

Milton leaned forward and hugged Sofia. "Looking forward to your next video. Tomorrow, right?"

She shrugged. "Maybe. It depends on if I'm called to do one."

Jude thanked Milton, and while completing payment with him, Sofia diverted her attention to the ceiling. She pinpointed her Leo sign and then wondered what Jude's sign was and if they were compatible.

Jude snuck his arm around her waist, looked up, and said, "Aquarius."

He kissed her on the cheek, further flustering her. Holding her hand, he led Sofia to a nook behind row 9. A scuffed-up wooden bench filled with tasseled pillows sat atop a Persian carpet in a bright pomegranate-red color.

He gave the book to Sofia. "Please, do the honors."

She held it in her hands for several seconds and felt a wave of calm envelop her body. She no longer heard him, only the beating of her heart and her breath. She carefully opened the book and landed on a random page—it was a book of symbols. There, staring at her, was one of the many symbols tattooed on Jude's fingers, the same as the ones she did a video on. Tears welled in her eyes; she had been searching for the meanings for the longest time.

She delicately handed the book over to Jude and excused herself.

"Are you okay?" He looked concerned.

"Yes," she mumbled. "I just need a minute."

She found a spot hidden from others and choked back her tears. She had finally accepted her solitude in this awakening journey, and now this man appeared. In two days, he managed to divert her onto another path. Her higher self pleaded with her. *Just go with the flow.* But her lower ego was screaming louder and louder. *Watch out.* Sofia learned over the years to tame that part of her mind. So, she breathed in for eight counts and breathed out eight more, as many times as she could, to ground herself.

Walking back, she stopped and peeked through a shelf filled with books to watch him. The book was still closed on the bench beside him. He was simultaneously staring at the ceiling and drawing something in his notebook.

As she approached, he swiftly stood and took her in his arms. No questions. No words. He held onto her for a few minutes. She held back a second bout of tears. Their energy was explosive. She felt his heart beating in unison with hers. He pulled away, and from the look on his face, Sofia imagined he felt the same thing as her. He rested his hands on her shoulders and gazed at her. His piercing green eyes melted into Sofia's aqua-blue eyes. The imprint was set. There was no going back.

FREE

The more you love yourself,
the more you free yourself.

The more you free yourself,
the more you love yourself.

6

He never let go of her hand once they hit the pavement. The whiff of steamed hot dogs churned her stomach, and the implausible film of exhaust clouded her vision. Or it could have been the rock-concert-like crowd vibrating with a fluctuation of high and low energies. Whatever it was, Sofia bulldozed her way out of it and headed into the nearest hellish alleyway.

Jude followed her. "What's going on, Sofia?" He lifted his hand and said, "No, wait. I know." He paused. "You always tell us to surround ourselves with white light. This is the city that needs that kind of protection."

He was right. She rolled her eyes and laughed out loud. "I felt so safe in that haven of books that I forgot we were in this city of madness."

"Let me do the honors."

He wrapped her in his arms and mumbled a protection prayer. She took advantage of the position to voyage to la la land, imagining them together in her happy place. But an onslaught of text messages interrupted them. He ignored them at first. As they continued ringing in, his arms tightened around her. She felt his heart beating so hard, the sounds of the bustling city faded into the distance. As she remained still in his arms, his energy simmered down.

He leaned into her, whispered an apology in her ear, and slipped away to take care of the rampage of messages. When he nervously tapped on the phone and brought it to his ear, it shocked her to hear the first word that came out of his mouth, "*Maman*" (Mom).

She walked away, even though she wanted to listen.

She stepped back onto the sidewalk and reveled in the power of the white light protection. Nobody approached her. They never once entered into her auric field. *Fait accompli* (mission accomplished).

It was another busy day in the city with screeching cars, queues of tourist buses, rowdy humans, and ear-splitting sounds. When she turned away and looked toward Jude, she was privy to another side of him.

Gone was the gentle soul that had catered to her every whim on this trip. Gone were the smiling eyes. Gone was the golden glow around him. A dark, heavy cloud now surrounded him, the same one that appeared in the lobby with Trinity. She rubbed her palms together, and with palms facing outward, she sent positive, energetic vibes his way. He looked up, and for a moment, Sofia could see the waves cloak his body. The waves rolled around them when they locked eyes, cocooning their bodies. As if hypnotized by her gaze, he removed the phone from his ear, hung up, and headed over to her.

He lifted Sofia's chin with a finger and said, "Thank you." He planted a soft kiss on her lips. He had a way of taking her breath away.

He adjusted the leather messenger bag Milton lent him for the book of symbols. "Are you ready for the next leg of our adventure?"

She handed over the reins to someone else for the first time in a long time and said, "I'm all yours."

7

The car dropped them off in front of Central Park. Sofia was more than pleased to spend the day in nature rather than in the hustle and bustle of the city. She didn't pry into his phone call, and he didn't share it with her. There was a side of Jude that intrigued and frightened her at the same time because it was that side that would propel her into rabbit holes.

They found their way along the perimeters of the Pond. Leaves in kaleidoscopic shades blanketed the walkway. By the time they reached the far end of the pond, the pandemonium of the city had tapered down to a tolerable, droning sound. They walked in silence. His hand never let go of hers.

Their trek led them to the iconic Gapstow Bridge, a breathtaking stone bridge that curved graciously over the pond's light green, calm waters. Sloping grass hills, towering leafy trees, and large carved rocks framed this picture-worthy spectacle.

They still hadn't exchanged words. Instead of worrying about it, she savored the downtime between them. An exchange occurred only when they passed through the throngs of children clamoring to go into the zoo.

"How is it," Sofia began, "that they still allow these animal prisons to be open?"

"Your guess is as good as mine." He looked toward her. "Since you're so connected, do you think it will be long before they free these creatures of earth?"

If he's trying to impress me, it's working.

She nodded. "We are all connected. But, soon, the entire world will change. I look forward to this time of healing on the planet."

Her higher self kicked in and whispered. *And you will be a part of this change, dear one.* Sofia ignored it, as she never really understood her mission on earth. She hit a brick wall called the ego whenever she tried to decode it.

They walked toward the Mall, a wide-open space lined with wooden benches filled with couples, teens perched on skateboards, and families devouring oversized pretzels and ice cream. It was buzzing with energy. Rows and rows of elm trees towered the pathway. She wondered where he was taking her, but left it at that. He took a sharp right, and before them was an open space of greenery.

He opted for a bountiful tree."Do you want to stay in the shade or the sun?"

She pointed to the side where a sliver of sun peeked through the deluge of leafy branches.

He pulled out a tartan blanket from his bag and settled under the tree. Sofia quickly removed her runners and socks and planted her feet on the grass. Jude followed suit.

She gazed out onto the green landscape. "It's rare to meet someone on the same journey as me." She paused and found the courage to face him. "I may have a popular YouTube channel, but it's been lonely harboring my inner-knowing from all the "non-believers," especially when most of them are my friends and family. It's been quite a few years of heartache and solitude."

He responded by moving closer and draping his arm around her. "I get you. This is why I'm drawn to you. I feel we're living the same life but with different circumstances."

She looked at him, expecting him to reveal his situation, but he wasn't quite ready. Her gaze returned to the luscious land and changed the subject. "Did you know they use forest therapy in Japan to heal depression and anxiety? Their patients hug trees or sit under them for an allotted time. The scent of the tree acts as a natural immune boost."

He nodded, shifting his gaze to the tree behind them and back at Sofia. He then jumped up and pulled her up with him. "Let's hug this tree and claim her as our healing tree."

They stood on either end of the trunk and coiled their arms around it, lacing their fingers together. "I hereby declare," Jude began, "this sacred tree as part of our coming together. We will protect her even if we are not around her. She will be our refuge when we are in this city." He paused and squeezed Sofia's fingers. "You continue."

She nodded and carried on. "In the highest and greatest good, we bless you with our love and welcome your energy to re-energize our power. And so it is."

They held onto each other for a few more minutes, absorbing the energy of Mother Nature. A vibrational stream of energy flowed from Sofia to the tree to Jude and vice versa.

When she released her hands from his, the pulsations slowly subsided. It took her a minute to collect herself. She stood in the luminous sun and embraced the rays. When his arms framed her body, she leaned against him. Her seventeen-year-old giddiness returned. The moment was not to be lost.

They returned to the blanket; Jude hunkered down by the tree. He pulled out the book of signs from the bag and placed it on his legs. Sofia sat beside him, as a normal couple would. Every single symbol in the book mesmerized her. She felt the energy rise in her every time he flipped the page. Of the ten symbols on his fingers, they found four of them.

"But, there are no meanings," she grumbled. "So, we're back at zero again."

Jude snapped his fingers, reached into the bag, and pulled out a mini booklet. He waved the book in front of her face and said, "Milton told me that this was published years later, and I believe the meanings are here."

Her eyes lit up. "Finally, we'll get some clarity." She rubbed her hands together and grabbed the booklet from his fingers. Sofia leafed through the book and found one of the symbols in the shape of a leaf. She exclaimed, "Aha, the leafy one signifies new beginnings."

Jude nudged her and smiled. "Appropriate." He whipped out his mini notebook and jotted down the findings.

"One of these days, I would love to see what's in that little book of yours!"

He looked up and handed it to her. "Here. It's a whole bunch of random thoughts and ideas."

Sofia waved her hand. "No, it's okay. I'm a journal writer too. It's fascinating to find someone like me, always writing down thoughts in a book and not a phone."

She gestured to Jude to flip to the next symbol. The next one was a spiral with a slight upturn in the center.

"This one means power and strength. We will have to do more research, but at least we're getting somewhere." She was elated that there was finally some concrete evidence of their findings.

The following two were more graphic. One was the heartbeat lines found on an EKG; the other was similar but the vertical version. The former signified creative expression, and the latter: truth.

"Well, we're moving along," Jude said as he closed the book and set it aside. Resting his hands behind his head, he leaned against the tree and turned to Sofia, who was lost in thought. He inquired about the pendant she was twirling in her fingers.

She pulled it out from underneath her top. While he inspected the copper pendulum tied onto a tattered leather cord, she told him that she inherited it from her mother, who inherited it from her mother, and so forth—a family heirloom.

"What's the crystal? I've never seen one quite like this?"

"It's called Andara. It's volcanic glass from Mount Shasta. These pale green stones hold the highest frequency within them."

"Is that why you are always so 'high vibe'?" he teased.

"Once you know me better, you will witness my not-so-high vibe moments. We are human, after all!" They both laughed.

"I look forward to getting to know you better." As he intently gazed into her eyes, her cheeks instantly flushed. It seemed she would always revert to teenage giddiness with him.

She looped around to face the park and savored the golden silence between them. She sat observing the father and daughter throwing a frisbee at each other. Sofia remembered a time when life was simple, when her mom was still alive, and there was laughter and joy throughout the house when she played catch with her dad and brother, and when she lived in pure love every day. She looked forward to 'new earth' for those feelings of freedom and unconditional love.

Jude traced his fingers along her arm. Sofia turned and was caught off guard by his wanting lips waiting for her. She willingly obliged. When they lowered their bodies onto the blanket, his phone vibrated. Incessantly. Jude tried hard to ignore it, but she felt his touch and kisses shifting from soft and gentle to harried. She lightly pushed him off her and sat up.

"Answer the phone or turn it off completely." Sofia exhaled a heavy sigh.

Jude lay down with arms crossed behind his head. The gleaming sun rays sliced through the leaves and shone down on him, drawing attention to his transcendental gaze. An orb of light radiated around his closely-shaven head. She was falling hard for this complex soul. He remained silent throughout the buzzing sounds. It never stopped. She tried to listen to his thoughts but got nothing. She was tempted to hurl his phone into the forest of trees behind them but chose calm and resignation instead.

He finally reached over his head and pulled the bag down to him. He checked his phone and sprung up to his feet like a cheetah.

Sofia said, "Now that, my friend, is athleticism!"

Jude acknowledged her sarcasm and groaned. "It's experience from dealing with the crazy women in my life." It was obvious by his grimace that he probably didn't want to reveal that much, but it was too late.

She once again chose the high road by remaining silent. Her ego was in full-speed-ahead motion delivering her a mixed bag of scenarios.

Meanwhile, Jude scanned the area.

He was on high alert for what? Was his mother here in New York? She battled with her ego when her higher self made it through and assured her that all was fine. It didn't seem fine. But her higher self was adamant, easing Sofia's mind to rest.

While he 'Sherlock Holmed' the area, she stretched her arm as far as she could to hook the corner of the book and slid it closer. She delved into the ancient symbols to better understand them. There were symbols she had never seen before, dating back five thousand years. *History.* Sofia rolled her eyes. *Who knows if these dates are even accurate?* As she flipped through the book, a piece of paper flew out. Jude was no longer in sight, so she scrambled to her feet and ran after it. It floated into the trees behind her. A gust of wind came out of nowhere and blew it deeper into Mother Nature's den. Fortunately, there was someone to snatch it mid-air. When Sofia extended her arm to grasp it from the woman's hand, the stranger held on tight.

"Thank you for catching it."

The fiery redhead stared at her with mischievous eyes, continuing to hold on tightly to the paper—*yet another crazy New Yorker.*

Something was not right about this woman. She didn't flinch and returned the icy stare. The woman handed over the paper, then framed Sofia's face with her fingers in an "L" shape as one would when taking a professional photograph.

Sofia didn't wait around for the rest of the interaction. She darted out of the woodland.

Once in the clearing, she looked back. The woman was nowhere to be seen. Was it a figment of her imagination? Perhaps the demons were out to play. After all, this city was their playground. She headed back to their spot, and Jude was still not there. It had been a long time since such negativity had touched her. Sofia tried hard on this journey to come from a place of love, not fear or anger, but that woman triggered something in her. She leaned against the tree, planted her bare feet on the grass, closed her eyes, and breathed.

When Sofia finally felt grounded, she felt someone's fingers at the side of her face, and she shrieked. Opening her eyes, she saw Jude.

"Why so jumpy?" he asked.

She stared blankly at him, unable to process into words the awkward encounter she had just experienced. That woman's glacial stare was a permanent fixture in her mind.

"What happened?" His teeth clenched so tightly that the veins in his neck were popping. "Did you see something? Did you meet someone?" He scanned the surroundings.

Finding her center first, she then divulged to him what had happened. His posture stiffened, and his eyes burned with fury. He pleaded with her to tell him every detail.

Then she remembered that girl's name from last night and asked, "Is this Gabrielle?"

He jutted his neck and cried, "How do you know her name? Did Etienne say something to you?"

He quickly pulled out his phone, but Sofia placed her hand on it. "You told me." She wasn't ready to admit she heard it while reading his mind.

"Impossible."

Standing squarely before him, she gently gripped his forearms and said, "It doesn't matter how I know her name. Can you give me a clue who she is?"

He exhaled a heavy sigh. He twisted his head from side to side as if he was getting ready for a boxing match before reaching out and holding her in his arms. His heart was beating like heavy rain crashing upon a window pane.

She unlocked herself from his inviting embrace. "I know we don't know each other. And I don't expect you to tell me the backstory about this girl, but it would be nice to know just one bit of information. She had a creepy vibe."

He placed one hand on the tree, further defining his muscular arm. She leaned against the trunk, waiting for his response. With his free arm, he caged her close to his body. Despite her best efforts, she couldn't hear what he was saying.

Sofia rolled her eyes and snuck from underneath his arms, out into the sun. *Enough is enough.* She wasn't going to deal with these uncommunicative men anymore. Her ego was having a field day—let's see which fears would come out from the past. She always pictured her ego as an evil blacksmith, welding new fears, anxieties, and doubts in her brain.

While deep into her own battle of the mind, Jude asked, "Did she hurt you?"

Did she hurt me? Who is this girl? She shook her head. "No. Is she someone I should be worried about?"

He looked away and mumbled, "Not for now." He took several breaths in and out to calm himself and repeated, "Not for now. She works for my uncle in the social media department. She's harmless. She has a small crush on me. Don't worry; she's my problem, not yours."

Sofia half-believed his story but went along with it to not ruin the rest of the day.

Tapping into her higher self, she still got the go-ahead. *Try not to look into this too much, Sofia. Enjoy your time with him.*

****

The day could have been ruined, but Sofia was well-seasoned with tucking away stressful situations neatly into deep pockets. Jude was just as proficient as she was. He gathered the blanket, shook it in the air, and wrapped it around the precious books. He carefully inserted them into the bag and grabbed his phone to text someone.

While he was organizing the rest of the day, she sat atop a boulder nearby and observed the man she had a crush on for so many years. Destiny had a funny way of weaving its way into their lives.

When Jude looked up from his phone, the glint in his eyes was back. Gone were the stress lines around his eyes. His smoldering gaze sent a kaleidoscope of butterflies into her body. It was overwhelming but magical at the same time. It had been a long time since a man had excited her as he did.

A melodic sound drifted from the greenery and through the leafy branches. Sofia tilted her head to see where it was coming from. She glimpsed a man sitting nearby playing the saxophone. Her eyes closed—she listened to the vibrational frequency of each note.

"May I have this dance, m'lady?"

She opened her eyes to find Jude's palm facing her. She giggled and said, "Why yes, my gentleman." She lightly placed her hand in his. He lifted her and twirled her in his arms.

They slowly moved to the gentle pulsations of the music. In the stillness, images of the redhead flashed through Sofia's mind. As quickly as the images came in, as quickly she rejected them. No more drama, so she placed her cheek on his chest. His heart beat just as fast as hers. She took it upon herself to make a move, nuzzling her face in his neck and flirtatiously kissing him. She felt his breath quicken as her hands slid down his torso.

He cradled her in his arms, and just like that, she tapped into his mind as he said, *I wonder if she feels the same as me.*

She pulled away from his chest and looked up into his eyes. He combed his fingers through her unruly hair, gathered her long locks into a makeshift bundle, and passionately kissed her. She welcomed his luscious lips onto hers. This was truly a fairytale moment until the ringing began. This time, he didn't ignore it. He pulled away from their embrace this time and enthusiastically picked up the phone. But whoever it was aroused laughter and joy, so not the redhead nor his mother.

He spoke French. His whole demeanor metamorphosed in a matter of seconds. Sofia penned him her 'chameleon.' He lifted a finger to her, excusing himself, and continued to talk to this person with delight. She watched as her 'chameleon's' aura fluctuated from gold to green to white.

As soon as Jude hung up, he rushed over and finished where he had left off. He drew her body up against his and lowered his lips onto hers. He was self-assured and loving at the same time. And, when Jude stepped away, he left her wanting more.

"Let's continue this later," he whispered.

She acquiesced.

With an arm around her shoulder, he said, "Shall we continue our trek?"

As soon as they hit the path, Jude's disposition became more gladiator-like, shielding her from eventual run-ins. His gaze darted from left to right with every step they took. In the distance, she caught sight of the 'Angel of the Waters' sculpture looming in the clouds. She tugged Jude toward the Bethesda Fountain. The crowds were spilling out from every staircase, pathway, and greenery. It was nonsensical.

"I changed my mind. There are way too many people," she said.

Jude nodded and cut through the grassy slope. As they maneuvered around the swarm of tourists, they followed the road to the Trefoil Arch. Upon entering the dismal tunnel, Sofia froze. She didn't much like tunnels ever since she did a video on the nefarious ways of the underworld. Feeling suddenly weak, Jude leaned her up against the wall. In doing so, he curiously examined the wall behind her and whipped out his phone.

He turned on the flashlight and shouted, "You need to see this, Sofia."

She twisted her body and spied the street art on the granular wall. The breathtaking mural depicted a fiery background with a dragon and phoenix spray painted at the center of the masterpiece.

Signs and synchronicities were what they believed in, after all. Jude warmly embraced her. They stood there as one in their bubble amongst the passersby and the cyclists. Electricity surged throughout their bodies.

She heard him say, *This just feels right. She's the one I've been waiting for my whole life.*

Tempted to divulge her secret superpower, texts from both their phones interrupted her.

She was content to leave the tunnel. Even though it housed a representation of Sofia and Jude, it still didn't jive with her. When they emerged into the sunshine, the light blinded them. But the sun was their friend, not their enemy. Within a few seconds, they adjusted to the brightness.

They strolled toward the lake at the edge of the Terrace. The scenic lake was set against formidable willow trees. Sweet humming sounds of the indigenous birds fluttered around them. Familiar voices echoed in the distance; Lola and Emma, with their New York friends, waved at them from pedal boats.

Jude squeezed her hand and whispered, "Surprise. I intended for this day to be special and not so frenzied."

"Nothing is ever as it seems. Especially on our journey."

Jude and Sofia made their way around the lake to the famous Boathouse Grill. Etienne was on the terrace by the waterfront with a boisterous group of people.

Jude whispered in her ear, "Their bark is bigger than their bite."

Jude and Sofia found their way to the best tables on the terrace despite the sea of colorful tourists crammed into the restaurant. Plates of tapas, cheese, and dips littered the tabletops. They were deep in conversation but greeted the duo with waves and winks. Etienne was most welcoming, sliding a chair out for Sofia. Jude remained standing and surveyed the table. He then grabbed two plates and handed them to one of the girls. Mid-speech, she understood his request and brimmed them with all the culinary delights. Meanwhile, he poured himself a glass of wine and prepared a tumbler with fresh Spring water and wedges of lemon, orange, and lime for Sofia.

As he settled into his chair, she witnessed Etienne and Jude making eye contact and communicating in code. Etienne caught sight of her and pivoted his head away. Jude shifted in his seat and reached over to Sofia, placing his hand on her shoulder.

"You boys can exchange what you need to," she told Jude. "I'm going to step away for a few seconds."

Etienne laughed. "The eyes have language everywhere."

"Etienne loves to speak in riddles and quotes." Jude looked over at Sofia, smiling from ear to ear. "You've been forewarned."

She placed both hands on their shoulders and said, "I have a feeling both of you will do a good job entertaining me."

She stood and went to the far side of the balcony, leaned over, and waved at Lola and Emma. They acknowledged her and made their way to land.

When she returned to the table, Etienne and Jude were engaged in a tense tête-à-tête with Etienne's words ringing loudly in her ears. "*Mais arrête. C'est pas vrai?* (Stop it. You're lying)." She sat closer to the others and introduced herself to them.

Sporting a platinum pixie cut, Daphne extended her wiry fingers toward Sofia. "We know who you are. We've been keeping tabs on you since we caught Jude watching one of your videos between shoots. We're some of your most devoted followers and even plan our photo shoots around your "live's" so we can stay informed."

Sofia beamed. "Wow. I'm honored. Does your boss know you are doing that?"

Daphne pointed to Jude. "You can ask him yourself."

Sofia turned to Jude and observed as he dominated the energy of the table, but most modestly. He took her breath away once again. He teetered on the chair's back legs—arms crisscrossed behind his head. A white light glowed around him—it could have been the sun, but she believed otherwise. When they locked eyes, he held the stare.

And then she heard him say. *I would love to kiss her again.*

Heat flamed her cheeks, so she turned away and continued chatting with his friends. She discovered that Daphne was a makeup artist, Mathieu was a lighting director, Rose was one of the models, and Melanie was the social media coordinator.

Sofia turned to Melanie. "Oh, so you must work with Gabrielle."

Jude's chair slammed to the ground. Everyone fell silent. They all veered their eyes toward Jude.

Etienne's panic-stricken eyes spoke loudly. He looked at Jude with deep concern but didn't wait for his friend to react and quickly jumped in. "Yes, she does. But Gabrielle is more of an influencer. She only works with us in Paris."

Sofia looked at Jude, then back at Etienne, and repeated, "Really, so she's not here in New York? She's back in Paris?"

Etienne turned fifty shades of blue and exclaimed, "Well, she was here for a special shoot, but she had to fly back."

Sofia didn't have to look at Jude to feel his weighty energy.

When she coiled her head to glance at Jude, she caught sight of her friends walking toward them. *Saved by the bell.* She sprung out of the chair and went to hug her besties.

Lola made her grand entrance and worked the table like the social butterfly that she was. Meanwhile, Sofia returned to her seat next to Jude. The rest of them played a bit of musical chairs before they all settled into their seats. Jude called over the waiter and ordered more food and drinks.

Sofia chose not to deep dive into the drama as promised, so she left it alone. Etienne was still perturbed but was quickly distracted by Lola's charisma and charm. The magnetism between the two of them was most potent.

When her eyes flashed back at Jude, he half-smiled. His fingers wildly tapped on the back of her chair. Sofia's emotional see-saw was back; as it lowered, so did her confidence, and as it went up, so did her remembrance of self. After so many years of being single, she didn't miss this aspect of relationships.

The conversation soared in no time to an animated one. With so many dynamic energies at the table, it was no surprise. And when they brought up the current status of the world, Sofia couldn't resist the temptation to disclose some of her findings. They listened intently. Both Etienne and Lola jumped in and refuted some of her theories. Lola was often the devil's advocate and was now joined by Jude's best friend. Sofia loved listening to opposing views. It helped her better understand where the collective stood.

Emma usually had an opinion but would never vocalize it in front of so many strangers, yet confrontation was once her strongest suit. On the other hand, Jude was more thoughtful when he asked questions; his critical thinking elevated the discourse to new levels.

Lola nudged Sofia and whispered, "He's totally turning you on right now, isn't he?"

She knew her too well. It became an orgy of beliefs and ideologies.

Etienne made a strong point against one of Sofia's thoughts; usually, she would have dove into battle. She found herself struggling with the "war of words." Even though her whole platform was based on years of research, she was evolving on this journey. She realized it was more important to relay her wisdom rather than her knowledge; in other words, her experiences rather than someone else's information. She was at odds. Where she once thirsted for victory at all costs, she would now rather sit back and be the observer. Still, she engaged with Etienne, but luckily they were interrupted by a gang of servers promenading toward them with buckets of champagne and sparklers. When they all clinked glasses, she turned to Emma and lifted her glass. Emma's response was robotic at best. And, when Sofia called her over, she refused.

Their friendship had spanned over twenty years, and there were moments of instability. When they first met, Sofia was angry at the world. She had just lost her mother to a five-year battle with cancer. She was hard on others and herself, too. In her attempt to bury her emotions, they were usually not kind when they escaped. Sofia was a rebel, constantly contradicting others. So was Emma, whom she met at an underground bar where a group of them would meet to discuss the "end of the world." Feisty and opinionated, Emma had a lot to say. They would lead street protests, with Emma screaming into the megaphone.

That's why it was so hard for her to watch her friend sit quietly and not say a word. Sofia vowed to stand by Emma's side through thick and thin as she did with her all those years ago.

The festivities continued. Pedro and Michael heavily flirted with the other women at the table. Lola was too enthralled with Etienne to notice, and Emma just sat back and brooded the whole time.

Sofia barely felt Jude slither his hand into hers. She only realized it when goosebumps formed on her skin. He moved in closer and nestled his face into her neck.

He whispered, "This thing we have will never be boring."

Before she could react to his words, his phone rang once, twice, three times. He let go of her hand to shut it off, only to get a slew of beeping texts. Lola curiously eyed him, then Sofia. He sprung from his chair and exited from the terrace to steer the attention away from him.

Sofia looked at Etienne and mumbled, "Maybe it's Gabrielle from Paris?"

Etienne squinted his eyes and furrowed his brows. He shook his head and bellowed, "You are a fiery one. You are exactly what he needs in his life."

Sofia accepted the compliment. Her heart skipped a beat at the thought of being in Jude's life. At the same time, she realized she was heading into precisely what she had tried to avoid in her life. Ah, the karmic lessons were never-ending.

When Jude returned, he apologized, blaming it on a work thing.

Everyone went along with the lie.

He then showed his smartphone to the table. "You need to head back to the hotel and set up. So, finish the food and the drinks, and let's go."

He called over the waiter, handed over his credit card without verifying the bill, and that was that. Sofia had been working on her shadow self for quite some time now. Allowing others to take care of her was on the list. One hurdle at a time.

8

The weather was changing. The clouds were moving in, and the wind was picking up. As they waved goodbye to Jude's team, he turned to Sofia. "There's one place I would still like to visit before we head back—Strawberry Fields."

Sofia had nothing but time, especially if it meant more of it with him.

"My dad is a die-hard Beatles fan. When you see his collection, you will understand me."

Well, let's see. If Jude's dad lives in Paris—will I visit them soon? She couldn't help but smile.

Etienne chimed in, "Nietzsche said it the best: Without music, life would be a mistake."

Jude rolled his eyes, laughed, and whispered in her ear, "I warned you!"

The trek to the John Lennon memorial was wrought with apprehension and angst on Jude's part. He seemed cool and collected in front of Sofia's friends, but she felt the variations in his energy field.

Hooking his arm into Sofia's, Etienne pulled her away from Jude.

Before Jude could react, Etienne yelled, "Don't worry, I just want some alone time with her!"

Jude retorted, "That's what I'm afraid of." He then wearily walked away.

As he swept her away, a whiff of his fruity and spicy cologne whirled around her. He was slightly taller than Sofia's 5 foot 7- inch height. His presence reminded her of the Knight of Wands in her tarot deck; he was brash, fearless, handsome, and had a way with women, too. While they walked on, Etienne chatted about nothing. The closer they got to their destination, he finally revealed to Sofia some of the anguish that followed Jude around.

"Look at Jude." He pointed to his friend.

When they both looked over, Jude was busy surveying the area, not enjoying the company of her friends.

"I don't think you understand what a breath of fresh air you are for him, em, for us." He smiled and continued, "I'm going to let you in on a little secret."

Sofia looked over and easily fell under the spell of Etienne's bewitching hazel eyes. "Yes, I'm all ears."

She could tell he required validation in his life. She wondered what kind of childhood he had but stopped her wonderment when she heard his words. "Jude has been waiting a long time to make his move on you."

Sofia's heart fluttered, and a new set of butterflies emerged from their cocoons.

"I'll let you in on another secret. But just between you and me, right?" He looked into her eyes and waited for her acknowledgment. "That girl, Gabrielle, is a problem, but we're working on getting her under control."

He looked up toward Jude and mischievously smiled. "I beg you to be patient with him. He's worth it."

The flutter of butterflies continued.

He hugged her and said, "Unfortunately, I come with the package, so you will be stuck with me, too."

Sofia dared ask him. "And what about his mother?"

Etienne grimaced. "We'll leave that one for another day."

Jude finally joined them. He snuck his arm around Sofia's waist and pulled her close to him.

He good-humouredly said, "Enough of this flirting. Can I have some time with her, please?"

Etienne was already way ahead of them and caught up with the rest of the gang. Arm in arm, Jude and Sofia strolled behind.

"I hope Etienne wasn't too intrusive?"

Sofia shook her head.

The park was precisely as she had "imagined" it to be. Rose petals in the most vibrant hues formed a peace sign within the tiled splendor. The sun barely peeked through the blanket of clouds, creating an eerie backdrop. People sat on the ground near the "Imagine" memorial. Silence fell upon them, with only the sounds of the rustling of leaves and soft murmurs between friends echoing among the trees.

She lightly caressed the tattoos on his fingers and said, "One day, we will discover the meanings of all these symbols. And maybe one day, it will help us remind us who we are."

Jude lowered his lips to her forehead and gently kissed her. "Who we are? Well, you already know that, don't you?"

She looked up and drowned in his luscious greens. She blushed all kinds of colors and nodded.

She heard him say in his mind. *Sometimes, she forgets how powerful she is.*

She couldn't help but blush even more. Jude laced his fingers into hers and squeezed them tightly. He was still very vigilant as he verified every entry point twice.

When a young man sporting a black woolen coat and tightly-laced combat boots jumped onto one of the many benches along the edges of the tiled wonder, he caught the passersby's attention. He remained silent, eyeing everyone as he raked his uncombed hair into a makeshift ponytail. And when he raised his arms most theatrically, words spilled from his mouth. "I celebrate myself and sing myself. And what I assume you shall assume. For every atom belonging to me as good belongs to you..."

Jude whispered to Sofia, "Walt Whitman."

Fascinated as she was about him recognizing the poem, she was further intrigued when Etienne slid by them and asked Jude to get up and read one of his own. Jude's immediate reaction was to shove Etienne away.

When the resident poet ended and curtsied, he invited others to express themselves. There was never a shortage of free thinkers in the city of Manhattan, so one by one, people of all ages and all walks of life recited poems, vented, or sang to the crowd.

Etienne would not take no for an answer and volunteered to go next. He snagged Jude's book from his back pocket and sprinted to the bench before Jude could react. When he yelled and attempted to retrieve his book, Sofia clutched onto him. "I want to hear. Please."

He gave in, and on went Etienne.

"She is the light. She is the star in the sky that winks at me night after night.

She is the sun that shines in my eyes, so bright.

She is the wind that caresses my   cheek,

propelling my heart to ignite.

She is the wave that helps me stay afloat under the moonlight.

She is the earth to which

my feet stand on tonight.

She is my daylight. She is my twilight.

She is my midnight. She is my light."

The thunderous clapping overshadowed the thunderous beating of Sofia's heart. And when she tilted her head toward Jude, she caught Lola and Emma blowing kisses her way—further flustering her. Sofia's seventeen-year-old self was getting the best of her, and she had difficulty looking into his eyes. He leaned in—his lips moved against her ear, "You are my light, Sofia."

Sofia didn't have time to respond when Etienne swooped in and handed the book back to Jude.

"You're welcome." He winked at Sofia and sped off toward Lola and Emma.

The leaves crackled around their feet. The branches swayed back and forth like a folk festival crowd. A gust of wind whooshed past them, soaring up to the next dimension. Was this a sign from the universe that all good things had to come to an end? People were running about, trying to catch the flitting petals from the peace sign.

He looked up at the sky. "We better head back. The clouds are rolling in pretty quickly."

Before they could gather with their friends, the torrential rain swept through them, and not even the plentiful leaves could shelter them from Mother Nature's wrath. Lightning lit up the sky, and the claps of thunder seemed to shake the earth. He led her into the wonderland of trees and shrubs surrounding the area. The rain was pouring down on him, soaking him thoroughly. She pulled him in closer, shielding him from the downpour. They were practically skin against skin.

He cleared the wet hair from Sofia's face, fixed his gaze on her, and softly said, "It's funny how we always find ourselves in these situations. Do you think this is all part of our blueprint?"

He was doing a fine job firing her up with all his wisdom.

Sofia hadn't been touched in a long time, and this was an opportune time to take advantage of it. It didn't take time for her forty-two-year-old self to appear. She whispered, "Let's go to your room."

He smiled at her request.

The rain felt like cold rocks on their skin. Their trek through the slick streets proved to be challenging. Jude's tight hold helped to coordinate her pace. The abundant raindrops crashed down, drenching their clothes. They ran under an awning for shelter. His teeth were chattering, and his lips turned a pale blue. She wiped away the droplets of rain on his face. His scintillating eyes studied her every movement. He swept her wet hair back and lowered his quivering lips onto hers. It didn't matter that half of New York crowded under this awning with them; as soon as his soft lips touched hers, everyone disappeared. It was just him and her, and the rain. His body was shivering, so she took the lead and ran for it.

9

As soon as he swung open the door, he did not hesitate to undress, peeling away his top and soaking wet pants. Sofia wiggled her way out of her top, too. And when he twirled her in his arms, she shrieked, "Warm shower. Pronto."

His teeth were chattering, and his lips turned varied shades of purple. Sofia covered his body with a blanket in full nurturing mode and escorted him into the bathroom.

Why did they have to make shower heads so complicated?

As she tried to figure out the hot and cold, he reached over her, turned the nozzle to the left, and shuffled right in.

Sofia's brain was in overdrive as she laid her eyes on Jude's flawless body. Her ego crept in, dropping synapses from left to right—filling her mind with endless insecurities.

As droplets of water gushed down the back of his head and streamed down every curvature of his body, all insecurities flew out the window. And she was in there with him.

Jude turned to face her. "You are never going to be able to take your jeans off—you do know that."

She did. He whipped her around and pinned her against the tiles under the cascading flow of water. He sneaked his head under the downpour and devoured her lips. His hands traveled all over her body. He was as passionate as she had fantasized.

And just like that, as was becoming customary for them—they heard the room door creak open. He swiftly shut the water, pulled her into his embrace, and tried to catch his breath. When Sofia looked into his eyes, the sheer panic in them was unsettling.

How is he living like this? It's not normal.

He released her, reached for a towel, and wrapped it around his waist. He then grabbed the blow dryer hanging on the wall and headed out. It was like a scene from a horror movie—the protagonist grabbing whatever he could find only to get sliced in half by the axe murderer.

Okay, zip it, Ego.

Then nothing. *Nada. Niente.* Now, what? She didn't know what to do. But, she was damn sure not going to wait for her 'Psycho' moment to happen in the shower, so quietly, she stepped out. What a feat it was to walk in her sopping, wet jeans. When she made it outside, it was only Jude in the room, slumped over on the side of the bed in self-defeat. She couldn't bend down for her life, so she stood by him.

Sofia asked him who it was. He shrugged his shoulders. And that was that.

She made her way back to the bathroom. While she squatted, lunged, and wriggled her way out of her jeans, her mind was abuzz with scenarios. *Is this something I want to get involved with? As much as I like him, is this the right move for me right now? And why the secrecy? Is it even safe for me to be around this?*

Her higher self was equally as chatty and swarmed her mind with, *Yes, he is worth it. Go into your heart, my dear, and lead from there.*

Her feelings forged forward when she let the water cascade down her back. She was indeed looking forward to making love to this man. She slipped into one of the neatly folded bathrobes when she got out of the shower. She twisted the heck out of her jeans and placed them near the radiator.

He was fast asleep by the time she made it out—his breathing soft and melodic. Gone was the tension in his body. Gone were the dark circles under his eyes. Gone was her self-reprimanding. Sofia lowered her body down onto the bed and snuggled up against him. He grumbled, turned to face her, and scooped her in his arms. His heavy arm draped over her body. It felt right.

Awakened by an incessant buzzing sound of a phone, Sofia reached over to shut it off but accidentally answered the call.

"Jude!" shouted the woman on the phone.

Disoriented, Sofia brought the phone to her ear. "Hello? Who's speaking?"

"*Mais, c'est qui ça? Bof* (Who is this? Wtv). *Écoutez, passez-le-moi maintenant*! (Put him on the phone right now!)," her voice shrieked in Sofia's eardrum.

She shook Jude awake.

He swiftly sat up. "*Quoi?* (What?) What? What is it?"

The woman's voice was as loud as a siren; he grabbed the phone and ran into the bathroom. This time, Sofia didn't sit idly by. This time, she sneaked by the door to listen in.

The woman was a drama queen—she went from roaring like a lion to crying like a lamb. "*Je ne sais pas pourquoi tu m'en veux, je fais juste attention à toi.* (I don't know why you get angry with me, I'm just looking out for you)."

"*Toujours la même histoire, maman. J'en ai sérieusement ma claque.* (Always the same story, mother. I seriously can't take this anymore)."

"*Tu crois que c'est facile pour moi d'être toujours loin de toi et ton frère? Je souffre énormément.*" (Do you think it's easy being far from you and your brother? I suffer greatly)."

"*Laisse ton histoire triste à tes amis. Ça ne marche pas avec moi.* (Leave your sob story with your friends. It doesn't work with me). Enough. *J'en peux plus!* (I'm done)."

The dialogue went back and forth like a Paris Masters tennis game. Sofia didn't have the patience to find out who would win match point, so she crawled back into bed.

As she lay there, her ego worked in overdrive—so much rage inside him, yet he seemed so put together on the outside. *Maybe I need to be listening to my ego on this one.* Her higher self zoomed in—*all is well. You will proceed slowly, but it's where you need to be.*

Amidst self-talk, the sound of her ringtone surprised her. She picked up. "Sofia!!! Where are you??" It took her a few seconds to understand who she was talking to.

Emma repeated, "Hello. Are you okay?"

As Sofia slowly came to, she whispered, "Yes, yes. Sorry. What's up?"

Emma replied, "Did you forget about dinner?"

She quickly glanced at the time on her phone. "Oh shit! I didn't realize."

She leaped out of bed and bolted to the bathroom. Despite the contention between mother and son, Sofia walked in to find Jude whistling a cheery tune. She got lost in la-la-land as she admired the man of her dreams rubbing after-shave on his face. His eyes lit up the moment he caught sight of her.

She snapped herself out of the schoolgirl daze and showed him the time. He acknowledged her by brushing his fingers down her face and then returned to his grooming.

He was turning out to be more enigmatic than she had ever imagined him to be. And what does a girl do when faced with such complexity? Why, she jumps right in with two feet, of course—just like the Fool card in the Tarot.

She removed her bathrobe and laid it on the bed. Sofia didn't have to turn around to feel his presence as she shimmied herself in her still-damp jeans, but she did anyway. He slipped on the tapered khaki pants neatly draped over the throne-like chair by the window. They perfectly outlined the definitions of his lower body. He wore those often back in Montreal. Sofia couldn't help but get lost in his every movement as he unzipped his garment bag and pulled out a charcoal crew neck sweater. The man had style.

He snaked his head back toward her and amusedly asked, "Aren't you in a hurry?"

Sofia nodded but didn't move. Setting the sweater aside, he reached his hand out to her. He twirled her into his arms and held onto her for a few seconds. She buried her face into his neck, kissing and inhaling his scent. He lassoed his arm around her waist. His firm grasp heightened her desire. She grabbed his head and kissed him. He heartily responded, skillfully unhooking her bra and pinning her against him.

Her phone rang again. Texts chimed in. They ignored it. The door swung open, and there stood Etienne. Jude quickly blanketed her body with an embrace and yelled out, "*Ouate de Phoque* (WTF). Give us a minute, *frérot (bro)*."

Etienne was already in the hallway. Jude rarely ever got upset at Etienne. It was interesting. And endearing at the same time.

As Etienne was having a full-blown, one-sided conversation with himself, Jude grazed his hand down the side of her body. "To be continued."

She pulled her top on and adjusted her hair as best she could; he went to the door to check on his friend. Then she panicked because her pendulum was no longer around her neck. She frantically looked on the bed, in the sheets, and under the bed. Nothing.

Etienne strolled in. "I kept telling Jude to get another room, but he was 'only coming for business' and 'not interested in hooking up with anyone.' Not that you are only hooking up, or maybe you are...."

Jude amicably slapped him on the arm. Jude moved forward, grabbed her hand, and pulled her in closer to him. "Hey, what's up? What happened."

She held back a waterfall of tears and pointed to her neck. "I lost my pendulum."

"Are you sure? It's probably here somewhere." He patted down the comforter and shook the pillows. He repeated the same movements as she did a few minutes earlier. And he came up with the same as Sofia.

Feeling defeated, sadness overcame her, and she sprinted to the door. Jude rushed forward and held her back. "We'll find it. I'll look for it. I will retrace our steps if I have to."

That pendulum had rested on her heart since her mother left the Earth plane. She felt the sincerity in his words, but it didn't matter. Losing the last bit of her mother was too much for her to handle. She couldn't keep it together, so she ran into the elevator.

Lola and Emma greeted Sofia in their hotel room, dressed to the nines and holding glasses of sparkling champagne.

Lola went into warrior mode. "What happened? What did he do to you?"

"N-no, it's not him."

Emma sat by Sofia and hugged her. "Cry it out and tell us when you are ready."

Sofia disclosed to them about the pendulum.

They comforted her with words of assurance. "We will find it. It will show up."

"Remember when you thought you lost it, and it just showed up?" Emma said. "It will be fine. And,"—she placed her hand on Sofia's heart— "she is always with you, regardless."

Sofia wiped away her tears and expressed gratitude to them while her inner self remained conflicted. Her higher self chimed in. *Your mother is a part of you. She's always inside you, my dear; that is more precious than an object.*

Before hopping into the shower, Lola mentioned they received a text from Jude about dinner plans. He invited them to accompany him to the restaurant in the hotel—he was doing the photo shoot in the lounge adjacent to it. Lola quickly added, "I mean, we couldn't refuse. It's one of the hippest eateries in the city right now. Plus, I want to see the decor."

Go with the flow, my child. Let these girls bring you back into the "now" moment. All will fall into place for you. You shall see.

As she dressed, she received a text from Jude inquiring about her status. She responded with an apology.

He texted:—Don't apologize. I would be upset too, but I will do my best to find it for you. Hope to see you later. xx J—

She resolved to wear her go-to outfit—a black fitted dress, her treasured textured heels gifted to her from Lola from one of her Italy trips, and the bejeweled cuff Sofia bought eons ago in a tiny shop in Cannes. Lola sported a red tulle skirt with a blue and white striped sweatshirt, and Emma was on the other end of the fashion spectrum in a silky gray jumpsuit. Their different styles and distinct personalities were a testament to their everlasting friendship.

Lola handed Sofia a flute filled with water and proceeded with a toast as they held their glasses up. "Cheers to Sofia for always being a trooper no matter what gets thrown at her. And also,"—she batted her eyes—" for maybe finding the one!"

That was one way to revert Sofia's attention away from the sadness, but she still shook her head, "Relax, my friends…."

Before she could continue, Lola shushed her and said, "We know that you had lost hope in true love, but you may have stumbled on it again, so why not revel in it?"

Emma continued the toast, "And if there is hope for you, then for damn sure, there is hope for me."

Lola rolled her eyes and lightly slapped Emma on her arm. Sofia just let out a heavy sigh.

SURRENDER

Shhh…
Listen.
Your soul knows.

10

The line-up at the restaurant's entrance endlessly lapped around the lobby. Lola tugged on Sofia's arm. "Come. Jude gave us clear instructions on who to talk to at the door."

As they zigzagged their way around the uppity, puffed-up patrons, a broad-shouldered man abruptly put his palm in their faces, stopping them in their tracks. His hand in her face miffed her, but Lola still conveyed kindness. She asked for Rebecca. He called out to the slender, unresponsive girl a few feet away. And when she looked their way, Sofia recognized her as the flirtatious hostess from the night before.

She waved her finger at the bouncer and waved them to the end of the line.

Sofia turned to the girls. "Let's go somewhere else. I am not going to take attitude from this girl."

Lola held her hand up and said, "Since when do you give up so easily? Let me handle this." She whipped out her phone, and within a few minutes, Etienne was by their side. He leaned in to talk to the hostess. She promptly fidgeted with her side ponytail while batting her eyes. He continued to flirt until Sofia snapped her fingers to get his attention.

He came to and said, "Yes, yes. Okay."

He pointed to Sofia. The hostess begrudgingly motioned to the bouncer to let them in. Unfazed, he unhooked the velvet rope.

She escorted them to the center of the room, which blossomed with booths in the form of petals. Velvet-covered seating donned every booth in hues from the most popular floral families. Wild-flowered wallpaper blanketed the ceiling. Shards of terracotta and patches of moss rolled along the walls and flooring. Wicker baskets overflowing with burro tails cascaded from the top. Lola was quick to touch on the placement and choice of each detail. Sofia listened to them both criticize and praise the decor, another reason she loved going to restaurants with them. As they continued on their lengthy rant, Sofia handed the girls a glass of the Rose

Veuve Clicquot waiting for them on the table. She then poured herself one too.

Lola looked at her. "You drinking tonight, my dear?"

"I think I deserve at least one glass of bubbly."

An impressive seafood platter arrived at their table, overflowing with luscious oysters, clams, jumbo shrimp, tuna ceviche, and scallops. Lola kicked Sofia under the table, veering her attention to Emma. She was never one to splurge on food or drink.

Sofia winked at Emma and reminded her, "We have to live our best life, right, Emma?"

She half-smiled.

A hip, twenty-five-year-old appeared before them. "Hi. My name is Jamal, and I will be your waiter tonight. I hope you don't mind, but your menu was pre-selected by Jude."

Their expressions propelled him to add, "And don't worry; it's all taken care of by him too." He winked and continued, "Feel free to stay as long as you want."

Lola was over the moon. Emma finally settled down. Sofia, on the other hand, was once again on that proverbial fence.

But her higher self kicked in and asked, *Can you just enjoy what is being given to you?* Sofia laughed inwardly.

Lola reached over and held her hand. "I can hear the wheels turning in your mind. You need to let this go, Sofia. You are always so quick to be generous with others. What do you always say? We are all mirrors of each other?"

The atmosphere became increasingly lively as the epic sounds of Ben Böhmer vibrated through the speakers. They went over the happenings of the day in more detail. Sofia recounted the encounter with Jude, but Etienne popped up as she was about to get into the nitty-gritty. He scooted right by Emma. Sofia didn't expect to see her blush; even Lola remarked on the change in her.

"So, what do you think so far?" he asked.

Sofia nodded but conveyed her concern at the expense.

He waved his hand at her. "This is nothing!"

Lola kicked Sofia under the table again, resulting in a shift of all the plates and cutlery. She pursed her lips together, and Etienne laughed out loud. As they shared a moment, Sofia witnessed a tinge of jealousy wash over Emma's face.

Sofia pondered for a minute. *If Emma is also interested, this will get into a sisterhood battle I'd rather not get involved in.* Her higher self chuckled. *Let's see if you can stick your nose out of this one.*

Jamal passed by and asked Etienne if he was going to join. He looked at them. "Well, it depends if the ladies want me to join?"

Lola welcomed Etienne with open arms while Emma quietly nodded. They ordered more champagne.

Sofia inquired about Jude's whereabouts. He slapped his forehead with the palm of his hand and exclaimed, "*Putain* (Fuck). That's why I came here, to bring you to him."

She shook her head. "Wow, it doesn't take much for you—a little flirtation, a little champagne."

His cheeks flushed. He grabbed Sofia's hand and said, "Come, I'll show you where he is." He turned back to the girls. "I'll be back."

Lola raised her glass. "We aren't going anywhere."

He led her across the way to a lavish nightclub with textured paneled walls, ornamental tiling, and over-the-top lamps. There were numerous rooms, each with its own story. They had set up Jude in the purple-lit room. There were massive light bulbs, racks of clothing, and tables of jewelry and accessories. Centerfold-worthy models decked out in haute couture leisurely stood around the room. His team waved at Sofia, propelling Jude to look up. As soon as they locked eyes, he amorously smiled. He called for a break and rushed over to her.

He pirouetted her around, pinned her arm behind her back, and growled, "I can't wait for this to be over."

Those damn butterflies were back.

"I hope everything is to your liking."

Sofia commented on his over-generosity, and he reacted much as Etienne did. So, she let it go.

"Let me return to work to continue where we left earlier this evening." He gently kissed her lips. "*A bientôt* (See you soon)."

Mesmerized by his creativity and focus, Sofia watched him in his element. His unique directing style opened her eyes to new perspectives she had never seen before.

Etienne joined her. "It's impressive, eh? But Jude makes it look so easy. He's a real master at what he does—a perfectionist. I love watching him at work."

"Right, that's why you are here to watch him and not the eye candy!" she said, nudging him gently.

He wickedly grinned. Before returning to the restaurant, she noticed Jude checking his phone and swearing under his breath. "*Bordel de merde* (For fuck's sake)."

She turned to Etienne and just stared.

He winced and told her he would linger a little longer with Jude.

The girls were in deep conversation while picking at the plates of risotto, ravioli, and roasted beet salad set before them. Sofia wanted to fill her besties in about the redhead. But Lola was deep into one of her colorful tales when she sat down. Tonight's topic *"du jour,"* was about her last boyfriend. He reached out to her a few days ago, and she couldn't get it out of her mind. Lola and Sebastian dated for three years. Both were very eccentric. Their bohemian lifestyles meshed well until he wanted to settle down and have children. She, on the other hand, was flying high in her career and wasn't yet ready for the picket fence life.

"Are you ready now?" Sofia asked.

Lola blankly stared at her. "Yes, and no. I want children, but that would mean taking a step back in my buying trips. I'm not sure if I'm ready."

Lola's hands rose and hid her face. "Does that make me horrible?"

And hence the dilemma women faced dealing within this society that claimed they were worthless if they didn't conceive.

Emma interjected, "There is no good or bad here. What do you want? It's not about him. It's not about the would-be child. It's about you."

"Either way," Sofia added, "we have your back. But also know that having a baby does not impede your career. Heck, you can take your baby with you on these trips. All you need to do is bring your favorite babysitters." She pointed to both herself and Emma.

Lola smiled. She made life more complicated than it was. And Sofia was bringing her together with Etienne, so she had to know. "The question here is, do you want to go back with Seb?"

Lola bit down on her lip and shrugged her shoulders. Then her eyes lit up. When Sofia twisted her head, she caught sight of Etienne. The plot thickened. They poured more champagne.

Etienne took over the conversation and regaled them with stories about his life growing up in Paris and his crazy Moroccan family. The more he rattled on, the more both girls warmed up to his beguiling ways. Sofia leaned back on the plush velvet, but the minute she closed her eyes to visualize Jude, the incident with Gabrielle replayed in her head. She spooked herself out, swiftly opened her eyes, and landed on Etienne's gaze.

He immediately reverted his attention to the girls. Sofia kept her eyes on him—they had an undeniable connection. Her higher self chimed in, *Yes, indeed. Stop thinking and enjoy, please.*

After the third bottle of champagne and dessert, Etienne waved his smartphone. "I just got the approval to bring you, ladies, to the lounge."

****

Subtle down-tempo beats simmered in the background. The wait staff huddled by the bar as their manager coached them, giving them their pep talk of the night. Jude's equipment and team were nowhere in sight. Two burly bouncers guided them up to a platform overlooking the dance floor. They padded them down and directed them to a booth closer to the tall window spilling over the Manhattan skyline. Not a moment too soon, a voluptuous waitress was pressed up against Etienne. Completely ignoring their presence, she listened closely to his every word. He milked every last drop of this attention. Meanwhile, back on earth, Lola was at it again, critiquing the interior design.

Sofia faced the cityscape, mesmerized by the seesaw of art déco and modern architectural buildings. She was quickly snapped out of her reverie by two servers who squeezed past her legs to place a shiny silver bucket on the table. Etienne waved at them, "Drink up, ladies!" Emma prepared all their drinks—she was the designated bartender whenever they had dinner parties. She had an eye for measurement. It didn't take long for others to join their booth—some of the models and the rest of the entourage, but still no Jude. As Sofia scanned the area, the club was filling up. It never took long for the "right" clubs to fill up with the "right" people.

She observed all the activity before her: Etienne heavily flirted with everyone, and Lola twirled around and danced alone. Emma sat pencil-straight at the edge of the seat, looking at everyone and no one. She imagined all the self-defeatist talk going on in her head. Sofia flew to her feet ever so graciously.

Snatching Emma's hand, Sofia said, "C'mon, ladies, let's go dance."

Before leaving the guarded area, one bouncer branded them with an invisible stamp.

There's probably a tracking device on my arm now.

She set aside her distaste for the 3D ways for the night and followed the strobing lights to the center of the crystal-gridded dance floor. She remembered the series she had done about Earth's crystalline grid anchoring the template of the New Earth. Lola was already dancing with a group of people. Emma joined in the fun. It was good to see Emma let go of her ego for a while. When both girls cocked their heads to the side and smiled, Sofia knew Jude was behind her. His arms encircled her waist, securing her body in his embrace. He leaned into her. Flames of heat rushed through her body. He fluttered sweet kisses on the back of her neck. She felt a white light encapsulate their bodies. It was just her and him in the Universe, and she was content to stay that way all night long.

Etienne made his way to them and danced with Emma first. Her stand-offish reaction didn't bode well for him. So he turned toward Lola, who was more receptive. This love triangle was becoming more intriguing by the minute.

When Jude swirled her around to face him, Lola, Emma, and Etienne were but a memory. Too entranced by him, she couldn't even remember their names. They swayed to the electro-soul beats, body to body, mouth to mouth.

She whispered, "Can we go back to the room?"

His hand journeyed down her body and back up again. "I can't go yet," he whispered. "I have to schmooze with the owners of the club." He frowned. "It's my least favorite part of the job, but I need to do it."

With the tip of her finger, she traced his lips. "If that's absolutely what you must do."

He gently bit her finger and moaned. "And they ask me why I'm attracted to older women."

He kissed her forehead, tapped Etienne on the shoulder, and jetted off to hobnob with the rich and famous.

Wait, what? Who were "they"? And how does he know how old I am?

Sofia's ego tried hard to penetrate her mind, but she was well-versed in stopping it in its path. She was also very good at letting it back in. No one said a spiritual awakening would be easy.

As she stood alone on the dance floor, her inner voice shouted at her to look back. She knew her higher self was very present when her head felt heavy. She turned, only to catch the redhead by the entrance.

Where's Jude? Why didn't Etienne see her coming right at me? Am I dreaming?

Sofia's heart was beating at lightning speed. When yet another New Yorker bumped into her, she lost her footing and almost hit the ground until Etienne broke her fall. Supporting her, he smiled but soon reversed it upon seeing the look on her face.

"Are you okay? Did you see her?"

Sofia nodded.

"Can you bring your girls to the booth, please?"

Sofia gave him a dirty look.

"Please. I would feel better if you were safe. I need to find Jude before he does something regretful."

Regretful? As soon as he went off to search for Jude, she had to devise a little white lie to tell the girls—but another lie meant another lesson. *I gotta do what I gotta do.*

She turned to the girls. "This place is too pretentious for me. I think I'm gonna head out."

"We just got here," Emma whined. "Are you sure? What about Jude?"

"He's not finished working. He needs to do his rounds with the owners and the V.I.P." Sofia rolled her eyes. "You know how I feel about that kind of crowd. But, you ladies can stay."

Lola curiously looked at Sofia."We'll come with you."

Once they pushed through the horde of club-goers, Emma grabbed Sofia's arm and pointed to the far left corner. There was Jude and Gabrielle. They were in a heated discussion. She was gorgeous—her red hair billowing past her shoulders. She almost towered Jude with her four-inch heels and perfect long legs. Young girls taking photo ops with them surrounded them.

Wow. What the fuck is happening here? Look at them; they look perfect together. Even when Sofia's higher self tried to comfort her—*You have nothing to worry about*—she still wasn't convinced. *I feel so sick right now. I want to scream.*

Emma grabbed onto Sofia's arm. "Let's go. Whatever this is, it is not where you need to be." She urged Sofia to leave.

Lola squinted her eyes and, without a word, lingered with Sofia behind the colossal plants. The starlet was causing a raucous. Sofia somehow felt the tension rising within Jude. The club owners loved Gabrielle's presence and all the hoopla that came with her. When Jude gripped Gabrielle's hand to bring her into a private room, Sofia's heart dropped, and when the redhead slipped her arm around his waist, and he allowed her to stay that way for a bit too long, Sofia had enough. *Am I seeing what I'm seeing? Is this another test? I'm floored right now. I can't. He doesn't seem so bothered by her presence. Have I completely lost all my Spidey-senses?* The flashbulbs were unceasing.

Sofia couldn't take her eyes off Jude and Gabrielle. Unfortunately, she also witnessed Gabrielle lean in for a kiss. He didn't pull away as quickly as Sofia had hoped. The paparazzi went wild. *I can't believe I got so blindsided by him. Fuck him. I'm so over this crap.*

"Oh, so maybe I still have a chance with your "not-yet" boyfriend!" Suddenly, out of nowhere, Trinity appeared. Her words pierced Sofia's heart.

As Lola tugged on Sofia's hand to leave the bar, Trinity held her back and purred, "They make a good-looking couple, though." She was on a roll, "She's a bit of competition for me, but I think I can work my magic."

Lola raised her voice, "Do you know this girl, Sofia? Who the hell does she think she is talking to you like this?"

She didn't wait for an answer and defended Sofia like the "badass" friend that she was. While Lola and Trinity bickered, Sofia unclenched her hand and headed straight to Jude.

Sofia wouldn't let this one go; instead, she barrelled through the muster of peacocks, only to come face-to-face with Etienne.

"Don't do it." He grabbed onto her wrist and constrained her. "Trust me."

Jude side-eyed Sofia and gestured with his hand for her to leave.

"I've played nice all weekend, but you don't want to get on my bad side." She relayed her message loud and clear to Jude's best friend. She peeled Etienne's fingers—one by one—from her wrist. The Leo in her was ready to show them who was Queen of the Jungle. Instead, she tamed herself and said, "I'm going to walk away now." Then she peered into his eyes, "The moment I turn my back is the last time you see me. That's it. I'm so done with you and with him."

He played me. Wow, Sofia, you can really pick them. Her higher self tried to squeeze in a message, but she wasn't in the mood, so she shut it down. *I fell backward into the Matrix. I did this to myself. And now, I have to regain my strength again. He wants to play in this illusion with Gabrielle; then, he can go right ahead. But there's no fucken way I'm gonna join their game.*

And anyway, he owes me nothing. And I owe him nothing.

She fled the club with Lola in tow.

11

Exiting the club, Lola and Emma dragged Sofia to a quieter corner of the lobby area and began drilling her with questions.

"What the hell is happening, girlfriend?"—"Who is the stunning redhead?"—"Who is the other girl?"—"What is going on with you and Jude?"

Sofia gnawed on her lower lip, trying to make sense of it all. Tears welled up in her eyes—her head about to explode—she gestured to her friends for some space. Request granted.

Once fully composed, she briefly went into the lobby encounter with Trinity and then into the Central Park encounter. She told them as much as she knew about Gabrielle; the rest were all assumptions.

"So, you think he's dating her right now?" Emma asked.

Sofia shrugged, shaking her head. "I don't know what to think. And quite frankly, I don't give a damn. It's why I've been single for so long. I can't deal with this crap." She quieted down and continued, "I mean, the time we have spent together would make me think otherwise. But who knows anymore? We've been duped many times in our past, right?"

Lola hugged her. "I still think you need to wait for his explanation. The way he looks at you and acts around you, I'm not convinced she's a current girlfriend. Maybe an ex for sure, but that's it." She paused. "And that Trinity girl, wow, she was unrelenting."

A silence descended upon them until Lola asked, "What do you say we continue this night and end this girls' weekend on a high?"

Emma rubbed Sofia's arms, smiling. "I think it's a great idea, right, Sofia?"

Lola suggested a bar she had visited on one of her buying trips, just a short distance from the hotel. Sofia was there, as long as there was no Jude, no redhead, and no drama. The energy in the city was buzzing. Her mood, not so much. Sofia believed in soul contracts, yet here she was in full victim mode, feeling sorry for herself. She went further into her ego mind and scolded herself for going down the rabbit hole of jealousy, fear, and doubt.

How could I be a mentor if I can't even follow my own teachings?

And the conversation pursued this way in her mind for a few blocks until Lola yanked her arm. "This is not going to work if you go into that dark place of yours."

"Lola! How can you be so insensitive?" Emma said, frowning.

Before this turned into a squabble, because they all knew why Emma was agitated with Lola, Sofia said, "You know what, Lola is right."

She fanned out her hands, and they each held one another's hand. They stood in a circle, looked into each other's eyes, and acknowledged the hurts, pains, and love. They had been doing these circles for over twenty years—it was their way of finding their way back to their center. Even the catcalls and snide remarks from some of New York's finest didn't deter them from their bonding moment.

Walking arm in arm, they reminisced about their meal, the music, and the people. They were careful not to mention any of the other players of the weekend.

They managed to snag a high table close to the bar. She preferred to stand, so Emma and Lola sat on the quilted leather chairs. Presented with an extensive cocktail list, they exchanged a knowing glance, realizing they were in for a long night ahead.

And so the drinking continued for Emma and Lola.

Was it a coincidence that Michael and Pedro showed up at the bar? Emma blushed and raised her shoulders.

Lola started singing aloud to the Beatles' song playing in the background, draping an arm around Sofia's shoulders. Meanwhile, Sofia couldn't help but bring up images of Jude. Just the mention of his name in that song, she was off into fantasyland. Sofia downed her water to clear away the incredible chemistry she shared with him. She wanted no part of that drama if he was involved with Gabrielle.

Emma squeezed her wrist and leaned in. "Sorry, I invited them. I needed some male attention tonight."

Sofia graciously smiled.

As if she was in Sofia's head, Emma whispered, "Don't give up so easily on Jude. Let him explain his side of the story. I'm sure you know what you have is special."

Oh, the power of carnal attraction. Pedro was quite the looker with smoldering brown eyes and curly brown hair; his masculinity radiated off him like a solar flare. Watching Emma's inherent, reserved nature battle with his overtly affectionate ways amused Sofia. She was handling it like a champ, though. Meanwhile, Lola, as bold as brass, had no qualms about flirtatiously dancing around Michael. They were doing just fine without her. So Sofia bid farewell to Emma, Lola, and their dates.

Once outside, she slipped in her earphones to drown out the city's liveliness. She selected her favorite self-healing playlist to quiet her mind. As long as her vibration was high, she was well protected. It still didn't stop her from surrounding herself with a bubble of light to shield her. Astonished by how the shield worked, she weaved around the throng of humans.

When she arrived at the hotel, she hesitated. The last thing she wanted to do was run into Jude, Etienne, or even worse, Gabrielle. Every inch of the lobby and open areas were jam-packed with people. *Okay, higher self, do your thing. Which is the best way in without getting noticed?* The answer came in quickly. *Go to the day concierge.*

Coincidentally, he worked the night shift and was overjoyed seeing Sofia. When she asked him to whisk her away from all the hoopla discreetly, he took his mission quite seriously.

He glanced around. "Are there bad people looking for you?"

She laughed inside but went along with his suspicion. "Something like that."

He skipped in his steps, grabbed her by the hand, and whispered, "Follow me."

He led her behind the quiet nook where she had spent the first night with Jude and into a secret doorway.

Always a secret passage for these elitists.

He then led her to a private elevator. He escorted Sofia directly to her room, eyeing each guest as they passed.

"Would you rather I set you up in another room for the night? That way, you are safe from the dark ones."

He had a wild imagination. Or perhaps he'd seen all kinds of bad behavior. *Hmmm...* Sofia wondered if she should talk more to him. But his energy verged on vampirism, and she wasn't in the mood to fend it off all night.

Privacy is what Sofia needed, so she accepted his offer. She gathered her belongings and followed him into the elevator up to the penthouse. She couldn't possibly afford this, so she politely declined.

He patted her arm. "Oh, honey, this is my gift to you. There's no one staying here tonight. As long as you're out by the afternoon—all is fine." He paused, gazing at her. "This is the least I can do for Divine Sofia."

His generosity touched her. Even though, technically, it wasn't him paying for it.

"Will Jude Christophe be joining you?" He blushed at the mere mention of his name.

Sofia grinned. "No, not tonight. I must be alone to work on my new episode without interruption." She winked.

He was all giddy, a smile widening across his face."Oh yes. Yes. I will leave you to it." Before leaving, he pirouetted and said, "Please, enjoy all there is to offer in the mini-fridge. It's quite a treat!"

As he turned to leave, Sofia stopped him and slipped him a tip to thank him.

"You are so kind. You don't have to." He took it, anyway. "Keep doing your wonderful work. It truly does help us on this journey." He stepped outside into the hall and blew her a kiss.

First, she texted the girls that she was staying in another room and bid them good night. She didn't have much energy to explore each room, but she did step into the bathroom suite. The square bathtub was inviting her, so as soon as she figured out how to turn on the faucet, she let the water flow.

She slipped out of her clothes and enveloped herself in one of the plush velvet bathrobes. Living the high life wasn't new. Her Italian-born father may have landed in Canada with a few dollars in his pocket, but his ambition far exceeded his circumstances. His hopes and dreams of the new world paid off, providing her and her brother a comfortable life.

She plopped down on the king-size bed in starfish mode. The opulent chandelier with etched glass pendants reflecting a constellation of stars on the ceiling mesmerized her. She was in her own little cosmos, far from the crazy of the real world. She remembered, as a child having a galaxy wallpaper on her ceiling. Every night, her mother would lie on the bed with her, and they would come up with stories about each star system. Sofia's mother was open-minded and learned in esoteric studies but only shared it with her clients and daughter.

Sofia's father and brother were a bit more conservative. They didn't take well to her mother's energy healing practice. Her dad supported her mother's vocation but never boasted about it publicly. It seemed the apple hadn't fallen far from the tree since Sofia continued where her mother left off. She missed her so much.

She wondered about Gianluca and how he was doing with his newfound family. It had been five years since she had seen her brother. Their last words to each other were insensitive and downright boorish. They never saw eye-to-eye throughout their childhood, so it was a given that Sofia's life choices would be ludicrous to him. Ever since their mother died, the family fell apart at the seams. They became the dysfunctional family often shown on the tell-lie-vision.

She snapped out of her dream state when her higher self shouted, *Bathtub*. She leaped out of bed and ran to turn it off. As she released the day's energies, she remembered why she was still single. She closed her eyes. Her mind went straight to the day in the park with her and Jude reading the book. It then skipped to the shower—how she reveled in those precious moments of tenderness and sensuality.

Yet, here she found herself at odds with Jude. Was he dating Gabrielle? Was he true to his word? Did she make it all up in her head? Her higher self responded to all the questions. *No. Yes. No.* And that was that. She didn't want to linger in the drama.

When she felt depleted, her higher self encouraged her to shower or jump into a pool—not only did it clear her mind, but it also reconnected her to her true essence.

Once finished, she prepared herself for bed. She looked forward to a peaceful night's sleep. Walking over to the mini-bar, she peeked inside. Oh, what a delight—filled with the highest quality spirits. She chose the ten-dollar water and low-vibe junk food.

An overabundance of fairy lights glistened through the white flowing curtains. Her curiosity got the best of her. When she slid the balcony door open, she discovered a mystical wonderland. Lined with evergreen hedges along the glass railing, the potted Oxalis and Goldenrod seemed to delight in Sofia's presence as they sprang to attention. The rattan bed and swing chair were calling her name. She snooped inside the tall wicker basket by the bed and discovered pillows and quilts. She pulled out the heaviest blanket and prepared her nook for quiet time. Before settling in, she grabbed her earphones, a sweater, and smartphone.

When her mind quieted, the city's energy continued reverberating in her soul. She always felt uncomfortable in the chaos of this city. She pulled out her phone and found numerous texts from Jude.

12:12 a.m.—Sofia, pls text me. You must know that there is nothing between Gabrielle and me. J—

12:22 a.m.—I'm getting reprimanded by Etienne–this is a first. Pls lmk where you are so we can talk. xx J—

12:34 a.m.—Are you ghosting me? I don't understand why you're not answering me. At least, let me explain. J—

1:01 a.m.—I thought you were different. J—

Is this guy for real? The last text hit hard—a rush of panic surged through her body. All went blank. *He thought I was different—different from whom?* She chucked the phone onto the cushion and tried to collect herself. Her higher self came in loud and clear. *Do not take this personally. You need to talk to him, my dear.*

It seemed she was shutting down her ego and her higher self tonight. Then a text chimed in—Hey! I'm at your room door. Are you here? J—

Sofia went back and forth on whether she should run down and talk to him or continue ignoring him.

She did one worse and texted him back in her unfiltered self:

1:53 a.m.—I'm not in the room. I'm out. And it's none of your business where I am and with whom. You've made it very clear that...actually, you've made nothing clear at all. I can't believe I fell for it and fell for you, either. Was this weekend all a game to you? Or, maybe this was one big lesson I had to learn. Wtv it was. Please stop texting me. S—

The phone went silent and stayed that way for the better part of the night until she received a text from Etienne.

2:25 a.m.—This is none of my business, but he's a mess, and I've never seen him like this...I mean, I have...but not over a girl. Please do me a favor and text him in the morning. Sorry for the late text. I hope I didn't wake you up, and if I did, my bad. Anyways, good night. xo E—

I seriously don't know what to think anymore. But it's only been a weekend. Why am I getting so worked up? I just need to relax and go back to living carefree and single. Relationships are not my thing, it seems.

Sofia shut her phone for the night.

MIRROR

Stand up.
Look at me.
Show me what I need to see.

12

When Sofia woke up, she had to re-acclimatize. Did she dream about the events of the last few days? Did she jump into another reality? Where was she? She looked at the alarm clock in the room: 7:17—the angel number for solid unions, twin flame love. When Sofia checked her phone, there were new texts. She slipped it under the silk pillow for the time being. A little more rest would have been nice, but it wasn't to be. Her mind was akin to a hamster wheel.

    Instead of enjoying her time in the deluxe pad, she jumped in the shower and then gathered all her things. A walk in the city would soothe her. Sunday mornings were the best times to explore busy metropolitan cities. Only Lola was there when she dropped off her stuff in the room.

    There was hardly anyone in the lobby. Sofia slithered past the concierge desk, down the escalator, and onto the sidewalk. The streets of Manhattan were silently chaotic. She disengaged her lower ego mind, which was very much in the mood to play. In quieting her mind, she played her go-to soul-healing music by her galactic sister, Mei-Lan Maurits. Her transcendental voice instantly soothed upset nerves. Gone were the worries.

    She sat on a random bench on a random street to go within. But her ego won today with the many questions and queries popping up in her mind: *What role did Gabrielle play in his life? Can I trust Jude? What's the deal with his mother? What's up with his mood swings? Is this a test from the Universe? Haven't I been tested enough in this lifetime? Why am I allowing my ego to be so prevalent right now? Have I not learned anything?* And on and on it went.

    With her eyes shut, she replayed all the weekend's events in her mind. She popped open her eyes, realizing someone had sat beside her. Gabrielle. Sofia didn't flinch. She was more curious than ever to hear Gabrielle's side of the story. As they sat in silence, they both observed one other. The color of her eyes mirrored Sofia's. Sofia's higher self warned her to tread slowly, so she did. When Gabrielle reached out her hand toward Sofia, she shook it.

"Hi. My name is Gabrielle."

That was pleasant enough. Sofia didn't offer her name. She noticed her perfectly manicured fingernails. And how the gold jewelry she wore gleamed in the early morning sun. Still, her higher self cautioned her.

"I don't know if you know who I am."

She waited for Sofia to acknowledge her. Not understanding the question, Sofia shook her head.

"Well..." She pulled out her smartphone and showed Sofia her Instagram page with 1.3 million followers. "...this is me. And,"—she scrolled a little more— "this is Jude."

It was a photo of the two smiling, arm in arm. Sofia's heart broke into a million pieces, but she kept her disappointment to herself. "And?"

Gabrielle scrolled lower and showed her more pics of her and Jude. "We are a couple. And you are in the way. He is the love of my life, and I am his."

She appeared erratic. Sofia reached over, placed her hand on Gabrielle's arm, and said, "I am not aware of your relationship. Jude and I are just two people getting to know each other."

If she could have stabbed Sofia with her eyes, she would have been bleeding all over the bench. Gone was Gabrielle's calmness.

She jumped off the seat and exclaimed, "No! There's no you getting to know him. He's mine. All mine." Then she came up into Sofia's face and yelled, "Do you understand?"

This was not Sofia's first rodeo dealing with crazy exes. As Gabrielle composed herself, she sat back down. Sofia remained quiet, although her insides were raging. She went right to her Higher Self. *Why would you encourage this union if he's dating her? I don't fucken understand anything. There's clearly a connection here, even if she feels off to me. Why would he lie to me? I don't know who to believe anymore. Ughhhhh!*

Gabrielle began to talk to herself. "No one loved me as he did." She corrected herself, "He does." She looked at Sofia with her piercing eyes. "He was, uhh, is so gentle and caring with me. I feel lonely when he's not around. I feel like ending my life at times. Life is worthless without him."

For a moment, Sofia felt her heart sink. Her empathic side emerged, and she listened with an open heart. Sofia's ego shrieked, *Don't fall for it! She's manipulating you.* Meanwhile, her Higher Self whispered, *She is troubled, dear child, be cautious. Stay calm.*

Gabrielle continued her sob story. "My family only loves me now that I have over one million followers. But before, when I had a measly hundred thousand followers like you have, they treated me like nothing."

Sofia did not engage. It all had become apparent. Gabrielle was probably the one who disliked her videos and left nasty comments.

"Jude was....er.... is the only man that ever truly loved me for me. Not for my money." She turned to Sofia. "Because I have a lot of that."

Sofia continued to listen to her rants. *I don't know how much more I can take of this. I know she's crazy, but why am I subjecting myself to her? But, most importantly, why did Jude leave these bits of information out?*

"You know that Jude is loaded, right? His family is very wealthy. And wealthy families only like to mingle with their counterparts. So, maybe he was playing with you this weekend because he was away from his family, but he could never settle down with you, ever." She mockingly laughed and then shouted, "EVER!"

Wealthy this, wealthy that. Who fucken cares? She's right about one thing—he's playing one of us.

At that moment, Sofia's phone dinged with a text message from the girls. Gabrielle violently cocked her head toward Sofia's phone. "Is that him?" she yelled.

Fucken psycho! She can keep Jude all to herself. I'm not interested in all this drama. They're perfect for each other.

Gabrielle leaped to her feet and shouted, "His mother wants me to marry him. There's no way you have a chance with him. He's mine!"

"I had enough of your bullshit!" Sofia barked back as she got up to leave.

"Where do you think you're going? I'm not done with you yet."

Sofia wasn't in the least bit afraid of her, even though she probably should have been. "Are you serious? You don't have control over me, woman," she said, eyes narrowing. "If I choose to leave right now, I will!"

Gabrielle lunged at her. "Over my dead body!"

Sofia stepped aside and shouted, "Don't tempt me!"

Gabrielle met her match. Reaching out, she scraped Sofia's cheek. Stabbing pain hit instantly, but Sofia didn't wait around for more. She spotted a cab from the corner of her eye, ran, and jumped right in.

Resting back against the seat, a rush of emotions flowed through her like molten lava. She hadn't been triggered like this in a long time. The pounding sensation in her heart weakened as the cab rolled down the street. Sofia felt the slow burn on her cheek.

The cabbie offered her a tissue box. "Please, no blood in my car."

Only then did she realize how deep the cut was. Lola and Emma were outside waiting for the car when he dropped her off in front of the hotel. She got out of the cab, fuming. "Guess who I ran into this lovely morning?"

"No way! What the fuck?" Lola embraced Sofia.

Emma pulled her away from Lola's arms. "Why are you bleeding? Did you physically fight with her? Come. Let me get you cleaned up."

As Emma dragged her wounded friend into the hotel, Jude intercepted them.

Sofia put up her other hand in his face. "I don't want to see you right now. Please, go away." It was hard for her to think clearly when he was around.

He tilted his head, staring at her cheek. "She did this to you?"

Lola nodded while Sofia ignored him.

"Fuck! *Elle est vraiment une connasse!* (She's such a bitch)." He roared. "Why does she have to get in my way every single time?" He regained his composure. "I'm so sorry, Sofia. I will straighten this up, I promise." His gaze pleaded for her understanding. "I know I'm asking a lot from you, but I want to see you again. Please, Sofia."

Sofia blankly stared at him. *He's so fucken hot. But, no, he can't get under my skin. Nope. Fuck him.* Her heart was still racing from the encounter with Gabrielle. *He doesn't get to play with my heart this way. I don't know who to believe.* Emma returned with a first aid kit from the concierge's desk. She pulled Sofia away from Jude and sat her down on one of the steps.

She tended her wounds as diligently as possible while Lola spoke with Jude and Etienne. There were some raised voices and then mumbled ones. Sofia had no idea what they were discussing but knew for damn sure Lola had her back.

When Lola's car pulled up, the valet pressured them to clear the space. Lola shoved all the bags into the trunk while Emma tried desperately to straighten them up. Sofia made her way to the car, but Jude stopped her. The valet yelled for them to move out of the way. Etienne slipped him some money, which shut him up for the time being.

Don't look into his eyes. Don't get sucked into his beautiful greens. Sofia thanked her ego for watching out for her.

When his fingers lifted her chin, she still kept her eyes downcast.

"Sofia, please look at me."

She bravely met his eyes and callously replied, "I just can't. I had one rule—no more drama, but it seems to follow you around." She sighed, "And you lied to me, too."

He fell silent. Sofia couldn't hear what was going on in his mind. "It is a lot. But I didn't lie to you. I may have skirted around the truth—it was only to keep you safe."

"Safe? It didn't work out that well for me, did it?" She pointed to her cheek.

His posture stiffened as he rubbed his temples and the top of his head with his hands.

At the corner of her eye, she saw Etienne make a beeline toward Jude. He called out to his friend, "*Réfléchi avant de parler* (Think before you speak)!"

Jude leered at him. He then twisted his body to face Sofia. His eyes were as empty as the hole in her heart the night her mother left the Earth plane. "You're right. There is a lot of drama in my life. It's been a long battle for me (and still is). The last thing I want to do is drag you into it." He forced a smile and then walked away.

Etienne breathlessly whispered to Sofia, "I will fix this." He sped off.

Sofia was caught off guard by Jude's glacial indifference.

As she watched him step onto the escalator, she screamed in her mind. *So, that's how you deal with conflict? You turn it around and blame me for your fucked up situation. Why are you such a coward?*

Much to her surprise, she received a response. *A coward, I am not. I'm not blaming you at all. You have no idea what I am up against. Maybe, one day you will better understand how I acted. For now, it's best that I take care of things on my end. I enjoyed spending time with you this weekend. But let's just leave it at that.*

She jerked her head right and left. Her heart raced as fast as a hummingbird's wings. *What is happening here? Can you hear me?*

A sole *Yes* resounded in her head. A big part of her wanted to run up to him and discuss this fantastic discovery. But the wounded part of her remained where she was. She hardly felt Lola and Emma's arms wrap around her as they ushered Sofia into the car.

The second she settled into the back seat, a deluge of tears cascaded down Sofia's cheeks. She thought, *When did he start hearing the crazy in my head? Why didn't he tell me?* Before Sofia continued in self-defeat, her higher self swooped in and reminded her that she didn't tell him either.

If we can both hear each other, our story is not over, then? The answer was *No*.

HOME

Twin flames are home to one another.
They awaken every room with their love.
They light the darkness with their power.
They ignite the hearth with their fire.

Home Sacred Home.

13

Just as Lola journeyed into the labyrinth of cars, cyclists, and humans, Sofia felt her body sink into the cushiony abyss of the seat. Any attempt to free herself resulted in more weighty energy. The only thing she could do was breathe her way out of the sinkhole.

Her ego was in complete control as reels of the weekend's events scrolled through her mind. All she wanted to do was cry but wasn't in the mood for consolation from her friends nor exploration into the why's and what's.

Lola caught her eyes in the rearview mirror and said, "Let it all out, Sof. It's the only way." She winked at Sofia and continued, "You know I'm right."

Then Emma offered her two cents, "I don't want to be a Debbie-downer, but you sort of provoked him to answer that way." She arched her eyebrows, looking at Lola for approval.

Lola shook her head.

Emma cried out, "What? It's the truth. Why is it that only Sofia can be forthright, but when I am, I get shunned by both of you."

Silence befell them, with only the pounding of the jackhammer at the nearby construction site echoing in the car. Sofia shut her eyes and quieted her mind. In doing so, she felt an old pattern rising within her—Jude's image was slowly fading, giving way to the black hole she believed to have buried long ago.

Instead of deep-diving, she re-focused her energy on the stinging pain gifted to her by Gabrielle. In doing so, Sofia chuckled.

Emma whipped her head around. "What are you laughing at?" She glared at Sofia.

Emma looked over at Lola. "I don't get Sofia anymore. One minute, she's laughing; the next, she's down in the dumps. One minute, she's in love; the next, she's aloof."

Lola quickly glanced over at Sofia and winked at her. She then veered her attention to Emma. "I don't get you, Emma. When did you become so insensitive? What gives you the right to judge her when you are the same?" She turned her head back to the road.

Oh, the mirror work was alive and well in the car.

Silence ensued a bit longer.

Sofia chose the high road and turned the conversation over to Emma.

"Can you regale us with one chapter from your last night with Pedro, Emma?"

No reaction from either of them. Sofia leaned over and coiled her hand around Emma's seat. She lightly played with the wispy hairs on the back of her friend's head. "C'mon, I don't want to fight. Let's change the mood, please."

Sofia's touch was calming to many. This gift came to light a few years back when she was involved in an altercation between strangers. When she placed her hands on both parties, they instantly subdued to her touch.

Sofia felt Emma's tension dwindle. Slowly, Emma recounted her sultry night with him. And that paved the way for more stories from Lola, as well. And before they knew it, they were already back in Montreal. They didn't need signs to tell them they were approaching the city—the roads were a clear indication as Lola swerved from left to right, avoiding the meteorite-sized potholes and endless rows of bright orange construction cones.

Sofia felt compelled to look at the graffiti under the bridge as they sat in traffic. Scrawled over the cement were the symbols Jude had tattooed on his fingers. Her heart skipped a beat. As they had been literally in a deadlock for the past ten minutes, Sofia asked to stop the car and swung open the door. "One sec."

She ran to the wall, snapping several pics of all the letters. She rushed back to several honking cars and waved her hand in apology. Emma groaned, "Why do you always have to disrupt our lives?"

Lola rolled her eyes. She looked at Sofia. "See, a small part of you still cares about him."

Sofia retorted, "It's for my research. It has nothing to do with him."

Lola pursed her lips together and nodded, "Well, I hope whatever you found there was captivating enough to upload a video for us all."

Sofia didn't have the energy to deal with Emma's snarky remark, nor Lola's "bright-side" thinking. Thankfully, Lola pulled up to her loft. She embraced them and said, "Ladies, this was a most memorable weekend." She reached out her hand toward Emma. "Still friends?"

Emma conceded and slipped her hand into Sofia's. "Friends."

Lola's eyes beamed with approval.

Sofia waved and shouted, "See you both, *mañana!*"

The door slammed behind her. As she stood in the darkness, fleeting strips of sunset shimmered through her shutters. As much as she loved adventures, she loved the comfort of her space more. Placing her carry-on aside, she slumped on the sofa amongst the sea of colorful pillows and throws she had picked up on her travels.

Having mastered heartbreak when her mother died, Sofia was used to being the rock, even if the earth was collapsing below her feet. She was the one that had to shelf her emotions to care for her father and brother. At the time, becoming the pillar seemed like the normal transition—it's what her mother would have done. Her grief and sorrow gradually gave way to responsibility and pragmatism. Sofia's fractured heart was so submerged that she learned to mask all that was painful—until she embarked on the awakening journey, forcing her to face her deepest wounds and fears. It still was a constant struggle—clearing the mind and living in the "now moment" had proven to be the most challenging task for every lightworker.

Heavy energies plagued her journey. As she was getting ready to build the Game-of-Thrones-sized wall around her heart, her higher self had another plan for Sofia. *You must know, dear one, the significance of meeting Jude this weekend. Surely, you felt the twin flame connection.*

It took Sofia by surprise. *Twin flames? Did I hear that correctly?*

Yes, my dear. And you know the predicament of twin flames on this journey—it's always a push and pull. It's the most challenging reflection of them all. But it's also the most profound one of them all.

Sofia had never put much thought into the twin flame journey regarding herself. She spent hours talking about it with her followers and friends, but with the slew of failed relationships behind her, she was pretty content with singlehood. Jude stirred up the dormant romanticism within her, but Sofia was still iffy about launching into this with him.

How was he able to shut me out so quickly?

Ahem, her higher self interrupted her, *two peas in a pod. Wouldn't you say?*

She acknowledged her higher self but wasn't in the mood to reason with it and shut it down. However, she was in the mood to drown in the darkness—her constant companion. Deep down, Sofia knew the lesson was showing up because it was time for her to confront the triggered, unhealed part of her. She could have thanked Jude for bringing this up in her, but tonight was not the night.

As the fiery reddish-golden sun bowed down to the glorious crescent moon, Sofia found herself in the depths of literal darkness. She had no energy to turn on the lights and remained still. As a child, the dark terrified her to no end. She later learned that all the monsters and shadowy figures that visited her at night were her angels and spirit guides attempting to awaken her from her slumber. Clicking into that realization years later changed her whole perspective. She waited for signs every night after that—they were few and far between, but still, Sofia held onto the hope of one day seeing or speaking to her team.

In adulthood, she resigned to settling with the "knowing" inside her heart—all she could do was trust in divine timing—when the time was right, they would present themselves.

The longer she sat in the dark, the emptier her mind became. And then, it happened. Her ego crept in and flooded it with an endless reel of images and conversations shared between Sofia and Jude. It was easy to fall prey to his grand gestures and the starry-eyed moments between lovers, but she was more seasoned than that.

Or so she thought.

The butterflies returned—stretching, squatting, lunging—ready to move into full acrobatics mode. If they were indeed twin flames, their story was far from over. Her high-school giddiness was back.

Sofia impulsively grabbed her phone to write an unfiltered text to the man that crushed her heart. Instead, she landed on an emoji-filled screen of hearts and praying hands from her besties. Not one text from Jude.

Her mind went back into overdrive. *Was this whole weekend even real? Was it all made up in my overactive mind? The twin flame journey is arduous—do I even have the stamina to embark on this?*

She diverted her attention to music before her higher self or ego could join the conversation. She selected the 528HZ healing and self-love soundtrack, shut her eyes, and switched everything off.

****

Sofia! The high-pitched whisper resounded in her head. *Sofia!* Her eyes flung open. That only happened when her higher self warned her of an upcoming event.

She rocketed out from under the galaxy of pillows and looked around her grid-like space: every room had its own multi-dimensional energy. She slinked around to every nook and cranny. Nothing. She cautiously climbed the ladder up to her open-concept bedroom, and still nothing. Then she heard a knock at the door and almost fell backward.

She immediately felt a wave of low vibrational energy sweep across her body. She strode toward the door and repeated, "I am a powerful being of light."

Peeking through the shutters, she saw no one. Her heart still pounded, but she found the courage to open the door. Still, no one. She popped her head out and was only met by the cool morning breeze as it touched her cheek. She didn't linger and shut the door behind her.

The sun was still sleeping, so Sofia joined the dreamers, too. She undressed, climbed up to her bed, and slipped into her favorite silk sheets. Not even the soothing aroma of Clary Sage infused in her pillowcase could appease her mind. *Who was at the door? It could be a late-night partygoer.* Sofia lived in the heart of the old city amid bars, restaurants, and tourist hot spots. Everything was possible. But still, her mind was a flutter, and of course, Gabrielle popped up.

Just the thought of her made the scratch on her face prickle. Sofia did not want to bring up the past events in her mind, so she gently placed her other cheek on the pillow and attempted to sleep.

It would not be so when notifications from her phone chimed in. A little part of her hoped it was Jude. But to no avail. It was Lola checking in. Usually, she would have picked up the phone even if it was 2:16 a.m. Lola was as much a night owl as Sofia. Post-partying days, they would stay up and keep each other company in their respective workspaces—with lots of coffee. They fed off each other's creativity—they did some of their best work together. Since Lola partnered with Emma, they spent less time with each other. But, still, they found a way to treasure every moment, even if it was a quick meet-up at the café.

Lola and Sofia shared many lifetimes; it was a given they would be together in this last lifetime on Earth. Reminiscing about their friendship was one way to relax her mind and nod off.

14

A whiff of ylang-ylang, patchouli, and musk floated under Sofia's nose. She didn't have to unwrap herself from the cocoon of Mulberry silk to know that Lola was right by her side. Her fingers fanned along Sofia's arm as she whispered to whom Sofia assumed was Emma. Eyes still shut, she felt one of them tend to her wound. Sofia was rather content in her solitude. Opening her eyes meant discussing the elephant in the room, and she had been good thus far, not bringing him up in her mind.

They were well-versed in dealing with Sofia's dark moods. The more awakened the lightworker became, the deeper the dive into shadow work—it was the biggest challenge but also the most rewarding one.

At one point, their hushed voices became rather high-pitched, compelling Sofia to snap open her eyelids.

"Sorry, did we wake you?" Emma murmured. "If we did, it's Lola's fault."

Sofia could just imagine the eye-rolling happening behind her.

Sofia rolled onto her back, twisted her head, and grinned, "Why are you being so mean to Emma?"

Lola smirked. "I'm not. It's just Emma being Emma. Right now, take your time. Get up if you want to. Stay in bed. Do whatever you need to return to the light, my darling." She glared at Emma and then walked to the top of the stairs. "I'm going down to fix you some food."

Emma followed her down the ladder—their bickering was non-stop. While Sofia usually enjoyed their banter, today, she only wanted to bring her higher self in to understand the twin-flame connection better. She also wanted to bring in her ego, so she could scorn Jude for being so cold and heartless with her.

The only thing that won was the fiery phoenix inked on her neck. She felt a burning sensation emanating from there, inciting her to rise. As so, she vaulted off the bed. She dizzily found her footing and shouted to the girls, "Stop what you're doing. I have a better idea. Let's go to the café."

The outdoor terrasse was bustling, with the regulars vying for the trio's attention. They stopped. They lingered. They chit-chatted. When they finally made it in, there were no free tables or space at the bar, or so it seemed. Lola stealthily grabbed one stool and slithered her way between patrons. When the barista noticed them, he snapped his fingers to one of the busboys to find two other seats.

After downing her espresso, Sofia immediately ordered another and a cornetto. As she awaited the missile of questions from her friends, she chatted and flirted with the young Adonis servers behind the bar. When one of them told her what day it was, Sofia looked at Emma and then shifted her gaze toward Lola.

They revealed to her that she'd been out for three days.

Emma touched Sofia's shoulder. "We knew you needed to process it all. It was a lot to take in one weekend." She paused. "Lola was the one who wanted to wake you up. She didn't want you sulking." Emma's killer smile was out. "Isn't that right, Lola? That's what you said."

Sofia patted Lola on the back. She then turned to Emma. "Three days is a long time. I appreciate you looking out for me, but I'm no longer the old Sofia you once took care of." She paused. "At least, I hope I'm not."

Emma recalled when Sofia shut herself from the world for three months. She went on to describe the state of her home during that time. She brought up how Sofia stopped eating, rendering her weak and skeletal. While Emma chronicled the play-by-play, Sofia was unable to relive the moment. She then smiled, leaving Emma dumbfounded.

Sofia consoled her friend. "I'm smiling because I don't remember any of it."

Emma wildly replied, "And that's a good thing?"

"Yes, Emma. I'm in the process of detaching myself from the past, so this is freaking amazing. All this hard work is paying off."

Emma was at a loss.

On the other hand, Lola shouted, "Well, this calls for a celebration." She called out to one of the baristas and ordered a bottle of Prosecco. She turned to Sofia. "One drink?"

With her higher self in snooze mode, the ego gleefully approved.

As the regulars slowly assembled around them, one bottle became seven bottles. They officially took over the bar area, occupying all the seats, much to the displeasure of the other patrons seeking quiet time. No complaints were coming from the owner— it was instead encouraged.

Charcuterie boards stacked with the finest Italian cheeses, meats, olives, grilled vegetables, bread baskets, and pasta bowls streamed out of the kitchen like a production line. It didn't take long for them to devour the plates, just in time for the chef to present the next delights.

The flow of conversation was as lively as the tarantella. The patrons shimmied from one to the other, talking, laughing, and flirting. Shot glasses lined up in a row were ready to receive Galliano, hot coffee, and whipped cream—a signature favorite for the regulars. Sofia turned hers away as they were doled to the already intoxicated bunch. It was not to be heard of—they wouldn't shut up until she downed the shot—she caved in.

While the barista poured another round, Sofia felt a tap on her shoulder. When she turned around, she was taken aback—Etienne was standing in front of her with the warmest smile. When she hugged him, her eyes landed on Jude. He was still by the entrance—two picture-perfect girls were talking him up. The moment Sofia looked his way, he did the same. There was no going around it, the butterflies were back, but his icy stare sent them fluttering back into their cocoons. Thanks to the man sitting beside her, she had little time to contemplate Jude's frosty response. The patron swung her around to take back yet another Hot Shot.

Etienne had already found his place ensconced between Lola and Emma. Sofia may have been tipsy, but she still felt Jude's energy sizzling within her. With her ego in full throttle, it won, and she continued to play the "*I don't care. I don't see you*" game. She made her way to the girls with a bottle of Prosecco.

"Etienne, are you ready to party with the girls?" Sofia cried out.

"I was born ready."

She topped everyone's glass with more bubbly. As they cheered, the rest of the posse cheered along with them. Tomorrow would be a day of regret, but Sofia preferred to enjoy the moment guilt-free. When she observed the girls—Lola was at ease in her element, and even Emma regaled in the merriment.

Etienne attempted a few times to call Jude over, but he never made it. Instead, he sat down with the flock of girls fawning over him.

"I thought you didn't drink?"

Sofia replied to Etienne, "Well, sometimes, it's easier to escape with this," pointing to her glass, "than to feel the heartbreak."

He reached over and placed his hand on her forearm and didn't expect to get an electrical shock, but they both reacted to it.

Lola interrupted the weird connection and whisper-shouted at Sofia, "Jude is here. Did you see him?"

Sofia patted her back and chuckled, "Yes, my dear." She called the barista and yelled, "Make Lola her favorite."

He confirmed. "Espresso with a triple shot of Bailey's. Got it."

Everyone joined in and clamored for the same.

While the barista prepared the next round of shots, Lola asked, "Why don't you talk to him?"

"I don't want to."

"You're so stubborn. You realize this is the beginning of a great love story, right?" Lola turned to look over at Jude. When she caught his eyes, she called out to him, inciting the whole bar to turn their attention toward him. Subtle, they were not. He acknowledged them but turned away.

Lola leaned into Sofia and teased, "It seems you're both very stubborn." It didn't take long for her to get distracted by the barista and the rest of the staff. And just like that, she was off, causing havoc at the other end of the bar.

As Sofia collected herself, Etienne motioned for her to sit down. His face went from silly to thoughtful. "We don't know each other very well, but it feels like I've known you forever because of Jude." He curved his lips into a smile. "I will repeat what I told you in Central Park. He is completely into you. And, despite appearances, nothing has changed."

It didn't matter how often a woman heard those words; it still had the same effect every time.

"Do be patient with him. He has been emotionally numb for a very long time. He hasn't felt this way about anyone in his entire life." He glanced at Jude and then back at her. "I'm sure he will regret this whole missed encounter."

Sofia listened to his every word but brushed them aside. *Yay! Another man with commitment issues.*

I don't have commitment issues. Stop listening to Etienne. Jude's stern delivery resounded in her mind.

She whipped her head around to face him. She had forgotten that he was in her head as well. She wanted to respond but shut down the telepathic exchange instead and returned to the party. Etienne's phone blew up with endless texts. After reviewing some of them, he swiveled the stool to face Jude and exchanged a back-and-forth of secret-coded gestures. Still, Jude remained seated. Sofia took it upon herself to physically twist Etienne back towards the bar and commenced the art of making her "not-boyfriend" jealous.

Lola and Emma caught on to her dalliance and joined in. Etienne was the perfect candidate—he was more than welcoming to any attention. There was no going back once the flirtation was set in motion, especially with Emma's apparent interest in Etienne and Lola's lust for life.

The result was most effective—Jude was no longer seated at the table. He was no longer in the café at all.

****

Vacating the café was a chore—if it were up to the regulars, they would rather set up tents to sleep there than leave their stools. So, they weren't going to be so relenting with the foursome. But they managed to slip out into the eerily quiet streets, anyway. August was a funny month in Montreal—as much as there were crowds of tourists, there were also moments of ghostliness. The glitches in the Matrix were real in this city.

They walked in different directions so no one would spot them and drag them back in. Once they turned the corner, they huddled in a circle discussing their next move.

Emma chimed in. "As much as I had fun, I must go home and sleep." She eyed both Lola and Sofia. "I'm not built like the two of you."

Sofia checked her phone. "It's only 7:30 pm, Emma. Come on. One more stop and that's it." She knew Emma was their only hope of staying out of trouble.

But Emma wasn't interested. She declined and clocked out, leaving Etienne, Lola, and Sofia to continue the party. If this was how the Universe planned it out, so be it. Sofia didn't want to go home, nor did she wish to host them. Lola neither. So, Etienne took the lead. While he organized the next destination, Sofia and Lola played hopscotch on the cobblestoned streets, singing their favorite oldies—out loud and out of tune.

Amidst the laughter, Lola received a text and walked away. Now alone, Sofia took a few minutes to go within, and as much as she disapproved of her choice to drink her sorrows away, she also remembered how comforting it was to feel nothing. Keeping her scorn for Jude at the surface level was easier for now. The longer she waited by the curb, the closer she got to joining Emma's rank—so she rocketed upwards and tugged on Lola's sleeve. "We need to go somewhere, or I'm going to go back into the darkness of my room." She pleaded with her best friend. "Please."

15

They zigged; they zagged through the maze of streets riddled with detours and potholes. They ended up in front of tall antique brass doors intricately carved with deities and animals.

Lola instantly gravitated toward the masterpiece and clicked multiple pics of it.

Sofia curiously asked Etienne, "Are we going to a temple?"

He smiled widely and shook his head. "No. Come."

Etienne entered a passcode, and they were in. But they weren't indoors just yet. It was a narrow pathway between two heritage buildings to the right and left. At the path's end was an entrance to another building. The door was just as impressive; it was all-black with a massive lion's head door knocker at the center. He keyed another code, and they entered a super sleek room—a man dressed in black from head to toe stood behind a black cube-like desk.

Lola was in heaven. She smiled and said, "Sofia, your favorite color all in one place."

The concierge politely greeted them. Etienne conversed with him while Sofia and Lola admired the Klimt painting of The Kiss hanging on the all-black painted wall. Sofia wondered if it was the real deal–real or not, it was one of her favorites. It brought her back to the hotel rooftop and reminisced about the kiss they shared under the canopy.

Etienne thrust his head between them and said, "Let's go upstairs."

The brass elevator door opened to a dimly lit, black-paneled elevator controlled by a key card—no floor numbers, nothing. Very mysterious, indeed. When they arrived at the door, he keyed in a code again. She was expecting to walk into Bela Lugosi's den, but the room was airy and bright, with the last streaks of sun filtering through the multiple stick-like windows lined along the bricked wall.

"This is someone's home." She looked at Etienne. "Yours?"

He grimaced, turned away, and headed to a wet bar by the open-style kitchen. Lola followed him.

Sofia heard them prattling on like two budgies in a cage. Out of nowhere, Afro-beat sounds streamed out of the speakers, and the party was on again. Sofia took time to drink in the decor—ultra modern with all-white and chrome everything. The mural on one of the walls struck her as odd but mostly intoxicated her senses. It was a photograph within a photograph within a photograph—three different scenarios all in one, sprawled on every inch of the wall.

Lola showed up right by her side, and when she handed Sofia a drink, she refused. Lola didn't insist. But Lola insisted that she stand in front of the wallpaper and pose. As the two besties snapped pics, Etienne made his way to them.

"I would never have pegged this style of decor for you. Jude, maybe," she paused. *Jude, for sure.* Then she opened the gate for her higher self to enter. The confirmation was quick. She twisted her head to stare into Etienne's eyes, but he was already missing in action. She firmly grabbed Lola's arm and asked, "Is this Jude's house?"

Lola averted her eyes. She tried changing the subject, but Sofia knew her too well. Before Sofia could react, Etienne interjected. "Yes, this is his home."

"What? No. I can't be here. You guys are so annoying."

He reassured her that Jude wouldn't be home for another few hours. "In the meantime, let's enjoy a drink or two, and then we can leave. Trust me; he won't be home for a while."

As much as she wanted to storm out of there in a huff, she also wanted to explore a little more. It was an opportune time to learn a little more about Jude. She wagged her finger at them and said, "Okay, only one drink, and then we're out. I don't want to see him this way."

Etienne and Lola exchanged looks, smiling.

Sofia turned to Lola. "And you, sneaky girl. You're supposed to have my back."

She replied, "I do," and winked at her friend.

She ignored them and continued her walk-around. Jude had a mezzanine with what she could only imagine as his bedroom. There was a winding staircase to get to it.

"You can go up if you want!" Etienne smiled.

She nodded and replied, "I'll go up to it when invited."

With no effort, the mood shifted from somber to lightheartedness as they teased each other, shared funny stories, and bickered about the playlist.

Sofia asked for the bathroom. He directed her down the hall. It was the most enormous guest bathroom she had ever seen. No, wait, she once went to a friend of a friend's house whose father was a mobster, and that bathroom was akin to a master bedroom—*Going off on a tangent again, Sofia?* She missed her higher self. *Even if you shut me down, I'm still here. You know that, right?* Sofia was ready to shut it down one more time. But, didn't.

The cleanliness and the high-tech gadgetry in his bathroom impressed her. She spent more time playing with the faucets and buttons than doing what she needed to do. When she stepped out, she turned right instead of left. She found herself in an alcove with photography equipment strewn all over a metal desk and a bulletin board with assorted photos and mementos. In the corner, she found an old record player with a record already inside—"Dis-moi que tu m'aimes by Ninho." *I never really pegged him as a fan of rap. You learn something new every day.* Sofia placed the cushioned headphones on and set the needle on the LP. A vibrational buzzing bolt passed through her body as she swayed to the music.

Is this the music?

No.

The answer didn't come from within.

Startled, she stood still. She then gently removed the headphones and placed them on the stack of records. When she twisted her body, her heart felt like it was beating outside her chest. Jude stood before her, as luminous as ever.

It turned quickly to darkness when he indifferently asked what she was doing in his space. Even with the coldness, the glint of gold shimmered in his eyes. He was still in there.

She barely looked at him and walked past him. They grazed each other—their energies zipped from one to the next. He followed.

You never allowed me to explain my side of the story. Why were you so ready to shut me down? He started their conversation with a bang.

When she entered the main space, Etienne and Lola sat silently for a change. They didn't dare look at either of the lover's eyes. Jude headed to the bar and fixed himself a drink.

"Does anyone else want a drink?"

Etienne sprang up from the couch and responded, "Two drinks for Lola and me."

Sofia ignored his request.

Just because I'm doing something doesn't mean I can't hear you, Sofia.

Sofia liked this petulant side of him. But, still, she remained silent.

He continued, *I don't know what Etienne told you at the bar, but I am not afraid to commit to you. I bared my soul to you in New York. You're the one who shut me out.*

Trigger number 33. Sofia answered, *So, you are blaming me, then? How 3D of you. This is why I don't do relationships.*

Don't you dare pull that Matrix shit on me, Sofia. If you weren't interested in entering a relationship, then you sure as hell fooled me.

Trigger number 34. Sofia cleared her mind before relaying the next message. She pretended to look at a magazine not to cause any suspicion from Lola or Etienne. *Well, I thought I was getting myself into a monogamous relationship. I don't do polyamory, like you.*

A loud shattering sound of glass smashed against the wood flooring. The Whiskey Sour splashed everywhere—on the furniture, the floor, the walls. Jude didn't budge. He didn't even look up.

When Etienne sprung up from his seat, Jude barked at him. "Sit down. I'll clean it up." Etienne flashed a look at Sofia. She shrugged her shoulders and looked back at the magazine.

Meanwhile...*Are you serious, Sofia? I'm glad my life is a big joke to you.*

It isn't, but if you don't talk to me and tell me what the fuck is going on, I can only assume.

He barrelled in again with yet another trigger. *Are you done yet? You, of all people, know that assumptions were created in this illusion. Or, maybe I'm just talking to drunk Sofia and not "light and love" Sofia.* The triggers were endless. She wasn't in the best state to fend them off, but she did her best.

You are just as trained in delivering low blows as I am. I'm not perfect, and neither are you, Jude.

Etienne interrupted their secretive communication and asked if they wanted to grab a bite.

Sofia and Jude simultaneously shouted, "No."

"Okay. Then, I will order food." He sauntered over to Lola. He turned on his phone, and they discussed their preferences.

Sofia continued her thought. *You can come at me with all the triggers, but it all boils down to you not being forthright with me about Gabrielle. Do you believe me to be so fragile?*

I don't think you're fragile, but maybe you are a bit naïve about what I'm really up against. My whole life has been a mess from the get-go.

Sofia let slip her sarcasm. *Boo hoo.*

Exactly, Sofia. That's why I don't date or engage in long-term relationships—for unfeeling responses like that.

Sofia retracted her snarky remark and immediately apologized.

It doesn't matter because we weren't going to work anyway.

Silence.

Jude continued his thought. *I don't think I can fight and argue with another strong-minded woman. Two are enough. It's just how it has to be.*

Sofia somehow understood his behavior—it made more sense to her that they were twin flames. At the same time, she didn't want to be near him. She only wanted to crawl into her bed and scream into her pillow.

Sofia whispered to Lola, "I'm heading out. I need some time alone. Please stay here and be my eyes and ears."

She hugged Etienne and left without even acknowledging Jude. Still, a message came through. *Take the fire escape, Sofia.* Even as she stepped into the elevator, she heard him. *Try to take a different route home.*

****

Tears streamed down her cheeks as she raced back home. She listened to his advice and took shortcuts—through the parking lots and narrow alleys. She had lived there for over ten years and never felt unsafe. The only danger she encountered were drunk partygoers, homeless people, and the occasional rat. Ultimately, Sofia never fed into fear; as a result, it allowed her to live life more purposely.

Cowering away into darkness was the only thing on her mind as she ducked into the back alley of a government building. Her higher self came in and tried to deter her from that passage, but Sofia was tired. Even when she heard footsteps behind her, she thought nothing of it until they neared at a hurried pace. The footsteps followed her to street level. And when she pulled out her phone to text Lola, her favorite redhead knocked it out of her hands.

How is it that she knows where I am?

She is Jude's stalker, Sofia. Where else would she be? Her higher self's sarcasm was real. *Try not to engage with her.*

Sofia urgently contacted Jude via her mind.

She fixedly stared at Sofia. Then she began her tirade, which consisted of: "What does he see in you?"— "Why are you still in the picture?"— "Do you know what happens to girls who don't listen to me?" And it went on. The last sentence didn't sit well with Sofia, so she did what her higher self told her not to do.

"What do you do to people who don't listen to you?"

Gabrielle grinned. She tapped Sofia's phone against her head. She then slammed her phone on the pavement and pierced her heel into the screen.

Sofia tempered her anger. *Who the fuck does she think she is? That phone cost me a lot of money, bitch! Jude, if you hear me, you better come now because "love and light" are not what is scrolling through my mind right now.*

Gabrielle was unimpressed with Sofia's non-reaction, so she continued, "Second, I let them know how I feel. Then I leave a scar to remember me by." As she reached over to touch Sofia's wound, Sofia flinched. She was about to push Gabrielle away when Jude skated between them. He restrained his stalker's arms and pushed her backward. He was fierce and fiery like the dragon that he was but compassionate and kind like the man she met only a few days ago.

Try lifetimes ago.

Sofia didn't have time to converse with her higher self. Instead, she yelled at Jude in her mind. *She's fucken crazy. If you don't do something, I will.*

I know you're pissed. You have every right to be. The best thing you can do is leave. I will take care of the rest. Now, go.

Sofia lingered a bit longer, just enough to hear them exchange unpleasantries in their native language. Gabrielle yelled, cried, and sweet-talked him all at once. She was a piece of work. Still, she sensed the deep torment in Gabrielle's energy.

Jude was not having it. He shouted in her mind. *Don't get fooled by her beguiling ways. The devil works in mysterious ways. Please, go.*

16

Sofia swiftly entered her apartment, slamming the door shut. She triple-locked the door. Her heart thundered in her chest. Fear tried to overwhelm her, but Sofia's higher self had other plans. *Sofia! How many eons have you lived on this Earth? You are a powerful master of light. Do the breathing exercises. That's right. Breathe in. Breathe out. Fear is what?* Sofia calmed down and answered. *Fear is a made-up construct. I have lived and died endless times. I got this.*

She went to the kitchen and dunked three chamomile tea bags into hot water. Her mind was a blur. *My human self is still freaked out, though.* Her higher self consoled her. *Just feel through it. You're never alone. I am here. And so is Jude.*

A knock at the door startled her. Her heart skipped a beat. *Was Gabrielle here to finish what she started?* As Sofia made her way to the door, she readied herself for whoever was on the other side. The closer she neared the entrance, the more electricity built within her. Without hesitation, she swung open the door, and there stood Jude—darkened circles under his eyes; his aura beamed, and he was still as handsome as ever.

He walked in, shut the door behind him, and confidently swept her into his arms. Just like that, Sofia turned into jelly. The strength of his grip around her body and the energetic vibe between them rendered her even more speechless.

He growled low in his throat as his body pressed against hers.

He moaned. "I've missed you."

When their tongues danced together, the power that surged through their bodies was magnetizing. A deluge of light swirled around them. When Sofia opened her eyes, the surrounding area appeared as waves of frequency: the walls, the shutters, the plant. And as they held each other in the cosmic field of energy, millions of questions arose: *Is it the right time for us? Is our union supposed to happen now, with all this drama in his life? How do I fit in all of this?* And so they went on.

He cradled her face, careful not to press on her injury. "We'll find a way. We'll figure this out together." Jude managed to calm Sofia as the anger slowly evaporated.

She lowered her gaze, but he lifted her face and whispered, "I don't like fighting with you. She is already coming between us, and we're not even dating." He brushed Sofia's dark brown locks from her face and placed them behind her ear. "From all the ramblings in your mind, I have understood that we are twin flames, so we are bound to each other." He planted another meaningful kiss on her lips. She melted into his embrace.

Sofia welcomed the closeness and vacillated between her higher ego and lower ego. Still, she pulled back. He relented and let go of her.

As he stood there drinking in every detail of her home, she reprimanded herself for quickly falling into his arms. She observed him as he lightly ran his fingertip along some of her antiques or unique pieces. He stopped before a filing cabinet, looked up, and asked, "Vietnam?"

She nodded. Everyone always assumed India. He was the first to guess it right on the first try. She remembered feeling an immediate connection to the hand-stamped wooden piece. An elder gifted it to her after a three-month volunteering program in Hanoi. The ninety-seven-year-old woman told her, "It's time to start remembering the fire that lives inside your essence, dear child." At the time, Sofia was still living in the illusion, unaware of her power. But she knew, innately, that she needed to accept her offer. It felt right.

He approved. "Very exquisite work. Did you carve one of our symbols here?"

Sofia arched an eyebrow. "What symbol?"

He re-examined the piece and lifted one tattooed finger. "This symbol."

She approached him, staring at his findings. "I can't believe this." Floored by his discovery, she continued, "I've had this cabinet for over twenty years, and I've never noticed this."

He draped an arm around her shoulder. "Nothing is coincidental, right, Divine Sofia? And maybe I was supposed to be the one to point this out to you."

She finally felt more relaxed and breathed easier. Still, she stepped away from his embrace and headed into the kitchen. She prepared him an espresso from her cherished Moka pot. Her mother faithfully drank coffee from this pot. While the coffee brewed, she surveyed him as he scrutinized every design element—touching, reading, and examining every book, artifact, tarot deck, crystal, and painting.

He was paradoxical to Sofia in a way that fascinated her—one moment King of Cups, the next King of Swords.

His phone rang a few times, and texts chimed in. He ignored them. But Sofia didn't. "Is that her?"

He nodded, then shut down his phone.

She brought out the pot so he could freely fill his cup. When he glided by her, she stepped away—there was only one thing whirling around in her mind—she wasn't ready to give in to him just yet.

"Don't worry. I won't make any moves, even if I want to." He muttered. "We need to talk first. I get it."

His listening to her every thought needed fixing. Alas, such was the plight of the twin flame.

Not every twin flame has the capacity to hear each other so clearly. Not yet, anyway. She had forgotten how chatty her higher self could be.

She sat down on the couch, hot tea in hand, and invited him to join her. He opted for the carpet instead. His presence always flustered Sofia. She couldn't think straight when he was around. But, she summoned up his bullheaded behavior as of late in her mind to remind her to stay afloat.

His phone rang again. He showed her the screen. It was Etienne. He still shut it down and tucked it behind one of her pillows.

"Maybe, it's important, Jude. Maybe it's about her."

He shrugged his shoulders. "Maybe. But tonight is about you and me."

As he faced her, she quickly got lost in his gaze. A rush of shyness sent color to her cheeks, but she kept her eyes on him. He reacted by leaning toward her and softly kissing her lips.

She pulled away. "Stop distracting me. I have a lot of questions, Jude."

He breathed in and out. "*J'suis là pour ça.* (I'm all yours)."

"First, hand me that," she pointed to her laptop on the coffee table. "I want to do a quick look into the symbol."

As she researched, she felt his eyes boring into her. She didn't dare look up for fear of falling into his embrace again. When she discovered the symbol's meaning, she turned the computer toward him.

He took it upon himself to read it aloud. "This symbol represents success and prosperity but also divine masculine and feminine union." He asked her to zoom into the symbol. The image of the dragon and phoenix whirling around each other rattled them.

Jude repeated. "Divine masculine and feminine union—dragon and phoenix. Hmmm…". He then pointed to the photos from the graffitied underpass, "What are those symbols?"

She recounted the anecdote related to the symbols in question. They laughed at Emma's insolence. "I did some research while I was in the car and found that this one," she pointed to the symbol with a vertical line with 3 horizontal lines underneath, "means grounding."

"Divine union, grounding; I can't wait to discover the others." He stared into her eyes.

She lost her train of thought but came to. "There was one question I've had on my mind for the past few days. When did you start hearing my thoughts?"

He told her that he heard snippets throughout the weekend, but it became crystal clear the day she left post-Gabrielle encounter. Since then, he had heard her even when they were not together.

What? How is that possible? Her higher self comforted her. *Calm down. Only sometimes, only when you address or call out to him.*

He asked her the same question, to which she answered.

He went on, "I wonder if we've always heard each other's thoughts but never acknowledged them as so." Jude's introspection was both refreshing and riveting.

The twin flames sat in reverence, hands intertwined, recollecting their past encounters.

An image of Gabrielle popped up and clouded her contemplation. She took it as a sign. "Gabrielle, what's the deal with her?" She paused. "You know, she showed me the both of you as a couple on her Instagram profile."

He grabbed one of her many pillows and fidgeted with the fluffy tassel. After a heavy sigh, he said, "There is so much to tell you; I don't know where to start."

"You don't have to start from the beginning, but can you help me understand your relationship with her now?"

"We were childhood friends," he replied.

Jude was back to talking briefly and concisely.

Sofia was determined to get more out of him. "I need to know more. She seems a little..er..a lot unhinged, and she knows where I live. I don't like it one bit. As masterful as I am, I'm still not a fan of things that go bump in the night. So, please, a little more."

He nodded and sighed heavily. "Yes. You deserve that much." He began. "She lived very much in the uppity social scene. When life blew up in her face, she came back to me for support, which I did," he pointed out, "as a friend." He continued, "In hindsight, I should never have gone out of my way to help her out, but," he grazed his fingertips along Sofia's legs and warmly said, "I truly believe that humans are all full of love."

He stretched his arms out. As he yawned aloud, he said, "My mother is a whole different species." He avoided contact with Sofia but still added, "You want crazy? My family is it."

His phone rang. This time, he reached behind the sea of pillows and answered it. She knew it wasn't Etienne when he swore in French, English, and a made-up language. He rocketed up from the carpet and was going to walk away, but Sofia pulled his top. She gestured for him to stay by her side.

He did so reluctantly. He then put it on speaker. It was Gabrielle.

She spoke seductively, unlike the Gabrielle that Sofia had encountered. "Jude, why must you make life so difficult for us? I only want to shower you with love like you once loved me. Why can't we go back to that time?"

Jude never once looked at Sofia. Instead, he rested his head against the sofa's cushion and stared at the ceiling.

She dominated the conversation. "I can't wait to buy a home in Paris with you or wherever you want to live. I will follow you anywhere."

It was slightly disconcerting for Sofia to hear, but Jude's apathy led her to believe he was not interested.

Then, her voice changed slightly, sounding almost possessed. "But, we can't do this if others are in the way of our happiness. Why can't you see that?"

He spoke up, "Gabrielle. *J'en ai marre.* (I can't do it anymore)."

She fell silent.

He hung up the phone. That was that. He had had enough. He slumped down on the sofa, exhaling deeply. "I'm so done with her and my mother." He wasn't talking to Sofia per se, but talking aloud. "I tried over the years to tame the situation for my mother's sake, for Lennon and my dad, but I can't anymore."

She didn't have time to comfort him when there was another knock at the door. *I'm famous today.*

She opened the door to a worry-stricken Etienne. "Hi, Sofia."

Jude ran to his friend. "What are you doing here? What has she done?"

Etienne waved him outside. Jude didn't hesitate. He pecked Sofia on the cheek. "I won't be long." He squeezed her arm and walked away with his friend.

And the drama ensued. Sofia shut the door and returned to the sofa. Her mind was racing with made-up scenarios until her higher self came in. *Stop thinking. Remember, trusting the plan is all you need to concern yourself with. You are his lighthouse right now. Stand tall and shine your light, my dear.*

She sent a message to Lola advising her that she had lost her smartphone. She then busied herself by responding to comments from her followers. "Where are you, Sofia? We miss you!"—"Have you been kidnapped by aliens?" They amused her. They did more than that—they were her soul family.

She shut down the computer and tried to quiet her mind. Eyes closed, she felt an energetic wave sweep around her. Jude traced his finger along her neck and down the side of her torso. To say that the currents were flowing between them was an understatement. When she looked into his eyes, his gaze was somber. He tried hard to feign his unease, but Sofia felt it in her heart.

She waited for him to talk. He interlocked his fingers into hers. He sat at the edge of the cushion, looked fixedly into Sofia's eyes, and disclosed the reason for Etienne's visit. Gabrielle reached out to Lennon.

"She is relentless, to a fault." Jude paused. "She knows my pain points. The only way I can get her out of my life...er...our life is..." A longer pause. "By me going to Paris."

"Like, for a few weeks?"

"No."

Her heart sank into the abyss reserved only for her mother. *Why does he need to go back home? What am I missing here?*

"You are not wrong to be feeling confused. The situation with Gabrielle is more complicated than what you heard on that phone call."

"Try me."

Jude lowered his gaze and played with her fingers. Her seventeen-year-old sappy self emerged when he looked up and stared deep into her eyes. Before shedding tears, she tried jumping up but fell back down and lost her footing.

They burst into laughter.

Between giggles, he said, "I can't possibly leave you alone. You will never survive without me."

"So, don't go," Sofia pleaded.

"It's something I need to do. If we have a chance at forever, I must do this once and for all."

Pain coursed through her leg when she tried to get up again, but she kept it to herself.

He helped her sit down on the sofa. "You don't have to hide it. It hurts you; I can feel the pain."

She glanced at him. "Seriously, you can't leave me now. I have finally found someone who talks like me."

He softly spoke, "I won't be gone too long. Maybe three to four months."

Thoughts whirled in her mind. Her lower ego came out to play. "That's a long time, Jude! A lot can happen. We just started this, whatever this is." She repeated. "Three to four months is a long time. If she's been such a heavy burden for you, why has it taken you so long to be proactive?"

He raised his eyebrows and stared at Sofia.

She replied. "Because of me. She's threatened."

Jude nodded.

But, still, four months will feel like forever.

He fluttered his fingers along her hands. "Absolutely. That's why I was wondering if you wanted to join me?"

Paris was always a soft spot for her. She often went there with Lola on her buying trips. But also, picking up and going to the city of lights with Jude for a few months was a bit too spontaneous even for her, who was usually up for any adventure. She declined.

"Just think about it. I leave tomorrow and want you by my side."

A sense of loss crawled its way up her body. She exhaled a heavy sigh, shaking her head.

"The quicker I get this done, the quicker I get to spend getting to know you and falling more in love with you."

Heat warmed her cheeks, hearing those words. Her butterflies were back doing all the acrobatics. And her higher self urged her to return the sentiment. But she couldn't. It wasn't formulating into words.

He grasped her hands and whispered, "Just think about it. Me, you in Paris—away from everyone." He stopped, then said, "Granted, we'll have to deal with my mother,"—he rolled his eyes—"but she lives in the South of France. I can deal with her on my own." His mood shifted to a more positive one, and he exclaimed, "And I want more than anything to introduce you to my brother, Lennon. He's another one of your die-hard fans."

It was tempting indeed. "And what about Etienne, your protege?"

He made a face. "Etienne will stay behind if that is what you choose. He will take care of you."

Sofia smirked. "I don't need a bodyguard."

Jude's lip curled to one side. "Really? After what happened tonight? She knows where you live, remember? She is fearless when it comes to getting me back. You heard her on the phone. Trust me." He groaned. "Hopefully, she'll follow me to Paris. And then I can settle all of the problems in one place." He looked away from her but continued, "In fact, maybe we can pretend you're coming with me to Paris. That will compel her to buy a ticket and follow "us" back home."

As Jude rambled on, it sank in that he was leaving in 24 hours. Instead of remaining on the higher ground, she started to fall into the black hole of victimhood, the same "why me" narrative that loved to come out and play with Sofia and most humans on the planet. Self-pity was designed to lead humans down the path of escapism with drugs, alcohol, food, etc. Facing the trigger or fear like a warrior was the only way to the light. Sofia needed the courage to stand up to the old wounds, trying to find their way in. Luckily, she had three to four months to conquer her demons.

17

A glimmer of light on Sofia's face roused her from her deep sleep. When she looked toward the source, the rainbow-colored spectrum of light peeking out from behind the curtain mesmerized her. She never pushed aside synchronistic signs and knew hope was calling her name.

She lifted herself and looked around her. *I didn't dream about last night's events, right?* The answer was quick. *Right.* She called out Jude's name. Nothing. As she lay sprawled on her comforter, fully clothed, she reminisced of the night before. Jude spent the night; they talked, laughed, kissed, and dreamed together.

Sofia felt no urgency from her higher self nor her ego to reach out to him, so she let it go. Instead, she agonized over his upcoming departure. Sofia hadn't realized how strong her feelings were for him, having convinced herself a long time ago that the idea of yearning for someone else's touch or hearing their spoken word would never play a significant role in her life. Shaking off the sadness and despair, she thanked the rainbow light and put on her favorite, uplifting music.

She danced and flitted around the room, made her bed, and jumped into the shower. Even though she felt torn about Jude's departure, she was thrilled to be back on track with him. Sporting her favorite army green fitted dress, she made sure to wear chakra-aligning colors. Most times, it was unconscious, led mainly by her higher self. Today, she needed to protect her heart. She made her way downstairs and dillydallied in front of the computer.

He left a note on top of her keyboard. *Went home to pack and finish up some errands. Loved our night together. Will be by later, xxx J*

She didn't have time to experience teenage girl silliness upon reading his words when she heard a knock at the door. She assumed it was him, but it was a trio of precious souls when she opened the door. Emma, Lola, and Etienne stood before her holding bottles of green juice, coconut water, and take-out food.

"May we come in?" Lola batted her eyelashes. "Unless you're busy, we can come back."

Amused by her friends' assumptions, Sofia welcomed them into her home. The music was still blaring in the background, compelling Lola to groove her way in. Emma walked past the dancing queen and did what she did best: prepare the food and drinks, making sure they were all taken care of. When Etienne hugged Sofia, a mild sizzling sensation ran through her body. They both reacted but didn't acknowledge it. Instead, he joined in on the dance fest.

She joined Emma in the kitchen, admiring her poise and maternal instinct. Sofia leaned onto the counter, peering into Emma's eyes. "So, what's going on with you and Etienne?"

She retorted, "Nothing. Why would you say that?" Emma glowered at Lola for a moment, then continued her thought. "It doesn't matter because he seems to be into someone else, anyway."

Sofia glanced back at the two dancing and wondered if Emma had a point. There was a fluidity between Lola and Etienne that felt both calming and dynamic at the same time. They exuded an electrifying energy. So much so that when he looked at Sofia, she experienced a tingling in her heart. He kept his eyes on Sofia until his cheeks blushed a deep red. He quickly veered his attention toward Lola.

Explain. What is happening here? Her higher self put her at ease. *No need to worry yourself. It's just admiration between friends.*

Sofia wasn't satisfied with that answer but let it rest and returned to Emma. "Don't give up. If you like him, let it be known." She looked into her friend's eyes. "Lola's not interested in him. She's just being Lola." Sofia hugged her.

Etienne and Lola made their way to the counter and nibbled at the plates of food. Emma reprimanded Lola, "How you can dance with a hangover is beyond me. Now, eat and drink as much as you can; later, we have a meeting to attend."

Lola listened as a child would a mother. Etienne followed suit.

They ate in silence until Etienne asked, "So, Sofia, are you going to Paris or what?"

Sofia jerked her head toward him and glared. He immediately realized he had overstepped his boundaries.

"What about Paris?" Lola asked.

Emma scoffed, "Are you going to Paris without telling us?"

As the questions flooded her way, she scowled at Etienne before finally giving in. "Jude is moving to Paris for a few months."

"More like a year," Etienne grunted.

Sofia whipped around and cried, "What?"

Etienne cowered in his chair. "He told you a few months?" He paused, looking ill suddenly. "Well, maybe I got it wrong."

Defeated, she rolled her eyes and then turned to the girls. "Well then, apparently, he's moving to Paris for a year."

Sofia's heart shattered into a million more pieces. She tried hard to keep it together but struggled with Jude's deception. *Is this guy for real? It's a fricken rollercoaster ride with him. How can I trust anything that he says? Who knows if Gabrielle and he are not playing with me? Maybe all these electrical currents between me, Jude, and Etienne are warning signs.*

Her higher self rolled in. *Don't start with your doubt. Do you trust me?* Sofia: *Yes.* Higher self: *Well, okay then.* Still, Sofia felt betrayed.

Lola reached over and cupped Sofia's hand, brushing away a stray tear from Sofia's cheek.

"Why didn't you tell us as soon as we walked in?" Emma asked, adding more fuel to the fire.

"Do you tell me everything happening in your life, Emma?" Sofia blurted out, feeling ire rising within. "Really? You want to go there with me?"

Emma lowered her gaze. Not one word.

It was up to Lola, this time, to alter the mood. "I have a great idea! I am going to a special showing of furniture in Marseille in January. Why don't we all visit Paris for New Year's Eve?"

Emma nodded approvingly. "I've never been to Paris in the wintertime."

Etienne twisted his body to face Emma. "I would love to show you around."

Instant blushing of the cheeks for Emma. Lola and Sofia made silly gestures to her behind his back, further embarrassing her.

While they were planning the whole trip, Sofia interrupted them. "I'm not going."

Puzzled by her response, Lola insisted, "Sofia, what's going on inside your mind? You always jump at the chance of traveling."

"I have things to do. I have a business that needs attending to. I have to provide videos to my community. I can't just up and leave for a man that can't even be honest with me."

There I said it. Are you happy, Lola? That's what you were fishing for.

"You must know that Jude is completely into you," Etienne said.

Lola squealed quietly, shifting in her seat. Emma reached over and squeezed Sofia's hand.

"Maybe he's overly ambitious and thinks he can follow through with that restraining order for Lennon from his mother in a few months. It's Paris—the land of bureaucracy," Etienne added.

Do carry on, Etienne.

He wasn't finished. "Jude is a man of his word. And a man of few words, fewer than me, that's for sure." He laughed.

"Jude will never go back on his promise. It's just not who he is." Etienne paused, laughter replaced by earnestness. "He's had a tough time fitting into his upbringing. He always felt like the odd man out. And now that he's found someone aligned with him, he will not let you go—like, ever."

Lola got all giddy, squirming in her seat. "How romantic! Come on, Sofia, just come. You have four months to do as many videos as you can. You're allowed some downtime too."

Emma pleaded with her friend. "You know you want to."

Etienne added, "Whether you go in December or not, you're stuck with me. I'm going to be your royal pain in the ass, friend. And you know why!"

Both Lola and Emma nodded. Lola said, "That makes sense. If Jude is gone, you're left with the crazy redhead."

"You see," Etienne interjected, "even your friend understands the situation."

When Sofia icily stared at him, he lowered his eyes.

Lola poked Etienne. "Don't be afraid of Sofia. She's just teasing you." She turned to Sofia. "Right, Sof, what happened to all your love and light?"

"Oh, and not to get on your bad side again, Sofia." Emma daringly asked, "A little birdie told us about an unexpected encounter with Gabrielle. What happened?"

She heavily patted Etienne on the shoulder and shook her head. Enough said. She recounted the run-in with her nemesis. As they consoled and hugged Sofia, there was a knock at the door. Etienne jumped up and saluted Sofia. "I will begin my bodyguard duty as of now."

There was no threat at the door. There was no one. Etienne looked back at Sofia. "Does this happen often?"

Sofia nodded.

But still, he took his duty seriously and stepped out to investigate. In doing so, they heard him scream like a baby. The girls were on high alert as they hurried to the door—only to find Jude bent over laughing as

Etienne regained his composure. When Jude came to, he quipped, "It seems you have some work to do, my friend."

Sofia had never seen Jude in such good spirits—she could get used to this side of him. When they locked eyes, the laughter subsided, and the world just disappeared. He handed over his bags to Etienne and promptly slid his arms around her body. They didn't exchange words or thoughts. The silence between lovers spoke for itself.

****

By the time they strolled back into her home, there was no sight of the trio; only plates of leftover food and drinks remained.

The first thing he did was pull out a box. "Here."

She opened it to find the latest iPhone, along with a case. She returned it to him.

"Don't be stubborn and proud. Gabrielle did this because of me." He was insistent. "Just take it, *s'il te plaît* (please)."

Her higher self was about to chime in, but she stopped it and accepted it.

He smiled and put the smartphone on the table. Sofia thanked him by resting her cheek on his chest and hugging him. The frequency around them soared. He leaned into her embrace. Even when the electricity raced through their veins, they remained unmoving. He swept her hair away from her neck with one hand, leaving butterfly kisses on any bare skin he could find. He whispered, "I will miss you," and "I want you in" her ear. Tears cascaded down her cheeks. She had been holding in her heartache but couldn't any longer, especially with the powerful magnetic pull on her.

He turned her around and used his sleeves to wipe away her tears. When she looked into his golden-speckled greens, more tears flowed.

He pouted. "You're going to make me cry, and I didn't want to, not before I leave." This time he wiped away her sorrow with his fingers. She closed her eyes, trying to imprint his every touch in her memory.

He mumbled, "You wouldn't have to memorize my touch if you just came with me."

Her eyelids flew open, and she exclaimed, "I can't leave for a year."

He stepped back and asked, "What are you talking about?" Then he shook his head and said, "Etienne."

"Yes. Why didn't you tell me the truth? Why do you feel the need to save me from something? I'm a grown-ass woman who has dealt with more than you can imagine in one lifetime. I don't need saving from anyone. Especially not you, Jude." She said, "If you lie to me once and then twice, how do you expect me to believe you the third time?"

He rubbed his eyes and sighed, "Oh la la, this is not how I wanted this day to be."

Sofia grabbed his top and brought him closer to her. She snaked her hands into his and held them tightly. "Me neither. But let's start with the truth."

"Etienne doesn't know what he's talking about because I haven't filled him into everything I'm doing. First of all, what do you know?"

Sofia told him she knew about Lennon and the restraining order.

He rolled his eyes. "I didn't want to tell you about that because it wasn't important in the grand scheme. But, yes, I've been working on this for over a year with my dad. She is an unfit mother. Try telling that to a French judge."

She ran her fingers along the stubble budding along his cheeks and down to the side of his neck. His whole body relaxed as he reveled in her touch.

He kissed her softly. He then wormed his hand into hers and led her to the sofa. They sat with a memoir of lost moments and an unwritten future. When his fingers caressed her lips, she kissed them. As he lowered his lips onto hers, she responded with yearning. When his hands traveled along her body, she encouraged his journey. When he breathlessly explored, she acquiesced and returned the love.

As they lay there in reverie, Sofia heard him say in his mind. *One day, I'm going to marry you, my divine phoenix.*

FLY HIGH

Come, my lightworker,
your dragon awaits.

Climb on top of me.
Off we go!
Your light will guide us.
Your light will shield us.
Your light will shine.

Fly high. Fly low.
It's your time to fly.

18

Sofia had always felt the presence of a dragon spirit around her ever since she could remember. She was drawn to both the dragon and the phoenix as a child—doodling them on paper as she listened to her teachers. It came as a big surprise when she learned about Jude's fascination with dragons, but was it such a big surprise? It seemed like their lives were inter-connected, and maybe soon, it would become more evident.

Whenever she traveled by air, she imagined herself on the back of a dragon powering through the high winds. Discovering that come dreamtime, her soul left her body to spend time learning new wisdom with her devoted masters and guides; she felt validated. All those times she "dreamed" about riding her dragon were for real. It was at times like these that she missed Jude. He was the only person she could confide in about these ethereal concepts without feeling judged or deemed insane.

When she turned away from the window, she caught Etienne gazing at her. She smiled. He smiled. There was a moment. She wasn't sure what that moment was, but she felt it in the depths of her heart. He was nestled in his business class pod, watching the screen. Sofia splurged on her flight to Paris. However, she believed that Jude may have contributed to some of the fare in dealing with his travel agent. Lola and Emma were going to join Sofia in a week. They were forced to stay behind because of a lucrative project that landed on their lap.

She returned to the blanket of pillow clouds set against the fiery orange skies. When she closed her eyes, flashes of the past four months streamed through her mind. All she did was work on videos and more videos. She spoke to Jude every night for the first month, but then it dwindled to three times a week. He was knee-deep in his mother's and Gabrielle's shenanigans. As expected, Gabrielle followed him back home, but not before terrorizing Sofia for a few weeks. Etienne and Sofia had to devise a plan to encourage her return to Paris. They played her at her own game and put Jude's strategy to work. Sofia used her excellent editing skills and uploaded pics of her and Jude against Parisian landmarks. It took less than three days for Gabrielle to fly home.

The quartet spent a lot of time together with Lola and Etienne's birthdays in November—one Scorpio and one Sagittarius—the celebrations were lavish and intoxicating. Sofia spent Christmas with the girls and Etienne. She did hop on a call with her dad and stepmother. And she managed to catch her brother, too. New Zealand was not a hop, skip, and away. It had been years since she had seen him. His newest addition to the family was born there. She had just turned three in early December. Sofia imagined how her mother would feel about this separation within the family.

She developed a strong bond with Etienne, convinced he was one of her soul mates. His purpose was to facilitate the unification of Sofia and Jude, with more details yet to be revealed. There was no movement regarding romance with Etienne, Emma, or Lola. But still, flirtations ensued when together; it was innate in Etienne and Lola.

Etienne became Sofia's missing link. She learned more about what he did in his day to day. He was more than Jude's friend. He also worked closely with Jude, assisting him with the Gabrielle situation. It was evident that he never had to worry about money. In this linear world where job status and positions were highly revered, Etienne adopted his own way of living. And Sofia admired that about him. He was "going with the flow" and living life as it presented itself.

They were often spotted around town or in the café together, chatting up a storm, bickering, or just being. Many even mistook them for a couple. At times, Sofia felt their closeness as something greater but swept it under the rug as a silly crush on his part—as expected when the connection was so profound. Sofia's love for Jude remained steady, and as she got closer to being in his arms, she couldn't help but awaken the dormant butterflies.

Etienne didn't take long to weasel more champagne and chocolates from the flight attendant. In the seven hours together, he commanded the conversation for about five of them. He spoke into the wee hours of the night, even when the other passengers repeatedly shushed him.

Sofia learned a great deal about Etienne's back story. His father was an elusive businessman—he didn't expand on it. His mother was a socialite who preferred hobnobbing with the rich and famous rather than spending time with her son.

"I grew up with a nanny my whole childhood. For the longest time, I thought she was my mother." He paused, and when he glanced at the neighbor's movie screen, he quickly got lost in thought. Sofia snapped her fingers at him. He twisted his head and nodded. He continued, "I never saw my parents—maybe twice when I graduated high school and university. They had to be in the photos, or else it didn't look good."

Sofia reached out and placed her hand on his shoulder.

"It's okay," he said. "I found a family with Jude." He changed tempo and asked, "Do you want to know how I met Jude?"

Sofia enthusiastically nodded.

He rested his head in his hands and pondered. "Let's see...how do I keep this short and sweet."

Sofia giggled. "Ummm...You never keep anything short. And we have plenty of time, so go slow and in detail, please."

He batted his eyelashes and began. "Many people imagine the lives of the wealthy to be all glorious and perfect." He looked over at Sofia, who was arching her eyebrows. "Well, most people.

"We had access to all the riches—the best schools, the best cars, the best clothes, etc., but that's it. And I luxuriated in that lifestyle along with your boyfriend. If I'm being honest, I still enjoy living in the lap of luxury, but back in the day, we lived in excess: excess of drugs, alcohol, sex, you name it—we did it."

Jude was part of that clique, but hearing it come out of Etienne's mouth created new insecurities she thought she released long ago. How was she supposed to move into a higher consciousness if she had to face her shadow every few weeks?

"And Gabrielle, was she part of your so-called friends? Jude told me they were friends when they were young, but were they friends throughout his lifetime?"

"Do you truly want to know?" Etienne said, peering into her eyes.

"Do tell. I'm an adult. I can handle it."

"Okay." He hesitated initially but continued, "As you know, she's been in Jude's life since they were kids and remained that way until their twenties. Their parents rubbed elbows together at the same parties.

"Speaking of which, that's exactly where I met Jude, at a shindig in the South of France." He cleared his throat and smiled at whatever memory came forth. "There were hundreds of pretentious and la-de-da people—young and old. As you can imagine, the chichi girls chased Jude all night.

"I, on the other hand, was the jokester and the clown, and I was fine with that role. I wasn't good friends with Jude, either. But we always seemed to show up at the same parties. He was always courteous with me and rather enjoyed my jokes." He smirked. "I was quite funny."

He leaned back and went on with his tale. "Lo and behold, I was graced by my mother's presence. She showed up unbeknownst to me, with not my dad but a younger man, probably in his early twenties, not that much older than me. At that moment, I thought nothing of it until I saw her snorting cocaine with him. And when he gyrated on the dance floor with her, I freaked out.

"I didn't have a relationship with my mother, but I felt compelled to save my father's honor, so I ripped through the crowd and peeled the guy off her. He didn't take too kindly to my action and began to punch and kick me to the floor. He was a heavier build than me, but also, I wasn't a fighter." He stopped and flippantly said, "I'm a lover, not a fighter."

"I pleaded for my mother to tell him to stop. She did not. Instead, she egged him on to teach me a lesson." He sighed. "And, whenever I think back to that incident, I can still see her laughing at me as I lay there bloody and beaten on the swanky terrace. The whole crowd was applauding and cheering for more blood."

Sickened by their behavior, Sofia uttered, "Isn't that a preferred form of entertainment for the elitist?"

He raised his eyebrows and affirmed, "You bet. But that's another story."

He took a swig of the champagne and continued, "I couldn't see through my bloody eyes, but then I heard Jude and his father berating the crowd for participating in this abomination. Jude barked orders at people. He was like, 'You. Stop laughing and help me restrain this low life.' I could hear the crowd dispersing at Jude's request. There was a lot of commotion. Not once did my mom console or help me. Jude's dad took me home. And I never left."

"Wow, that is one story. How long did it take you to recover?"

"Five months, no joke. Her boy toy cracked four of my ribs. And I had to get surgery on my cheekbone and nose." He whipped his head around and boasted, "That's why I'm so handsome today."

Sofia chuckled. "Jokes aside, you didn't only suffer a physical beating, my friend. That was an emotional beating." *And a karmic lesson for him and his mother.*

Etienne gave a half-smile. "Tell me about it. And, this is only the tip of the iceberg, as you say in English."

"Not gonna lie, your mother sounds like a troubled soul. What about your dad? Did he find out about the incident? Why didn't he fight for you?" Sofia was on a roll.

He held up his hands. "My father didn't dare stand up to my mother. So, forget about standing up for me. They stayed together. She never stopped cheating on him. Eventually, he did the same." He peered into Sofia's eyes. "This is the way of the wealthy.

Sofia said, "I'm sorry you had to grow up in a loveless environment."

Etienne warmly smiled. "My nanny at the time raised me. She showed me love in her way. And, when Jude's father took me in, I found my place in a loving family." He paused. "I'd rather not live in the past."

She loved that about him. He lived in the present moment.

He continued, "I stopped talking to my mother after the incident. When she showed up at my university graduation for her photo op, her presence floored Jude. He would have called her out if he could have, but I allowed the facade to ensue."

He sighed heavily and took a few minutes to collect himself. He leaned into Sofia. "Jude's mother—now that's another piece of work," he exclaimed.

Sofia replied, "I had the privilege of listening in on one of her rants."

He grimaced.

But she still wasn't sure she had it in her to hear another deranged story. So, she declined. Whatever happened to the divine feminine? What happened to mothers protecting their children? Just listening to his story made Sofia miss her mother. She wished Jude could have met her.

19

Sofia barely recognized Jude when she came rolling out of customs. His hair had grown out into soft and lush waves. His hair was darker than she had imagined. The circles under his eyes were disconcerting; still, he took her breath away. As he scribbled in his mini notebook, she called out to him in her mind and said, *I'm here by the plant.* His gaze darted right at her. When their eyes met, a wave of frequency flowed between them and meshed into her heart. He bolted right at her. He took her in his arms and enveloped her whole being. He showered her with butterfly kisses on the top of her head.

Your hair always smells like Summer to me. She missed hearing his thoughts. *I've missed you so much. I'm happy you are here. You are my beautiful treasure.*

She reciprocated and mindfully told him she never wanted to be apart again.

He whispered in her ear, "Did you pack for a long stay, then?"

She didn't have a chance to answer when Etienne joined in on the hug fest. He teased, "Oh, how I've missed you, my Jude."

Jude wriggled out of Etienne's embrace. "You know you did. I missed you too, *frérot* (brother)."

Etienne did not deny it. After all, they had been tied to each other's hips for twenty years.

Jude stretched out his arms and took Sofia's hands in his. "It feels like forever since I've laid eyes on you. *Tu es ravissante!* (You are ravishing)." He twirled her right back in his arms, prompting him to purr in her ear, "I have a surprise for you later."

The butterflies were back, coupled with a snake stirring in her sacral chakra. She felt her body temperature rising. She coyly gazed at him and muttered, "I look forward to it."

Etienne shouted, "Hello, I am here. You seem to forget that when I'm around you."

Jude kept his eyes on Sofia while simultaneously mussing up Etienne's hair. Then he took her luggage in one hand while holding her other. "Shall we be on our way?"

She remembered how rambunctious the French were as they maneuvered through the flock of people waiting for their family members, lovers, and colleagues to come through the doors. It was part of the reason she loved this city—they expressed themselves outwardly. The electrical waves continuously pulsed throughout her body. It was a phenomenon she would have to get used to. His hold on her was commandeering but gentle at the same time.

It felt like the car was a gazillion miles away in that maze of an airport. She was not in a hurry and was content being in his presence. There was nothing she needed more than that.

Jude acknowledged her thought and trumpeted his love for Sofia throughout the airport, *"L'amour est tout ce qu'il y'a dans la vie* (Love is all you need in life)."

He was regaled with affirmations and cheers by some bystanders.

They arrived at a black Mercedes-Maybach S600. A tall, lanky, handsome man with dark brown skin leaned against the car. He wore a crisp white shirt that perfectly fit his dark denim trousers. The moment he caught sight of Jude, Etienne, and Sofia, he adjusted his stance and opened the doors for them. Sofia was introduced to Xavier. He had been with the family for over fifteen years as a chauffeur and right-hand man to Jude's father.

Sofia settled onto the butterscotch Nappa leather seat with six different massage buttons. She tried every one of them as the men chatted it up with Xavier. She further distracted herself by scrolling through social media. It wasn't a coincidence that she felt compelled to turn on the phone as the first message to pop up was a message from Gabrielle to her Divine Sofia account.

She clicked on it, and it said,

—He's mine and will always be. I can't wait to meet you again on the street or in a dark alley. Oh, and you can try to block me, but I will always find a way in. xo Gabi.—

Sofia closed the phone and shut her eyes.

****

The slamming of a trunk jolted her awake. When she opened her eyes, she was in the back seat of the car, with only Jude's musky scent remedying her disorientation. She removed his jacket that swaddled her body. She beamed joyfully when she looked out the window and spotted a man on a bicycle with a basket overflowing with baguettes.

She gathered her things and glided to the other side. As the door opened, Jude was there to help her out.

"Why didn't you wake me up?"

He padded down her unruly hair. "You were in a deep sleep." He gazed into her eyes and playfully said, "Plus, I'm pretty sure that Etienne kept you up the whole flight. He's not a fan of flying, and talking makes him forget his fear."

"Where are we?"

"I brought you to Etienne's family home for now. It's not safe at mine. His home is tucked away and more secure." He muttered, "I hope that's okay with you."

"Will you be staying here with me?"

He bent over and kissed her on the lips. "*Oui.* (Yes)"

Sofia felt weak at the knees. She wanted so much to make love to him.

Jude swung open the towering, black iron gates into a small courtyard—enormous terra cotta vases lined the wall. A trellis hung above, adorned with browned leaves dotted with delightful pink flowers. Branches and vines twined around wooden columns and slats. Positioned by the door sat a fancy, wrought iron chair. A modest wooden bowl with colorful yarn rested at the feet of the almost ostentatious chair.

She tugged at Jude's arm. "I thought Etienne was estranged from his family. Why does he live in their home?"

Jude laughed. "He sure talked a lot on that plane ride. His father felt bad about the whole mother debacle and handed the deed to Etienne many years later, with only one stipulation—when visiting, if they, either he or his wife, chose to stay in the home, they could by giving him a one-week warning."

There is faith in humanity, after all.

She held him back again and asked, "So, what's with the knitting gear?"

He snickered. "You are a curious one. I guess that's what makes you an amazing researcher." He kissed her again. "Come, I'll introduce you."

Jude opened the door into the kitchen—a rustic area with an old wood stove. The solid oak table was peppered with homemade foods—

the smell of freshly baked bread filled the house. A fairly robust woman rambled in, hugged Jude, and buoyantly roared, *"Bienvenue ma Canadienne."* (Welcome, my Canadian). She wore her salt and pepper hair in a bun high on her head. Her rosy cheeks and glowing smile were most welcoming. She called out Etienne's name. "Where is that boy, always running away and hiding." She continued, "He used to do that all the time as a kid." She nudged Jude and teasingly said. "No one blames him with a mother like he had." She boisterously laughed.

Etienne came running down the stairs. "I prepared your room."

Yolande rolled her eyes. "Excuse me? Who prepared her room?"

He blushed and repeated. "Sofia, I see you met my other mother. And yes, she did a wonderful job. It's fit for a queen."

Yolande eked out an "I miss you" to Etienne but whined in typical European motherly fashion. "You gained a bit of weight. You've been indulging in American food. How long are you staying this time?"

All eyes went to Jude. He raised his palms in the air. "I can't give you an exact date. Things are day to day."

"Well, the more time I spend with both, er, the three of you, the happier I am." She looked over at Jude and Sofia. "She's the best one so far."

Sofia glanced at Jude, who was shaking his head. He immediately draped his shoulder over Sofia's. "She is my only one."

Even Yolande teased him; she reflected on his words and said, "She better be. I have a good feeling about this one." She wagged her finger at Jude. "You better protect her from the other one, too."

"Okay, enough yelling at us," Etienne said. "Did you get it out of your system yet?"

She smirked and opened the fridge. "I've cooked a good week's food for you ungrateful boys." She opened the freezer. "And there's more here."

Etienne and Jude both reached over to hug her. Yolande was not an overly affectionate woman. She didn't do well with compliments and just shooed them away. "Call me when you need something. I'm not far away." She turned to Sofia. "If these boys are too hard to handle, contact me. I know how to put them in their place." She gave Sofia a once over and added, "But, I think you can handle them alone."

Yolande picked up her basket of yarn and left. She called out from the courtyard, "Oh, and I'm taking the car." When Xavier tried to open the door for her, she waved him away and bickered. He laughed, went to the driver's seat, and they left into the streets of Paris.

Meanwhile, the boys were already nit-picking at the food on the table. As Sofia watched them feast on the homemade goodies, she felt at home with the two of them. She felt like this scenario had happened in a past lifetime. Or was it a future one? When Jude looked up, he immediately rushed to her side. "The food can wait. Shall we go see our room?"

Etienne looked up from behind his brioche. "I brought up all your luggage already. Take a "nap" if you want. Later, we'll go out into the city. Sounds like a plan?"

Sofia nodded.

"Let's go to Guillaume's," Jude said. "It's a good way to introduce Sofia to our Paris." Etienne agreed.

Jude slipped his hand into Sofia's and led her up the rickety, carpeted stairs. When they got to the top floor, there was a labyrinth of doors to choose from. They walked to the far end of the hallway and turned a corner to a secluded room. He lifted the heavy velvet curtain before the door, opened it, and waved her in. As Etienne said, Sofia sashayed into what felt like a boudoir fit for royalty. It wasn't difficult to miss the view from their window: the iconic Eiffel Tower—she always had a love-hate relationship with this landmark. As she examined the rest of the room, the pastel blue and ivory jacquard print seemed to be a favorite for the interior decorator. It was on the chairs, the walls, and even the headboard. She imagined Lola and Emma scrutinizing every detail. A vintage watering can overflowing with pretty peonies was fashionably posed on the nightstand. And on each pillowcase lay lavender stems tied with pale blue ribbon.

How old is this room? I can certainly feel the energy within the walls calling out to me.

Jude leaned in and said, "I feel the same energy. Did you bring your smudge sticks with you?"

Sofia thought of everything. She had filled her luggage to the brim with crystals, singing bowls, journals, tarot cards, and other tools for energy cleansing. She opened her suitcase, pulled the bag out, and handed them to Jude. He opened all the windows and lit the sage and lavender one.

He went to the middle of the room, said a prayer, and cleared every corner. He swooshed all the energy out the windows. The room felt lighter. It worked. He placed it in a ceramic ashtray and headed over to Sofia.

He pulled her to him and growled, "I can now feel only your energy traveling up and down, and in and out of my body."

She wrapped her arms around his waist and leaned her cheek against his chest. "I missed you. I had gotten used to having someone listen to my wacky stories without thoughts of locking me up in an institution." She backed away and said, "But before we go any further, I must shower. Airplanes are the worst."

He concurred. "I'll go down and catch up with my friend. Unless you want me to join you?"

She was tempted but declined the offer. Jude did leave her with a longing kiss—one she didn't want to break free from, but alas.

20

Refreshed and ready to hit the streets of Paris, Sofia sported her haute winter gear. Paris was not as cold as Montreal temperature-wise—with its cemented homes, dampness was not her friend. She heard Jude and Etienne chatting up a storm. Setting up an altar was customary everywhere she traveled—first the altar cloth, then the rest of the paraphernalia. She recited a sacred prayer to protect her valued pieces and to shield Jude and herself from any energies that would want to come out to play. After all, Paris was just as energetic as New York.

A swoosh of high energy wrapped around her. Jude's hands journeyed up and down her fitted knit dress. Jude nuzzled his face into her neck and murmured, "*Je kiffe* (I love it)!"

With one swift move, he twirled her around and kissed her. The strength of his embrace, the confidence of his lips, and the magnetism of their energies heightened her desire. His touch stirred up dormant feelings of lust within her. She always read about the kundalini awakening but never experienced it in her lifetime. There would always be a first time.

"I want you so badly," she admitted.

He cupped her face and stared intently into her eyes. "I've wanted you since I first laid eyes on you." He lowered his lips onto hers again and hungrily devoured her lips.

She pushed him back onto the bed, which he gracefully landed on. As he lay there as delicious as ever, a bout of insecurities washed over her. Her ego listed all the reasons she shouldn't take her clothes off— how he would eventually break her heart: the usual linear mind traps. He lifted himself and brought her down on the bed.

"Stop listening to all those thoughts running through your mind. Who are you?"

Sofia frowned.

He repeated, "Who are you? You are Divine Sofia. You are a beautiful luminous being that shines her light wherever she goes. Wipe away those thoughts. They are not becoming of your greatness."

Sofia cracked a smile and combed her fingers through his silky hair. She whispered, "It feels creepy now to make love to my biggest fan. Maybe we should keep this platonic."

He laughed and brought her back down with him on the bed. "There's no rush, even though I can't wait to see how our energies will merge." He growled and canvased her body with more kisses."I can't seem to keep my hands off of you."

"Then don't." She climbed on top of him. She felt a sharp pain in her inner thigh when he lifted his torso. "What is that?"

"It's my surprise for you." He fell back on the bed, reached into his front pocket, and pulled out a silk pouch. When he returned to his upright position, he dangled it before her.

Like a giddy teen, she untied the knot and pulled out a soft leather rope with a green and black stone shaped into a pendulum. She grazed her fingertip along the engraved symbol on the metal casing at the top of the crystal. "Which symbol is this?"

He showed the tattoo on his fourth finger and said, "We haven't figured it out yet, but it felt right." He explained that he couldn't find the Andara crystal but was called toward the Nebula Stone, symbolizing spiritual growth and kundalini awakening. It's also symbolic of the "Cosmic Circle of Life."

He took it from her hands and fastened it around her neck. Then he reached under his T-shirt and displayed a replica of the necklace.

Tears spilled down her cheeks. He inched closer and swept his fingertips along her cheekbones, wiping away the tears. He then placed his hand on her pendant and rested it on her heart. "Now, we continue the legacy."

Sofia placed her hand on his heart and whispered, "You really are a romantic."

He smiled from ear to ear. "What can I say? After so many years of surfing the waves of emotions, my heart feels safe to open itself up again."

She grazed her fingers along his face and leaned in to kiss him. He responded by bringing her body close to his and reclining back onto the bed. He explored her every curve and pleasure point—it was easy to fall under his spell until they heard Etienne stirring in the hall, prompting Sofia to hold back.

Jude whispered, "Soon. Just me and you, alone."

They lay on the bed together, holding hands. Sofia said, "Can we just stay like this until the end of time? Heart to heart. Lips to lips, without the complicated world out there?"

He reached over, caressed her cheek, and sighed, "Seems like a fine plan to me."

They stayed quiet for a while until Sofia asked, "When we're together, especially pasted up against each other, do you constantly feel the current traveling between us?"

His eyes sparkled a luminous green. "Yes. All the time. Even when we hold hands, I've just gotten used to it. It's like my blood is rushing through your veins. And vice versa. It's miraculous."

He lifted himself and asked, "Did you want to go out and about? Because if we stay here, there's only one thing I want to do, and it doesn't include talking—well, maybe some talking."

Sofia laughed and peeled herself off the bed. She lifted him to his feet, and he sprang into her arms.

"I can't wait to have my way with you." His soft lips cushioned her lips. He pulled away and muttered, "Let's visit my city."

****

Leaning up against the car as honking cars whizzed around him, Xavier waited for them in front of the gates. He would sometimes answer back to the catcalls, but he often ignored his fellow countrymen. When Xavier saw them walking toward him, his eyes lit up. He opened the door for Sofia.

"I hope these boys are not giving you any problems. You can always call me if you need help." He winked at her. He seemed not much older than Jude, somewhere in his thirties. And he spoke perfect English. There was a soothing vibe about him.

The boys greeted him with their handshake. Jude joined Sofia in the back seat, and Etienne went up front to do what he did best—chit-chat.

As Jude joined the bro-fest, Sofia appreciated the magnificent Haussmanian buildings with intricate limestone facades. In observing the buildings, she remembered some research she did a while back on their "true" history.

Jude was mid-speech when he paused, leaned in, and said, "I remember that episode. It was eye-opening." He continued blabbing away with his mates.

Whoever said men never listen, this proves them wrong. I'll need to be careful what I'm thinking, too.

She realized she wasn't tapping into his thoughts as much anymore. Her higher self advised her that it depended on her state of mind. *No big deal.* Okay, well, if my higher self says so!

She went back to admiring the Gothic architecture. Every street corner had a boulangerie, croissanterie, and patisserie. The streets were chock full of men and women, young and old, high-fashion and no fashion.

Sofia remembered how much she disliked this city when she was younger and less connected to her light. Their arrogance and snobbery affected her until she could see past that. Now, she was able to observe their essence, their auras. Being "awake" made her a pariah, but she would not have it any other way.

Jude lounged on the leather chair and slung his arm around Sofia. He brought her closer to him. "I'm sorry if it feels like I'm listening to your every thought, but I am." He chuckled. "Like you always say, you can't unsee what you see and unknow what you know."

Sofia rested her head on his chest, her fingers playing with the buttons on his military-style jacket. "You are the best gift the universe has given me in a long time."

He kissed the top of her head.

Not even the Eiffel Tower or Arc de Triomphe persuaded her to look up. She was in no rush to relinquish this closeness with Jude. The rest of the ride was spent listening to Etienne and Xavier's heated conversations about soccer and politics, the usual, while Jude and Sofia remained in silent reverie.

They arrived at the iconic Notre Dame Cathedral. Sofia couldn't help but stand facing the church in deep contemplation. She remembered doing a series of videos revealing the darkness and unholiness found within many iconic structures worldwide. It was one of her most popular videos. Since then, she has come into the innerstanding that she, along with the rest of the starseeds and lightworkers, were, in fact, responsible for the "evil" in the world.

Jude added. "I've always felt that somehow. In your last video about polarity, good and evil exist side by side. So it makes sense. You must do a follow-up series with this wisdom." Jude draped his arm around her shoulder.

"It would be a challenging one."

"That's never stopped you before." He kissed her on the cheek.

Etienne made a face. "I have no clue what you're talking about, but you guys should do a podcast together."

"Well, maybe next week, we'll go live together," Sofia said. "What do you think about that, my love?"

He twirled her in his arms, smiling. "My love? Well, my love, I think that's grand!"

"I'm serious. I know you are apprehensive because of Gabrielle."

"I don't care about her anymore." He paused. "I mean, I do, and it's still ongoing, but nothing changes if nothing changes."

Etienne shook his head and said, "Wow, you guys are meant for each other—talking in riddles and metaphors all the time."

Jude raised his eyebrows. "This coming from the man of literary quotes."

Sofia noticed the market along the Seine and pointed a finger. "Can we go there, please?"

"Yeah, sure, but you know they're going to rip you off," Etienne grumbled.

Jude grabbed Sofia's hand and walked toward the kiosks overflowing with souvenirs, art prints, books, and trinkets. She spotted a stand with records. The silver-haired man wearing a Pink Floyd t-shirt was setting up an old record player. She reminisced about her first record player and the care she took with all her 45s and 12" LPs. When she recounted her story to the boys, Etienne giggled. "Maybe you shouldn't be declaring that out loud. It ages you."

Jude slapped Etienne's arm playfully. "And, what's your point? I have the same memories, and I'm younger than her."

Sofia laughed. "I am not that much older than you. Regardless, I don't care about my age. It is but a number in a linear world."

"I literally only understand twenty percent of what you say to me," Etienne replied.

There were records and CDs from all genres of music and eras. Jude talked to the owner while she flipped through the 80s and 90s faves.

Sofia tested Jude. "Can you guess which song I want to…?"

Before she could finish her train of thought, the song flowed through the speakers, and Jude rushed to her side. "You were saying?"

It was uncanny how he lived in her head. Out poured Chris Cornell's voice. His cover for Sinead O'Connor's "Nothing Compares to You" always struck a chord with Sofia. She felt it deep within her soul.

He encircled her in his arms, and they swayed to the music, inciting the man to increase the volume, and soon enough, others were doing the same.

Meanwhile, Etienne sat on a nearby bench and lit a cigarette for the old man beside him. Sofia looked up at his gesture and turned to Jude."I haven't seen you with a cigarette in a while. Have you stopped smoking?"

He nodded. "I'm trying to quit. I know how much it lowers my vibration. Plus, you don't much like it."

"I never said anything to you about it." And then she remembered she didn't have to because he was in her head. She placed her cheek back on his shoulder and drank in the lyrics to the rest of the song.

Jude then asked the same question. She listened closely and chose his song with a spring in her step because if it was the right song, then she undeniably found her twin flame.

As Michael Hutchence's voice echoed onto the streets of Paris, Jude looked delighted. More bystanders crowded the stand, swaying to the music.

"When I first saw you, this is exactly how I felt. "Nothing, as the song says, can tear us apart," Jude said, wrapping her back into his arms.

She didn't care how many shades of red flashed on her cheeks. Jude lifted her chin toward his face and leaned in for a sultry kiss. A tidal wave of energy coursed through her body. By the look on his face, she knew he felt it too.

"That was intense—it went from my feet above my head. You?"

She nodded. Was it part of the process of the twin flames? More research was in order.

Etienne came running over to them. "Whoa. Did you see that?" They both looked at him. "There was like a flash of light that ripped right by you guys."

Jude winked at Sofia. And then placed his hand on Etienne's shoulder. "What have you been smoking?"

Sofia mimicked Jude's teasing. "Have you been sleeping enough?"

Etienne narrowed his eyes, staring at them. "You're screwing with me, right? In any case, I'm hungry. Shall we go over to Guillaume's? It's walking distance from here."

Jude and Sofia strolled hand-in-hand. They couldn't keep their hands off of each other. When Jude stopped mid-walk and kissed her, Etienne whined.

Sofia teased, "Does Etienne need some lovin' today?" She broke free from Jude's embrace and put an arm around Etienne's shoulders. Jude came around the other side and did the same.

He replied, "Well, that's better. Come to think of it, it's been a while since I've had some one-on-one time." He paused and turned to Sofia. "So, when are your friends coming to town again?"

Sofia wondered which one he preferred. Her superpower did not yet extend to others outside of her beloved. Time will tell.

21

It was a typical Parisian bistro, what one would expect to see in a movie. The chairs were black with rattan covering. Mirrors replaced the walls, the menu was on a colossal blackboard hoisted onto the wall, round light bulbs hung low, and the tables overflowed with locals. There was a line-up, but they snuck in by the side entrance. The wait staff acknowledged Jude and Etienne, and so did several patrons. They sat at the only free table by the bar.

One minute in, an older man pulled up a chair beside Sofia. Tied in a ponytail—the salt gleamed brighter than the pepper in his head of grays. All dressed in white with grease stains across his buttoned-up jacket, Jude introduced him as the chef and owner. She extended her hand to him. Guillaume wiped his hand on his pants and shook her hand. "It's the first time Jude has brought in such a classy woman."

Etienne snickered. Jude ignored him. Sofia did not.

He droned on about how Jude brought in all the most beautiful girls. He joked that his wait staff fought over his reservation to serve his dates. Sofia's lower ego was having a field day.

Jude nervously twitched in his seat, and mid-way through Guillaume's tales; he cut it short. "Let's change the subject."

Guillaume chortled, "Oh yes, of course." He winked at her. He then changed the subject and filled them in with the latest gossip—this one cheated on her husband, that one got into a fight, the other one stopped talking to her, etc. She studied Jude. He was courteous, but she felt his energy deflate with every gossipy tidbit. On the other hand, Etienne fully engaged with every rumor with laughter.

Then silence fell upon them for a few seconds until Guillaume turned to Jude. "So, what's going on with your mother? Have you found a way to delete her from your life?"

Jude squirmed in his seat. "*C'est plus exigeante que prévu* (It's more challenging than expected)."

Guillaume consoled Jude. "*Allez, ne te dégonfle pas. Rien n'est perdu : il faut que tu te bouges, point barre.* (C'mon, don't give up. It's not lost yet: you have to step it up. Period.)"

He told Sofia that he'd known Jude since he was a boy. His mother was never really a mother to him, nor was she a good wife.

"I knew his mother when we were younger. And let me tell you, she was a knockout." He leaned back in his chair, arms crossed, reminiscing. "But she knew it, and her vanity got the best of her." He paused and said, "When she met Jude's father, I was weary for him." He laughed out loud. "Michel managed to keep her in line for a few years, but again she strayed back to her old ways."

Sofia kept her eyes on Guillaume but mindfully asked Jude, *Old ways?*

He replied. *Guillaume is a master storyteller. The story is far from over. He will give you all the details, my curious one. But just for you...* Jude addressed Guillaume, "Do you wish to grace us with a story to help Sofia better understand her "old" ways?"

Guillaume whipped his mane back and jutted his chest out. "It would be my pleasure." He dove right into Coco's, short for Claire, upbringing in the land of the rich and famous and how it eventually shaped her. "She only dated men that could adorn her with jewels and take her to the best restaurants. To be fair, she was just a product of her environment. Her parents treated her like a porcelain doll. They brought her to all the parties to show off her beauty, never praising her for her smarts. You know, she had a university degree. They shunned it until it suited their needs for a certain event."

Jude was silent throughout. Sofia listened intently. Etienne scrolled through his smartphone.

Guillaume continued, "When she started dating Michel, her parents were not impressed. He came from a good-standing family but was not exceedingly wealthy like hers. Jude's father was more humble than her; let's just put it that way. At first, I never understood the union, but it made sense; he welcomed her ways and gave her free rein with her ideas and beliefs. Michel never judged her for being outspoken. As for him, he was escaping the humdrum life and entering Coco's version of life. But, eventually, life got boring for her. And she went back to consorting with the elitists."

Guillaume heartwarmingly glanced at Jude and said, "When Jude was born, she had no idea how to be a mother. She hired nanny after nanny until Michel put an end to it. He quit his job and became the caregiver." He cleared his throat and looked over at Sofia. "It was just not done in those days. But, he didn't give a rat's ass and did it anyway." He paused and nodded. "And to tell you the truth, I had the utmost respect for that man from then on. He gave up his job as a scientist and brought up this boy." He pointed at Jude. "And he did a fine job, wouldn't you say, Sofia?"

She approvingly nodded. "Yes, but I'm sure Jude was a handful."

Guillaume chuckled and said, "Well, actually, he wasn't. The handful was Lennon." He twisted his head and asked, "Have you met our golden boy yet? You will understand when you see him. My waitresses always fight to serve him." He reflected on his following words and said, "Despite being adopted, it's uncanny how much he resembles Jude."

Jude shifted in his seat.

Guillaume looked at them and exclaimed, "*Bon* (Alright, then). I must return to my kitchen. Who knows what *bordel* (mess) they are creating in there. I will prepare some plates for you." He peered into Sofia's eyes. "*Enchantée et bienvenue à la famille* (Pleased to meet you and welcome to the family)." He was gone in a flash.

Sofia debated whether to bring up the latest information but opted against it. Instead, she sat quietly, waiting for Jude to explain himself.

As customary, Etienne and Jude spiraled into another conversation completely off-topic.

Why would he not tell me about the adoption? What is it about keeping all these secrets? So much drama. But why would he tell me if I keep telling him I don't want drama?

Jude leaned into Sofia and relayed. *So much thinking going on in that brain of yours. What happened to not "overthinking?" I promise to explain later.*

Rather than pursuing it, she changed the subject. "Why aren't you being harassed by Gabrielle like you were back home?"

Etienne jumped in, "Oh, he's still harassed."

Jude shot him a look. "I love you, brother, but man, we'll have to work on your tact." He tapped him on the shoulder and said, "It's thirty-six years you've been on this planet, so we can't expect miracles."

"I think you may have to give up on that one!"

They chuckled. But Sofia waited for an answer.

Jude turned to her. "We have more leverage in Paris. Here, we have access to her parents and therapists." He paused. "It's not, by all means, easier to handle her, but she understands her boundaries a bit more. And the consequences would not be pretty for her."

"Well, why don't you approach the parents about this whole situation and get it over with, once and for all?" she asked.

Jude briefly exchanged looks with Etienne and sighed. "It's more complicated because it, somehow, involves my mother. She lived with Coco in her early twenties. I never quite understood the reasoning behind it. Since my mother was not very...." He lowered his eyes and continued, "Anyway, it's unimportant. When I went out seeking answers, I always got the runaround. When they say Paris is bureaucratic, it's also the same for family life."

Sofia was more than intrigued. She was ready to embark on a digging expedition on her own until Jude intercepted her thoughts again and said out loud, "No, you don't."

Etienne swiveled his head from side to side, staring at them.

Jude continued, "You have no idea how powerful her parents are. And you haven't the slightest clue how insane my mother is. She will stop at nothing or no one to get what she wants." He placed his strong hand on hers and pleaded, "I beg you to leave this fight for Etienne and me."

Sofia backed down, but this story was not over yet.

Jude patted Etienne on the shoulder. "Without you, I don't know how I would have survived all these years."

Etienne's aura beamed, and his smile stretched wide across his face.

Their exchange was interrupted as plates of food steamrolled in filled with roasted root vegetables, hearty sausage, and duck confit. A charcuterie board with seven varieties of cheese accompanied by a basket of piping hot bread was Sofia's highlight.

As Jude served them, Sofia thought, *I can't wait to meet this man who raised three boys alone. He unquestionably did something right.*

As he placed the plate in front of her, he said, "He will love and embrace you as his own."

Etienne smirked. "Why do I always feel like I'm losing parts of the conversation?" He curiously eyed them and waited for a response.

"You're not listening to us because you are always too distracted by the beautiful women around you."

"Like the one at the table." Etienne let that slip out without him even realizing it. He blushed a deep red and looked away from Sofia's gaze.

Jude curiously eyed Etienne, then reached over and swept his fingers along the curves of her face. "She is, indeed." He lowered his mouth to hers and longingly kissed her.

When his lips touched hers, she quickly forgot about the awkwardness of Etienne's remark and got lost in Jude's incandescent energy. She no longer heard the rowdy clientele and chatter around her. She felt like she was in a chamber filled with muffled sounds. When his lips displaced themselves from hers, she was brought back to the present moment with the high-pitched sound of clinking glasses.

She heard him say to her. *Oh, what a journey we are embarking on, my divine phoenix.*

IT JUST IS

Your love doesn't need to be justified.
IT JUST IS.
Your journey doesn't need to be justified.
IT JUST IS.
Your truth doesn't need to be justified.
IT JUST IS.
Your dream doesn't need to be justified.
IT JUST IS.
Your way of being doesn't need to be justified.
IT JUST IS.

22

As soon as Sofia stepped outside, the cold air smacked her in the face. She zipped up and tucked her face inside the warmth of the woolen tube of her jacket.

Etienne laughed. "Oh la la, Canada is much worse than this."

He was right, but regardless, Sofia was never a fan of the cold, no matter where she was. Jude circled her waist and brought her closer to him. "I will keep you warm, my Canadian ice queen."

Etienne rolled his eyes. "In the wise words of Albert Camus, In the depth of winter, I finally learned that…."

Sofia continued his quote, "Within me, there lay an invincible summer."

Etienne dotingly looked at Sofia and bashfully smiled at her.

Jude amicably shoved Etienne to the side. "Sofia, you better watch out. You may have more than one of us crushing on you!"

Xavier pulled up right in time. Etienne jumped in and waved to the two of them as he gallivanted into the Parisian night.

Jude mumbled to himself, "He is a funny one, sometimes."

Sofia didn't overthink it. Instead, she wormed her arms around Jude's waist and buried her head into his cashmere scarf.

He chuckled, "Are you still cold?"

The moment he returned the affection, their energies plugged in. It created a flush of heat that traveled throughout their bodies. Jude kissed her on the forehead.

"Well, that solves that. Do you want to go for a walk in the park?" He pointed to the wintery forest postcard scenery up ahead.

December in Paris was magical, with most city streets and monuments illuminated with lavish holiday lighting. As they walked toward the park, gone were summer's lush landscape of manicured shrubs replaced instead with winter's offerings of towering, bristly trees. Still, the statues and fountains gracefully stood in their stark elegance.

Jude and Sofia walked hand-in-hand in silence. She had a long list of questions for Jude but favored the tranquility. The sound of their footsteps echoed into the woodland around them. She leaned in and whispered, "Do you normally walk in the park in the dead of winter, or are you doing it for me?"

"I know you love nature since you keep telling your online community to hug those trees." He smiled. "But I prefer connecting to Gaia as much as I can. Most of the time, I prefer greenery over humans."

Sofia gripped his hand and held him back. She gazed into his eyes. "Where have you been all my life?"

He embraced her and purred, "I'm here now." He pressed his soft lips against hers. The strength of their magnetism and their desire to be one with each other made it difficult to disentangle from one another. They both listened to their higher selves and simultaneously loosened their grip.

Jude rested his forehead against hers. "I want you so badly. My place isn't far, but…." He paused for a long while.

"But, Gabrielle."

He sighed. "Yes." His mind was racing while his hands were roving up and down her body. "But, I can sneak you in from the back alley. What do you say?"

"I'm in. I'm not scared of her."

He peered into her eyes, "My love, no need to be your brave warrior self. She is not to be trifled with. She is more dangerous than you think."

Sofia nodded. She distracted him by brushing her lips along his neck.

Jude glanced at his phone and said, "It's faster if we walk. Paris traffic is a nightmare. It will take us about eighteen minutes or so. Is that okay with you?"

Sofia smiled and whispered, "Like you always say, we have a lifetime ahead of us. There's no rush." She traced her finger along his lower lip.

He playfully bit her finger and bestowed another kiss but broke away just before the magnet fastened them again. He latched onto her hand and steered her toward the street. They walked away from the austere backdrop into a turbulent concrete jungle full of lively humans, a zillion cars, and a deluge of lights cascading from the trees and lampposts.

She heard him say. *Now you understand why I can't spend too much time in this city.*

She squeezed his hand. As much as she adored nature, she also loved the méli-mélo of European cities, or perhaps the ancient architectural setting made the difference. She tugged on his arm. "Do you live in the Latin Quarter?"

He shook his head. "Not quite. But I'm right at the edge. I live in the 6th—Saint Germain-des-Prés."

Sofia remembered a time when she came with Lola, and they ended up in a tourist restaurant in the Quartier Latin that served raclette. The waiters ended up taking them out on the town. And they took them out for the duration of the trip—no expectations, just fun times.

Jude said, "I can't remember the last time I lived so carefree. Soon, I will fix the problem and return to a normal life."

Sofia's higher self kicked in with advice: *To avoid him always in your mind, create a wall of light so that he can't tap into your private thoughts.*

Sofia sincerely asked, "Do you make it a point to listen to my thoughts, or is it an organic process?"

Jude hung his arm around her and smirked. "The latter. I would rather not always hear what you say, especially your memories with other men. I don't know how to control it just yet."

As they passed café after café—she bemused that even in the dead of winter, the French didn't let cold weather deter them from their coffee and croissant. Before turning the corner, Jude held Sofia back. He surveyed the road ahead. He turned off his phone. "The coast is clear for now. I will bring you in by the front door. Come."

They arrived smack dab in front of a busy bookstore. Sofia's eyes feasted on the multitude of books displayed in the windows. Delighted, she exclaimed, "Oh, what a wonderful shop. Is this where you live??"

He nodded and pointed to the door right beside the bookstore.

It took a few minutes to unbolt the numerous locks and slide open the second gated door. Once locked inside, Jude turned on the light, led her up a flight of stairs to another heavy metal door, and punched in a code.

He removed her jacket and purse and hung them on the hooks. She took off her booties and made her way around his apartment. She was astonished to see how many full-length windows lined the space. It was a similar vibe and color palette as his home in Montreal, but this one was more impersonal. It was an ample, open space. All walls were pristinely white with accents of shades of wood or black throughout. No table, only chairs tucked into a kitchen island. His energy was only half there. Both north and south-facing windows overlooked the city rooftops. He lived in a postcard.

A tornado of energy whipped around and propelled her to face him. He was sitting on the bed, observing her every move. When she slinked her way toward him, he reached out his arms and ushered Sofia into his embrace. As their bodies molded into each other, a fiery current quickly uncoiled itself and erupted from the base of the spine toward her crown chakra. She lifted herself and removed his sweater. He did the same and slipped her dress over her head. When fully naked, there was no shyness. Sofia's butterflies were nowhere to be found either. There was a sense of familiarity between the two of them. Their energies began to swirl and dance all around them.

Goosebumps formed all over her body when his hands swept down her torso. Skin to skin, they explored each other with tenderness and enchantment. "Your skin is so smooth and velvety, Sofia." The electricity between them was surging at a rapid rate. Every kiss, every touch, and every movement brought forward a memory of their past lives together. The images weaved into every moment of ecstasy. It felt like they were no longer on the earth plane; instead, they transitioned into another realm—their bodies guided by the waves of rapture. When they neared full arousal, a prism of colors encapsulated them. As the rainbow of energy pulsated throughout their bodies, their movements flowed with purpose. And when it was time for Sofia to relinquish her Divine Feminine power to Jude, they did so while encompassed in a golden ray of light.

They lay side by side for the rest of the evening—no words, just togetherness. Their bond was sealed. There was no going back to what was—they were now ready for their mission as one soul in two bodies.

23

Sofia woke up to the sound of Jude's steady breathing. The warmth of his skin against hers was welcoming, with the early morning chill lingering in the air. She lay in his protective embrace, listening to the surrounding quiet. Something felt different, but she couldn't quite pinpoint it as yet. Rather than going into a full-blown analysis, she focused on the man before her. When she softly kissed his chest, she tasted the saltiness of his skin. He stirred but only to tuck her closer into his arms.

Her higher self kicked in, or was it his higher self? *Let him sleep. He hasn't done so in months.*

She reveled in their oneness as images of last night played in her mind. Their union felt so natural. When she climaxed, she remembered seeing visions of their past, present, and future selves converge into one. The more she immersed herself in that moment, the more connected she felt with him. She absorbed his fatigue. And she could feel that it was his, not her own. So she gently disentangled herself from his strong arms and glided to the edge of the bed. The thought of assimilating with Jude was both thrilling and frightening at the same time.

She immediately asked her higher self. *Will we feel each other's feelings more and more?* Yes was the answer. *Do not fret, my dear; it will get easier to manage.*

She covered his body with the crisp white sheet and noticed a warm gold glow hovering around him.

Am I seeing what I'm seeing? It was a yes. *It's also around you, my dear.*

Amid her self-talk, she heard Jude's voice. *Don't be scared, Sofia. We are in this together. I am never leaving your side, ever.*

Yet, when she gazed at him, he was still sound asleep.

The talk-fest continued for a few minutes until she felt Jude's hand resting on her arm. "Why are you so far away from me? Come in closer, please."

She slid back to her original position and nestled into his body.

He mumbled, "Now, that's better." And before shutting his eyes, he whispered, "Stop with your crazy thoughts. We are twin flames, which means we are one and the same." He bent down and kissed the top of her head.

And that was that. He fell back asleep. She wouldn't fight it any longer and lowered her eyelids.

24

A waft of coffee found its way under the cloud of Egyptian cotton that enveloped every inch of her body. She heard Jude busying himself in the kitchen. Sofia was too comfy to move a muscle, so she called him over using their mind connection. But nothing. She still heard him clinking pots and pans. But before she could doubt her skills, she felt him sneak under the duvet.

"I had to turn off the coffee pot." He settled in a position facing her. He reached over and caressed her arm as they lay as two sides of a heart. "We can stay here all day long. I have nowhere to be but here."

Sofia's butterflies returned. Jude made a face and asked, "Is this what you feel whenever we're together?"

"What are you feeling?" she curiously asked.

"I feel fluttering inside my belly."

Sofia was awe-struck. "I guess this is something we need to get used to. What a ride this is going to be. Are you ready for it?"

Jude slinked in closer. "Am I ready for this? I've been waiting my whole life for you." He scooped her face into his hands and devoured her lips. His hands sculpted every curvature of her body. And when his body etched into hers, an eruption of lights cascaded around them.

In unison, they both giggled. "Fireworks, every time."

They lay breathlessly, side by side. Then Jude lay flat on his back in beautiful splendor, inciting Sofia to plaster him with kisses from head to toe. He stirred at her every touch. She pleased him. He pleased her. Every moment of arousal was duplicated by their energetic connection.

She looked over at him. "I'm down for a coffee." She purred as she grazed her lips over his body.

Goosebumps spread like wildfire all over his skin. He growled, "You're not making it easy for me to get out of bed." He grabbed her again and kissed her.

But this time, Sofia pried her lips away from his. "Okay. I promise no more teasing." She leaped out of bed. Jude had neatly placed her clothes on the chair. She slipped on the most accessible thing—her dress.

He observed her every move, and when she turned around to look at him, she asked. "You like watching me, don't you?"

His lips curved into a wide grin. "I do. I find you fascinating. It's like I'm watching myself but in a female body."

Sofia rushed to the bed to recount her experience from the morning, how she felt like they were the same person. He nodded in validation. They went over their explosive moment the night before, as well, all the while touching, caressing, and hugging each other.

Jude raked his fingers through her hair and declared his love to her. "I don't think we've said that yet to each other."

Sofia longingly kissed him. He pulled away from her lips. "I don't want to be apart from you ever again."

Sofia got lost in the moment. "I'll move to Paris if you want."

Jude's eyes sparkled, and his whole body relaxed. "Or we can move somewhere else to live in peace."

"Yes. I'm in! Where do you want to go?" Sofia asked.

Jude grabbed her hands and said, "Let's say where we want to go in one, two, three.."

"Malta," eked out of both of their mouths.

They sat eye-to-eye, hand-in-hand, heart-to-heart—both speechless.

He rested his forehead against hers. "Maybe one day we can look into our Akashic Records to see if we ever lived in Malta together. It must be significant to our soul to want to go back there."

Sofia remained silent. She was in deep conversation with her higher self, his higher self, or their oversoul; she had no idea what was happening anymore.

Jude embraced her and sighed. "I'm so happy to have the privilege of being in your beautiful mind."

He calmed Sofia's nerves. She snapped out of her astonishment and confided, "Everything that is happening between us is all my research coming to fruition. It's not just an idea I have or a knowing from my inner voice. It's like me, and you are the proof I've been searching for my whole life— that we are not crazy." She quickly reverted to talking to her mother. *Oh, how I wish you were here, so I could discuss this with you.*

Jude hugged her and whispered, "Remember, she is still around us. Like you always say, we will see them again one day soon. Keep the faith, my love, as you have faith in all of us."

25

While Jude was in the shower, Sofia tidied up the bed and the kitchen. As she peered out the window and onto the streets of his neighborhood, she fell more in love with the antiquated streets and buildings. Sofia most definitely could envision herself living here for a time. Or perhaps, she already had. When she twisted around to the space before her, she remarked he had no sofa.

As was becoming more commonplace between twin flames, Jude chimed in. *Go to the wall and press hard against the concrete block.* She did and out popped the entire block. She slid open the length of the wall, and lo-and-behold, there was a built-in sofa with a coffee table and more photos on the wall. She immediately looked around for more empty walls and pressed on them. *Voilà, more hidden nooks.* She expected to find a TV directly across the couch but instead found a computer workstation. He was a man of many secrets.

Dressed in slate blue cotton joggers and a relaxed-fitted hoodie, Jude made his way to the center of the room. "You've discovered my secret spots, except for one." He pointed to the wall closest to the workstation. He pushed against the wall, and out popped another station with shelves of books, old records, and trinkets.

Impressed by the discoveries, Sofia patted the cushion beside her and said, "Come, join me, my love. Let's talk."

"Oh, oh! Did I do something wrong?" He boyishly smiled.

"I don't know, did you?" She smiled. "Come, I need you to sit on my feet. I can hardly feel my toes."

He cupped her feet into his hands and blew hot air onto her toes. "I know you want to know about these windows. They are tinted so that no one can see inside, but I can see outside." Jude swiveled to look at her. "So Gabrielle can't see anything." He gently lifted her feet, placed them on the sofa, and went to the kitchen. He returned with tea and cookies.

He settled into the sofa. "I know you've been dying to know more about Gabrielle. Shall I begin?"

Sofia was all ears.

"Better yet," he said, "let me tell you all about it in my mind. Are you up for that challenge?"

Nodding, she sat in a lotus pose facing him. He did the same. They wove their fingers together and stared into each other's eyes. But instead of hearing his Gabrielle story, something else began to occur. An energetic wave spiraled around their bodies. The revolutions seemed to amplify in speed as they tightened their grip. There was no fear, only wonderment. The snake was back, and it was slithering up in a rapturous manner. Heat emanated from their hands and coursed through their bodies like a bushfire. With their eyes affixed on each other, a vibrational stream of light formed between the two of them and seemed to pulsate from heart to heart. Their bodies fused into one. When she closed her eyes, she felt an energetic pulsation burrow its way out of her crown chakra. They both released a euphoric sigh. Once they unclenched themselves, the wave subsided to an amorous energy current that harmoniously flowed around them.

They remained motionless, still facing one another. Neither could hear the other's thoughts. There was emptiness but togetherness.

When Sofia leaned against the cushion, she realized the coiled energy continued unraveling. She was still fully aroused. Jude sensed it and inched closer to her. He gently touched her heart and whispered, "You want more, *mon amour* (my love)?"

She did but waved him away, needing time for the current of energy to slink back down her vertebrae and into her root chakra. Jude did what he loved to do most—observe the love of his life as she slowly found her way back into her body.

Remaining idle for a few more minutes, she twisted her body to face Jude. She traced her fingers along his face and raked them through his hair. The immense love Sofia felt for this man was immeasurable. She wanted him to know how much he meant to her just by her touch. A waterfall of tears spilled down her cheeks, tears of joy, tears of lifetimes of release. He leaned in and kissed her eyes, then her cheeks, then her lips.

She laid down, placed her head on his lap, gazed into his sea greens, and said, "I have never experienced anything like this in this lifetime and any other one, I think." She grinned.

He brushed his fingers across her cheeks, wiping away the remaining tears, and replied, "Me neither, my fiery phoenix."

They spent the better half of the morning discussing their tantric moment until a repetitious buzzing sound interrupted them. He vaulted off the couch and checked his phone. "*Merde* (Shit), she's early!"

Sofia was wondering where Gabrielle had been all this time. "Early? Is she coming over?" Sofia made a face.

He promptly flipped open the laptop at his workstation and clicked away. The buzzing stopped. Sofia saw Gabrielle standing by his door, looking directly at the camera. Sofia went to the screen and inspected her nemesis while Jude was busy doing whatever he was doing. A chill ran down her spine. Gabrielle's venom seeped right through the pixelations. She used a technique learned when confronted with lower frequencies: she breathed in and out and found her center, then she filled her heart with love and returned to the screen. She attempted to send loving energies to this woman who only seemed to want to harm her and Jude.

Jude shook his head, looked at Sofia, and muttered, "It won't work. I've tried it multiple times. She's too entrenched in anger. It's not easy to tear her away from that energy. She almost thrives in it." Looking back at the screen, he said, "You see." He pointed to Gabrielle as she gestured diabolical signs at the camera. But abruptly stopped and put on a fake smile when a teenage girl approached her for a selfie. He rechecked the phone and said, "Okay, she'll be gone in ten, nine, eight…" Gabrielle walked away.

He shut the computer, reset his alarm code, and tucked the station into the wall. He then grabbed Sofia's hand and led her to the bedroom. "Come, it's time I fill you in about Gabrielle."

As they propped themselves in the billowy Nirvana, he reached under the bed and slid open a drawer. He pulled out a patchwork quilt donning all the colors of the rainbow. "I hear your comment, and yes, it is very colorful for me, but it was my grandmother's. She gave it to me right before she passed away." He paused. "My dad's mother was as tough as nails but as soft as this blanket." He caressed Sofia's arm. "Much like you. She was a grassroots kind of woman. She didn't much like my mother's love for money and fame. She taught me to treat everyone with respect and love, regardless of status."

He leaned back on the headboard and went on, "My grandparents worked hard for their money and lived affluently, but she volunteered every weekend at the homeless shelter or lent a helping hand to her neighbors. There was no hierarchy with her or my grandfather." A lone tear rolled down his cheek. "She was truly a blessing in my life." He looked over at Sofia. "And right before she transitioned, she told me, 'Take this quilt and share it with your one true love. She will be here shortly, my boy. Take care of her, for she is you.'

The impassioned flow of energy between them was unceasing.

"I never really understood what she meant by that until this morning." He lifted the quilt and covered their bodies with this miraculous gift.

Sofia rested her head on his shoulder, and they lay sheathed in happiness for a few minutes. Until she sat up, still cloaked under the quilt, and said, "Okay, I'm ready. Before you tell me the story, I want to know how you knew she would walk away in ten seconds."

He laughed. "Nothing goes past you. She always comes at the same time every day. But today is the only day she visits her parents, so she can't harass me for that long. You know the way serial killers are so precise? Well, she's the same way."

Well, that's not a great analogy to use, Jude.

He cracked up. "It's how I feel about her. She's out of control yet very calculated. *En tout cas* (anyways), are you ready?"

"Yes, but if she's here at the same time every day, why can't you call the police?"

"It's more complicated than that." He inhaled deeply, cracked his knuckles, and said, "Shall I begin?"

Sofia nodded—with both enthusiasm and dread.

He reverted to his childhood when he would play with her on the beach in the South of France. Every summer, his family would go down to Saint Tropez so that his mother could mingle with her socialite friends. And Gabrielle's parents were part of that elite group. He cleared his throat. "My mother made it a point to stay connected. Sometimes, I felt like she was offering me as a prize for their daughter. It was strange. I'm so grateful that my dad always had my back."

He reminisced about excursions he would take with his father while his mother was shopping and eating lunch at the finest yacht clubs. "He would rent a scooter and then randomly drive us to neighboring villages—'the more remote, the better,' he would say. Nine times out of ten, we ate in strangers' homes or farms." Jude beamed while talking about his father. He went on, "I learned so much from that man. I don't think I have ever told him how those moments shaped me later."

Sofia picked up on his warm-hearted emotions. Her whole body tingled with tiny love bugs.

Jude looked up at the ceiling and paused. "He was once so wild and free. When my mother moved away from us to the South of France, he became more of a recluse. My dad took over during my formative years, but when it came to my early teens, she was adamant that I consort with the country club set. My father went along with it for my sake. I believe he was protecting me, at least trying to, but," he rolled his eyes, "you know how these people roll—sly and conniving and inauthentic."

Jude continued to chronicle how his life intersected with Gabrielle. "As I said, my mother was more interested in me being "seen" with the right people than me dating a good girl. And she went out of her way to bring Gabrielle and me together whenever I visited her in the summertime."

He sighed and continued. "Gabrielle was withdrawn when she was young. She was the apple of her father's eye. He would gift her with all the riches and praise. She didn't like being center stage, and her mother was quite happy assuming that role. When Gabrielle turned twelve or thirteen, it became clear that her mother competed with her for her husband's affection. And she did what all high-society mothers did; she sent her away to boarding school."

Sofia was not surprised.

Jude smirked. "Exactly. But guess who was sent to boarding school too? That's right. That's where I met Etienne. What a ride that was."

Sofia wanted to hear more but was also hesitant.

Jude reached out and placed his hand on her shoulder. "Remember, we had to find our way to each other by living out these moments with others."

Sofia found herself dipping into her insecurities more often than she wanted. Alas, this could be part of her journey as well.

Before continuing, he took a moment to breathe. "I'm not going to lie—well, I can't anyway!" He let out a laugh. "I tried hard to keep up with my father's standards, but rich kids and school away from home equate to only one thing—bad behavior. There was no way around it. Every kid, even the academic ones, was on prescription drugs, recreational drugs, and alcohol." He shook his head. "And we all know it was mostly to numb the pain from our parents' lack of nurturing and affection."

Sofia interrupted, "But your dad was not like that."

Jude shook his head. "He was not, but when he learned about my behavior, he shut down, became indifferent to me, and allowed my mother to take a more proactive role in my life. My father left me at the hands of my mother because he could not A: control her and B: didn't want to control me. But, don't worry, unbeknownst to my mother, after a couple of years, he came down to see me once a month, and every week, he reliably sent me a care package with handwritten letters. He made up for his momentary lapse of judgment." Jude sighed and lovingly said, "I never blamed him, ever. He did the best that he could."

He stretched his arms and legs out. Then he motioned to Sofia to lie next to him. "I'm going to take a break. So many mixed feelings here."

She played with the string hanging from his hoodie. She looked up at him. "Do you want to continue this another day?"

He lifted his head and peered into her eyes. "We're getting to the good part. No, I want to get this over with—the sooner, the better." He reached over, hoisted her body, and pressed his lips against hers. She welcomed his affection. They rolled around and kissed and relayed sweet nothings to each other.

"Shall we eat while you recount the rest of the story?" Sofia was feeling a little bit peckish.

"Yessssss. I'm so hungry. I wasn't sure if I was hungry for you or food." He growled into her neck. "It's definitely both."

Sofia playfully pushed him away, and they headed to the kitchen.

He opened the refrigerator and took a second or two to look inside. "I don't have much since I haven't yet done the groceries, but this will do." Jude pulled out a brick of Brie, a jar of Apricot jam, and country-style bread from the freezer. He sliced and talked at the same time. "Okay, so where did I leave off? Oh yes, I never really dated Gabrielle, nor did I ever date other girls. They were mostly flings. And the amount of intermingling between couples was nasty. But the more I rejected their lifestyle, the more girls liked me."

Sofia interjected, "But also because you are a "lightworker." And it was probably making them uncomfortable. They wanted to unconsciously or consciously vampire your energy and light."

He glanced up at her and affirmed, "Yes. If only I knew then what I know now."

He slathered the slices of bread with the butter, then added them to the grill. "I guess I became friends with Gabrielle because we had our parents in common. But also, I am inclined to help those in need. I listened to her and tried to guide her the best way I could. But she delved into the harder drugs and the harder partying, and we eventually parted ways. But, *on s'entend* (if we're being real), we were always in the same confines of the school, so we still crossed paths." He gazed into Sofia's mind and said, "No, I didn't partake in their recreational activities. I tried a whole bunch of stuff but didn't pursue it."

He lifted his hands in the air. "It is what it is, right, Sofia? We can't go back, only forward." Jude removed the bread, shut off the grill, and added the jam and slices of cheese. He sprinkled thyme on top and a dash of rosemary and served Sofia. "It's not fancy, but it's something."

Sofia showed her gratitude by wolfing down the first slice before he ate. He smirked. "Hungry, are we?"

She leaned in and kissed him on the cheeks with her sweet lips. "Yes. And thank you."

He snickered and continued his story, "After high school, we went all of our merry ways, except for Etienne. He came to live with us because he was fortunate to have a "mother of the year" as well."

Sofia mumbled, "I heard that story."

Jude said, "Yup. The first chance I got to move back home to Paris, I took it. My mother tried to do everything in her power to keep me in her tentacles, but I was eighteen, so no can do." He rolled his eyes. "Thank God."

Sofia inquired. "So, why the stalking? I don't understand."

"Patience, my dear." He chomped down the second slice. And then put the kettle on to boil.

He poured the hot water into two cups with freshly squeezed lemon and grated ginger and waved his hand up. "Shall we head back to the bed or sofa?"

Sofia pointed to the bed. His eyes twinkled in approval.

He propped all four pillows up against the headboard and continued his tale, "As you know, my mother came from an affluent family, and she pulled all the strings she could to get me into the Ecole des Beaux-Arts right here in my neighborhood. I wanted to attend the local art school, but she couldn't have her only son attend a 'plebeian' school. I rejected her offer, but my father convinced me to attend. He said, 'Son, just play her game and get the best education while you're at it.' He had a point, so I went. But it wasn't because I wanted to learn art that she did it—she did it so I could be in the same classes as Gabrielle. She truly was and still is a piece of work, my mother."

Watching him for a moment, Sofia thought. He *drinks hot water just like me.* He sipped the piping hot water with two hands wrapped around the cup. She laughed inside. He heard her and stuck out his tongue in jest.

He set the mug down and continued. "I got closer to Gabrielle in the first year because we shared the same classes and worked on projects together. By our second year, her parents had different plans for Gabrielle and pulled her out of school. I tried to reach out to her, but she never answered. She was full speed ahead in that world again. I started seeing her in the socialite columns and on Insta at all the "right" parties with all the "right" people. And when I would bump into her, she would always be coked up and hyper-flirtatious with everyone around her—

man or woman." He pondered on that moment. "I guess I, like you, always felt this need to fix people. My life also took a detour; Gabrielle was no longer in school, so my mother stopped paying the exorbitant tuition fee. I couldn't afford it and wouldn't dip into my trust fund, so I had no choice but to quit."

Sofia interrupted him. "Your dad couldn't afford it?"

Jude replied. "Probably, but I didn't want to ask. And, anyway, it was the best thing because then I could take back control of my life, or so I thought. I went to work for a local photographer who taught me the ropes. It was the best training—I truly flourished there."

"So, why are you working for your uncle now?"

Jude smirked. "You don't know how the elite go about their business, do you?"

Sofia widened her eyes and shrugged. "I guess not."

He sighed. "Well, my mother heard through the grapevine that I was working for an unknown photographer, and she came for a visit. And not even two weeks later, he apparently had to close his shop for a gig in Los Angeles." He shook his head.

Perplexed by her behavior, Sofia asked, "Why wouldn't she want the best for you? I've understood her to be controlling, but she's still your mother."

He put down his cup, reached over, and patted her hand. "She's no mother. She's a selfish woman who manipulates everyone for her stature." And just like that, Jude's eyes lost their sparkle.

It dawned on her right then that they both suffered from maternal abandonment, but how interesting that his storyline had a neglectful presence. She would not have this woman diminish his light, so she whispered, "Have you worked on forgiveness with her? That way, she no longer has her claws in you."

He grabbed her hands and held them to his chest. "I thought I did forgive her, but it seems I haven't."

"I may never be a mother in this lifetime, but as long as you're on my team, I will love you always and forever."

He wrapped his arms around her, and they remained there for a few minutes.

"I'm at the last stretch. Let's finish this and go out since we know Gabrielle's preoccupied all day and night." He sat up and continued the tale. "My mother made it difficult for me to find a job anywhere, so I reluctantly took the position with my uncle, her brother, who is just as nefarious as she is." He paused and gazed into her eyes. "I can hear you. Yes, I could have searched high and low, but my father intervened again and made another good point, 'better be in the devil's lair than outside of it.' It made sense to me at the time."

"Father knows best, it seems." She offered a small smile, feeling the angst he went through.

He squinted his eyes. "Are you being sarcastic?"

"No, I'm giving props to your dad for taking care of you." She lay her hand on his.

"Sorry, I don't mean to be defensive. My father has been a rock to all of us—in the best and the worst of times." He took a long pause and went on. "To no surprise, Gabrielle started working at my uncle's business in marketing—just a facade. That's all. She had built up her own following and tagged him for their wicked games. I put up with it and let it slide off my back. Until one fateful night when we all went out to an event, I bumped into my photography mentor, who never closed up shop and never moved to L.A. It was just another facade."

He squirmed and looked away from Sofia. "So, I took a hit of cocaine which I later found out was laced with MDMA or Fentanyl. Gabrielle was there. And I am pretty sure something happened with her."

She looked at him warily. "I mean, you would know, right?"

Jude lay down and stared at the ceiling, recounting part of the story. "I blacked out. I don't remember anything from the night. People told me they saw me go into a private room with her. She was high and returned to that room with other guys during the night. It was a crazy night that I'm not proud of, but I was just done with everyone. Honestly, I didn't care about my life at that point. If someone had offered me poison, I would have taken it." Tears welled and streaked down the side of his face. "I was just done being lied to, controlled, misguided. And upset for choosing this direction in my life. I was out of service for a whole week after that party. Etienne and my dad helped revive me back to the best version of me again."

He paused, taking in another deep breath. "Oh, and I continued working at my uncle's, but I took control of the situation and arrived with demands which were all met. A few weeks later, Gabrielle went to a fancy rehab. And I was at peace for a while until she returned. When she did, she was a completely different person. No drugs but very....uhm....how can I explain....like how she is now, needy but empty, like void of emotions."

"I'm so sorry that you had to go through this. " She rested her hand on his. "But one question: her parents don't see her bad behavior?"

Jude made a face. "Of course they do, but they don't have time for her. They just give her money, and then she's free to do whatever she wants. And when she gets out of hand, she always knows she can be sent away again without hesitation. So, that's on my side. What's not on my side is that she is in cahoots with my mother, so God knows what schemes they come up with."

He let out a heavy sigh and rolled to his side."Now, I'm done. I don't want to focus my energy on them anymore." He combed his fingers through Sofia's hair and asked, "Shall we head out?"

Sofia kissed the tip of his finger, which led to more frolicking in the bed. One kiss was all it took for them to engage in a union of the minds and bodies.

WE ARE THE ONE

We meet each other only to find each other again.

26

Jude escorted Sofia into the Art Deco building where his father lived—the opulence of the lobby area caught her eye. The chevron-patterned floors in black and white mazed their way around jet-black marble columns. Tarnished gold decorative accessories littered the space. The ostentatious chandeliers above hung heavily along the high ceilings.

Hmmm…How rich is rich?

Jude squeezed her hand and said, "My father is not pretentious like this decor. He is very down-to-earth. You will see."

But you didn't answer my question.

He remained quiet and just winked at her. He led her to an elevator door engraved with a golden sunburst motif. As the door opened, she had to whip out her phone—the purple velvet-covered interior dotted with trapezoidal mirrors warranted a photo that she immediately sent to her besties. *They would have an orgasm in this lobby.* Jude smiled as he beeped them up to the 17th floor.

He stole a kiss before the elevator opened into the apartment.

It was a grandiose space with the highest ceiling she'd ever seen in a home. Books and frames lined the left wall, and old trinkets punctuated the right wall. At the center was a rectangular wooden framed contraption with hanging plants—a hydroponic garden. When she wondered how the plants received sunlight, Jude clicked on a remote control that slid open ceiling coverings that exposed the night sky. She wanted to linger, but Jude lured her deeper into his childhood home.

They passed another table in oxidized copper scattered with journals, pencils, rulers, and a crate brimming with odd objects. Sofia turned to Jude. "Is your dad a quantum physicist by any chance?"

"Why don't you ask him yourself?"

There stood a stately man with silver wavy hair. Thick black-rimmed glasses sat atop his head. His aquamarine eyes sparkled against his tan skin. Sporting a marine blue cashmere sweater with a crisp, white shirt peeking out at every opening, he was more sophisticated than Sofia imagined. Jude got his looks from his dad. Michel kissed her on both cheeks and then warmly embraced her. "Welcome to the family. We have been waiting a long time for you." He hugged his son, and they exchanged pleasantries.

He waved them into the lair. "Come, come. Lennon is very excited to meet Divine Sofia."

Sofia blushed. She often needed to remember that everyone had access to her via her channel.

The apartment was never-ending, with more paraphernalia hanging on walls. His Beatles albums and instruments were as impressive as Jude had mentioned. They reached a central room with curved walls and windows. A teal velvet scalloped sofa mirrored two accent chairs in similar shades. Plants of all shapes and sizes occupied much of the space.

As Sofia scanned the retro decor, her eyes fell on waves of blonde hair. Lennon's hair hung below his shoulders, and he had the brightest green eyes. He flung himself toward her and shouted, "Finally, I get to meet you!" He hugged her for quite some time until Jude pried him off her.

Jude chuckled. "He can get a little too clingy." He turned to his brother. "Right, Len?"

"Well, especially with the women," Michel chimed in.

Sofia wondered what kind of relationship Lennon had with his mother. And also wondered why there was such an age gap.

Lennon was just as tall as Jude, lankier, but quite a looker for a sixteen-year-old. His personality filled the immense space. He incessantly chatted with his brother about current events and this girl and that girl. While the boys talked up a storm, Michel took it upon himself to usher Sofia into the kitchen. He prepared a cup of tea while asking her about life back in Montreal. Jude's father was a cordial man with a calming way about him.

He peered into Sofia's eyes and said, "My scientist mind saw right through your reaction to Lennon. I'm surprised Jude didn't tell you how young he was." Then he laughed. "Of course, he didn't. Jude is so private."

Michel opened up to her about Lennon's adoption—his wife felt guilty about how she raised Jude and wanted to give it another go but through adoption. "Initially, I was hesitant, but I gave her the benefit of the doubt." He paused. "I believe in people too much, or maybe just her."

Sofia then asked about the uncanny resemblance. Michel relayed that his wife took her time finding him. "She is a very persistent woman. She always gets what she wants."

He never once talked maliciously about his wife. Instead, he excused her lousy behavior, blaming it on her upbringing. He leaned his elbows on the island. "I'm not going to lie. It was rough at the beginning. But truthfully, I would not have changed one iota of my life. These boys are my treasures." He stood straight, flattened his palms on the marble, and continued. "At one point, you understand the bigger picture—that there is more to life than just a career and a house. That's why I enjoy your videos so much. You have managed to open up this linear mind to far greater possibilities."

Jude sneaked up on them. "And you can thank her for starting you on your quantum physics journey." He bent over and kissed her on the cheek.

Michel replied, "Yes." He looked over at Sofia. "As I was saying, your research has opened up a whole new world for me, and I would love to sit down with you one day and exchange wisdom if that's okay with you?"

Sofia nodded, elated. "Of course. It would be my pleasure. I've tried to grasp quantum anything, and it's quite the challenge."

He was all smiles. "That it is, indeed. I still don't know everything, but that's the beauty of its multidimensionality."

He was saying all the right words. She was almost tempted to remain there longer to get into his mind. Then she heard Jude say. *If you plan on living here for a while, my love, you'll have plenty of time.*

Lennon joined in and rolled his eyes. "Is my dad boring you with his science?"

Jude reached out and messed up Lennon's hair. "Be nice to the man who saved you from spending the holidays with the wicked witch of the South." They both cracked up.

Michel shook his head. "She's your mother. She may not have always raised you, but she still loves you."

Sofia heard Jude loud and clear in her head. *Why must he defend her every single time?*

Jude turned toward his brother. "So, where can we go out so early?"

Lennon spewed out a list of cafés, lounges, and restaurants. Sofia asked if Michel was joining them, and Lennon burst out laughing. "My dad is not coming out with us!" He turned to his father with an apologetic gaze. "Sorry, Papa, I love you, but…."

Jude lightly tapped Lennon on the head. "We need to fix that filter of yours."

Lennon then opened the invite to include his father. Michel smiled but declined and directed his reply to Sofia. "I would much rather stay home and do more research than be out with this one." He pointed to Lennon.

During the lively conversation, Etienne and Xavier rambled in, further elevating Lennon's energy. Michel turned to Sofia. "You better get used to being around men all the time."

"Don't worry. I lived with my dad and brother most of my life. I got this covered." She winked at him.

Etienne made his way to Sofia. He kissed her on both cheeks and timidly said, "I've missed you." Sofia hugged him.

When he returned to chatting with the boys, Sofia caught Michel staring at that exchange. He leaned against the stove, with arms crossed, and nodded. When Sofia acknowledged his perception, they both chuckled.

Jude slinked his way beside her. "Why are you two laughing?"

"Nothing," she said.

His father feigned ignorance—the first bonding moment of the night between her and her future father-in-law.

Jude arched his eyebrow but let it slide. "Okay, mon amour, shall we go?"

Sofia stared at Jude and, for a moment, felt a wave of sadness wash all over her.

He placed his hands on her shoulders and shuddered. "What was that?" he asked.

Everyone stopped talking and just stared at the two of them. Sofia's cheeks reddened. She tried desperately to release it from her energy, but it lingered. Jude enveloped her in his arms, and the energy recharged with the help of his power. Silence still floated in the air. When Sofia unlinked herself from Jude, Michel reverted the attention to Lennon. It didn't take long for Lennon to take over the conversation again.

Michel made his way to both Jude and Sofia. "Fascinating, you two. I could see the energy swirling all around you. You will decidedly be my next test subject."

Jude jokingly pushed his father away. But Sofia heard Jude recognizing the genius of his father.

"It would be our pleasure to be part of your experiment," Sofia said. "That way, I can have scientific findings on twin flame energy for my subscribers."

Michel nodded, his face brightening with a smile. "Indeed. I will get right on it."

"Twin flame energy?" Etienne asked. "Is that what you are? That makes so much sense." He loosely hung his arms around both of them and giggled. "Of course, you must explain that further to my small mind."

Jude got up from the chair and clapped his hands. "Okay, if we don't leave now, Sofia will get sucked into our father's wormhole. Let's go!"

Lennon, Etienne, and Xavier made a beeline to the door, but not before hugging or secret handshaking Michel. Jude followed while Sofia lingered behind and whispered to Michel, "Definitely to be continued."

Jude grabbed her hand and lovingly pulled her away from his father. He bent down and kissed her. "I knew you were going to love him and vice versa."

27

They breezed right past the two heavyset bouncers and zipped through the swarm of people waiting to enter the swanky lounge. But instead of remaining in the club area, they passed through royal blue velvet curtains and downstairs to an intricate wooden door. Etienne knocked three times and said, *Serpent de Mer* (Sea Serpent). The massive door creaked open, and in they went.

A gargantuan snake statue at the entrance welcomed them. The low blue lighting lent itself well to the ominous, oceanic theme. It was a narrow space with round tables along the walls. There was no bar, which was curious; only an elevated stage at the far end with musicians playing electro-jazz and what seemed like a dance floor at the center.

They crammed into two tables. It was buzzing with people, but only at partial capacity. Xavier joined them, which added to the testosterone at the table. Sofia loved observing human nature; she knew she was in for a treat with these boys. When she looked over at Jude, he felt distant in his regard. She slithered her arm around him and whispered, "Is everything okay?"

"No. I've been ruminating on that dark emotion that came over you earlier, and it felt apocalyptic to me."

Sofia loved that he divulged his true feelings to her instead of brushing them off. She laced her fingers into his. "I don't know where that came from, but let's not worry about it now. Let's enjoy this night with your brothers." He gently squeezed her hand and nodded. But ever since their energies collided, he was transparent to her now; she knew he was with a heavy heart.

They ordered drinks. Sofia ordered the French version of a hot toddy with cognac. She would nurse it all night as she did when she went out with most friends. Lennon was a breath of fresh air, chatting up a storm. When more patrons filed in, the boys' attention fell on all the women in the club.

How will it be outside of this matrix? With telepathy being a norm, the whole cat-and-mouse game will never stand a chance.

Jude chimed in. "I've often thought about that. It will be the new normal." He softly kissed her on the lips. "It will be wondrous."

He pondered the thought and grabbed her hand, lifting Sofia to her feet. Jude navigated around a group of girls inching their way slowly to the table and led her to the circular space. He whirled her in his arms and swayed to the music. Body to body, mind to mind, soul to soul—a golden glow haloed around them. This time, Sofia felt their bodies interlink into one. She no longer had control, yet felt anchored to the ground. He steered her body from right to left. He was the captain for the moment.

When his lips pressed against her forehead, an intense, energetic current blazed through her body. Jude stepped back but still held on tight. "Did you feel that?"

She had no words and simply nodded. She wasn't sure if her skin was burning or his.

He whispered, "I think it's both of us. Is it me, or do you feel a deeper connection happening right here?"

She said, "Yes, I feel like we probably need to be alone next time you kiss me."

He swept her in his arms, making him more irresistible to her. She couldn't quite comprehend what was happening but wasn't hating it. She realized they had been stationary when she felt someone poking her arm.

Etienne was standing by them, looking distressed. Jude tensed up and asked, "Where is she?"

Etienne said Gabrielle was upstairs in the lounge area. They immediately devised a plan of distraction. Sofia waved goodbye to Lennon. Fully immersed in the art of seduction, he still pried away and made his way toward Sofia. "*C'est naze* (It's stupid) that you have to go so early. I hope to see you soon." And he kissed her on the cheek.

Xavier motioned to Jude if he wanted a lift. Jude waved him away. Before opening the curtain, Etienne said, "Don't worry. I'll take care of her tonight. You two go off and enjoy your twin flame-ness!" He was an expert at diffusing tense situations with humor. "Wait for my text."

Etienne made his way into hell to fight off the demon.

Meanwhile, Jude's mood went from calm to agitation. He tried hard to keep his cool, but Sofia felt him losing his way again.

"No, no, no, don't worry about me. I am going to get this under control. I promised I would, my love." He nestled her face in his hands. "Please, trust me." He stared brazenly into her eyes. She once again almost lost her footing from the intensity of his stare. The text came in that the coast was clear, so he grabbed Sofia's hand, and they slipped out of the darkness.

The crowd amassed into a mob, making it more challenging to maneuver their way out. With Jude's every step, the group seemed to part like the sea. His captain mode was still in full effect. Once they reached "shore," he turned back to ensure Gabrielle didn't follow them. His movements were erratic, so Sofia took the lead and marched around the corner away from the line of sight of the club. She leaned against the side of a building and gripped his hands. When they locked eyes, she worked her magic on him. His shoulders relaxed, his jaw loosened, and his eyes slowly returned to their shimmering green. He raked his fingers through Sofia's hair, and when he gently kissed her, a tirade of texts came roaring in.

Before he could lose his shit, Sofia grabbed the phone and slipped it into her bag. "Nope, she's not going to rain on our moment. Let's pretend it's music playing in the background."

He grimaced and reached into her bag for the phone. "Unfortunately, I need to see where she's at. Because if she's loose, we need to know."

As he scrolled through the infinite list, Sofia asked, "Do you think it's too late to go back to your dad's?"

His eyes shot up from the screen, and he rubbed his chin. "Never have I ever been asked this question from a girl I've dated." He looked at the time. It was 11 p.m. "My father is a night owl. He does most of his research until the wee hours of the morning. Are you sure that's where you want to go?"

"Yes. I'm interested in hearing what he has to say about our connection in quantum terms." Her eyes widened. "Is that weird? If you prefer, we can go home."

"No way. My dad will be thrilled to have a conversation with a like-minded soul for once. Let's go."

Michel hunched over his table as prescribed, calculating and measuring objects. His eyes lit up when he saw Sofia and Jude walk toward him. Also, a streak of terror sailed across his face, and he asked, "Did something happen? Why are you here? Is Lennon okay? Etienne? Xavier?"

Jude patted his dad on the shoulder. "Everyone is fine." He dangled his arm around Michel's shoulder, sat beside him, and exclaimed, "You will never believe who wanted to come back to talk to you?"

He turned to hug his son, took off his glasses, and raised his hands in the air. "Hallelujah! Someone just as eccentric as me."

He exited his table, half-tidied his objects, and headed to the main room. "Come. I'll boil some water, and we can discuss whatever you want, my Divine Sofia."

And that they did, into the wee hours of the night. She went into some of her research on twin flames—how one soul divided into two and how part of it remained beyond the veil when the soul decided to drop into the human body. Part of the soul also chose to be their guides, and if there was to be a twin-flame connection, then one part dropped into another body. Sofia went on, "Apparently, you cannot merge until both have completed their karma and have cleansed through their traumas."

Jude described some occurrences between him and Sofia. Michel listened intently, never once interrupting, never once rationalizing it. He listened and observed. Then he went into his scientific findings of quantum entanglement: two particles separated by time and space; what affected one affected the other simultaneously, no matter the distance between them. According to science, twin flames shared an energetic signature—mirrored souls. Michel rolled over a marker board where he attempted to illustrate some of his theories to the curious students.

At one point, he asked, "Do you see the energy around you or just feel it?"

Jude and Sofia mutually replied, "We feel it."

Michel laughed aloud. "You are so adorable together."

Sofia smiled widely and asked, "Why, what do you see?"

Michel eyed them and answered, "I see waves of light. It's more than just your skin glowing; it's an energetic wave floating around you. It's quite magnificent."

"By the way," Sofia said, "if you can see us, then that means, my friend, that you are a wayshower, definitely a starseed."

He beamed. "That I figured out as soon as I watched your video describing each star system. Which star system do you both come from?

Sofia quickly went to her higher self to get his origins and smiled. "You're from the same star that we are from—Sirius. But, I believe we've also experienced life in other star systems." She shrugged. "But, who knows anything? We will find out the "truth" of who we are soon enough."

Michel's eyes twinkled, and he grinned. "That's why I have such a close connection to my son?"

"Possibly, or you just love him for being such a wonderful soul."

Jude's cheeks blushed a crimson red. He leaned into Sofia and kissed her on the cheek.

Michel lifted his hands in prayer and rested them on his lips. "Yes, that must be it." He winked at Jude and said, "She's a keeper."

Sofia noticed tears in his eyes as he turned his gaze toward his charts.

The mood was serene, with both men at a loss for words and reveling in the gentleness of the moment. Sofia decided to change things up and brought up one last topic. "So, one last thing." Michel twirled to face her. "Let's talk about these symbols that cemented our union together." She took Jude's fingers and showed them to Michel.

In doing so, she noticed one of the symbols fading—the exact one he had engraved on their matching pendulums. She showed him, and he acknowledged her observation.

Michel nodded. "Yes. Yes. Jude talked to me about this as soon as he arrived." He turned to his son and said, "And I forgot to tell you, I've contacted some collector friends and may have found a book for you. It's coming from Egypt. I believe it's written in an old scripture. I can't be certain."

Sofia's body tingled, and she relayed to Jude. *Maybe it's the book I wrote in my past life?*

Jude nodded. "Maybe. That would be interesting."

Michel's eyes ping-ponged from Jude to Sofia. "This is the same thing that happened earlier. Does that mean you are both telepathic, as well?"

Jude looked over, and she gave him the okay to divulge the secret. But Michel was one step ahead of them, and he shouted, "This is marvelous. You are a living example of the future, my dears." He put his hand up. "Yes, Sofia, I know we live in simultaneous timelines. But you know what I mean!"

Sofia added even more insight by explaining they were all from the future, rectifying the "wrongs" of the past/present. "We annihilated the planet because we allowed Artificial Intelligence to take over. In essence, we became robots."

"Are these new findings?" Jude asked. "I haven't seen any video talking about this."

"Have you memorized every video that I have done?" She couldn't help but smile.

Jude tilted his head to the side, nodding. "Pretty much."

"Well, you're right. This is part of a series I'm working on. I've been getting downloads on and off about this, and I just want to piece them together before I present it to the masses."

Michel launched into his scientist-self and asked question after question. Sofia answered as much as she knew. When she informed him that their souls were actually off planet on a different broadband frequency and, in the now moment, they were mere soul fractals activating the magnetic grids and anchoring their light, Michel's interest peaked even more, and he gestured her toward his work table.

When she turned to talk to Jude, he had already dozed off. He swiftly grabbed her arm as she gently rose and pulled her down. And when his lips brushed against hers, he took her breath away as always. The fluttering pulsated in the pit of her stomach. And the reverberations of her heart echoed in her eardrum.

"I heard almost every word you said, Sofia. You make me feel so alive." He kissed her again and lay back down on the sofa.

There would be no sleeping that night for Sofia nor Michel as they huddled around the worktable and continued their foray into the twin flame phenomenon and the planetary changes Gaia would go through in the upcoming years.

28

Sofia woke up to a rumbling sound. She was on Michel's sofa, underneath a blanket, lying next to Jude: that was a good start. But there was another body near her; Lennon was at her feet. The moment she moved, so did Jude. He wrapped his arm around her and brought her closer to him. As his hands cruised along her body, she got caught up in the early morning ravishment but still managed to point to his brother.

He snickered."My brother won't hear anything," he whispered. "You can bang a drum in his ear, and he won't wake up. So, where was I?" He continued maneuvering his hands in all the right places but abruptly stopped when the elevator door opened. He tenderly bit down on Sofia's lips. "*À suivre* (To be continued)."

Michel made his way to the kitchen with bags of groceries. Jude bounced off the sofa and went to help his dad. Michel shooed him away and mumbled something. They bickered like an old married couple until Sofia made her way to resolve their silliness. Sitting by the island, she asked, "Can one of you grumpy old men get me some coffee?" They smiled and immediately calmed down.

"I've been meaning to ask you," Jude told her. "When are your friends coming in? Will they be here for New Year's Eve?"

Sofia had forgotten about that. "I'll check in with them later."

Jude told Sofia all about their family tradition; every New Year's Eve, they had a pot-luck dinner where each family member or guest cooked their favorite meal of the year. It was a way to say goodbye to the past. Then, after midnight, they had to prepare a dessert or share a story of what they wanted to bring into the new year.

"How long have you had this tradition?" Sofia asked.

"Ever since Jude was, maybe, seven years old." He looked over at his son for confirmation.

"About that. It was my father's idea. It was the time of the year people were extra nice to us just to get invited to this shindig." Both Michel and Jude rolled their eyes. "But in the past few years, we've gone low key, and now that,"—he reached over to poke Sofia on the nose—"you're here, we decided to keep it more intimate."

"Keep what, more intimate?" Lennon pulled out the stool beside Sofia and sprawled himself over the island. "Why are you shouting this morning?"

Michel tapped him on the arm and ordered him to tidy up the couch and jump in the shower. "What have I told you about smoking?"

Lennon lifted his head, smelled his clothes, and turned to Sofia. "Do I smell?"

Sofia sniffed, hiding a smile. "Yup. Get in that shower, boy!"

Lennon sprung from the chair and bolted to the bathroom.

Michel leaned in. "You are welcome to stay in this house anytime." He returned to unpacking the food while grumbling about his son.

Meanwhile, Jude received a call from his alarm company informing him that the red-haired woman had tried breaking in again.

Michel reached over and placed his hand on his son's shoulder. "Go. Xavier should still be downstairs."

A dark shadow passed over Jude's eyes. He tried to restrain his anger, but Sofia could see and feel right through him. She placed her hand on his heart. "Go deal with her. I'll be fine here."

He kissed her and left to deal with Gabrielle, leaving her to navigate through her own hodgepodge of emotions.

"That woman is a thorn in our sides," Michel grimaced.

She tried masking her turmoil.

But the scientist saw right through her. "Don't worry too much about her. Jude is a smart man. He has this somewhat under control. Getting things done in Europe is always a bit slower because the bureaucracy and corruption are more prevalent than where you are." He patted her back and reassured her, "Come, let's go to the other room."

He slid open the door to a palatial room filled with light. A massive alabaster table sat at the heart of the space with solid gold metallic chairs, each with a different fabric. A variety of photographs in every shape and size camouflaged the walls.

She pointed to the photos. "Jude?"

"Yes. He has such a beautiful eye. He captures the emotions of each person, landscape, and object." She watched Jude's father admire the photos with pride.

Moving to look at them, she noticed a photo of her—it was her in the café with a book in hand, staring out the window.

Michel came to stand beside her. "This is one of my favorites. Your regard is contemplative and far-reaching."

"How long have you had this photo of me?"

"Did you not know about this? Oh, then, I love it more. It's been a few years, for sure."

Her higher self kicked in. *Do you see it now? You were not the only one with a longstanding crush. It has been in the works for a long while.*

Her seventeen-year-old self came out to play as she sheepishly smiled.

He left her in the room to observe more of Jude's work. Before long, he returned with a tray full of goodies: croissants, butter, jam, a bowl of fruits, a pot of coffee, and one for tea. He set it up on the table with grace. "Let's eat in peace before the Tasmanian devil joins us."

Sofia sat down. Peace is not what she felt, for she could feel Jude's anguish even from a distance. Her heart felt squeezed and her belly in knots.

Michel filled her in on the Gabrielle story she knew about, adding some of his observations. "Unfortunately, Jude takes after me in that. He has too big of a heart. No matter what she did to him, he would never hurt her or strike back in a way that would ruin her life. He had many chances to release her to the wolves—her parents or the authorities—but didn't because a little part of him wants to believe she will awaken from their stronghold."

It made sense, but still; she wondered if he could ever detach himself from her. And she immediately received a message from Jude: *It's over. I will now take the measures against her that I should have taken long ago.*

Michel extended his hand and placed it on her forearm. "Are you okay?"

Sofia came to. "Yes, why?"

"A light encapsulated you for a few seconds. What happened?"

She told him, and he pulled out a mini notebook from his pocket and entered the findings. Sofia chuckled. "So, we really are your next research project?"

He winked at her. Before they could go further into the Gabrielle topic, Lennon galloped in with his half-wet blonde curls bouncing in the air. He darted right to the food. "Oh, I'm starving." Between bites, he asked, "So, what's the plan today?" He batted his eyelashes at Sofia. "Can I spend the day with you?"

"That's a great idea," she said. "I haven't been to Paris in a few years. Maybe you can show me your favorite spots."

Michel jumped into the conversation. "In about an hour, I must go into the city because I'm meeting some old colleagues. I'll drop you off, and you can come home with me or do what you want. Sounds good?"

Sofia accepted the offer but asked to be dropped off at Etienne's for a quick change.

****

Xavier dropped Lennon and Sofia off in the Montmartre neighborhood. It surprised her that he would frequent this very touristy spot. Lennon led her toward a Christmas market with the famous Sacré Coeur Basilica looming in the background. He went straight to the mulled wine vendor.

"Care for some hot wine?"

Sofia glared at him before she hooked her arm into his and dragged him to the hot chocolate stand instead. He sulked but didn't argue. They strolled through the picturesque kiosks overflowing with Made in China goods. It was an eye-sore in such a historic part of town. She bought hot roasted chestnuts and marrons glacée. They made their way toward the antique carousel at the base of the church and sat on a bench.

He stretched his legs out, rubbed his hands, and blew into them. It was a bit nippy, but Sofia was used to much worse. He told her he loved going there because it reminded him of the happier times with his family. Lennon was a charmer as he flirted with every girl that passed.

Sofia nudged him, "Are you sure it's not for the pretty scenery?"

He pouted and batted his eyelashes. "I don't know if you know, but I'm in boarding school. I see the same people every day." He rolled his eyes. "Plus, I have to catch up to my brother. He's been with all the pretty girls." He laughed aloud.

Sofia laughed along with him while attempting to tame the ego from unleashing the insecurities. Her higher self stepped in and distracted her. *You have met your match. He's just as and maybe more unfiltered than you.*

The two remained on the bench nibbling on the chestnuts. Lennon often shifted in his seat—fidgeting with the stack of leather bracelets on his arm or playing with his bouncy curls.

He broke the silence. "I'm going to tell you a little secret." He twisted his body on the bench, knees bent, to look at her. "I hate boarding school. I can't wait to live with my dad again. He's so cool, even though I make fun of him." He kept his gaze trained on her. "They constantly reprimand me at school for being a troublemaker, but I'm just speaking my mind and questioning their policies. Isn't that what I'm supposed to do—be a critical thinker, like you say in your videos?"

"One hundred. If something doesn't feel right, then by all means, speak your truth. But, if you're rebelling against authority for the fun of it, then I'd say reassess."

For a moment, when she caught Lennon's gaze, she felt a strange energy zip right through her. It was similar to the electricity felt with Jude, but much less intense. Meanwhile, Lennon shared stories of his trouble with fellow students and teachers. "It means a lot that you don't judge me, being that you're older than me. Why is that?"

Sofia snickered under her breath. "Because what is age, anyway?" She winked. "You could be older than me—your soul, that is." She rested her hand on his shoulder. "Sometimes I think that I stopped aging at seventeen years old." She wasn't by her mother's side when she took her last breath, but she always felt like the night her mother left the earth, somehow part of her soul remained within her. She could never explain it to anyone without being made fun of, so she shelved it. As an adult, Sofia realized she felt a deeper connection with those younger than her. It never even crossed her mind, people's ages—ultimately, they were all ageless souls.

Lennon chugged his hot chocolate and chuckled. "So technically, you're only one year older than me!" He paused, then hollered. "You're way too young for my brother. You can date me instead!"

She shook her head and gently pushed him. "You're crazy."

He rose to his feet, curtsied, and said. "Madame. Oops, Mademoiselle. Shall we take a walk?"

She followed her tour guide toward the cobblestoned pathways lined with quintessential brightly painted homes. He nervously looked around. "There is something I want to tell you, preferably away from prying ears and eyes."

He pulled out a joint from his back pocket. "Do you mind?" Before she could respond, he added. "My dad doesn't know, but Jude does."

She smiled. "If Jude knew or not, I wouldn't stop you."

"Super cool." He lit up and offered her a hit. She shook her head.

Sofia patiently waited for his big secret. She cloaked her mind with white light from Jude's uncanny talent of listening into all of her thoughts. "You had something to tell me?"

"Yes. I'm getting to it. I need to talk to someone impartial like you because I can't tell my dad, Jude, or Etienne. They are too involved in it."

Lennon unloaded all his feelings about his mother. He was half-crying, half-angry when revealing some of her unmotherly behavior to Sofia—how she always sided with the school, never with him. And that she allowed them to punish him the way they saw fit.

At one point, she interrupted him to ask for details about the mishandling at school. He divulged that they left him without food for three days, only water. And his mother approved it. "I've been in detention more times than any kid in my school. It's normal for me. And then when I'm sent home, my mother grounds me."

"Has she ever hit you?"

He hesitated. "I mean, she's slapped me. And once she hit me with her handbag. Most of my friends get punished in that sort of way."

Sofia tried hard to mask her thoughts so Jude could not feel the distress in her mind. "Why don't you tell your dad or your brother?"

"Because I know how my dad doesn't like confrontation regarding my mom. And if I tell Jude, he will lose it on her, and then the whole family will break more apart." He lowered his gaze.

"How long do you have until school is over?' Sofia inquired.

"I finish in June."

"If you're asking for my advice, I would tell your dad and get out right now. I would not return to that school. I would press charges against them for withholding food from you. Unbelievable."

His story continued. He then disclosed the most disturbing part of it. "One of the times I was sent home, I overheard my mother talking to Gabrielle on the speaker phone; she was giving her Jude's work schedule."

Sofia was speechless. When she found the words to speak, she said, "Lennon, I need to tell your brother this part of the story. This is bad. This woman is stalking your brother, and your mother is a common denominator."

Lennon pleaded with her but finally conceded. "Okay, I will tell him. But can we do this after New Year's?"

She shook hands with him. "Deal." Her mind reeled with all she heard. She let out a long-winded sigh. "Is there anything else you need to get off your chest?"

"No, I think it's enough for one day. Can you fill me in on what's going on in the world? I want to know everything. I told my friends you were dating Jude, and they're all jealous I will spend the holidays with you."

It was strange to hear that about herself. She was never the prettiest girl in the school, nor the smartest, for that matter. Nobody wanted to be her. It took time for the black sheep to shine, but when they did, their presence made a difference.

She told him about her latest aha moments and the most recent mainstream takedowns. He was attentive, never interrupting or invalidating her, a trait that seemed to run in the family.

The higher they walked, the cooler it got. Then Sofia attempted to contact Jude via her mind, and it worked. She heard him say, *Hey beautiful, I hear you in my head. I can't wait to see you later.* This telepathic communication would be a great video segment, but she wasn't ready to reveal their secret yet. It was also a fantastic way around A.I.

There was a raucous up ahead, so naturally, she walked toward it instead of away from it. Her higher self kicked in and said, *Walk away from it now.* As much as she trusted her inner voice, she went straight into the fire pit. Gabrielle was smack dab in front of them with little girls taking selfies with her or asking her questions. Even if Sofia wanted to turn away, Gabrielle had already spotted her. To make things worse, three girls recognized Sofia and ran up and asked to take photos with her. Lennon jumped at the chance of being in the picture.

Gabrielle stormed through the crowd and came face to face with Sofia. She mumbled while still putting on a pretty smile. "Are you following me?"

Sofia didn't mean to laugh aloud, but she did, further frustrating her.

"Next time I see you, I will kill you," Gabrielle muttered.

Lennon said, *"Elle est completement ouf! On doit y aller."* (She's fricken crazy! We have to go). He grabbed Sofia's hand and fled the scene of the "almost" crime. They ran down the hill like two bandits, laughing the entire way down. This was far from over. Gabrielle was going to strike again, and soon. They reached the park again, and it seemed the coast was clear.

When she thanked him for the great escape, he snickered. "You can thank Jude. He ingrained in my head that I needed to run away as fast as possible whenever she showed up." He shook his head. "Such a crazy life we lead, eh? Did I hear right? She said she was going to kill you? *Psssii* (Fuck). She sure is a nut job."

Sofia had to catch her breath for a second. Her nostrils flared while inhaling deep, calming breaths. "Yes, indeed. Hopefully, we'll be able to control her so Jude can live a "normal" life again."

Lennon kept nodding his head, smiling. "You legit love my brother?" She beamed. He instinctually hugged her and said, "I'm so happy you're here."

Jude's family showered her with an abundance of love. She couldn't wait for the girls to meet them. Then it donned on her—she didn't text the girls. She received confirmation that they were already on the plane.

Sofia told Lennon it was better they left the area in case of another cameo appearance from Gabrielle. He agreed and immediately texted his dad to meet them at a famous sandwich vendor across the street. "Come, I'm hungry. You have to eat this when in Paris." It was a baguette slathered in sweet butter and layers of ham. Sofia removed the ham from hers and gave it to Lennon. He shrugged his shoulders. "No ham. Next time I know."

While enjoying her buttery goodness, she was caught off guard by a swoosh of red hair that smacked her in the face. And there stood Gabrielle, up close and personal.

"I told you not to get in my way. I told you to stay away from Jude."

Sofia was stunned for a second when she heard Len*non's voice in her head. What's her problem? Should I text Jude? J'sais pas quoi faire.* (I don't know what to do).

He pulled a "Jude" and came to her defense, yelling French cuss words. This time, Sofia wasn't going to walk away. This time, Sofia was going to stand up for herself. This time, she was going to show Gabrielle who she was dealing with.

She thrust Lennon to the side. "I'm going to take care of this one."

She came eye-to-eye with her nemesis. "I'm not afraid of you, Gabrielle."

Her face contorted. Sofia's anger caught her off guard. But Gabrielle didn't take long to conjure up the malevolence within. The raging energy whirling around her felt dark and sinister. Sofia got lost in thought. *Hmmm....if she's a reflection of me....is this dark shit inside me, too?*

She was swiftly knocked back into reality with Jude's voice howling in her mind. *Sofia! What the fuck is going on? Where are you? What's happening?*

The battle of words between foes was ruthless. Neither was backing down. When Lennon tried to intervene one more time, it enraged Gabrielle. She lifted her arm to strike him. Sofia promptly stepped in to receive the blow. When Sofia hit her head against the pavement, all went dark for a moment until a tornado of energy swooped around her. She had a hard time orienting herself, unable to lift herself. Voices became muffled. A heavy metal soundtrack played ever so loudly in her head.

My head is pounding.

Her higher self kicked in. *Lay still, my child. Help is on the way. Quiet your mind.*

Easy for you to say. You didn't get assaulted by a psycho stalker.

Jude's voice came in sporadic, electrically-charged bursts.

She tried to cloak him, but nothing was working.

When Michel's voice echoed in her ear, she knew they were safe. Her body lifted off the ground and carried into what she assumed was a car. She heard Xavier whispering to her, "Everything is okay. You'll be fine."

Once seated, she felt someone patting her head with a cloth. She kept her eyes closed because the hammering sensation was relentless. The adrenaline pumped through her body. *I hope Lennon is okay. She better not have touched him. This is not normal. How is she roaming the streets so freely?* She could feel everyone scrambling around her. Then the car was moving. Someone slipped his hand into Sofia's for comfort. Michel could be heard mumbling to himself. She opened one eye, but the light of day was too painful, so she quickly shut it and squeezed Lennon's hand for reassurance.

She relayed a message to Jude. *Your girlfriend has gone too far. You better find a way to fix this, or I will.*

She's not my girlfriend. And yes, this is the last straw. Now, stop thinking about her and try to calm your mind, my love. I will be here when you get home.

****

Sofia awakened to hushed voices around her. She was lying comfortably on her back, her head propped up on multiple pillows, but the moment she moved, hard-thumping beats played in her head. Her eyes winced. Then she felt the weight of a hand on her forehead. It was Jude. His energy helped slow down the roaring tempo. Sofia tried hard to open her eyes, but all she could see were laser beams of light.

She closed them again and muttered, "Jude, can you help me up?"

He slid one hand under her back and the other behind her head, gently lifting her. She felt someone else adding more pillows behind her. She unglued her eyelids and focused on the face directly before her.

It feels like a lifetime since I've seen him. Etienne's worry-stricken face made her smile.

She reached over to Jude and brought him closer to her. He moved in and slung his arm over her mountainous headrest. She comforted Etienne, "Your face is priceless. I'm not dying. I just got a scratch."

Etienne made a face and then looked over at Jude. Then she heard Jude say, *It's more than a scratch, Sofia. Your face slammed down on the sidewalk.*

"Can I have a mirror, please?" Sofia asked.

Nobody moved. *Am I that bad?*

Jude sent Lennon to fetch one. She cracked a few jokes to lighten the somber mood. "C'mon, boys. I'll survive. I just need to learn how to defend myself better. Nothing like another injury from the crazy bitch to add to my growing list."

When she rolled her eyes, the stabbing pain ripped right through her. She screamed out.

Jude immediately placed his hand over her eyes to soothe her. Pain and hostility overwhelmed all her love and light. She fought against it, but it was too powerful.

Her higher self kept repeating. *It's all part of the plan you devised, dear one. Let the anger flow right through you. And breathe. Remember, the pain is all in your mind.*

She tried listening to the advice by breathing in, but it wasn't working as well as she had hoped. She reached out to whoever could hold on and felt Etienne's clammy hand slide into hers. In doing so, a burning sensation seared through the side of her body, and she relinquished his grip.

"I will fix this, my love," Jude replied in a commanding voice. "This is the last time she does this to anyone in my family. Her time is up."

Lennon was quiet. He paced up and down the room the entire time. Etienne, too, just sat by Sofia.

"Okay, so where is this mirror? Let me see her work."

Lennon handed the mirror to Jude.

Glancing at her reflection, she gasped. "Wow, she did a number on me!" The whole side of her face, shoulder, and arm was bloodied and bruised. Her face swelled with each passing minute. In her mouth, she tasted blood. "Did I lose any teeth? I will be a sight for sore eyes this

New Year's." When Sofia chuckled, pain coursed through her body, but still, she appeased them with a half-smile.

Gabrielle is not going to get me down. I don't care how bad I look. That bitch is going to pay for all of it. You hear me, Jude?!

I hear you loud and clear, my love.

When Jude asked them to leave the room, he propped himself in front of her. His incensed expression spoke volumes. There was a wickedness in his eyes she had never seen before. Gabrielle brought up the worst in all of them.

"What happened?" she asked.

"According to Lennon, Gabrielle pushed you, but when doing so, she tripped you."

Sofia interrupted him and joked. "We know how coordinated I am!"

Jude lowered his gaze and replied. "Yes, my love. And I should have been there." He remained silent for a few seconds, then continued. "She lingered trying to make amends with Lennon, and when my father showed up, she fled." Jude's ire returned. "Of course, no one in Paris bothered to help you or my brother. Sometimes, I wonder how humanity will ever find its way into a new energy when it can't even lend a hand. It's mind-boggling."

Jude wasn't done with his displeasure. He looked fixedly at Sofia. "And you!" He sprang up from the bed. He rubbed his face with his hands. "How often have I told you not to engage with Gabrielle?" He exhaled a heavy sigh. "I don't know how to convey to you how dangerous she is."

His fury was only worsening her pain. Deep down, she knew he was right—she provoked Gabrielle.

The 'more compassionate' Jude appeared as he settled by her side and pleaded with her to refrain from triggering Gabrielle further. He inched his hand over hers. "I promised to deal with it. Can you trust me to do that?"

A single tear cascaded down her cheek. "I trust you, my love."

Jude lifted her hand to his lips and kissed her fingers. He said, "Our family doctor checked on you while you slept and may come back later to ask a few questions. I know you're not a "doctor" person, but he's a good man and will help you *sans* pills."

It was challenging for her to speak at length, but she mentioned she tapped into Lennon's thoughts. "Maybe I was in a stupor and didn't hear right."

Jude continuously swept his fingers along her temples and forehead. He eyed her and relayed, *You may be on to something. I've also heard his thoughts, but it's very sporadic. I just assumed we were extending our gifts to those we love. It's not important now. Now, I need you to rest.*

She nodded.

She couldn't help but rev up her mind when she shut her eyes. Sofia whispered. "I'm ruining New Year's for everyone."

"Are you kidding me right now? Gabrielle is. Not you. You are another casualty in her cat-and-mouse game."

Another? Why, there's more than me?

"Yes. She's come into contact with some of my friends in the past. Never so viciously like this. This time, she's out for blood because she sees what you mean to me."

The playlist was back, a mash-up of tracks thundering in her brain. She asked him to remove one of the pillows. When his face was close to hers, she kissed him. "How is Michel? I'm sure all this shook him?"

Jude grunted, "My father was married to my mother. He's been through worse than this!"

"Okay, my love, I'll sleep a bit more." Before she shut her eyes, she asked her guides to come in and heal her. She thanked them, and slowly, her eyelids tapered down to darkness.

****

Sofia's eyes flashed open, her heart beating at lightning speed. She gasped for air. Darkness surrounded her. Her parched throat made it unable for her to scream. Her higher self came in and told her to calm down. *Breathe in and out.* And after five breaths, she found her center. Soon enough, she noticed flickers of light twinkling by her body. She still spoke to her cells for extra help and spoke aloud, "Divine I Am Presence, please recalibrate and align my vessel to the highest timeline frequency of my ascended being."

Though she yearned to join the boys, guidance from her higher self urged her to remain in her position. So she did. And then she heard Jude's voice. *Are you up? I feel tingling all over my body. Is something happening?*

The door creaked open, and Jude poked his head in. She waved him over. When he looked over, he asked, "Am I seeing what I'm seeing? Is there a glimmering light all along your side?"

She gently twisted her head to face him and whispered, "I've never seen them work on me. Amazingly, they are presenting themselves to us. This is huge. I'm so excited. I can feel them equally overjoyed."

"What are you feeling?"

"Tingling, like you said. But it's also vibrational and burning a bit. I'd be happy if they could heal me, even a little." She looked deep into his glossy greens and said, "I've also asked them to work on healing your heart because I know it is broken from today's events. So, stay close to me. Let's enjoy this miraculous moment together."

He swept his fingers across her cheek and placed his hand on her heart. "You are everything to me." He lay glued to her as their healing guides worked their magic on the twin flames.

****

Someone screaming in her ear jolted her awake. *Sofia!* She was privy to a glimmering figure of light when she opened her eyes. When she focused, she felt her mother's energy and heard her mother's voice. *The time to integrate is coming soon. Do not be afraid when it happens. You are both ready. We are here for you. You are so loved, my child.* And then the light faded away. She tried to call out Jude's name but couldn't speak. But he heard her and was already by her side.

When she recounted what happened, he asked, "What do you think that means?"

"I don't know, but the energy was very loving, so whatever it is, it will probably be a good thing, I hope." She wasn't entirely convinced. Deep down, she knew they only came to her when there was a significant event or change about to occur in her life. She surrounded her thoughts in a white bubble of light, so her beloved couldn't tap into her worries.

She managed to sit up with minimal discomfort. His fingers lightly traced along her arm and up to her face as he examined her scrapes. "How do you feel? They've done a wonderful job at healing you."

Before getting up, she entwined her fingers into his. "We are blessed to have such a wonderful team around us, but it still doesn't take away from the harm Gabrielle continues to carry out on all of us. She must be dealt with, my love."

"I'm way ahead of you already. I promised to take care of her, and I will. I am going to go right to the source." While Jude tidied Sofia's messy hair, he assured her he would immediately take action.

She was ready to go home and change. Whatever was to happen would do so, but in the meantime, Sofia wanted to enjoy her time in Paris. As she made her way outside the room, Michel and Lennon both jumped to their feet. Michel stopped Lennon from rushing to Sofia.

"You healed quickly," Michel exclaimed. "Is there another intervention at play here?"

Sofia loved that about Jude's father. His mind was always working, just like hers. She winked at him.

Confused, Lennon interrupted, "Who are you talking about?"

Jude gestured to his brother that he would tell him later. Then Michel made space on the sofa for her. "Come, sit."

She politely declined and told him it was time she headed back home. He made a long face but said, "I understand. We will do everything in our power to remedy this situation." He placed his hand on Jude's shoulder and uttered, "My son has overreached his kindness. It's time to remedy the situation, once and for all.."

Jude scowled, "I will take care of this."

"I know you will, my son. You've always taken care of your family."

Michel turned back to Sofia. "This is your home too. Now that you are part of this crazy family, know that from this day forward, it's an "us" problem."

Before heading out, Sofia hugged Lennon. "Thank you for saving me from her. If I were alone, it might have been worse for me."

The spunky boy had a comeback that didn't bode well with Jude. "Now that you are officially part of this family, she can't kill you anymore."

Jude stepped forward and yelled. "Kill her? Why would you say that?"

Lennon's eyes flickered from Jude to Sofia. She tried to brush it under the rug by appeasing Jude. "She may have said that to me before actually striking me. No big deal."

"No big deal!" He deafeningly repeated, "No big deal! It's a fucken big deal, Sofia." His eyes turned jet black, and gone was the fluttering heart. He fumed and berated both Sofia and Lennon. "If you haven't noticed, she doesn't care about your life. She's not sane. She's not in her right mind. From now on, no more hiding anything from me." He eyed all three of them. "Everything that she says or does gets reported back to me. Are we clear?" He wasn't done. "You need to take her more seriously. She's not playing around, as evidenced here." He walked over to the window and muttered something while glancing outside.

Michel consoled Lennon. Meanwhile, Sofia made her way to Jude. She looped her arm around his waist and stood by him as he calmed down. "You are right, my love. We should have told you this."

Jude's eyes remained affixed on the Parisian cityscape as he mumbled, "Don't underestimate Gabrielle." He turned and looked steadfastly into her eyes. "Nor my mother."

REMEMBER

You've forgotten who you are.
All you need to do is look within.
It's time to remember.

29

Rhythmic beats flowed onto the sidewalk with Lola and Etienne's voices layered amidst the musical notes. She held him back once Sofia and Jude set foot in the courtyard. His anger had still not subsided. His thoughts were streaming in his mind at warp speed.

No one will come between us, ever. We are stronger together than apart.

Yes, we will get through this. She saw right through his automatic response but let it go.

Lola was the first to burst through the door to greet the couple. She didn't waste time and darted right at Jude. "What are we going to do about this bitch?"

Jude let out a sigh but acknowledged her words. He then released Sofia's hand while Lola cautiously hugged her best friend.

Leaning into Lola's embrace, Sofia tried to choke back her tears but couldn't hold back. Waterworks tumbled freely. The situation felt more natural with her longtime friend present. Emma crept in and slithered an arm around Sofia's waist. "Let it all out. She's not going to bring us down. Not now, not ever."

Jude instinctively pried her friends' arms away from Sofia, but Etienne pulled him back. Sofia heard Etienne say, "Let them take care of her for now." Jude recoiled. He kicked one of the pots in his way before making his way inside.

As her best friends relayed words of comfort and consolation, she could hear Yolande's raised voice blasting both of them in French. "It cannot go on like this anymore! She doesn't deserve this. And you, Jude, it's enough. Your life is a living hell. It's time you do what you've always needed to and go up against your mother. I will help you. You know that."

Etienne caught Sofia's eyes from afar and shut the kitchen door behind him. Before doing so, he winked at her.

When Lola and Emma stepped back, they began to inspect her scrapes. Lola furrowed her brows and said, "Etienne described your injuries to be much worse."

Sofia briefly recounted the energetic intervention, inciting Lola to clap her hands and Emma to contort her face. Emma was always skeptical of Sofia's world, but they never made it a "thing."

As the girls escorted Sofia into the kitchen, Yolande stopped yelling and rushed over to the injured soul. When she embraced Sofia, more tears spilled. Yolande may have been more emotionally-reserved than the women in Sofia's life, but she still had a heart of gold. She murmured in Sofia's ear, "The next time I see her, I will not only give her a piece of my mind but also make sure to scare her into submission."

Yolande reached her limit of affection. She called Jude over. "Come, wrap your arms around this one. She needs you now more than ever."

He speedily obliged. As soon as his arms wrapped around Sofia, a current rushed through them. Neither one of the twin flames spoke, nor did they tap into each other's minds.

Yolande waved everyone to the table and served her French fare. To lighten the mood, Lola regaled them with past stories about Sofia. It led to other personal stories as well from the others. It didn't take long for them to go from low vibe to high vibe.

Jude's voice crept back into her head. *You have remarkable friends, my love. When Lola came at me before, I was a bit taken aback, but I loved every moment of her mama bear posture.*

Sofia replied. *Everyone has been great. If I'm being honest, Gabrielle has shaken me up in an "I'm angry" way, and it doesn't feel good to be dipping in that energy.*

Etienne leaned forward and exclaimed to the table, "They're at it again, folks. They are talking among themselves." He pointed to his head. He praised himself for decoding their secret.

"Admit it, you're a bit jealous that you can't hear them," Yolande teased Etienne.

He waved his hands at her, but it was obvious to the table that she had hit the nail on the head.

While everyone poked fun at Etienne, Sofia felt an electric shock zip through her body. As she tried to keep it under wraps, Jude felt the pain and jumped out of his seat. When he cried out, he turned to Sofia. "Ouch! How are you keeping this pain inside? That was intense."

Sofia held her breath in an attempt to endure the agony but released it after his declaration. Leaning in her chair, about to tumble sideways,

Jude swooped her in his arms and brought her to the sofa in the living room. She winced when his arms brushed up against the side of her body. She heard the shuffling of feet and murmuring behind her like children playing hide and seek.

He gently examined her face. Before she could even ask for a warm towel, Yolande handed one to him. He gently placed it on her wound. She gladly accepted the warmth on her skin.

Jude twisted his head toward Sofia and asked, "Did you just relay a message to me?"

She shook her head.

"Well then, guess who else has just connected to his higher self?" He smiled. "I've just been told to warm my hands and place them above your wounds." So he rubbed his hands together, blew hot air into his palms, and then worked his magic. His touch sent shivers from her feet up to her crown and beyond. When she sneaked a peek at him, his eyes glazed a golden green. It was as if he was no longer in his body anymore. He knelt by her side and transferred his restorative energy by moving his hands melodiously along each scrape and bruise. She realized he was drawing their symbols when she fixated on each movement.

Do they see the glimmer of light emanating from his hands?

She placed her head back down and reveled in the curative energy sweeping across her body. In a hushed voice, she called out to whomever was nearby, asking for someone to record whatever was happening.

Etienne exclaimed, "Already on it."

It felt like it lasted a few hours when, in fact, it was only a few minutes, according to the bystanders. When Jude returned to his body, he breathed heavily and fell back onto the carpet like a starfish—completely drained of energy. Sofia didn't think twice and effortlessly vaulted off the couch to kneel beside him. When she placed her hands on his body, she returned some energy to him. His olive complexion was restored, and as his eyes fluttered open, his sea-greens had returned to their normal state.

The crowd never left. Mouths agape, they were speechless for once.

Jude cleared his throat and asked, "What happened?"

"What do you remember?"

He went on to describe his out-of-body experience to them. Sofia was the only one giddy about the occurrence. Everyone else was shocked until Yolande commanded, "Okay, back to the table. The food is getting cold. They will explain to us later. Let's leave these lightworkers to themselves."

Sofia jerked her head up toward Yolande.

As she shooed everyone else into the kitchen, Yolande bent down to the twin flames and said, "There are more starseeds in your entourage than you may be aware of, my dears. We are here with you, walking through the densities and activating the light along with you."

Sofia curved her lips into the broadest smile.

Jude propped himself on his elbows. "I knew there was something special about you."

She winked at them and said, "Okay, now let me go back and feed these humans." And she was off.

Jude inspected Sofia's face and declared her fully healed. As his fingers searched for any traces of scarring, he was just as mind-blown as their friends. He listened intently to her every word as she shared her experience.

A message flowed in from their higher selves. *And it has begun.*

****

Michel summoned Etienne and Jude to pick up some last-minute New Year's Eve items. It worked in the girls' favor because their jet lag had already kicked in. Emma had already retired to her room while Lola tried to hang on, but her eyelids had difficulty staying open. She waved goodbye and motioned to Sofia. "Are you coming?"

Emma and Lola's room were right next to each other. They had an adjoining door between them. When Sofia drew open the curtains, a picturesque view of Paris was laid out before them. Lola and Sofia took a few moments to scan the far-reaching cityscape. Lola's room was similar to Sofia's, except Lola's colors leaned more toward pink. A bouquet of freshly cut roses in bright red rested in a glass vase on her nightstand. It didn't take long for Lola to be in her pj's and under the covers.

She patted her hand on the bed. "Come, Sof. I want to hear about everything."

Sofia rested her back against the headboard and offered a brief rundown of the past events. They heard a light tapping on the door as they chatted and giggled. Emma popped her head in and said, "Can I join?"

"What kind of question is that?" Sofia said, laughing along with Lola. "Come. I'm just going through the past few days."

Emma sat at the edge of the bed, stiff as a board. She nervously folded and unfolded the comforter's corner while attempting to seem normal to her best friends. But Sofia and Lola eventually got her to relax.

The conversation zigzagged in all directions as they tried to cover all bases. Lola reconciled with Sebastian in the past week, and they worked things out again. Emma never heard from Pedro again. She was still heartbroken and seeking the "one." Then the conversation centered on Gabrielle; Sofia summarized her upbringing and the relationship between her and Jude. They listened on in dread. Their expressions were slightly disconcerting to Sofia, but she carried on. When she recounted her and Jude's intimate encounters, their eyes lit up, altering the overall mood.

At one point, they were all lying flat on the bed, staring at the ceiling, when Emma squeaked out, "What's with the wallpaper covering everything?"

They glanced at one another and heartily laughed. "The more you look at it," Lola said, "the more creepy it feels. Almost horror-like."

Silence fell upon them. Sofia quietly filled the space with white light, protecting them from any unaligned energies.

It didn't take Sofia long to realize that her friends were fast asleep, so she lifted herself quietly from the bed and covered them with the blanket.

When Sofia returned to her room, the Eiffel Tower shone brightly in the night sky with its golden Holiday lighting. She stood facing the mirror. She inspected her face and body for any scarring, but Jude (and her guides) did a magnificent job. There was only slight bruising; otherwise, there was no trace of Gabrielle's assault. She shut the lights in the room, lit a candle and an incense stick, and stood in front of her makeshift altar, thanking her team for the healing. Sofia also expressed gratitude for bringing Jude and her together at this time in her life. The stillness in the house was peaceful, yet chills still ran down her spine. She listened to her higher self. *Don't open the door if the doorbell rings.*

Well, that's not very reassuring!

Sofia slipped into her nightgown, kept the curtains open to allow the Parisian night sky to illuminate the room, and shut her eyes, praying to fall asleep before she had to deal with any crazy.

****

A clanging of pots and pans woke Sofia up. She could faintly hear Yolande bitching at Etienne. When she stretched her arm beside her, there was no Jude. She wondered if he ever came home at all. With no desire to get up, she lingered a little longer in bed. New Year's Eve always felt like a Sunday, no matter what day it was. She pulled the blanket over her head to camouflage the early morning commotion.

Not five minutes later, Jude stealthily snuggled into her cocoon. He peeled away any fabric that clung to her. Skin to skin, his hand gently swept up and down her body. "My divine phoenix, are you ready to rise from the ashes?" He kissed her everywhere. He touched her everywhere. He loved her everywhere. And when Jude entered her, the fire inside her blazed a trail right through her body. He consumed her as any dragon would, and when done, the love of her life swaddled her as any warrior protector would.

They lay in each other's arms for the better part of the morning, soundless but deep into each other's thoughts. Their telepathic work was excelling every day. She heard him say. *I have a surprise for you, my love.*

She spiraled her body to face him. "Ohhh, I can't wait. What is it?"

He took her breath away when she caught a glimpse of his whole being. His soul shimmered under his skin, and his eyes scintillated in the darkness. She told him mindfully. *I wish you could see what I'm seeing. You're a beautiful, glittering star.*

He whispered, "I'm not the only one, mon amour. Every night, I feel like I'm embracing a sparkling orb."

As the twin flames further examined their light, they couldn't help but merge their energetic bodies once again into one shooting star.

****

By the time Sofia got out of the shower and dressed for her cooking session, she hadn't even thought about what she would prepare for New Year's Eve, but she wasn't worried. One of her favorite pastimes as a child was sitting around and watching her mom cook up feasts without any use for cookbooks. Even when her dad showed up with impromptu guests, she whipped up some of the most delicious Italian fanfare. She was in her element, as Sofia and her brother would sit back and watch her weave her culinary magic.

Jude sat cross-legged on the oval carpet by the altar. He waved her over and stared at her briefly as she kneeled before him. Leaning in, he planted a kiss on her lips. She had no problem spending the day with this man in this position. But he reached behind his body and handed over a newspaper-wrapped present tied with a raffia bow adorned with dried flowers. She carefully pulled the string and then ripped through the paper. An outpouring of joy escaped her heart and flowed throughout her body upon glancing at the first name, "Alice."

He beamed. "You haven't even unwrapped it."

He bought her the pricey *Alice in Wonderland* book from the bookshop in New York City. No words materialized from her joy.

He clapped his hands together. "I asked Lola to bring it over. It was the second shipment from Milton, but I left too early for Paris."

Sofia smiled widely. "Well, funny that Lola brought this for you because my sneaky friend also brought something I ordered for you."

She leaned to the left and reached under her altar for a box. "I was going to wrap it later, but it feels like a good time to give it to you now."

His cheeks flushed red. He placed the box in between them and lifted the cover. "Two gifts?" Glossy eyes looked up at her.

Purchased from her favorite local bookshop in Montreal, it was a limited edition book dedicated to Rumi; his poetry always spoke to her on a deeper level.

He placed the book on his heart and asked, "I can't believe you bought this. This is so crazy. How do you know he's my favorite poet?"

Sofia leaned in. "Let's call it a twin flame innerstanding."

He pulled out the second surprise—a mini faded black leather notebook embossed with a fiery phoenix. When he flipped open the book, he landed on a page that Sofia wrote in.

"You are so random, and that's why I love you."

"We're a bunch of nerds, aren't we? We both got each other books."

He smirked. "I'd like to think of ourselves as light beings with a quest for higher wisdom."

"Oh, fancy words!" Sofia teased him and then fell into his arms. It had been a long time since she could fully and completely give herself to someone. The last person she trusted with her soul was her mother.

He pulled away and framed her face in his hands. "I know you're missing your mom today. And it mustn't be easy to live so far away from your family, but know this, my love,"—he ran his fingers through her hair—"you are my family now. You will never be alone, ever again."

A knock at the door startled them.

Etienne opened the door and said, "I don't want to be a pain in the ass, but you guys have to start cooking. No one wants to be late for Michel's dinner party."

Jude nodded and turned to Sofia. "He's a bit of a stickler when it comes to time. Everything is planned out, so when it hits midnight, we are ready." They simultaneously raised their hands in the air and mimicked Michel. "It's a science!"

The girls were already taking up all the space in the kitchen, but it didn't stop Sofia and Jude from squeezing themselves in between their mess. Etienne put on the music. They laughed, danced, sang, stirred, diced, fried, roasted, and they loved. It was a glorious moment.

I AM YOU

The one true light is ME.

30

As Jude buttoned up Sofia's vintage dress, her head hung low, listening to the harmonic sounds of shuffling feet between rooms and the sweet-sounding beats streaming out of Etienne's bedroom.

What about the end of the year gets everyone so worked up?

He softly kissed her neck before looping the last button and whispered, "I often think of that, too. After all, tomorrow is just another day. Plus, is it really New Year's? Or is this just another linear construct?"

He untied the loose bun on her head, allowing it to fall loosely around her shoulders. While he set her hair, he caught her smiling widely.

She leaned in. "You know how to turn me on, Mr. Jude."

He growled. "New year or not, I can't wait to spend the rest of my life with you."

He was self-assured as those words spilled out of his mouth, but it caught Sofia off guard. Her butterflies swooped from the depths of her belly to the top of her head. As her cheek rested on his spruce green knit sweater, she remembered their first night at the gates of Central Park. His heart was beating at the same intensity.

When Sofia unclenched her body from Jude, he resisted and mumbled, "Can we just stay this way forever?"

She loved this romantic side of Jude—tonight, he was her Knight of Cups and her fiery King of Wands.

The buzzing energy spilled into the hallway as Lola weaved in and out of the bathroom. Emma hummed to the music, and Etienne found his way to them, holding up two velvet jackets in the air. "Purple or black?"

The twin flames didn't have to consult with each other when they both blurted out, "Purple."

Before turning back, he remarked how beautiful Sofia looked in her dress. Jude remained silent, which escalated into an awkward moment for them. Etienne turned and dashed back to his room.

Sofia returned to her position in his arms to mask the tension and heard Jude say, *I'm way ahead of this, Sofia. The time will come when I will talk with him.*

He then twirled her around. "But not tonight because it's Michel's special night."

Sofia's chameleon clutched her hand and chose a high vibration instead of wallowing in pettiness. He sang out loud, further elevating everyone else's spirits. Emma stepped out in a striking periwinkle lace dress at that moment.

Jude outwardly complimented her, inciting Etienne to pop his head out, also in agreement. "Indeed, that color compliments your beautiful blues." He nervously darted his eyes at Jude and then back at Emma.

Jude laughed. "You're already flirting so early in the evening." He then pointed at his phone and said, "Chop, chop, you can be a charmer at Michel's, but we need to go soon."

Sofia tapped on Lola's door. "The same goes for you!"

Lola swung open the door and yelled, "Surprise! I'm ready." She wore a mustard yellow dress that only Lola could pull off in the middle of winter. She radiated like the sunshine that she was.

The energy was high as they piled into the car, and the flirtations ensued. A familiar, incessant ringing began in Jude's pocket. The music was too loud for the girls to hear, but the trained ears heard it. So Xavier and Etienne went into distraction mode while Jude checked his messages. He shoved the phone back into his pocket and stared out the window.

Jude's attempt to avert his attention failed. She reached over to grab his face but got startled by the pain shooting through her body. *It seems like "phantom pains" are real.* When she grasped Jude's thigh, she released a barely audible squeal not to ruin the merriment. But that didn't work. Now all eyes were on her, and her friends' words of concern came rolling in.

Jude placed his healing hand on her cheek, and Sofia relinquished her pain to him. When she laid her head back on the leather headrest, she didn't expect to feel equally anxious about the phone call from Gabrielle.

Jude chimed in. *I'm sorry that you have to feel how I do. The best way to release her from your mind is to go into your heart and remember the good things in your life.* He squeezed her hand, leaned his body in, and pecked her on the cheek. *It's temporary, but at least it's something.*

Following his advice, she replaced the tension by filling her mind with images of the fusion of their bodies and souls.

Jude whispered in her ear, "Now, that's what I'm talking about."

All it took was one sweet moment for the twin flames to reconnect.

They pulled up a few minutes before 8 p.m. Etienne rushed with the girls to the elevator. Jude waved him to go on ahead. He wanted to spend a few minutes alone with Sofia in the elegant lobby. He leaned Sofia against one of the columns and hypnotically looked into her eyes.

"Gabrielle is not just going to go away, my love. She is going to come in stronger next time. She is not well. You are a challenge for her, and she seems to thrive on that. And my mother is on her side, which is not good."

Sofia tried to say something, but he gently placed his finger on her lips and continued, "Please, let me finish. Now that we feel the same intensity, we must be smart about this together. Let's find a way to shut them both down. We can work as a team, but we need to get this done because," he stuttered, "because I want to settle down with you and just live the life that we've fought and died for, for the past thousands of lifetimes. And the only way to get this done is by letting me take the lead. Can you do that, Sofia?"

She half-smiled and bowed her head.

Before planting a mind-blowing kiss, they were interrupted by Lennon screaming at them from the elevator. "Come in the elevator. He's having a shit fit."

Wow. Michel takes New Year's Eve seriously.

"We weren't joking," Jude replied. "You'll soon see for yourself!"

****

Dressed in dark denim, a white T-shirt, and an army green jacket, Lennon came from the same family of chic. He hugged Sofia as soon as she entered the elevator. "How are you feeling?" He examined her and said, "Wow, you healed completely. My father is right about you. You are an angel."

The door opened to Michel standing squarely in front of them. Lennon sneaked past him. Jude poked his dad and said, "Papa, we're here. Don't worry about it." He kissed him on the cheek and glided around him. They left Sofia to deal with his ire. She apologized and hugged him while her eyes feasted on the abundant red, yellow, and orange fairy lights streaming along the ceiling and walls.

"Wow, this is so magical." She released herself from his arms and rejoiced in the splendor around her.

His eyes lit up. "You like? This year, I changed it for you. I know how much you love the fantastical worlds." He stood proudly facing the decor and boasted, "I'm dedicating this celebration to the two of you. Jude's gift to you inspired me."

Sofia was awe-struck at the details and the unconditional love this man had to offer her and his family. The energy was vibrant, with Lola, Etienne, Xavier, and Lennon making most of the raucous. Emma made an effort as she designated herself as the bartender; there were wine, champagne, and spirits galore. There was another beautiful energy among them. Sofia was introduced to Xavier's girlfriend, Yasmeen.

Michel didn't waste time. He escorted Sofia into the main dining area. A fiery red fabric with gold and yellow accents adorned the table. Chinese lanterns hung down from the ceiling. A shiny gold fortune cookie sat on each plate. Amongst Jude's photographs was a more oversized frame covered with a red cloth. Sofia tried to sneak a peek, but Michel tapped her hand.

Michel wagged his finger, "Nuh-uh-huh! You shall see later on. Shall we join the others?" He placed his hand on her back and swiftly pulled back. "Oh, I forgot you are injured."

She shook her head. "Not anymore. I'm surprised no one told you. Jude healed me last night."

He stopped her before entering the party zone. "What do you mean he healed you?"

Sofia chronicled the healing process from her guides, then to Jude's participation. "I made Etienne take a video for you so that you could see your son at work. He's a natural-born healer." She winked at him.

He waved Etienne over. As the three silently viewed the magic, Sofia noticed another luminous figure beside them but kept it to herself. Michel wept through the whole video. Jude walked over to the huddle, peeked his head in between, and whispered, "What's going on here?"

When he remarked on his father's emotional status, he draped his arm around him and asked, "Why are you crying, Papa?"

Overjoyed with emotions, Michel cried out. "This is glorious, my son. You are a healer."

Sofia nodded. "Yes, he is. That is why there is never too much discord in this home. He is the reason why many flock to Jude. It's not because of his money but because he is calming and full of light. He is also the reason why Etienne is here with your family." When she looked up, both Etienne and Jude stared at her in wonderment. "There are no coincidences in life, right, Jude? Isn't that what you always say? You, my beautiful twin, are the glue that sticks everyone in your life together. And once you realize that, we will be a force of nature."

Michel wiped away his tears and punched his fist in the air. "Pow. And she is the other half of that strength. I love all of you so much. You bring this old man much joy."

He summoned everyone to the table. Before sitting down, Michel designated everyone's seat. He started with Sofia to his left with Jude, and when Etienne went to sit next to Jude, Michel vetoed his choice. "*Debout* (Get up)." He waved Lola over and then pointed to Etienne to sit down. The number of eyes rolled at that moment was picture worthy. Sofia had a blast watching them all obey this warmhearted physicist—Emma next to Etienne, then Xavier, Yasmeen, and finally Lennon.

"Why don't I get two women side by side?" Lennon whined.

Everyone giggled. Michel said, "You always have two women on each arm, so tonight, you must go it alone." More laughter.

The night went on with chopsticks and everyone's fare. As part of their tradition, each chef had to describe their dishes and why they made them for the end of the year. Xavier presented Chicken Yassa, a favorite chicken and rice dish from his hometown in Senegal. "My dream is to one day open a restaurant and have my favorite chef flown in from home—my mother."

Jude, Etienne, and Lennon banged their chopsticks on the table and roared, "Yes, Xavier! One day soon."

Yasmeen shared her couscous dish from Tunisia. She blushed, held out her diamond ring, and said, "Hopefully, soon, I will only be cooking Senegalese food."

Michel rose from his chair. "*Ah bon? C'est magnifique!* (Really? It's wonderful)." He rushed over and congratulated the couple.

Jude yelled, "*Félicitations, frérot* (Congrats, bro)." Everyone else cheered for them. Another heartfelt moment.

When Michel returned to his seat, he asked Jude if he knew about it. Jude shook his head. Then Michel patted Sofia's hand and winked at her.

Jude veered the attention away from the topic and explained his dish. "I chose a dish that outlines this past year. Tofu is the main ingredient—it's rather bland on its own, which describes my life for the past, er, for many years now. The peanut sauce feels homey to me, representing my dad, Etienne, Lennon, and Xavier. And the chili is the spice that has come into my life." He turned to look at Sofia and said, "Because of you, I can feel again. I can savor life again. I can love again." He winked at her and added, "And she's intense like a chili pepper when mad!!!" Claps and cheers from everyone at the table. He handed over the reins to Sofia.

"That's a tough one to follow!" She shared her simple but delicious lasagna al pesto with everyone. "I chose lasagna because of its multi-dimensionality."

Etienne echoed, "Can you speak in simple English, please?"

Lola laughed out loud. Sofia rolled her eyes and continued, "Anyway." She looked at Etienne and spoke slowly, "For its mul-ti-lay-ers." She smiled. "Each layer represents someone important in my life; that's why it was so thick. The first foundational layer is for my mother, then my father, brother, Lola, Emma, Etienne, Michel, and Lennon—eight layers of people dear to my heart. Some of you may not know, but basil, for me, is what chocolate is to most people. I love, love basil. So the creamy and delicious pesto represents my one and only. He's what keeps the whole dish savory until the last bite. The top layer of cheese is me because I'm the "top cheese!!!" More laughter, more claps, more cheers.

Michel crossed his arms, sat back, and cried throughout each story.

Etienne was next in line to share his dish with the table. "I made, um, let's be real, Yolande made...." Booed, he calmed them down and said, "I had other things to attend to."

"Yes," Michel said. "He was busy running around for me. Cut him some slack. He's always cooked the other years."

Etienne described the scalloped potato dish she made and how it reminded him of his childhood. Half of the dish was plain and creamy, as he had eaten it as a child. The other half of the dish had colorful peppers, onions, and eggplant. "I have Sofia to thank for this part. She helped me forgive my parents for being nonexistent in my life. Without my mother's bad behavior, I would never have met Jude and been part of this remarkable family." He turned to Michel and pointed to the right side. "This side is for you. Thank you."

Michel's tears were unstoppable. He cleared his throat. "You're welcome. We must thank you too, Etienne, for you brought life into a broken home." He chuckled. "So much laughter. " He then pointed to both Jude and Etienne. "And between the two of you, so much trouble."

Lennon screamed across the table, "And what about me?"

Michel rolled his eyes. "How could I ever forget the biggest troublemaker? Yes, the three of you."

It was Lola's turn to share her dish, Armenian Manti. "I have to thank Etienne for going out of his way for me and finding an Armenian bakery. It's a traditional fare that we serve during the holidays, but for me, it represents my father, who has since passed. We used to make these together. It was our thing. As we usher in this New Year, I realize I must let the sadness go and accept him as always being with me. I must thank Sofia for opening this path and helping me understand that there is no death, and he will always be around me."

This dinner was a cry fest, it seemed. Emma was next. As she twiddled the chopsticks in her fingers, her voice quivered. But she pushed through it and remained poised throughout. "I prepared a typical Canadian dish—Shepherd's pie. Since the theme was about letting go of the past and moving into the new, I let go of my traditional ways of thinking and will try to embrace life as my friends do, without a care in the world. My time with Lola, Sofia, Jude, and Etienne has shown me that there's nothing more important than friends. And like Sofia's dish, these layers are a mish-mash of all my friends' personalities. They have shaped and stuck by me, and I will do the same for them this year."

Tears cascaded down Lola's and Sofia's cheeks. And when Emma locked eyes with them, tears also welled in her eyes.

Chopsticks banged on the table—two left to go.

Lennon volunteered himself. "I roasted sweet potatoes, one for each of you." Everyone banged their chopsticks.

Michel interrupted them, "Wait, he's not finished. Listen carefully to what he has done, this boy."

Lennon blushed and continued, "Every single potato has a specific spice according to your hometown or preference: Xavier's has peanut shavings, Yasmeen's has tabil spice, Lola's has za'atar spice, Emma's has maple syrup—which is the best one, by the way— Etienne's has Ras El Hanout, Jude has spicy chocolate because he's weird that way, Sofia has pesto because I have good sources, and my dad has the finest French herbs: chopped parsley, chervil, and chives. I've cut them up so we can all try the different spices."

The tears were endless at that table.

Michel was last. He stood up and left the table, returning with a rolling table filled with various dishes. Each was covered with its golden dome. He picked up a tureen and said, "This soup is for Xavier. You have been more than just my right-hand man. You have comforted my boys when they were down and provided me with companionship when these three were gallivanting about. I can't thank you enough, my son." He turned to Yasmeen. "You are truly blessed to be marrying this man. He is one of a kind."

The boys cheered and showered Xavier with loving words.

Michel then lifted one of the domed plates—spring rolls. "This represents my youngest boy. He is not just a pretty wrapping; he has many flavors—spicy, savory, and sweet. And he's crunchy, too!" Lennon flipped his golden curls from left to right, putting smiles on everyone's faces. That was his forte.

Then he uncovered another dish. "This one's for Etienne." It was a plate of dumplings with many different sauces. "Every time you bite into a dumpling, you never know how it will go. Will the sauce squirt in your eyes, dribble down your cheek, or will the filling fall out of the dough? This is our Etienne. He's a dumpling full of surprises, and each sauce represents his moods." Laughter and tears erupted.

"This last dish is for both Jude and Sofia." He lifted the dome to reveal a medley of Chinese vegetables and spices. "This story starts before Jude meets Sofia. After our little talk,"—he pointed to Sofia—"I got to thinking about the aha moments in my life as you asked me to." He paused. "And this extraordinary moment came to my mind, triggered by what's behind this red fabric,"—he pointed to the concealed area. "It was one day when Jude was only six years old. We were in Saint Tropez, and, as many of you know, it wasn't my scene, so I would whisk Jude away to visit the real French countryside. Give him an authentic taste of *la vie française* (the French life). So, we happened upon a tiny Chinese restaurant in a rural village." He snickered and turned to Jude. "Do you remember the old man and his wife?" Jude nodded. "Anyway, so on the menu, there was a dish called Phoenix and Dragon."

Sofia shrieked, "No way!"

Michel affirmed and went on. "This is the best part, Sofia. I'm not sure Jude remembers this, but he turned to me and said, 'One day, I'm going to meet my phoenix because I don't know if you know, but I'm a dragon.'" He looked over at his son. "Do you remember that?"

"Oh, I remember it. That precise memory flooded in when I saw Sofia's phoenix tattoo." He leaned to the side and kissed her.

"Of course, at the time, I thought he just had a wild imagination. So, I indulged him. But knowing what I know now, I probably would have delved deeper into it since he was probably telling me the truth." Michel turned to Sofia. "I believe it's you who told me that from birth to seven years of age, we all somewhat remember where we come from, right?"

"Yes. Our memories are wiped as soon as we enter the womb, but our minds are free from programming until we get into school, etc." She looked around the table and disclosed, "At this age, we usually talk to "imaginary friends" who are your guides, angels, elementals, and ascended masters. It's a wonderful trek down memory lane if you want to go there."

Michel spoke directly to Jude. "I'm sorry, *mon fils* (my son), if I didn't take it seriously. But who knew we would discover that we've been dragons, fairies, mermaids, etc., in our past lifetimes."

Etienne stared, wide-eyed. "Are you guys freaking serious?"

"It's time you listen to what she says in her videos instead of pretending to listen," Emma said to Etienne. Her comment was well received by everyone at the table. Even Etienne shared a laugh.

They ate. They drank. They shared stories. They ate some more. They drank some more. They laughed some more. It was a lively and vibrant feast, indeed.

Michel then asked Lennon to get the easel in the closet and motioned to Jude. "Shall we reveal what's under this cloth for all?"

Jude acknowledged him and got up from his seat. He stood before the frame and said, "As many of you just heard, Sofia and I unknowingly connected with our phoenix and dragon tattoos back in New York. According to Chinese culture, the union of the divine masculine with the divine feminine makes the perfect couple. I wasn't expecting this story from my father, but it has made a great segue into this reveal. So, when I got back to Montreal, I knew that Sofia had a good friend who was a painter. I visited her studio a few days before returning here and commissioned her to make this painting for us. And it was just delivered a few days ago."

Jude turned to look at Sofia. "This is my promise that the dragon inside me will always fiercely protect and passionately love you. I know the phoenix inside you will illuminate our lives with wisdom and beauty. You are my yin to my yang."

He unveiled the masterpiece—a painting of a dragon and phoenix mirroring each other. Each had its personality and beauty but was powerfully connected. Sofia's heart exploded. She ran up to Jude and hugged him. They were lost in each other's arms until everyone started teasing. "Don't start kissing. You know the way you both get."

They ignored their friends while, hand in hand, admiring the painting for its artistry and symbolism.

Jude relayed a message. *Are you seeing glimpses of all our lifetimes in this painting?*

Yes, yes, and yes.

Etienne shouted. "Are you both doing your telepathic thing and talking to each other so we don't hear you?"

They didn't respond. Etienne went on, "Are you really?" He made a face but continued to tease them, "What are you saying about me? Are you telling each other how much you miss my presence in your life?"

Jude turned around, grabbed one of the wrapped fortune cookies on the table, and chucked it at Etienne's head. Before they knew it, fortune cookies and rattles flew across the room until Michel ended the childish behavior. "Oh la la. How old are all of you?"

Still, a cookie went flying across the table. Michel shouted, "*Ça suffit* (That's enough). Let's go to the main room, my unruly children."

31

Sofia hadn't noticed how close Michel's home was to the Eiffel Tower. The colors red, white, and blue undulated up and down the iconic statue. Crowds of people filled the streets in anticipation of midnight. It was only 11 p.m., but the Parisians were ready to party. And so was Michel.

He rolled out table after table of desserts. Michel motioned to Etienne to put on the music and ordered Lennon to get the glasses. Jude was the champagne popper. Xavier got up to help, but Michel instructed him to stay put. "You work hard enough for this family year-round. Tonight, you will enjoy this family time with your future wife."

Michel kept looking at his watch. Sofia jokingly said, "There's still an hour left to go. Don't worry."

He mischievously gazed back at her and said, "Ah, yes. You are right."

Sofia asked Jude. *What is your father up to? I can see right through him.*

Jude replied, *Who knows? I told you he's obsessed about this night!*

Michel gathered everyone around the table and explained that he had ordered a special dessert for every guest. He looked at Emma and Lola. "Even the newcomers. But, for now…" He looked at his watch again and looked up at Jude. "I will let Jude take over." Michel turned to the girls and explained that come dessert time, they all have to divulge what they are looking forward to in the new year. "This year, Jude wants to go first." He looked at his watch one last time.

Sofia's curiosity was on a high. Even her higher self was quiet. Nothing about her time here in Paris was normal, so she waited to hear Jude's story with delight. He positioned himself facing Sofia and grabbed one of the plates from the table. It was the only one covered with a gold dome. He looked at his dad, and Michel nodded.

He lifted the dome, and there sat a ring. Sofia stared at the golden piece of metal that shined against the white porcelain, then up at Jude's virtuous eyes. She looked to her friends for support. Lola was jumping up and down. Emma clapped her hands. She turned to Etienne—he winked at her. Michel clasped his hands in glee. Lennon danced around. Xavier and Yasmeen encouragingly smiled.

She went back to the ring, then looked back up at Jude.

He told her. *You knew this was coming at one point. The time is now.*

She picked up the ring. It was not a diamond. Nor was it a gemstone. It was an exquisitely sculpted phoenix in gold. When she lifted it, there was an inscription inside the wide band. "Lovers don't finally meet somewhere." It was half of a Rumi quote.

He reached under his shirt and pulled out his chain. There dangled the green stone and a ring with a dragon instead of a phoenix. He unfastened the necklace, grabbed it, and united the two bands—perfect fit. The inscription in his ring read the last part of the quote, "They're in each other all along."

Then he set aside his ring, took the band from Sofia's fingers, and said, "I've been waiting for you my whole life. Are you ready, Sofia, for this divine union?" He paused. "Because I am." He slipped the ring over her finger. He held her hand as she collected herself. The tears flowed one after the other.

She looked around at all the eager faces and whispered, "I'm ready."

Claps and cheers and singing erupted from their friends and family. While everyone celebrated their union with the clinking of glasses, Sofia and Jude remained calm as the flaming energies blazed through their bodies. An energetic wave orbited around them as they clutched each other's hands.

Jude followed the wave with his eyes and mindfully said to Sofia. *Look.*

Sofia answered. *The dragon and phoenix flying around us?*

There was a message too. *This union is a blessed one. We have been waiting for lifetimes. Take heed, dear ones, of those around you with daggers and swords. The power of your union is absolute.*

And then all went back to normal. As Jude and Sofia looked around at their friends, no one noticed these mythical beings' presence. The only people who were in shock were Lennon and Michel. Lennon still joined the fun as if nothing was happening. But he sent a message across the room by pointing his fingers to his eyes and then back at them. Michel whisked the couple into the kitchen.

"What was that all about?" he inquired.

Sofia asked Michel what he saw. He only saw whirling energy but not the dragon nor the phoenix. Lennon made his way to them and confirmed seeing only the dragon. She asked if he heard a message, and it was negative.

Most interesting, your family is, Jude. Did you know they were so connected?

He answered. *I had a feeling, but not to this extent.*

The boys called Jude over to congratulate him. The girls rushed to Sofia's side to inspect the ring and celebrate the moment. Sofia asked Michel why he was so worried about the time. He told her Jude wanted to ask her at a significant time, and he chose 11:11. She leaned into Michel. "Your son is one of a kind."

Michel regaled them with the whole scenario of getting the ring on time. And that the painting almost never made it through customs, but Etienne paid off one of the workers. Michel spoke nonchalantly about it as if bribery was usual in France.

It was nearing midnight, so they huddled together with glasses of champagne, ready for the New Year to begin. 10..9..8..7..6..5..4..3... and the lights went out all over Paris, even the Eiffel Tower. Silence fell upon the city for a few seconds until they heard people screaming in the streets, *"Bonne Année!* (Happy New Year)."

In the darkness, there was still light. People continued to celebrate in the streets as fireworks colored the sky.

Jude and Sofia glowed in the darkness, which was also evident to the human eye.

Etienne remarked, "You guys are lit up, like for real. Are you wrapped in lighting?"

Sofia and Jude's higher selves rang in simultaneously and said, *Now we are one.* They looked into each other's eyes, and Sofia instantly felt the click. Then they heard. *Are you ready to jump on your mission?*

They both responded out loud. "Yes. We are ready."

Etienne asked, "Ready for what? Because I'm ready to party even in the dark." He lit candles, turned on his phone, and played music.

Everyone cheered and wished each other a Happy New Year. When Lola and Emma came by Sofia's side, they whispered, "We need to talk about all of this tomorrow."

Sofia wrapped her arms around them. "Yes. I wasn't expecting this at all, but it feels right. Right?"

They squeezed her and shrieked, "Right!"

Etienne joined in the huddle because he couldn't help himself. "What are we celebrating?"

They looked at him curiously, and Emma asked, "Are you serious?"

He batted his eyelids and apologized. "Yes, yes. The proposal."

Etienne clumsily hugged Sofia and whispered modest congratulations.

Lola was quick to remark. "That's it? As her bodyguard and friend, I expect much more from you."

He camouflaged his reserve by wrapping his arms tighter around Sofia. "Is that better?"

The girls favorably responded while laughing. Meanwhile, Etienne and Sofia caught Jude watching their interaction across the way. He immediately released himself from the embrace and directed his attention to Emma and Lola.

A FaceTime call came in from Jude's mother. Lennon picked up, but it was too loud for her to hear. She was upset at him for not caring.

Michel nervously told Lennon to go into the next room. "Don't upset your mother. Go, go." Then he signaled to Jude to go and talk to her, too. Jude rolled his eyes and nodded but remained seated.

Lennon came back with a worried face. He beckoned Jude to join him. Whatever he was telling Jude was getting him very antsy. But, at one point, Jude laughed out loud. Michel asked Etienne to lower the music and asked his boys what was happening.

Jude bellowed, "Lennon just told Coco that I was getting married." He raised his eyes in disbelief. "And guess what she asked—with Gabrielle?" Sofia felt the seething rage building up inside him. A visible vein throbbed in his neck. Everyone fell silent. He looked over at his dad. "How you expect us to be kind to this woman is beyond me. I am letting you know, and everyone else here, I am done with her antics. I am done with her. If she comes between me and the love of my life, she will play no role in my life, nor will she play one in my brother's. Do you understand, Michel?"

Sofia was not going to calm her dragon down. Instead, she stood by him as the phoenix she was and let him assert himself; no more allowing anyone to dim their light.

Michel bit down on his lip and nodded. Silence ensued until he said, "I am with you, my sons. I have always chosen you over her and will do so if that is what you want. You are my whole life."

Sofia pushed Jude to go to his father, and he did. She also pointed to Lennon and Etienne. They also obliged the quiet command. She played the music and tried to pick up where they had left off.

The lights never came on for the rest of the night, but it didn't stop Michel from keeping the party going, even with the minor hiccup. Everyone disclosed what they were looking forward to in the New Year.

Everyone ate their desserts. Everyone drank their champagne. Everyone talked. Some danced. Some sang. Some laughed.

While they reveled in the dark, Sofia looked into the Parisian night and wondered if this blackout was a telltale sign of what was to come for the New Year. Jude snaked his arm around her and whispered, "We are the light, remember? We will shine no matter how dark the darkness gets. I promised to be your protector, and I will. They will have to slay me first before they come between me and my phoenix."

YOU ARE ME

The one true light is YOU.

32

Sofia pulled up her socks and zipped up her hoodie before burying herself under the knitted blanket she found in Yolande's wooden chest by the door. As she rocked back and forth on the chair, flashes of the night before fluttered in her mind. She twirled the ring round and round on her finger as she inwardly spoke to her mother. *I wish you were here to be part of this union.*

She felt a cold breeze swoosh in. *I am here. I've always been by your side, my child,* said the voice in her head.

A lone tear escaped and rolled down her cheek. As she exchanged words with her mother, she realized she hadn't called her family. Immediately, she hopped on the phone with her dad, who was always an early riser. He was adamant about meeting the young man and asked them to visit him when she had time. He spoke of his garden and villa—the lemon tree was doing exceptionally well that year, but the fig tree not so much. His daily walks along the sea were still a part of his routine. Sofia's dad lived on a schedule, unlike her and her mother—but she was happy if he was happy. She dearly missed him.

It was a perfect time as well to call her brother. There was never a "right" time to call him. They were busy with work, the kids, or an adventure.

"Well, hello, sis," he answered in his Kiwi/Canadian twang. Sofia's heart melted at the sound of Gianluca's voice. It had been too long. He was, in fact, on his way to climb a mountain for sunset. She relayed the good news. Gianluca warmly conveyed his congratulations. "Next time you FaceTime, please put him on so I can personally congratulate him," he chuckled, "and warn him about you!" He continued to tease her as any younger brother would. "I guess he knows you're crazy if he's marrying you. But, I need to see with my own eyes the man who has agreed to take you on." They chit-chatted about his kids and his wife. They rarely spoke of her channel, until he said, "My oldest, Stella, is addicted to your videos." He paused. "Honestly, I was hesitant for her to watch, but she does it anyway. She's a bit like you." They shared a laugh. Sofia hadn't had much time to spend with his family but rejoiced, knowing there was another rebel in the family.

The sun was peeking out of the clouds. Dampness settled further into her bones. She dared not remove the blanket, so she snuggled deeper into the woolen wonder. Once she found her safe space, she basked in the alone time and the quiet of the city streets, post-mayhem. She hadn't checked her emails or social media messages in a few days and did so to her discontent. Gabrielle bombarded her with endless messages of hate and hostility. She couldn't help but feel the knots in her stomach tighten, even though Jude advised her not to let it seep into her heart. She tried hard to calm her mind, but Jude was already in her head. *It takes a lot of practice. Don't blame yourself, my love. You have every right to feel angry right now. Let it flow through you like you tell all of us. Where are you, by the way?*

I'm back in Canada—that's where I am. Can you bring me an extra blanket when you come down, please?

There was something about the weight of wool blankets in Europe that far outweighed the blankets back home. As he lay it down and tucked it around her, gone was the chill of winter; gone was the aggravation too. Instead, she took pleasure in the heat. "Why is it so warm?"

"I put it on the radiator to be extra toasty for you." Jude loomed over her. "Are you gonna scooch over and let me sit next to you?"

"I love you, but I'm not moving." She grinned.

He shook his head but still found his way under the blanket. She welcomed the additional warmth. As they lay swaddled in the wool bundle, she asked him, "How did you pull this proposal off without me listening in?"

Jude's eyes twinkled. "I learned a trick from this girl that does videos. She mentioned we could cloak ourselves to avoid people listening in or sponging off our energies. I'm not sure if you are familiar with her work." He poked her.

Sofia smirked. "Well done. I had no idea at all."

Jude grazed his fingers along her face. "That's why I needed to do it quickly. It was easier when you were not around me." He kissed her lightly on the arm. "It's over now. We will hear our thoughts no matter what. But I don't mind; I have nothing to hide from you anymore."

Sofia thought long and hard about that. "I'm not sure I always want you in my head. You may have a change of heart." She giggled but, deep down, was serious. Had she been candid about everything with Jude? *This is unequivocally another test of divine oneness.*

Their serenity fell short when they felt someone sit on top of them. Jude rolled his eyes and tried to push Etienne off the chair.

"I didn't remember Yolande's chair to be so bumpy!" Etienne yawned loudly, saying, "Come on, lovers, let's eat. I'm hungry."

Sofia resurfaced from her haven and gently slapped his head. "Is this how you treat your injured friend?"

He rocketed out of the chair and apologized profusely. Sofia made her way out of the blanket, draped her arm around him, and mumbled, "I'm just teasing."

Etienne blushed. "Okay. Still, sometimes I have no sense. Come, join me in the kitchen."

As they entered the kitchen, the table was brimming with food, drinks, and flowers. Yolande stood behind her handiwork with arms wide open. "Come here, my beautiful lights. Congratulations."

Sofia turned to Jude. "You didn't see her when you came downstairs?"

Jude shook his head. "I mean, I smelled some goodness and assumed she was here. But I didn't expect this wonderful spread with all my favorite things—croissants with almond paste, her homemade apricot and raspberry jam, and creamy cheeses from her farm."

Yolande smiled. "I also made some homemade bread with spicy chocolate and basil. A little bird told me these are both your favorite flavors. In truth, it's savory. I will add this to my menu."

Sofia thanked her profusely. Yolande shooed her away. "It's my pleasure, my dear. You are family now. Why don't you go call your friends."

Sofia nodded and went upstairs, but Etienne ran past her and advised her to wake up Lola first. Sofia made a face and understood right away. She went to wake up Emma first, but she wasn't in her room. "Oh, where might Emma be, Etienne?" She giggled.

She let him be and went to wake Lola. Inside Lola's room, she whispered in her ear, "Wakey, wakey. Guess who slept with Etienne last night?"

Lola shot up. "You did?"

Sofia winced. "No! Why would you say that?"

Lola lay back down. "Oh, Emma. Yeah, I figured. She drank too much last night, even more than me."

"Come, wash up. Yolande prepared us a delicious breakfast." She kissed her on the cheek and went back downstairs, not before peeking into Etienne's room and waving at Emma. "Come down. We're eating." Her friend's cheeks flushed a rosy pink shade while nodding.

Why would Lola think I would sleep with Etienne? How can she even think that?

It's not what you give off. It's the energy he gives off.

Sofia peered at Jude as she walked into the kitchen. He pointed to the side of his head. Sofia smirked. From now on, she would have to take her advice and do some cloaking.

They feasted like kings and queens and everything in between.

33

Sofia slipped away from the rowdy bunch to gather her thoughts and prepare for a "live." She would do a Q&A; that way, no material was necessary. She prepped her face to look half decent and jumped on an impromptu session. In less than five minutes, there were over five hundred viewers. She talked about her spur-of-the-moment jaunt to Paris. And then answered questions about the new earth, timelines, dreams, and current events. As the chat rolled, she saw Stella, her niece, pop on, so she did a shout-out to her. Jude walked in mid-way, and she invited him on screen. Sofia introduced him to her viewers. The heartwarming comments poured in: "You make such a gorgeous couple,"— "You look so happy," and "Relationship goals."

Sofia chuckled to herself when she read: "I told you he would look good on your video, girrrrlll." - TrinityLovesHerself369

Then Gabrielle showed up on the chat, discrediting the twin flames. It was a rare occasion that Sofia involved herself in the drama that ensued in the chat, but today was different. She would not sit back and allow Gabrielle to interrupt the flow. She handed the reins over to Jude, knowing he had the insight her followers would appreciate. Then she called Gabrielle out in front of the now 4400 viewers, "Hey everyone! There is a newcomer on the chat today. Let's give a shout-out to Life with Gaby. It seems she hasn't watched last week's video about mirror work. Also, you all know how I feel about haters. If she continues to shoot me and my fiancé down, I will block her."

Her keen followers chimed in. "What do you mean fiancé?"—"Are you getting married to that handsome man?"—"Congratulations!" The messages flooded in.

And so began the tirade of messages on Jude's phone as well. He shut his phone. Meanwhile, Sofia mouthed an apology to Jude for announcing it to the world.

He did one better and kissed her on the live, knowing Gabrielle was watching. He added, "I love this woman as much as she loves every single one of you. And that's a lot. You must know that!"

The chat box exploded with an outpouring of love. They continued the "live" together as a couple for the next three hours. The viewers didn't drop off but grew. She invited people online to ask questions. Sofia was in her element. Jude was in his, as well. When she ended her "live," it was hard to leave her online family. She promised another one in the coming days. "I'll do another Q&A, so get your questions ready. I truly do love all of you. Keep sending me questions in the comments; I'll try to answer as many as possible. But, you can understand that I prefer to spend some alone time with my man." She winked at them and blew them a kiss. The "live" ended.

On a high, they fell on the bed. "My fiancé. Where did that come from?" In one fell swoop, they were both undressed and entwined as one.

He shuddered her mind. He caressed her body. He kissed her soul.

****

Jude dropped Sofia, Lola, and Emma off in the Le Marais district so they could wander the streets of Paris as tourists. As much as she loved spending every waking hour with her man, she also craved some girl time.

That district drew them in because of its multiculturalism and the vast array of restaurants. It was also one of the districts jam-packed with art and history museums. Lola loved the amalgamation of people. Sofia loved the architecture. Emma loved the unique shops. The streets were rather barren, being New Year's Day. Most of the quaint stores and restaurants were closed, but that didn't stop them from exploring the neighborhood.

As they roamed the ancient pathways, Lola asked Sofia, "Now, with all the wisdom you have gathered over the years, do you see these monuments differently?"

"Yeah, I guess," Sofia replied with a nonchalant shrug of her shoulders.

"What kind of answer is that?" Lola lightly tapped her on the arm.

"I mean," Sofia replied, a hint of self-awareness in her tone. "It's like I catch myself rambling on, and I wonder if I'm just trying to prove something. Sometimes, I just want to be a part of the conversation without feeling like I need to have all the answers." She mused, "Besides, who am I to really know everything?"

Emma interjected with a mischievous grin, adding. "Yeah, she's got a point. Sometimes it's like, 'Okay, Professor, enough with the lecture.' It can be annoying."

And that was that.

Sofia felt a genuine connection to Emma's straightforwardness, her words striking a chord deep within. Rather than taking offense, she found herself appreciating her friend''s candidness.

The friends continued their stroll through the neighborhood, arm in arm in sweet contemplation.

You are not annoying to me, said the voice in her head.

Jude, you're just saying that because you're my boyfriend!

Your boyfriend? What happened to fiancé? She could actually hear him chuckle. He continued his message. *People will always find you annoying because you're not like them. Embrace it, mon amour.*

Alright, thanks for the pep talk but can you please stay out of my head until we see each other? Or else, I'll come into yours!

Okay, my little phoenix. I'll leave you alone. Just wanted to tap in and remind you how much I love you.

Sofia blushed and answered out loud, "I love you, too."

She caught the girls staring at her. "Are you doing the telepathic thing with him?" Lola clapped her hands. "It's kind of exciting, no?"

She filled them in when she first heard his thoughts in New York City. Lola grabbed her hand and pulled her to the nearest bench. They sat and bombarded her with questions. Sofia answered what she could.

"Mind blown, my friend. Absolutely mind blown," Lola repeated over and over again.

"And why didn't—" Emma started.

"Don't even dare ask her that question." Lola shut her down quickly.

"Why are you always defending Sofia? Why are you two always against me?"

Sofia held Lola back, who looked ready to give Emma a piece of her mind. Instead, Sofia reached out to Emma and wrapped her in her arms. Emma crumbled into her embrace, and she shed tears. Wiping her face with the cuff of her sweater, she turned to face Lola. "I need to be upfront with you." And she confessed all of her pent-up emotions with Lola. The exchange was a long and arduous one for Emma, filled with tears, long pauses and moments of introspection.

She also admitted to Sofia that she was jealous of her relationship with Jude and hated feeling that way. "I know my sadness stems way before Jude. I'm just disappointed in myself for allowing people to make decisions for me, for not standing up to my ex-boyfriends, and for living surface-level instead of diving deep into my emotions, as both of you do. I'm just not cut that way. But I'm trying to be a better person. Really, I am." And that was all that one could ask from their friend—acknowledgment and reparation.

The trio sat together in a moment of shared silence.

Then, Sofia exchanged a meaningful glance with Lola and turned to Emma. "You said you want to be upfront, so why are you not discussing last night with us?"

Lola lightheartedly interjected, "Seriously Emma, we're practically on the edge of our seats here. Spill the beans, already!"

Emma blushed. "Well, nothing happened. But, he's a damn good kisser, I tell you!"

The girls giggled. "Do tell us more," Lola said.

Emma timidly talked about her night. "He was a gentleman."

"Really?" Sofia asked. "I would have imagined him to be wild and crazy like he is in his normal."

"I think he's like that, but he seemed preoccupied most of the night. Then he confessed that he reserved his heart for someone else, so he couldn't go through with it, which I found sweet, in a way. We kissed and frolicked, but nothing more than that."

Lola arched her eyebrows and glanced at Sofia, but she remained silent for fear of Jude listening in again.

"And how do you feel about it today?" Sofia asked.

"Good. I think I'm ready to move on from the bad boys. I think it's time I work on myself, so no men for now."

It was the best thing she had said in a long time. Lola chuckled. "I wonder how long that will last."

"I'll prove you wrong. Let's bet on it. I'll stay without a man for the next six months, no, four, um, three months." They all laughed.

"You're so keen on laughing about my 'man' situation. Why don't you tell us about you and Seb, Lola?"

Lola smirked. "I deserve that. Okay. Uhm, nothing much is happening—we are taking it slowly. I'm still on the fence about giving up my career." She raised her hand and said, "Before you get all preachy on me that I can keep my job, blah blah." She shifted in her seat and gazed at them. "If I bring children into this world, I want to spend every moment with them. So, that's where I'm at right now." She leaned back.

They dove deeper into that one, laying out all the possibilities. Sofia never had the opportunity of having children of her own and would have loved to have had a chance at being part of a little human's life. She had very little connection with her nieces in New Zealand, which always saddened her. Alas, she believed in the Divine plan and knew that it was all for the greater good.

Changing the conversation, Lola reached over and patted Sofia on the arm. "Oh, I've meant to ask you since we got here. What was that zing that you laid on Gabrielle on YouTube today? Aren't you afraid that she's going to retaliate again? We were surprised Jude went along with it."

"Jude and I have decided to go up against the beast together. Come what may, we are in it as a team. I believe we need to bring down the master first."

Lola and Emma rolled their eyes and said in unison, "His mother."

"I'm surprised he allowed you out of his sight right now," Emma said.

Sofia made a face. "Well, I'm an adult and have you guys for protection. Today she's visiting with her parents, and we have one free day without her crazy."

They huddled closer together and observed the locals shuffle around in the snow-less wonderland.

Emma interrupted the quiet contemplation. "I also have something to ask you, Sof. I noticed one of the symbols on Jude's finger fading. Isn't it the same one that he made the pendant with? Isn't that strange? Do you know what it symbolizes?"

Emma's quality of observing things didn't surprise Sofia. "I noticed that a few days ago. I thought it odd, too. But to tell you the truth, this time in Paris has been odd, so nothing surprises me anymore."

Their conversations jumped from one topic to another. They laughed. They cried. They antagonized. It was what made their friendship so solid and so long-lasting. They touched on their future plans. Lola and Emma were leaving the next day to go to Marseilles for a private interior design show. Lola mentioned leaving earlier than planned because she wanted to travel to Spain and Italy.

"No matter where we are in the world, my dear friends, our bond will remain forever and a day."

****

For Lola and Emma's last night in town, Michel invited everyone for a casual dinner. He was not waiting for them in front of the elevator or bustling in the kitchen. Nope. Instead, hunched over his work table, he toiled over a science experiment. Etienne and Lennon were in charge of dinner. But neither was in the kitchen.

When the elevator door opened to Guillaume and another younger man holding boxes and bags from the bistro, Michel swiveled his chair toward Etienne and Lennon and shook his head. "You are something else, you two." He then waved them over to help with the packages. Michel greeted Guillaume and invited him to stay for supper.

"*Merci, mon ami* (thank you, my friend), but I can't stay away from my baby. You know that!" Guillaume turned to the newly engaged couple and said. "I hear congratulations are in order."

News travels fast. Sofia thought.

You have no idea. Paris is a small village in a big city.

Guillaume buoyantly hugged both of them. "From the moment you walked into the restaurant, I knew you would become part of this family. God knows they need a positive female figure in this house."

Jude glared at his father and vigorously nodded his head. Michel avoided his son's eyes and agreed with his longtime friend.

Guillaume's phone rang, and he shouted to whoever was on the other line. He bitched under his breath and grumbled, "Duty calls. This is why I can never step outside my restaurant."

He summoned his assistant and waved everyone goodbye. But, then swiveled back around and said, "Oh, Michel, I almost forgot. Thierry dropped this off a few nights ago." He reached into his leather satchel, slung over his shoulder, and handed a book to him. "He was closing his bookshop for a month and figured I would see one of the boys before returning from his vacation. *Et voilà!*" He promptly disappeared into the elevator.

Michel then entrusted it to Sofia. He cupped her hands and said, "This is the book I was talking to you about. Thierry is a longtime friend who happens to be a serious book collector. I trusted him with some of the symbols. I would love to flip through the book alongside you, if possible?"

Sofia clutched the book in her hands, staring at it in awe. "Of course! Let's look at it later or tomorrow when there are fewer humans." She giggled.

Jude pulled it out of her hands and asked, "May I? I'm curious about this tattoo that keeps fading. Maybe we can find out what it is."

He flipped through the pages but to no avail. Sofia did spot one of them they hadn't found yet. It was the one that most resembled fire, and it represented freedom.

Sofia whispered, "I like the sound of that."

Lennon summoned them into the dining room. Jude shut the book and placed it on his father's table. "Three more to go."

Jude and Sofia walked into the four of them, screaming, "Surprise!" Metallic gold balloons crammed the ceiling and the floor. A gold hand-painted banner hung along the window panes—it said, "Wishing you many more lifetimes of happiness!" Equally surprised, Michel called over his boys and hugged them. "You are the best pains in the asses any father could have."

Etienne ushered them in. "We didn't get to celebrate with you last night. So since the girls were leaving, we wanted to honor your upcoming union."

The gold-colored cutlery, plates, and goblets on the table glimmered brilliantly. Sofia mouthed a thank you to Lola and Emma for contributing to the overall styling.

Jude already greeted his brothers and hugged the girls.

They ate the food. They drank the cocktails (and mocktails). The laughter was endless.

Jude leaned in closer to Sofia and whispered, "You know all this is for you. You are the saving grace of this family."

She gently pushed him. "But you are the glue, my dragon." She poked him on the nose, "And don't you forget it."

He growled and bit her finger. And then comments from the peanut gallery came rolling in. "We eat at a table; we don't always kiss," Etienne snickered. Jude's response was to kiss Sofia so amorously even she pulled away. She noticed Jude and Etienne share a mutual glare.

No, no, no. I don't want to come between you two. I will not have it, do you hear me, Jude?!!! Sofia screamed in her mind.

Michel immediately sensed the discord and quickly veered the conversation to a story about him and Guillaume from the past.

She continued berating Jude in her mind. *He's your best friend and brother. He would never go against you. It's just a silly crush. You know, it will pass.*

He remained silent. Instead, he got out of his chair and pointed to Etienne. "Let's go. We need to talk."

Sofia implored him to be kind. *I will listen if I have to.*

Jude bent down and whispered, "Relax. I've known him longer than you. I know how to talk to him." He pecked her on the cheek, then left with Etienne to the other room.

Lennon, meanwhile, was oblivious to everything. "What's going on? Is there another part of the surprise?"

They continued eating and talking. Lola launched into story time with her colorful yarns of travel. Emma joined in as well with stories of clients. The night rhythmically flowed, despite Jude reprimanding Etienne in the other room. Sofia overheard Jude say. *You are soul mates. I know that for a fact. I heard it from her thoughts, like how she's listening to me right now.*

"Sofia!" he screamed from the other room.

She mischievously smiled. Michel asked, "You're listening in? So what are they saying?"

"I can't make out anything.." She fibbed, lifting her hands, and laughed some more.

She tuned him out and veered her attention to Lennon. He was a bright spot in this family—so lightweight and funny. He ranted about a new girl he was interested in and how she always teased him, never giving him an opening or confirmation. So he asked the three women at the table how to handle it. He received three different answers. With a confused look, he turned to his dad. "Is it always like this with women? They just made my life more complicated."

"Women are to be loved, not to be understood," Etienne directed an Oscar Wilde quote to Lennon. He was in good spirits when they strolled back into the room.

Jude glided beside her. "Sneaky. Sneaky. Did you hear everything?"

"No. Only that bit, and then I switched it off. You can tell me later if you want." She raked her fingers through his longish hair.

When she glanced over at Etienne, he gave her a big smile and winked at her. The divine masculine was set back in balance.

Sofia cleared her throat and tried to get the attention of the table. "So, now that all is settled, I need your input. I worked on a video on The Art of War a few months back. I'm sure most of you are familiar with it."

"Uhm, no…is it a video game?" Lennon asked.

Jude almost spat out the water he was drinking.

"I guess not," Lennon mumbled.

"Yoo hoo, Professor!" Emma waved at Sofia from the other end of the table. "Please regale us all with a lengthy explanation."

Both Lola and Sofia's eyes sparkled with amusement as their friend playfully put Sofia on the spot again.

She raised an eyebrow, feigning seriousness and spoke in a most scholarly way, "It's a timeless masterpiece written in the 5th century by a famous Chinese military strategist, Sun Tzu." Her tone became more relaxed as she continued, "I've been thinking a lot about it lately for a certain situation in our life. It's about how to win a war without fighting head-on. Instead, we play their game but at a higher frequency and use that energy on the attack, so they, in turn, use it against themselves."

Jude leaned back in his chair and fanned his hands behind his head. "I know where you are going with this. I don't think I like it."

"I think I do," Etienne said.

Lola also concurred, adding, "If anyone could play at their game, it's you, Sofia, and with Jude's help, you could win the war."

Lennon felt lost. "What are you guys talking about?" He got up. "I'm going to get some more drinks. I think we need to be less serious at this table."

Michel waited for Lennon to leave the room and then inquired, "Are you guys talking about Gabrielle?"

Sofia affirmed but added, "And your wife."

They eyed Michel for his reaction. He wasn't shocked. He wasn't upset. Instead, he nodded. "*Fais ce que tu dois faire.* (Do what you have to do). I trust you both will do what is necessary." He eyed Jude and said, "Let's keep Lennon out of this as much as possible. Because we know he would gladly join in, but for now, let's be discreet."

Jude agreed but told him he would do so when it came time to fill him in. "There's nothing more dishonorable than to be left out of a plan that involves you."

Lennon strolled back in. "What plan?"

Etienne patted him on the shoulder and reverted the conversation by joking. "The plan to lock you up in your boarding school and throw away the key."

Lennon whipped his head toward Sofia. "Did you tell them?"

"No. I haven't said a word, Lennon."

Jude leaned forward and asked, "What do you need to tell us, Lennon…and Sofia?"

Sofia wasn't going to lie. Jude would hear and feel her vibration lower, anyway. "Lennon, you promised you would tell him today, or I was going to do it, so now is as good a time as any."

"We can leave if you want," Emma said, slowly rising from the chair.

Lennon looked defeated. "No. It's okay. Stay. You're family now." He finally disclosed the story about the boarding school and his mother's reaction, or lack thereof.

The dragon beside Sofia was slowly erupting—she felt the flames rising in his soul. She interlocked her fingers into his. "Let him talk. It's hard for him to tell you this."

Etienne bolted from his chair and swore. Michel fidgeted in his seat and buried his face in his hands. Lola and Emma motioned to Sofia and left the room. Sofia got up from her seat and sat by Lennon. "It feels better, right? We'll take care of this for you. This is a little part of the Art of War we discussed."

He nodded and pointed to Jude. "Cool. But I don't think he's taking this very well."

Sofia returned to Jude, kneeled by his chair, and said, "Look in my eyes." He was too furious, so she gently grabbed his chin and forced him to look at her.

"Who are we?" She didn't wait for a response. "We are lightworkers. And how long have we been on this planet? Millions of years."

A slight crack in his ire evaporated.

"That's right, so whatever we need to do, we will do together." She pointed to the others. "With their help, as well. We have been through way worse than this in our lifetimes. And together, we are better, right?

"Lennon was looking for the right time to tell you. And is there a right time? No. We cannot undo what has been done. We can only meet her where she's at and overtake her."

A wave of calm settled in him, his eyes glistening with approval. He caressed the side of her face. "We will fight the right way." He looked up at his dad. "Are you ready to face the beast, Papa?"

Michel slanted his head to the left and stroked his chin for several seconds before replying. "I'm ready."

"Can we, like, call ourselves something?" Lennon asked, a youthful energy beaming with excitement. "Like, Four Dragons and One Phoenix?"

He managed to calm the nerves of everyone at the table. Jude got up from his chair, approached his brother, and apologized for his mother's behavior. "Next time, you tell Papa or me right away. No more being courageous. We need to stick together. Okay?" He hugged him.

Etienne hollered, "Definitely not a boring family, right, Sofia?"

Michel invited everyone to the main room. "On that note, let's go have leftover dessert to celebrate our eccentric family."

Jude kept Sofia behind while the others entered the dining area. He shut the door and cradled her in his arms. Jude didn't say a word. He didn't need to. She felt him and heard him. *We're taking on the beast for real, my love. We need to be strategic, strong, and heartless. Are you truly ready for this?*

I'm ready, and I already have my first play. But we can talk about strategy tomorrow. Let's eat and enjoy this last night with my friends, please.

He smiled, pulled her closer, and longingly kissed her. The energetic currents surged through their bodies, and those butterflies came out to play.

ART OF WAR

THE PLAN

Deception is the name of the game.

34

Bundled in layers of clothes, Sofia settled onto the bench, her gaze fixed upon the oddest tombstone. Jude selected the spot in the Père Lachaise cemetery—he always loved the sculpture of a man lying down holding the face of his beloved (with a tear dripping from her eye). Sofia had never heard of the French actor Fernand Arbelot, but the more she stared at the work of art, the more it felt ominous. Alas, the macabre setting was probably the best place to meet her archenemy.

Jude remained hidden behind the countless tombstones close by. Etienne was on call in a car just outside the gates. Sofia kept her thoughts uncloaked in case of any aggression. They spent the entirety of one day and night devising the perfect game plan with Etienne and Michel's help, too.

They had to consider every angle, every consequence, and every reaction.

This is it. The target is approaching, Sofia said to Jude.

Jude replied laughingly, *The target? I'm glad you are taking this seriously, though. Be careful, mon amour.*

Offset against the gray tombstones and drabness of winter, Gabrielle stood out in her head-to-toe blood-red outfit, and with her flowing red hair, she was a devil "not" in disguise. As she sashayed over, she surveyed the area.

"Jude is not here. It's just you and me."

Gabrielle narrowed her eyes and stood in front of Sofia with crossed arms. "What is the meaning of this?"

Sofia motioned for her to sit on the bench. "I want to talk to you, woman to woman. I feel like we have a lot in common. For one, we have the same taste in men."

Gabrielle gritted her teeth. She huffed and puffed for a few seconds but eventually sat, glaring at Sofia. Knowing her twin flame was near fueled Sofia with the power she needed to go against this woman.

Even when Gabrielle stretched her arm along the bench and lightly grazed Sofia's back, Sofia did not flinch. With her other hand, she calculatingly tapped her mouth as if to warn Sofia of her next move, but

Sofia smiled and continued to reassure her she was not here as an aggressor.

When Gabrielle fake lurched toward her, Sofia did not recoil.

Jude's cautionary voice echoed in her head. But then subdued when he witnessed his girlfriend react like the phoenix she was.

"Why is it that you trust me now?" Gabrielle screeched.

"I don't. If you want to kill me, it's a perfect place to do it. That way, my friends won't have to run around too much." She played with fire by smirking at her enemy.

Gabrielle pursed her lips together, holding back her laughter. Sofia playfully winked at her.

For a moment, Gabrielle's demeanor slackened. But it didn't take long for her to revert to her spiteful disposition. "So that you know, just because you are being nice to me doesn't mean I'm not going to try to win Jude back from your clutches."

"I know. I'm not here to change your opinion or your tactics. I'm here to get to know you. I only know you from what Jude has told me."

Gabrielle's eyes twinkled at the mention of his name. Looking unsure how to react, she asked, "So, what do you want to know?"

Jude rang in, *And she took the bait. Good going, my love.*

Sofia asked her about her childhood and her friendship with Jude.

"Why do you want to know this? Are you recording this?"

They knew Gabrielle was clever when devising this plan, so Sofia provided the correct answers. "I have nothing on me, not even my phone." She got up, unwrapped herself from the warmth, emptied her pockets, and even showed her ears for any devices.

"So, you just want to get to know me, for me?"

"Pretty much. To be honest, I get your devotion to Jude. He is a good man with a good heart. And from what I've heard, you had a rough childhood, so I want to understand better why you would be so adamant about hurting me." She continued, "And why do you think hurting me would make Jude love you? I don't quite understand that line of thinking."

Jude was having a field day in her head. *Burn!!!!*

Gabrielle appeared irked by her frankness. She stared at the tombstone, contorting her face at the morbid statue. She then turned to glare at her. "How else am I going to win him over? He doesn't answer my calls or want to see me. I need to catch his attention somehow." And from gentle, she swiftly switched to menacing, "You're just his *plat du jour (menu of the day)*, so I will just wait for the next time he is free of you." Briefly pausing, she mumbled, "She told me I would be his one day, and I'll wait. I'll do whatever it takes."

Wow, Jude, you are so right about your mother.

Gabrielle's perfectly manicured fingers peeled paint off the arm of the bench. Sofia sent her waves of calming energy and reverted to asking Gabrielle about her childhood with Jude.

She vaulted from the bench, flicking paint chips off her clothes like bugs crawling all over her.

Be careful, my love. She's not all there.

Gabrielle composed herself and gracefully sat back down. She dipped her head and leered into Sofia's eyes. "Jude was my savior. I had a horrible relationship with my mother. She didn't know how to love me and my father; he didn't know how to either, but Jude did. He knew how to love me. Jude took care of me like no other. Like, he's probably doing for you. But, it's all a show for you."

Don't get influenced by her nonsense.

Sofia tried hard to suppress the pangs of jealousy springing up. She weathered through them like a champ, listening to Gabrielle talk about him as her gladiator. She incessantly talked about how Jude would hold her every time she cried and defended her against the bullies in school. And how he kissed her when she felt terrible. It was torturous to listen to, but Sofia did it for the sake of the plan.

Gabrielle touched on the fact that she suffered from abandonment issues throughout adulthood. "I don't know if Jude told you, but he and I went to university together. It was one of the best months of my life. Jude was my friend, and I abandoned him then, so I need to make things right."

"By stalking him and violently injuring his girlfriend every time you see her?"

Gabrielle jerked her head forward, eyes narrowed. "Why do you keep calling yourself his girlfriend? You know he's mine. I'm allowing this time to pass; it will be him and me forever." Gabrielle leaned into Sofia's face. "You're nothing."

Sofia backed away from her, twisted her head, and rolled her eyes away from Gabrielle's line of vision. "Yes, okay, I'm-I'm nothing."

You're doing great, my love.

That's all it took for Gabrielle to calm down. She sat once more and stretched her long, scarlet legs. She reflected upon her time as a late teenager into her 20s as forgettable moments. "I hardly remember any of that time. I was so drugged up. It was all a blur. If I hadn't rejected him, Jude would still be in my life." She angled her head and peered into

Sofia's eyes. "I can see why you want to defend your position with him, but I've known him longer than you, and I deserve to be with him, not you."

"I understand. But our interactions don't have to be so uncivilized in the future. Instead of being agitated the next time you see me, let's talk it through like normal people. What do you say?"

Gabrielle grinned. "Well, why don't you stop being friends with him? It will make our life easier."

Tread slowly, Sofia. Don't agitate her.

Sofia chose to be honest. "I can't do that. I love Jude as much as you love him. I don't want to lie to you because I consider you an equal."

"Equal? In what sense?" Gabrielle looked confused.

"Well, Gabrielle, we are both women. We are both headstrong. We are both beautiful. We are both smart." She continued to flatter her ego. "We are both...well, you're more famous than me. And we both love the same man."

Gabrielle lifted her chin in a peacock pose and pondered Sofia's words. "Sometimes I wish I could find another man to fall for," she confessed. "I don't know why I feel compelled to stay with Jude."

Sofia listened intently.

"But then I'm reminded by...uhm...of how loving he was with me and that it's to my benefit to stay with him."

"Who reminds you? Coco reminds you?" Sofia overstepped her boundary, and she knew it.

Gabrielle bolted off the bench and scanned the area. "Why are you saying her name? Is she here? Does she know I'm talking to you?" She was panic-stricken.

I'm coming in closer. You've hit the nail on the head. Be careful, please.

"I'm sorry for bringing up her name. I'm sorry if it made you so frightened. Come, sit. I won't bring it up again."

Gabrielle regressed into a shrinking violet, in her case, a poppy. Sofia touched on a sore spot. She didn't want to lose her semi-trust, so she invited her back onto the bench. "I'd love to know more about your relationship with Jude."

Gabrielle slinked back on the bench and dreamily recited one of their childhood moments, building sandcastles on the beach.

Meanwhile, Jude was getting antsy. *Okay, I think it's enough. She's not very stable, as you can see. Let's end this, my love.*

Sofia graciously waited for her to finish her story, and when she did, Sofia softly said, "I think we did well today. Maybe we can meet again soon. What do you think?"

A wave of tenderness washed over Gabrielle's face, but something came over her, and she immediately metamorphosed into a demon. Beyond Sofia's better judgment, she stayed to help her through it. She sent her another wave of loving and compassionate energy. She enclosed Gabrielle in a bubble of light, much like Sofia cloaked herself in from the beginning of their chat.

End this, Sofia!

Out of nowhere, Sofia fell into a trance and began drawing out symbols toward Gabrielle, always sending her love. Gabrielle's diabolic energy subsided *tout de suite* (immediately), as they say in French.

"What was that all about? Are you a witch?"

Sofia came to and called in for backup because she was feeling extra vulnerable. But when she composed herself, she told Jude to stand down. *I will end this right now.*

"Aren't all women witches and shamans?" She gently placed her hand on Gabrielle's shoulder. "It's just a friend helping another friend. Does that happen to you often?"

Gabrielle, incredulously, calmed and lowered her head. "To tell you the truth, I don't even remember what happened. But, whatever you did hopefully helps with the severe headaches I suffer for days after. So, thank you."

Sofia nodded. "Hey, why don't we all go for coffee sometime?" Gabrielle curiously eyed her. When Sofia gave her the date, time, and place carefully pre-selected by Jude and Etienne, she most ardently accepted.

"So, I will see you in two weeks, then? Will Jude be there? This is for real?"

Sofia nodded. "Yes. How else can we fix this if we don't communicate like the adults we are? We're friends now, right?"

Gabrielle's gaze bore into Sofia's. "Right." And she leaned in to hug Sofia.

Jude was not having it and warned Sofia that he would intrude on the love fest if she didn't finalize the meeting and walk away.

Gabrielle walked away but kept returning to wave or check if Jude would appear. All the same, Sofia remained until confirmation came in that she was outside of the gates. Without hesitation, Sofia darted behind one of the tombstones and into the arms of her dragon.

WAGING WAR

Treat the wrongdoers well.
The trap will set itself up on its own.

35

Jude's motivation for victory outweighed his apprehension as he walked to the café. The soldiers were positioned and ready: Etienne sat across from them in a nearby café. Michel waited in the car near the meetup point while Lennon stayed home for now.

That morning was a temperamental one for both Jude and Sofia. More so for Jude. He was coming face-to-face with his stalker and had to play nice. He tossed and turned the whole night. Sofia tried to work her healing magic on him, but he was on a rollercoaster of emotions. She spent most of the night holding him and reassuring him that they had diligently strategized this part of the plan. They had spent weeks on it after coming up with the initial scheme. It was a fail-safe plan, especially since Coco had already taken the bait.

Jude's mother found out soon after their meeting and came in hot. She called Jude, demanding to speak to Sofia. She was livid. "Your girlfriend has no place in our lives!! How dare you lower the family's status with a nobody like her. Gabrielle may have failed for now, but we will soon remove your beloved wife-to-be."

Jude played his role very well. He didn't cuss her out as he usually would. He didn't even hang up on her. Instead, he listened and recorded every word. Coco didn't take long to return to her doting mother role. "I'm doing all this for your future, my son. It's all for you. You will thank me one day.".

Gabrielle was already seated at a table for two. The weather was warmer than usual. Her flowing hair was billowing in the wind. Impeccably dressed, she looked radiant and ready for war. As she posed for selfies with some fans, she spotted Sofia and Jude across the street and confidently waved at them. Sofia returned the wave.

We need to play the game, my love. I know you can do this. Think of the grand prize—no more stalking, no more mother, just me and you in Malta, Sofia said.

Jude tightened Sofia's hand and muttered, "That's the best thing I've heard all week. Yes, Malta."

They made their way through the jammed-in terrace. Jude picked up a chair along the way and placed it on the other side of Gabrielle. He sat in the one farthest from her, much to her dismay. He indifferently greeted her and faced the street.

You can do better than that. Remember, this is just a piece of theater. And we are the actors.

He consequently twisted his body and asked Gabrielle how she was doing.

She replied with enthusiasm and zeal. And when Sofia asked her a question, she rolled her eyes. "Can't you see, Sofia, I'm trying to talk to Jude?"

Jude was the one to come in now and sarcastically say, *Yeah, Sofia! She's one step past crazy, this one.*

Gabrielle went in for the kill. "Why don't you answer my calls or texts? Why are you always ignoring me? Why are you here? What's going on?"

Jude grumbled a little. "Do you think it's normal to call someone a hundred times daily?"

"Well, if you don't answer me after three times, yes."

Sofia inwardly laughed like a hyena.

Jude shook his head and replied, "Well, it's not." He pointed to Sofia. "You can see I'm in a…."

Sofia lightly kicked him under the table.

"A friendship with Sofia. And we're spending time here while she's in Paris, so why can't you back off for now?" He paused and leaned back in the chair. "If you were civil about things, we could be friends."

The waitress came to get their order. Gabrielle shooed her away. "I would like that. So when Sofia leaves, we can be friends again?"

"We can be friends with Sofia too. You've never had any good girlfriends before. Isn't that what you've always wanted, someone to confide in and do girl things with?"

He struck a nerve in her because, ultimately, Jude knew her the best. He knew where her soft spots were.

She longingly thought about it and replied, "Yes, that would be nice. But, first, me and you. And then she can join our friend group."

It was a laborious conversation. Gabrielle rehashed her life story to Jude. She talked continuously about her socialite life; she dropped famous people's names and elitist clubs. She droned on about her millions of followers and how much they adored her. "But I can drop it all for you, Jude. I will do it if you prefer to live as a pauper like her." She reverted to glaring at Sofia.

Jude placed his hand on Sofia's and grasped it before she could pull it away. Gabrielle stared daggers at the twin flames. "Listen carefully, Gabrielle. This pauper over here is my fiancé." He showed her Sofia's ring. "I will be marrying her one of these days. I want to be honest with you."

That statement unhinged her. Jude continued talking. "I have no intention of ever leaving Sofia's side, ever. She is the love of my life."

Sofia was confused by his approach but trusted him.

Jude released Sofia's hand and grabbed Gabrielle's. "Do you remember when we were in university?"

She instantly blushed and nodded like a child would.

"We had a nice friendship. Why can't we go back to that time? Why must we be a couple or nothing at all?" He freed his hand from hers.

Gabrielle faced the glowing sun and remained quiet for a few minutes. Jude side-eyed Sofia and told her, *I got this.*

"It's because of your mother," Gabrielle whispered. "She told me I had a chance. I should keep trying because that was the only way to get to you." She looked around fearfully and slanted her body towards him. "She said you would eventually cave because your heart was always bigger than your smarts."

Jude was swearing all kinds in his mind. But to Gabrielle, he responded ever so calmly, "Isn't it time you step back from that woman? Isn't it time you start living life on your own accord?" He looked over at Sofia and back at her. "We can help you if that's what you need."

A lone tear rolled down her cheek. "Why would you do that for me?"

Jude replied, "Because we are your friends, and that's what friends do."

Game on.

THE STRATEGY

Stand guard at the enemy's gate.
Attack when provoked.

36

As Jude and Sofia admired the fluffy white snow carpeted alongside the highway, she reminisced about winter back home. She described in detail her snowy adventures with her family. Jude listened attentively to every word. He never interrupted her and relished every moment.

When she was done, he softly kissed her on the lips. Since their plan took off, Jude had been more affectionate and more loving. He tried hard to stay calm while in the trenches with Gabrielle. Their goal was Malta; they needed to stay on course to achieve that.

They passed through a picturesque village with painted storefronts and narrow cobblestoned roads. It was a typical village found everywhere in Europe, but one Sofia dreamed of living in one day. The thought of living in a small community overlooking the pristine sea brought her the utmost joy.

Jude rang in. *I look forward to that too, my love. Soon, me and you and peace.*

Xavier pulled onto a long, winding, gravel road lined with sky-high wiry trees. When they reached imposing iron gates, he spoke into a speaker and announced the arrival of Jude for *Monsieur* (Mister) Lavigne. The gates opened to an immense estate. Snow powdered the landscape, but she imagined the green grass below was perfectly manicured, much like the garden of statues before them. The house was rectangular, with five shuttered windows at the top and more at the bottom. The white stone seemed to fade into the snowy backdrop. Nonetheless, its presence was known.

Etienne rolled down the window and winked at them. "Everything is going as planned. You guys are doing great. Xavier and I will head into the village. Just text us when you need us."

Unlike the pomposity of the exterior, the interior was more casual and contemporary in decor. As Jude and Sofia weaved through the high-end kitchen and around a study with shelves of books, the butler ushered them into the solarium at the back of the house.

There sat M. Lavigne on a chair with a blanket draped over his knees. He was leisurely smoking a pipe and staring outside. As soon as Jude walked in, he wearily got up from his seat.

Jude said, "*Pas de souci.* (No worries). Just stay where you are." He went over to him and shook his hand. "Pierre, I would like to introduce my fiancé, Sofia."

Pierre asked Jude to help him up to shake her hand properly. He hugged Jude, taking him by surprise. The stately man with sharp gray eyes motioned them to sit.

"You've turned out to be quite handsome, my son. Now I understand why your mother has always wanted to bring you and my Gabrielle together. So, what brings you here?"

"Speaking of mothers, is your wife not here today?"

He was surprised Coco hadn't informed him that his wife had passed away a few months ago. Jude and Sofia offered their condolences. He graciously accepted but spoke very frankly with them. "She was not a very easy woman to deal with. Since she's gone, the house staff is much calmer and more cheerful."

There's no bullshit with this man, Sofia relayed to Jude.

He went on. "We told Gabrielle, but she hasn't acknowledged it. Or maybe she has and doesn't care. I can't blame her. My wife was not a nurturing mother." He took a moment to survey the land outside and applauded a squirrel who jumped from one branch to the next. He returned to the conversation. "I tried my best with my daughter, but I failed. I didn't have much time when she was younger, and now, I fear, she is lost in her world."

Jude was about to say something but was interrupted by Pierre again. "And I have just become aware of your situation from my own sources. I must apologize for her persistence." He shifted his gaze to Sofia and said, "And apologies for your recent incident. I just don't understand why she is that way." Pierre was on a roll. It seemed he hadn't anyone to talk to. "Are you here because of Lennon? I've been waiting for you. I'm surprised it took you so long to come."

"What do you mean? What has he done?"

Pierre angled his body forward and looked fixedly into Jude's eyes before reclining back on his chair. He shook his head. "You have no idea. Your mother is one exceptional lady." He looked at both Jude and Sofia. "And I don't mean it nicely."

Jude was more than curious and urged him to disclose his information.

He let out a heavy sigh. "Well, it's better if it comes from me than your mother. She told me that she revealed the truth years ago."

While he stalled, Sofia and Jude were deep in discussion in their minds.

Whatever it is, Jude, we will face it together.

"Do you remember, Jude, when we shipped Gabrielle to the rehab for her drug problem?"

Jude nodded."It was like fifteen years ago."

Pierre cleared his throat. "More like sixteen years ago." He cocked his head forward.

Sofia clicked in right away. Pierre saw that she understood. They waited for Jude to click in, and he only did when he read Sofia's thoughts.

He jumped up from his seat and asked, "Is Lennon mine?"

Pierre nodded.

Jude clasped onto the back of a chair and swore under his breath.

Sofia quickly texted Etienne.

—Come now. You won't believe what Pierre revealed to Jude. Move your butt.—

A barrage of Jude's emotions discharged and filtered right through her. She didn't dare console him just yet. His temperament wavered as it hit all sides of the cyclone. They were in the eye of the storm, and not even Sofia could find her way to calm. She waited it out and called in for help from their higher selves. When she made it safely to the ground, her heart felt like it had just been stampeded. Now he was tied to Gabrielle, whether they played the game or not.

Once hearing her thought, Jude looked up and asked Pierre, "Does Gabrielle know?"

He motioned for Jude to sit down. Jude stayed put. "Please, sit down. It's better to hear the whole story to comprehend better the decisions made."

He sat next to Sofia and fidgeted with the multiple rings on her fingers.

She repeated, *Let's listen to his story, my love. I'm here.*

Before Pierre could begin, Etienne breathlessly ran in. "Is everything okay?"

Jude hugged him, saying, "Come, sit down, *frérot* (brother). Listen to what Pierre has to say."

Pierre looked over at Etienne. "You've grown into a fine young man. Michel was a good influence on you."

He called out to one of his assistants and asked them to bring in some drinks and a box of tissues.

"Okay, so where was I?" He gave them a brief rundown of Gabrielle's life of debauchery, greatly encouraged by his wife. "I don't believe she pushed my daughter to drink or do drugs, but it was what "they" did, so she had to follow." He rolled his eyes. "I do not blame my wife for all of this. I acknowledge I had a hand in this as I didn't speak up for her." Pierre shifted his gaze towards the wintery scene. "The more she spiraled into the socialite world, the more challenging it was for her to see clearly." He then leaned in and peered into Jude's eyes. "There was a glimmer of hope when Gabrielle spent those months at school with you. But, then, it was interfering with my wife's elitist ways, and she could not have that.

"One night, Gabrielle collapsed at a party." He turned to Sofia to explain the ways of the rich. "It is customary not to call an ambulance but to bring in the "family doctor." He notified me, but I sent my wife since I was out of town for work. Later that night, she texted me that she was admitting Gabi to a rehab center. At the time, it sounded like a step in the right direction. So, I agreed.

"Instead, my devious wife dragged her to a doctor friend with a private clinic outside the city. It was there when she found out that Gabrielle was 27 weeks pregnant. She was barely showing signs of a baby bump, so my wife underhandedly orchestrated a plan to keep the pregnancy under wraps. They administered general anesthesia to Gabrielle and performed a Cesarean section. The baby was born healthy, but they kept him detoxing his system for a week.

"By the time Gabrielle was sent home, she had no recollection of giving birth. She had a scar on her belly but was told that she fell while under the influence, and she believed it.

"Anyhow, do you remember that one party, Jude, you attended?"

Jude ashamedly acknowledged him.

Etienne was in complete shock, and even though he only heard bits and pieces, when Sofia looked his way, she knew he had put it all together. He side-glanced at her, and she appeased him with a wink.

Jude remained calm throughout. Her dragon was taming his fire.

Pierre continued. "While she was under the knife," he sighed heavily. "My wife looked over the guest list and reached out, in confidence, to three or four of the boys' mothers and asked them to supply her with a strand of hair from them. It was you, Jude. You were his father."

Still puzzled, Etienne asked, "When were you ever with Gabrielle? Like with her, with her?" He glanced at Sofia, then Pierre, then back at Jude. "So, Lennon is both of yours? Oh, la la."

Pierre nodded. Etienne slung his arm around Jude. "*Mec* (dude), this is both absurd and amazing."

Sofia leaned over and gave Pierre the go-ahead to continue the story. She interlocked her fingers into Jude's and conveyed words of calm and encouragement.

"I strong-armed Coco to adopt Lennon and keep it under wraps until the time was right. I dangled the only thing that mattered the most to her: her status." Pierre rolled his eyes.

Jude mimicked Pierre's reaction. "Did my father know about this?"

Pierre shook his head.

The fire started to blaze within him slowly. "How did you not tell your daughter? It's inhumane."

Pierre agreed with Jude. He apologized profusely. "I left it in the hands of my wife and your mother, thinking that as women, they would do the right thing. I thought having Lennon with his birth father within the household could at least give you time to spend with him. Unlike my daughter, who has lived a miserable life because of my wife and Coco." He did not make them fully accountable; he also took responsibility.

The flame within Jude blazed and then rescinded. His vibrations raised then lowered. Having Sofia and Etienne on both sides helped with composure.

"Gabrielle needs to know. But then what? Then we have to fight for guardianship? She will make it impossible for me," Jude bitched out loud.

"My opinion," Pierre interjected, "is to keep it mum for now, from her. I love her, but she's unfit to be a mother at this moment in her life. She would only cause more problems for you and Lennon. And that boy doesn't deserve that." He sat back and reflected. "I've followed him throughout his years. Such a formidable boy, so full of life." He turned to Jude. "He's a carbon copy of you. And he has Gabrielle's determination. We mustn't disturb his life right now." He looked into Jude's eyes. "Of course, Father knows best."

Pierre gestured in the air and called to one of his aides, "Ana Maria."

She rushed in and politely nodded to them. He asked her to get him a specific file on his desk.

Jude's head was about to explode with the river of thoughts streaming in and out. The tornado of emotions continued to swirl within him.

The petite-framed woman promptly returned with a few files. He propped his glasses on top of his nose and leafed through some papers, and shouted, "*Voilà!*"

He pulled out a legal document, quickly scanned through it with his fingers, and then exclaimed, "Jude, you won't have to worry about any opposition from my daughter. My wicked wife declared that Lennon's mother agreed to grant full parental control to the father who is,"—he looked up—"you, Jude. So, you are his sole guardian according to the law."

"But how could she lie about that on legal documents? And how come Jude was left in the dark? Who gave Coco the rights?" Sofia was on a roll.

Pierre shifted his gaze from Etienne to Jude. She took one look at the smirks on their faces and understood. *It seems the movies don't exaggerate when they depict the ways of the elites.* Acknowledging her thought, Jude gently squeezed her hand.

He irked a smile but was still overwhelmed. "So, as a lawyer, do you think the exchange should be simple?"

Pierre bit down on the frame of his glasses and rocked back on his chair. "Ah, yes, it could be simple, but it's your mother we are talking about." He reassured Jude that he would meddle if necessary.

Jude reached out, shook Pierre's hand, and thanked him for his time. He then stepped outside.

Sofia didn't bother interrupting Jude's moment of hysteria. Instead, she looked to Pierre for guidance. He solemnly sat in his chair. "Jude has always been a survivor. He will be fine. And so will the rest of them." He curiously eyed her and asked, "You are very calm about all of this. Are you sure you're okay?"

Calm, she was not. Sofia was livid that the woman who physically assaulted her would be in her life. And that same woman would play a pivotal role in Jude and Lennon's life going forward. No, she was not happy. And she relayed it to Pierre in a most restrained manner. "What would it accomplish if I were angry and vindictive about it? It would keep us in an endless loop of emotions. Your daughter is unwell and has caused much tension in our life, but ultimately, we can't change what has happened. What's done is done."

Pierre listened intently. She stared out at Jude and continued her thought. "In the end, I truly believe that everything happens for a reason.

It's just one more lesson placed in our path. I will always stand by Jude. Hopefully, we'll find an amicable way to solve this."

Pierre rested his head on the leather chair and approvingly said, "I see why you are with Jude. He was always more emotionally elevated than everyone in his entourage." He, too, looked over at Jude and warmly said, "You make a good couple. I know Lennon will thrive with the both of you." He leaned closer. "If I may ask a favor from you. It may be far-fetched at the moment, but one day, when my daughter is of sound mind, would you be able to include her in Lennon's life?"

The request surprised Sofia. She shrugged and told him, "It will be up to Jude."

"Yes, yes, I understand. I know Jude will do the right thing for her. She is undeserving at the moment after what she has put him through. I will see to it that she gets help." He reached over and placed his frail hand over Sofia's arm. "You are a good woman. Hopefully, this will all turn out for the best." He removed the blanket from his legs and said, "Can you help me up, please? I need to tend to do something."

She lifted him, and Etienne dutifully walked him to the next room.

Meanwhile, Sofia stood at the window, eyeing Jude. She felt the torment in her twin flame's heart as if it was hers. *May I join you, my love?*

She stepped outside and felt a lone snowflake fall on her cheek. A flurry of crystalline wonders sprinkled all around her when she looked up. She settled by Jude, sitting on the step, and weaved her fingers into his ice-cold hands. He looked at her. His face streaked with tears. "Now, what? The Art of War has become a full-blown battle of the heart."

"Now we don't think strategy. We take a few days off and spend time ruminating over this one. We need to be strong when we tell your father because we know he won't take too well to the news about your mother. But our numbers are growing. Having Pierre on our side is a big plus. And one that will rattle Coco." She reached over and wiped the tears from his cheeks. "You are not alone in this. Not now, not ever. It's me and you and now, Lennon, against the world."

INNER BATTLE

Try not to fall prey to the 4 archetypes:
Hero/Savior/Victim/Villain

37

Jude stared out the window the whole ride home with occasional tears streaming down his cheeks. Etienne was silent for the first time. Xavier didn't question either of them and kept his eyes on the road. Sofia followed suit but kept her mind open for messages whenever he was ready to talk.

She laid her head back and recalled the whole conversation in her mind. When she gave props to his mother for accepting to adopt Lennon to keep him in the family, Jude whipped his head around and glared into his twin flame's eyes. His eyes were black as the night sky; he shrieked. "No! She doesn't get any credit here. She did this for her place at the table and not for us. Do you understand me?"

Etienne was startled but remained quiet. She placed her healing hand on Jude's thigh and kept quiet for the remainder of the trip.

He was still cordial with Xavier when he got out of the car. He whispered something to him. Sofia only caught the tail end of it. *Don't tell Michel, please.* Sofia made a beeline to Etienne and hooked his arm into hers, and they walked quickly indoors. In a hushed voice, Etienne stared at her blankly and said, "Won't he hear us?" He pointed to her head.

"I've cloaked him for now."

He arched one eyebrow and repeated, "Cloaked? Still stumped." He raised his hands in the air. Sofia patted him on the shoulder.

He leaned in and disclosed how thrilled he was about the news.

Sofia's eyes widened, and she bobbed her head enthusiastically. "It's truly a gift, but it's also a huge betrayal for Jude by his mother again. And also to Gabrielle."

Etienne concurred, but still, they reveled in the fact that Lennon was a part of Jude.

"Ahem!" Jude cleared his throat.

They both looked up to find Jude leaning against the door frame at the entrance with arms crossed. Although tears remained, his glow was back. He curved his lips into a smile and exclaimed, "I'm a dad. I'm a father. It's pretty miraculous." One by one, the tears spilled down his cheeks. He then crumbled to the floor.

They rushed over to him and knelt beside him, huddling together.

They hardly noticed Yolande shuffling in behind them. "What are you three doing on the ground? Did one of you drink too much again?"

Etienne jerked his head toward her and mouthed something at her. She tiptoed around them and placed her bags on the counter. She approached the trio, bent over, and asked, "How can I help make this better?"

Jude chuckled under his breath. "You can help me up, for one." He stretched his arm out to her, and she effortlessly lifted him.

She noticed Jude's tears but didn't pry. Instead, she offered to warm up some hearty soup.

Etienne jumped to his feet. Jude helped Sofia to hers, and she held him tightly in her arms. Her healing energies outweighed his sadness; as they remained linked, she felt his suffering gradually diminish.

Yolande pitter-pattered without a word. Etienne lingered and kept reaching for his phone and putting it down. Sofia lifted her hand and sent him waves of calming energy. He eventually stretched his legs out and fanned his hands behind his head. *One down*, Sofia thought.

With eyes closed, she performed the symbols behind Jude's back and waited for the heaviness in his heart to subside. He bent down and kissed her forehead. *Let's go away for a few days, just me and you, before we tell Michel and Lennon. What do you say?*

It's a great idea. Let's celebrate our engagement correctly. She treaded slowly with the next comment but said it anyways. *And also our new addition to the family.*

He cupped her face and gazed deeply into her eyes. Sofia teased. *Don't stare too deeply, my love. I may just have a tantric moment.*

He let go. "We wouldn't want that!"

"I hope you know it's bizarre to be around people who sputter out words so randomly and spontaneously." Etienne was back to his old self.

Jude walked over to Etienne. He sat by him, stretched his hand onto his shoulder, and exchanged pleasantries and brotherly love. Yolande, meanwhile, waved Sofia over to sit at the table and served the soup without an inquisition. She also joined them. She recapped her day, purposefully diverting their attention from the tension. If anyone wanted to understand the divine feminine's power, it was right at that table.

RENEWAL

Sometimes it's important to preserve your
energy for the last battle.
Do what you need to do to recharge.
You never know how strong the enemy will be.

38

The excuse to take a short trip to celebrate their union worked for Michel. He had no reason to suspect anything. The decision to bring Etienne along with them was a precautionary one.

Jude organized the whole trip, ensuring no one but the trio knew their whereabouts. He surprised Sofia with a mini-retreat to Malta. It was only 2 hours and 40 minutes from Paris—with Etienne in tow; the flight felt short and sweet.

The ferry ride from the mainland to the island of Gozo was nippy. Thankfully, the energies between Jude and Sofia were alive and well—the transmission of heat was non-stop. When Etienne wasn't talking up a storm, he was making friends with two German girls.

He works fast.

Jude replied, "I've always admired that about him." He observed him in his element and smiled. "I hope one day he meets someone who will treat him like the star that he is."

As Jude observed his best friend, Sofia admired the ancient city of Malta with its sandy-colored fortress walls as it faded into the distance. She didn't expect it to be so crowded and big city-like, with its cramped buildings lined all along the shoreline. The splendor of the turquoise seas took her mind off the brief disappointment.

Jude rented two adjacent homes in the town of Nadur. As the ferry approached the port, it already felt more open.

Jude hadn't mentioned Lennon since they left Paris. He was still processing it in his mind, and Sofia allowed him the time to gather his thoughts. When they got off the ferry, Sofia stood by the sea, inhaled the salty air, and welcomed the cool breeze on her cheeks. A private car was waiting for them a few meters away.

Etienne sat in his usual seat at the front with the driver. The ride took them from the lively city to a landscape of dark green grass amidst rocky terrain. She gripped Jude's hand and said, *"Thank you for taking me to Mother Nature. She is so vibrant here."*

The driver dropped them off on the side of the road. It was too treacherous to drive any further. He recommended they use the path around the hill for safety, but it would take seven minutes longer.

They didn't have to look at each other to know they would be trying their luck over the hill. They all sported sturdy boots, so what if they had to lift their carry-ons on the steeper parts. Their trek did not disappoint. A few minutes in, they were overlooking the never-ending sea of blue. The feathery clouds seemed to loom right over them like angels guiding them to their destination. Jude instinctively knew where to go as he led them toward a lavish estate. It had a Moorish design with its flat roof and portal doorways. Locked and boarded up for the winter—Etienne and Sofia curiously eyed Jude. He was unfazed as he crossed the grandiose courtyard through a rocky archway to a circular tower adjoined to a square house.

He handed Etienne the code for his door. "Sorry, bro, I didn't think it would be that far from the city. You can look for a place closer to the action."

"Nah, I think I need some quiet time too."

"In any case," Jude said, "I rented two scooters." He pointed to two Vespa scooters parked at the other end of their courtyard.

Jude escorted Sofia into the tower part of the home. They had to bend their heads to go through the rather cramped doorway, but the beauty before them was worth the effort. A Renaissance-style fresco plastered the entire high ceiling, colorful patterned tiles bejeweled the flooring, and typical Maltese limestone scaled the walls. At the far end of this tubular home was an intricate staircase with an iron railing.

Before taking a tour of this fairytale home, Sofia and Jude had made a pact on the plane ride that they would completely shut down their phones for the length of the trip. He notified his uncle and extended his vacation for another week. They advised Michel, Lennon, and Lola— Etienne was the emergency contact. No Gabrielle. No mother. Nobody.

Once that was complete, the exploration continued, and Sofia climbed the stairs only to be wowed even more.

"Jude, you need to come here."

He double-stepped up the spiraling stairs and exclaimed, "It's more beautiful than the pictures."

A window curved around the whole second floor, revealing the most breathtaking view of the sea, the mountains, and the sky. It was an open space with exposed beams and a frosted-glass enclosed bathroom. A stately bed fitted with multiple blankets sat in the center of the room. Multicolor carpets dotted the floor. Along the facade ran window seating with pillows covered in various shades of blue. Sofia climbed on top of the bed and lay facing the Mediterranean Sea. Jude made his way right by her side. It didn't take long to fuse into each other's energies and bodies. They lay there in silence, and as she whispered gratitude, he whispered his undying love to her.

****

Sofia lifted Jude's arm and gently slipped off the bed. He was sound asleep, so she covered him with one of the heavier blankets on the bed and crept downstairs. Upon checking the refrigerator, she was pleasantly surprised with the neatly shelved, fresh produce. There were enough fruits and vegetables to satiate them for their stay. A towel covered a casserole dish with a note on top that said, "Minestra—Heat me up! Best eaten with bread." And on the counter lay a basket filled with baked goods. Sofia helped herself to a stuffed bread delight, wrapping it into a napkin and putting it in her pocket. She pulled out her favorite hoodie from her bag and headed out.

Etienne sat by the edge of the cliff. The view was magnificent. The sea stretched out endlessly from rugged ridge to ridge. When she pulled out the sandwich, Etienne's eyes lit up. He leaned in and confessed. "I already ate one of mine. You go ahead and eat yours."

Sofia still handed over the other half. As he tore into it, he said, "Did you know these are called ftira's? They are typical Maltese sandwiches. I have been doing my research."

Sofia smiled. "What else did you find in your research?"

He went through the list of activities—diving, hiking, and sightseeing. "There's a lot of history on this island and the mainland. I hope you and Jude get out to visit these sites. I will be doing it tomorrow with my new friends." He winked at Sofia.

He inched in closer to her. "I'm sorry about making things weird between us. I would never have made a move on you." He blushed. "It was just a silly high school crush, I guess."

Sofia loved that he was so blunt. She flung her arm around him and rested her head on his shoulder. "No need to apologize. We are soul mates, so you were right about feeling something. We are here to teach each other a lesson. I hope you know I will always love you, but not in the way I love Jude."

He nodded and brought up the whole telepathy thing. He giggled. "Do you think he's listening in right now?"

"I sure am," Jude said with a straight face.

Etienne's eyes almost popped out of his head, and he nearly choked on the bread he was chewing. When Sofia looked up, she caught sight of a radiant being wrapped in a blanket, looking down at them. Jude messed up Etienne's hair, sat by Sofia, and warmly covered the trio.

The flow of energies traveled along the three of them as they sat staring out at the vastness of the sea—and still, neither one spoke of Lennon or Gabrielle. Etienne rambled on about something and nothing. Sofia laughed and listened. Jude remained silent.

39

Jude revealed an oversize, brass skeleton key from his jacket pocket and dangled it in front of Etienne and Sofia's faces. "Do you want to explore the main house?"

Wide-eyed, Sofia asked, "How did you get that key? And isn't that someone's home?"

Etienne replied, "If he has the key, I don't see why not." He jumped up, raring to go.

Jude stood up and helped Sofia to her feet. He told them that the person in charge left the key in case of an emergency. He glanced over at Etienne. "I think it's an emergency, you?"

They both snickered like teenage boys and urged Sofia to join them. She caved in and followed the duo.

When Jude slid the key into the heavy wooden door, it opened to a vacant but charming space covered in multicolor Maltese-patterned tiles. In the middle of the home sat a courtyard with a glass dome roof that climbed two stories high. Natural sunlight illuminated the entire house. Sofia instantly felt a connection to the home. When she glanced at Jude, he had the same expression as her.

She tapped into her higher self, but it was hushed. *Are you feeling something here, Jude?*

Yes, but maybe it's just us loving the space so much.

They continued to check out the home. There was no furniture except for wooden benches that lined the sanctuary. The plants thrived and seemed well-kept, but every room was empty. The kitchen was a little piece of heaven overlooking the panoramic view of the sea.

They casually scanned the rooms, each with spectacular views, whether it was the cliffside or the greenery. When they went to join Etienne on the second floor, they found him lounging in one of many hammocks hanging from the ceiling. His eyes were closed so they didn't disturb him.

It was a loft-style space with top-to-bottom windows that framed the whole facade. At the center, the climbing vines from down below coiled around columns. The wooden slatted floors resembled a dance studio.

There were multiple rooms toward the back of the house, and it opened up to a massive balcony overlooking their tower and the whole of Gozo.

Jude twirled Sofia in his arms. "Maybe we should ask if we can rent this space for our wedding. What do you think?"

She wrapped her arms around his body. "It would be perfect, my love."

He bent and kissed her head.

Etienne sashayed right by them and asked, "Are you hungry? Because I'm starving."

Jude and Sofia laughed and shook their heads. Jude said, "You're lucky I love you so much. You sure do know how to ruin precious moments." He walked over to Etienne, hugged him, grabbed Sofia's hand, and walked toward the door. "Let's eat."

****

After cleaning their bowls of hearty soup and polishing off the freshly baked bread, olives, and cheeses, they reclined in their chairs and shared a smile. Etienne kept the mood lively throughout the meal with stories about everyone but Lennon. Jude also chimed in, but still, no mention of the Pierre reveal. Sofia was patient until she wasn't anymore. She reached out both arms toward Jude and Etienne. The second her hands settled onto theirs, Jude fidgeted in his seat, and Etienne stared at Jude.

Sofia took it upon herself to bring up the elephant in the room. She turned first to Etienne. "I enjoy listening to your stories, but it's time." She then peered into Jude's eyes and heartwarmingly spoke, "My love, it's time. It's time we talk about your new role as a father. It's time to talk about telling your father and your son. It's time to figure out what we will do with your mother and Gabrielle. We can't ignore this anymore. It's miraculous, like you said a few nights ago. It truly is. Let's celebrate this gift. And move on it, so we can enjoy the next step."

The silence was palpable. Jude removed his hand from under hers and piled the dishes and cutlery in a neat stack. He got up, went to the sink, turned on the faucet, and rinsed the plates. Sofia looked over at Etienne for help, but he shrugged his shoulders. She rolled her eyes and left the table. Sofia rummaged through her bag, swathed herself in the warmest clothes, knowing they were both staring at her, and walked outside.

Enough is enough. Deal with this however you want. I'm out. She told Jude the minute she stepped out into the chilly night.

The stars were aplenty, ready to guide her into the dark but dreamy landscape. She meandered along the craggy soil, always keeping the sea as her guiding light. Thanks to the shining stars above and the luminescent jellyfish down below, Sofia made it to a clearing without tripping or falling. Up ahead was a massive smooth rock spanning the size of the hand-crocheted mandala carpet she got in India. Sitting crossed-legged on the stone, she took pleasure in the astounding panoramic view of the seascape and night sky by lifting her hands. Paying homage to the mermaids, the selkies, the sylphs, and all the other sea elementals felt right to do at that moment. She searched in the sky for the Sirius star and transmitted a message of love to her home and soul family.

No one said it was easy being human. Her higher self always showed up when Sofia experienced a "3D" moment.

As long as there was a body of water and Mother Nature, Sofia always felt loved and at home. She never needed anyone else to make her feel whole until she met Jude. She talked extensively about twin flames and soul mates in her videos but never fully understood the profundity of their roles in her life. In her spiritual teachings, they always said that this was the lifetime in which the twin souls would unite because their energetic power would unite the whole rather than keep us all in oneness.

The only way we can be of spiritual service is if we are together, united, mon amour.

Jude cloaked her with a heavy quilt. He sat crossed-legged beside her. He then swiveled her body to face him. As their energies coursed through their veins, he leaned his forehead on hers and said, "Thank you for kicking my butt all the time."

Sofia didn't have time to respond when suddenly, she felt a surge of energy swoosh around them. And an extraordinary fusion of the soul occurred between Sofia and Jude. Neither had governance over the happenings. A stream of images inundated her mind, and, in a flash, she was living in another timeline but as a mother to a young Jude. When she asked what period it was, her higher self told her *1910. Where? Malta.* It was the only time they connected as twin flames on Earth in thousands of years. They were brought together for Sofia's sake—she had suffered many lifetimes of tragedy and discontent. To get her ready for this lifetime, she was reunited with Jude in the form of a son to remind her that she was loved unconditionally. A camera roll of photos showcased birthday parties, road trips, and lazy park days.

Then she saw that very rock they were sitting on—mother and son swinging their feet over the side. Out of nowhere, a tidal wave crashed against them. Sofia picked her son up and threw him onto the dry ground where he would be safe. On the other hand, she got swept away by the waters, and as she hung on to the edge of the rock, she felt in her heart that it was her time to go. She yelled to her son, "I'm always with you. Remember: we are in each other all along." As the sea's embrace swallowed her, the words, "Mama, don't go. Come back. Mama! I can't live without you," rang in her ear.

She was pulled out of the dream state by Jude. Tears flowed down her cheeks, but her heart exploded with joy—nothing like she had ever felt. She hung onto Jude, and when he opened his eyes, he experienced the same sad but blissful state as her. They clung to each other for the next few minutes. And when they looked into each other's eyes, they simultaneously said, "Rumi."

Jude added, "And Malta." He scooped her face in his tingling hands and longingly kissed her.

They spent the remainder of the night reliving their past life and tapping into their higher selves for more insight. They realized how powerful they became atop that cliff when they plugged into each other.

"Do you feel like they are testing us for something greater?" she asked.

His luscious greens sparkled in the night sky as he eyed her. "I know you are cloaking your thoughts. Why? What are you hiding from me?" He paused, bore into her eyes, and said, "Ahh, you think Gabrielle is our next grand feat?" He gazed into the depths of the ocean. "Well, if you feel that, then it is probably so because you're almost always right." He poked her in the arm and laughed.

She smiled and then got serious. "Perhaps we need to work on our capabilities and ensure we're ready for her wrath when she finds out about this lie. Who knows how she will react and who her rage will target."

He fell silent again at the mere mention of her name. She didn't pursue it, but at least her seeds were being planted. They remained in each other's arms, reveling in their experience as mother and son and as twin flames.

Right before the stars went to sleep, Jude took her into his arms and whispered, "With the sea, the stars, and the rock as my witness, from this day forward, everything we do is together. You are my heart. You are my soul. You are my one true love."

40

One practice Sofia diligently kept, no matter where she lived, was ensuring the sun showered her with high-frequency rays every morning. She always kept a crack open in the curtains or shutters to ensure her day started with powerful solar energies. As she basked in the morning delight, Jude peacefully slept beside her. Remnants of last night's past-life experience still lingered in her heart. But as she looked at him, reels of the night before also played in her mind. Jude's fiery masculine and Sofia's sacred feminine energies merged into one—the magnitude of their unification was one for the ages. The more integrated they became, the more she felt the presence of their spirit animals.

When she turned to face the sun, Jude growled, "Come back, my little phoenix. The replay in your mind was getting me riled up for round two."

They fooled around a little more until they heard a rock banging against the window. It didn't deter them from their morning activity until they heard two more with a faint voice echoing from down below. They stopped what they were doing and looked at each other, "Etienne."

Jude rocketed out of bed and to the window to see Etienne waving and talking. He put on his pants and went to the balcony. Jude and Sofia discovered the owners of this place had added a lower outdoor deck that wrapped around the tower—it wasn't noticeable from the outside but a beautiful addition, indeed. As they shouted at each other, Sofia went to take a shower. It didn't take long for Jude to join her, and it didn't take long for him to continue where he had left off. He devoured her body and sprinkled her with kisses. He then leaned into her and whispered, "Remember New York, it seems like forever ago, and sometimes it feels like yesterday."

Sofia thought. *It's because our timelines are converging.*

He laughed under his breath. "There's always a lesson to learn from you, my soul teacher."

****

Breakfast was waiting by the time she went downstairs—a basket of piping hot pastizzi—typical Maltese puff pastries stuffed with ricotta and a colorful spread of strawberries, mandarines, and winter melon. Jude served her a quick espresso. "For my Goddess." He kissed the top of her head.

"So, are we going to play tourist today?"

"Yes, today all day, sightseeing, and then tonight, we will talk about Lennon and Gabrielle and my mom and, and, and…."

As she downed her espresso, she felt the resurgence of energy in her body. He was back to his confident dragon self, making plans and setting up their life with Lennon.

Sofia hadn't accompanied someone on a scooter in the longest time. The choice to hang on to her beloved while taking in the splendid views of Gozo was easy. They lucked out with the weather. It was abnormally warm for the time of year. Since they had no phones, they relied on their higher selves for directions. And they were off.

They were guided inland, and as they swerved along the country roads, what struck her the most was the rawness of the landscape. Nothing about the island was structured. Mother Earth was in her pure glory. She squeezed Jude and said, *How beautiful is this island? This is how I imagine heaven on Earth to look like.*

Do you mean New Earth, Sofia?

Yes, exactly!

I know Lennon will love it here when we do live here.

Sofia's heart smiled. *I hope you're right. That's a significant change from a big city to a small island. But where there is love, there is happiness.*

Their trek led them from a sea of green to a sea of yellow. The cluster of limestone buildings and endless churches brought Sofia a short-lived rush of claustrophobia. As they breezed through the historic town, the energy felt more expansive, even though there was hardly a soul in the streets. The colorful balconies jutting from the homes made for a scenic ride within the city walls. The further they drove in, the more enchanting the city became for them, with its medley of architectural styles from Neolithic to Baroque.

Jude stopped by an open flea market lined with kiosks along the gray cobblestoned streets. When stationary, the sunshine was balmy and almost felt like Summer. Before heading to the stalls, Jude held Sofia in his arms and amorously kissed her.

They weaved in and out of the kiosks, chatting with the local vendors: many gave them tips, others asked questions, and some offered their delights for free—just some of the perks when traveling in the off-months. When they found themselves in front of an antique dealer, the curious man remained seated and nodded. The older man observed them briefly before reaching into a treasure chest by his side. He rifled through a stack of books and pulled one out in triumph. He called them over to the side and handed them the book. "I noticed your tattoos on your fingers. I think you will appreciate this book. One word of caution, be gentle with the pages, please."

Sofia thanked him and carefully flipped through the pages to remarkably find two of their symbols. When Jude went to pay for the book, the man shook his head. "Oh no. I'm not selling this book. It is worth a lot of money. It's dated 1910, an important date in our Maltese history. Feel free to take photos but from far away."

Sofia and Jude had a moment, and flashes of last night's past life whirled in their minds. They discreetly worked together to subdue the energies.

When she came to, Sofia's higher self kicked in and relayed a message to tell the older man. It was becoming increasingly frequent to share the love from beyond the veil with other lightworkers and starseeds on the planet. She leaned in and whispered, "Esmerelda wants you to know that she has so enjoyed watching you tend to all your antiques, especially her favorite jewel-toned box. It was a good run. This is the moment I talked to you about many years back. It's time." Sofia stuttered with the next word but repeated it how she heard it. "*Inħobbok* (I love you so much)."

He remained speechless before falling back onto his seat, releasing a silent deluge of tears.

Jude teased. "Why are you always making people cry?"

The neighboring seller came rushing over. "Charles, are you okay?" She leered into Sofia and Jude's eyes, assuming they were the culprits for this reaction. She was half-right.

He waved her away and grumbled, "Go back to your stand, woman. And don't be rude to my customers."

She walked away wildly-talking to herself. Meanwhile, the man collected himself, went to one of the glass-encased displays, and pulled out a tiny metal box hand-painted in emerald green. "This was my daughter's. I never had the heart to sell it because Esmerelda left this earth a few years ago, and it's all I have of her." He reached out to Sofia and asked, "May I?"

Nodding her head, he placed his hand on hers. Sofia looked at Jude and felt the energies of this man surge right through her. She didn't pull away but integrated his emotions into her being, subsequently allowing Jude to feel the sensation.

He reluctantly removed his hand and said, "Thank you for giving me back the power that dissipated when I lost her."

Sofia eyeballed Jude—he was just as confused as she was.

The man explained, "When she was at the precipice of dying, she turned to me and told me that one day two twin flame lightworkers were going to present themselves at my kiosk to help me on my mission. I had no idea what she was talking about at the time." He shrugged. "But I have since done my research, and now I understand. So, I thank you kindly." He bowed multiple times. "Thank you so much for that wonderful message. It's now time for me to close my shop, and hopefully, within the next few days, I will receive the guidance I've been waiting for." He grabbed the book from Sofia's hands and wrapped it in beautifully textured paper. He then handed it back to her. "This is my gift to you both. Oh and,"—he jotted down his name, number, and address on the paper— "whenever you come back to town, I would love to have you over."

Jude slipped him some money. He outright refused. Jude then gave the man his business card and returned the favor if he ever turned up in Paris. The old man politely accepted the card.

He then said, "Oh, I forgot. I also have a message for you." Turning his back to them, he rummaged through papers on the tiny table behind him and finally pulled out a mini leather book. Charles placed his glasses on his nose and searched the scribblings with his calloused fingers. "Aha, here it is!" He stood up and leaned in toward the couple. "Whatever happens is meant to be. It is part of your story. You are stronger as one than as two. And so it is."

The old man thanked them profusely and commenced to pack up his tent, leaving Sofia and Jude bewildered and confused by his parting words.

*****

They didn't linger in the city but headed out to the sea. Their minds were on overdrive, indecipherable to even each other. Instead of enjoying their surroundings, their egos had a field day, immersing them in a cyclone of energies. Jude pulled over to the side of the road. He shut off the engine and sat idly for a few minutes. Sofia felt the deluge of thoughts parading in his mind but remained still. She rested her cheek on his back, observing a lone butterfly dancing in the shrubs.

When he returned to the road, he thanked her for the silence. It was a long journey, but they made it to the Wied Il-Mielah Window—a must-see natural archway formed by limestone protruding into the sea. The azure waters were calling her name.

He lifted the seat and pulled out the jackets and sandwiches he had brought from home. He lifted Sofia's chin and planted a tender kiss on her lips. It was sweet gestures like those that still brought back her butterflies.

They walked down the steep steps to the archway. They felt the winter breeze right through to their bones, but that didn't stop them from proceeding to the top of the "window." They huddled and satiated their hunger as they propped themselves on one of the smoother rocks. The scenery was breathtaking, with a view of the infinite sapphire blue sea and miles and miles of rocky and verdant cliffs.

The beauty of their union meant there was no need to fill in the space anymore. They were one with each other's thoughts and emotions.

Sofia exclaimed, "Maybe that's what he meant. We are no longer two souls but one in two bodies."

Jude nodded to appease her, but Sofia could see and feel right through him; she couldn't blame him either—the news of Lennon had been a whirlwind. Having inhaled his sandwich, he reached into his jacket pocket, and out came the mini notebook Sofia had gifted him. While he scribbled, she noticed his sea-greens metamorphose into a deep turquoise. She was thrilled to be witnessing first-hand their amalgamation.

He then jumped to his feet and whipped out a camera, snapping photos of the splendor around them. He then propped the camera on the rugged terrain facing them. They made faces and playfully kissed each other for the duration of the timer. They acted like a "normal" couple for the first time in their relationship.

Next stop, they briefly visited the Salt Pans, a beehive-like pattern of geometric-shaped salt beds. In the short time they were there, Sofia pondered if there was a correlation to sacred geometry.

"There's a purpose for every curve, shape, and formation in nature." She prudently walked along the narrow ledges between salt formations and went on, "Like the flower of life. Did you know it's said to contain the blueprint of all creation within it?"

She sure did miss creating her videos and delving into research. Jude grabbed her hand and then pointed to his camera. "Yes, I know all of this because of your videos. I will have enough photos here for tons of video content." He lowered his eyes to meet hers and said, "I can't wait to collaborate with you. And when we live here, imagine the backdrops." He stole a kiss from her. "Come, my mastermind; I want to take you somewhere else." And then they were off to Tal-Mixta Cave.

When they parked the scooter, a young couple from the Netherlands warned them the gusts of winds were strong. They politely acknowledged the caution but didn't need to look at each other to understand they would be going all the same. As they descended the rough and rocky staircase, the wind picked up speed and knocked Sofia to one side.

She laughed. "If this is how I will go, so be it. It wouldn't be the first time in Malta!"

Jude narrowed his eyes, hooked his arm into hers, and accompanied his uncoordinated fiancée down the stairs. It was not an easy task, as he, too, battled the torrential gusts. It was worthwhile by the time they reached the cave. The heart-stopping view over the Maltese terrain and crystal blue waters was the closest to paradise Sofia had ever seen. Down below was the famous Rambla Bay with its red sandy beaches. Thanks to Jude's photographic skills, he took some stunning photos. It wasn't conducive to sitting on the ledge that day, but if they were going to live there one day, they had plenty of time to return.

The trek back up was equally as treacherous. "Do you mind if we head back home, mon amour?" Jude asked once they reached the clearing.

Etienne was still gallivanting with his newfound friends, so they had the courtyard to themselves. While Jude set up the double lounge chair overlooking the sea, Sofia rushed to grab more blankets and put some water to boil. By the time she came back out, he had stretched out on the chair with eyes closed; the book from the antique dealer lay clutched in his hand.

She lay one heavy blanket on his lower body and the lighter one on his upper torso, then set up the hot water with lemon zest and a sprig of rosemary on the circular table by Jude. She snuggled by him, rested her head on his chest, and soaked in the last activating rays of the sun. Whenever their energies were so close, the electrical pulses magnified and rippled from body to body, soul to soul.

"Let's look at the book before the sun sets, mon amour."

She would much rather have stayed glued to his body but was curious about the symbols. The book overflowed with riveting characters and fonts from ancient lands and beyond. They meticulously scanned each page to find the two symbols they had discovered at the market—the spiral symbol meant inner knowing, and the linear one meant connection.

As they researched other symbols apart from theirs, she casually inquired, "Do you find it strange that the one symbol that we have yet to find is fading now?"

Jude inspected his finger. "It is odd. I'll get it filled in when we go back home." He kissed her head and said reassuringly, "Stop analyzing so much. It just didn't take, I guess."

****

The thunderous clouds rolled in at lightning speed. Daggers of rain crashed down on them, waking them from their slumber. Jude hastily slipped the treasured book under his sweatshirt and snatched up the blankets. Sofia grabbed whatever she could. The razor-sharp raindrops pummeled her skin. As soon as they rushed indoors, Jude secured the book by wrapping it in one of the dry dish towels hanging off the oven door. In the meantime, Sofia stored the cups and saucers in the dishwasher. Their damp clothes clung to their skin. When they caught each other's eyes, they couldn't help but laugh.

The rain was incessant as it pounded against the walls of the tower. Jude grabbed Sofia's hand and led her upstairs. The view was perilous from up above. The sheets of rain blanched the seascape. Sofia had a love-hate relationship with thunder and lightning.

"Same," he said. "I used to cringe as a child, but still, l I would sit by the window and face the fear. I cried every time the thunder rumbled and the light cracked down, but a small part of me loved it."

She closed her eyes and transported herself into his memory. It was getting easier to do. There were moments when she felt like they were the same, but there were still moments of disconnect.

Jude leaned in. "We are a work in progress, my love."

He gently laid her down on the bed and kissed her. The electricity sizzled up and down at the touch of their lips, inside and outside. The torrential wind was not letting up as it violently thrashed against the tower.

At one point, they both shot up from the bed and looked at each other. "Etienne."

They darted downstairs. Jude frantically searched for his phone, neatly tucked away in Sofia's zippered pouch. When he turned on the phone, an overflow of notifications rang on his screen. He looked at Sofia briefly and shook his head but quickly returned to his phone and dialed his best friend. It rang and rang, and no answer. Sofia sent him a wave of calm, which he gladly accepted.

Sofia watched on as a mother would a child. She clicked in and said to her higher self. *Thank you for always showing us the way when we fall in and out of higher levels of consciousness.*

Her higher self replied. *That is why I am here. How else did you expect to awaken in this lifetime?*

Etienne answered via text. He was still in the city and sheltered from the rain.

Sofia then reached out the palm of her hand. He gave her the phone, and she hid it from him.

By the time they went back upstairs, the last of the sun was eking out from the darkened clouds. Specks of blue and green peeked through the blanket of gray. There was hope. Surprisingly, everything stayed put except for the scooter. It was lying on its side. Jude was unfazed.

Sofia stood at the window looking over at the spot where the ocean swept her away over a century ago. She couldn't help but wonder why they showed her and Jude that experience. Jude slipped his arm around her waist and brought her in closer. When their energies fused, everything seemed to make sense. She was Jude. He was Sofia. They were one.

****

Their flight home to Paris was late afternoon. Thankfully, the weather was cooperating with them at a balmy 19°C. Etienne would join them once he departed ways with his roommate.

When they arrived at the clearing, she noticed the stone had a pale pinkish hue and was much larger than she remembered. When Sofia looked over the cliff, she couldn't imagine why she would have allowed her eleven-year-old son to dangle his feet over the side. And when Jude neared the edge, she yelped.

He wrapped her in his arms. "The sea level may have been higher back then. Or maybe back then, you weren't so scared of heights." He planted kisses on her forehead and cheeks. "And you were teaching your son to be adventurous."

She unraveled herself from Jude and continued setting up the picnic before they had to leave for their flight. "I died and left you at a young age to fend for yourself."

He removed the plates from her hands, grasped her hands, and said, "Remember, these are all lessons that we needed to learn. You didn't die, right? And I must have turned out okay because we are here now, living our life to the fullest." He stole another kiss from her. "Maybe, you needed to be a mom to practice for this lifetime." His eyes twinkled. "Come, mon amour." He pulled her toward the edge. She resisted.

He sat on the rock and motioned her to do the same. "Do you trust me?"

She nodded. Jude pointed below. "Look, there is another level, so you will likely hit the grassy terrain even if you fall. Unless someone pushes you, then that's another story." He laughed out loud.

Not a time to be funny, my love.

Her higher self chimed in and gave her the green light. Carefully, when her feet swayed below, an overwhelming feeling of peace swept all around her. Jude held her close to his body, never once letting go. They mused over their past life and recreated conversations they may have had together as mother and son.

"I can't imagine a better view than this. Do you love it here? Do you still see us living here?"

Sofia curiously answered, "Yes. Why are you asking?"

"Well, I have a confession to make." He paused and caressed her fingers. "We came to this specific home because it's for sale. All of it, even the boarded-up house."

Sofia forgot about the danger of the cliff, contorted her body to face his, and excitedly said, "Is that why you had the key? You are always full of surprises."

Jude's eyes twinkled. "Well, the moment we discussed Malta, I got on the phone with my real estate agent, and she found me this beauty along with others. But this one caught my eye. And it makes sense now."

Goosebumps formed all over their skin when they realized the home was where they lived in 1910, too. Jude fell back onto the rock in wonderment. The glowing sun flickered all around him. He was beside himself with destiny at play. She bent down and canvassed him with kisses.

Once he calmed to her touch and affection, he propped himself on his elbows and continued. "We are here because I wanted to see if you loved it. If so, I was going to put an offer on the home. Lennon, Michel, and Etienne can live here any time of the year—there is plenty of space and more."

Sofia wanted to jump up for joy but wouldn't dare. With her luck, she would end up at the bottom of the sea again. "It's perfect, my love. So perfect."

"What's perfect?" Etienne rolled in. "I'm hungry. Have you been too busy kissing and not preparing the food?"

Jude and Sofia instinctively opened their arms to welcome him in their embrace.

"Ah, you guys are the best!" Etienne nestled in their arms while Jude and Sofia coddled him.

"Sofia, you're not only inheriting one child but two. Are you cool with that?" Jude teased.

She squeezed them both. "Honey, I'm adding you to that group as well. You don't get off that easily."

Once they finished laughing, they each pitched in, setting up the food. Etienne pulled out a Bluetooth speaker. "We can't be without some beats!"

"Bluetooth is very detrimental to your brainwaves."

Etienne shook his head and slapped his hand on his forehead. "You know I love you, but you're freaking annoying sometimes."

Sofia clenched her teeth."I know. I can't help it." She lifted her hands in the air.

Jude diverted the attention back to the house. And when he divulged the news about the place to Etienne, he asked, "Why didn't you tell me?"

"Why do you think you're on this trip with us?"

"What a great move, Jude. And it's not too far from Paris." He turned to Sofia. "But, a little far from Canada."

Sofia reached over and placed her hand on his shoulder. "Well, my dad lives in Italy, so I'm probably closer to my family than I was there. And Lola and Emma will always have a home in Malta."

While they ate and discussed plans with the house, Sofia reposed against one of the many boulders, drinking in the Maltese sun.

You're so beautiful, my divine phoenix. Malta suits you, indeed.

Sofia kept her eyelids shut. *Malta will be good for the whole family. I love you with my heart and soul, my divine dragon.*

Etienne rolled his eyes. "You guys are so obvious to me now. I see when you are communicating with each other because of the childish smiles on your faces. What are you saying?"

Sofia's eyes flipped open, and she joked, "We are talking about you and your roommate."

He blushed multiple shades of the rainbow. But then reverted to his cheeky self. "I did great." He roared in laughter. "To be honest, it had been so long. I almost forgot what to do!"

They all cracked up. Amid laughter, Jude checked his phone for the time and focused on the infinite scroll of voicemails, messages, and emails he received from Gabrielle. "For entertainment purposes, look at what I've missed while I was gone!"

Etienne filled them in on Gabrielle's shenanigans. "I was called by both the police and the bookstore owner that she was disturbing the peace." He turned to Jude. "Oh, and she got through the first caged door but failed on the second one."

Jude was unperturbed by the recount. He stared out onto the blue sea, nodding his head every once in a while.

"Your mother called a few times, but I never picked up. She didn't leave a voicemail either."

Jude thanked Etienne for allowing him a few days of peace. He then faced them. "This is a good segue into my next move. I will reverse the guardianship to me when we return to Paris."

"Yes," Etienne said, "and then we'll work on a plan to tame your mother."

"If you look into that, it will alert your mother, right?" Sofia asked.

"Yes, I know. I want to make sure that the legal process is simple. If that can happen, the rest is just dealing with emotions. Knowing how bureaucratic France is, I may have to tell Michel in the meantime." He turned to both of them. "What do you think about Lennon? Should we tell him right away, or should I wait?"

They went over all the pros and cons and decided to reveal the truth to Michel, and he could then help with the Lennon decision. He brought up Gabrielle as well. It seemed Jude was concocting a plan the whole time he was on their getaway.

"Sofia and I will continue to play the game with Gabrielle. It will agitate my mother. Maybe we will go as far as having dinner with Pierre and his daughter. That would take her over the edge." Jude's mischievousness came out to play.

"Do you think your mom would tell Lennon before you had the chance to?"

"She would be a fool to do that," he said. "She would lose everything and everyone."

Their discussion followed them back to Paris. Even when they arrived home and defrosted one of Yolande's home-cooked meals, they still ran through the master plan.

By the time the stars came out to play, they were all talked out. Etienne retired to his room, and so did Jude and Sofia.

Jude enveloped Sofia in his arms and held onto her tightly. He kissed his twin flame and whispered, "You are my everything."

ARTFUL

Take the enemy by surprise.
Strike them where they have taken no precautions.

41

Jude lightly caressed Sofia's fingers as he casually conversed with Etienne and the Uber driver. They were on their way to reveal all to Michel. It seemed Sofia was the only one feeling uneasy about the encounter. Something was off because her higher self had been elusive for a few days. When she inquired about the upcoming tell-all, she got the message to tread slowly and to cloak themselves. When she relayed that information to Jude, he brushed it off as their higher selves being too protective.

As she listened to their animated conversation about soccer, Sofia reminisced about a video she had done about how soccer was yet another form of programming unleashed onto the masses. It did a fantastic job in Europe and South America.

It was a challenging segment to watch for a die-hard fan like myself. Do you remember all the hate comments you got? That must have been a rough ride for you. Alas, this awakening was never going to be an easy one for humanity. Jude brought her in closer to him and planted a kiss on her cheek.

The moment they entered the elevator, Jude panicked. He turned to Sofia. "Do you feel that?"

Sofia felt a tightening in her chest. She instantly cloaked the three of them.

Etienne was in charge of Lennon. His job was to take him out for the night while Jude and Sofia broke the news to Michel.

But as soon as the elevator door opened, their plans changed. Jude instinctively shielded Sofia from the sight before him. He could not hide his displeasure. Michel appeared visibly shaken; his face had lost color, and his eyes lacked vitality. Before them stood Jude's mother. She was smaller in stature than Sofia had pictured; still, she exuded an overbearing presence. The jackhammer reverberated in her heart and mind—she was either absorbing Jude's energy or empathically sponging Coco's energy.

As they moved closer, Lennon sat on the couch, quiet as a mouse. His legs bounced up and down, his cheeks stained with tears. Jude attempted to go to him, but Coco had other plans. "You haven't seen me for months, and you're running over to your brother?"

Jude whipped past her, almost knocking her off her feet, and went to check up on his son. Coco huffed and puffed until she caught sight of Sofia—and just like that, her little fit was gone. She darted right to Sofia, completely ignoring Etienne's presence. He rolled his eyes and greeted Michel.

Jude was about to run back to Sofia, but he stayed where he was when he heard, *I got your mother. Don't you worry about me. Her wicked ways can't penetrate me. Stay with your son. Oh! I love saying that!*

When Sofia cracked a smile, Coco smirked and said, "Don't smile at me. You are the reason why this family is a mess."

Sofia was not afraid of this woman. Towering over her, she looked deep into Coco's beady brown eyes. "You should be ashamed of yourself."

Coco took a few steps back and frowned. Michel wanted to intervene, but Jude yelled, "Don't do it, Papa."

Coco didn't cower away. Sofia went on, "Your manipulative ways stop here, right now. We don't tolerate your bullshit in this house."

Hissing sounds were heard in the background from both Etienne and Jude.

"Excuse me? This is my house."

"I don't care if this house is in your name. But, I do care about all the people living in it, something you don't quite grasp yet." Sofia said in an angry tone.

Jude's mom tried to get help from Michel, but he remained silent.

Sofia had had enough of this woman. "You disgrace all women who have fought hard to keep their families together. You have only brought division within your own family."

She's something else, this woman. How can she not see what a beautiful family she has? How selfish can one be? Ugghh, she makes me forget about my whole spiritual path.

An eerie wave of darkness emerged from Coco's eyes. Sofia instinctually placed her hand in front of her face to ward off her evil. In doing so, she felt her hand hit a dense energy field. In her mind's eye, Sofia performed the symbol that cleared the energy. She felt Jude's energy power through, amplifying the clearing.

"Oh, now I see!" Coco raged at Sofia. "You're a witch, and you've put them all under your spell."

She went to swat Sofia's hand away when Lennon sprung off the sofa and darted between both women. "Sofia has only brought peace to this household. You have only brought gloom and doom. If you loved me like you say you do, then you would allow me to make my own choices. It doesn't matter that I'm only sixteen years old. I choose Papa and Jude and Etienne and Sofia." Lennon looked at every single one of them in their eyes.

"I am your mother. She's not." Coco leered at Sofia.

Sofia slanted her vision toward Jude and unleashed her phoenix inside while defending Lennon. "His mother?" Sofia laughed under her breath and then eyed her. "His mother that allows a psychopath to put her sons in danger?"

Sofia shook her head and stepped into her Mama role. She snapped her finger at Etienne and signaled him to follow the plan. She whispered to Lennon, "Thank you for standing up for yourself and me. Please go with Etienne. The Art of War has begun."

He flashed his bright whites, kissed her on her cheek, and left with Etienne amidst Coco's mini temper tantrum. Nobody was listening to her. Not even Michel.

When Jude marched up to his mother and asked her why she was there, Michel told him that he had taken Lennon out of school and enrolled him in the lycée in Paris to finish his school year.

Jude approvingly nodded and hugged his father. "You did good, Papa." He turned to his mother. "Now, that's how a grandfather should treat his grandson."

Sofia widened her eyes and tightened her lips between her teeth. *I love it when you fiercely go into dragon mode, my love.* She went by his side and interlaced her fingers into his. Michel slanted his eyes first at Jude and then at Coco.

Jude's mother's face was priceless. She quickly answered, "I don't know what you're talking about." She turned to Michel and tried to blame it on Jude, that he was trying to deter from the situation. She laid out a list of excuses.

Jude didn't care about the Art of War then; his warrior self was out for blood.

Michel stood there in disbelief. "What did you say? Can you repeat that, please?"

Jude replied. "*Grandpapa* (Grandfather). You heard right. And I have the proof."

Michel walked away from them, heavily breathed in and out, and wildly flung his arms in the air to calm himself down.

And then Jude went in for the kill. He looked fixedly into his mother's eyes and said, "I visited with a friend of yours in Marly-le-Roi."

She stumbled backward and quickly grabbed onto the counter. Her first instinct was to run to Michel to explain herself, but he didn't have it. "Pierre Lavigne? Gabrielle is the mother?" he roared.

Jude walked over to his father and hugged him. As they embraced, Coco looked daggers into Sofia's eyes, but Sofia didn't flinch. She kept her eyes on Coco until her higher self kicked in and advised her to steer clear of her energy. Sofia then snuck her arms around the two men. She whispered, "Isn't it amazing that Jude is a father?"

Michel couldn't help but smile amidst the disillusionment and sadness.

Coco cleared her throat. "I don't want to interrupt your love fest, but now that you know, when are you planning to tell Gabrielle?" She was as cold as ice.

Maybe your mother is a shapeshifter. She's scary af.
I told you. There is no maternal DNA in her at all.

Coco messed with the wrong dragon. The fire blazed within him. He unlinked himself from his father and sprinted to his mother. She flinched and let out a scared gasp. He asked Sofia for the copy of the contract. She pulled it out of her purse and handed it to him. He was inches apart from his mother as he read the part about him being the sole living parent. Michel approached Jude and slipped the document from his hands as Jude continued his rant on his mother.

"Wow, Coco, you asked about Gabrielle but not even about Lennon?" He turned to his father and said, "This is what you're married to." He shook his head.

In the thick of the drama, Jude remained poised but stern, eloquent but calm, heated but indifferent. Sofia reveled in the emotions that he bestowed. She tried to keep him as cool-headed as possible. It seemed to piss Coco off when Jude delivered his anger in a collected manner. She tried everything she could to set him off, but he wasn't playing her games anymore.

"I will tell Gabrielle when the time is right." He looked into Sofia's eyes and back at his mother. "Now that we are friends with her, I'm pretty sure it will go smoothly."

The dragon was relentless. He was not going to let her down easily. He added, "It's time for you to think wisely. I know it's challenging for you to reason. But, if you tell Gabrielle, you will lose us as a family, and

Pierre will strip you of any dignity or status you have left in your community."

The last statement struck a chord in her. She savagely lashed out at Jude, but before the palm of her hand landed on his cheek, he seized her wrist and brought her to a kneeling position. Michel's glacial stare said it all—he was no longer defending her. She cried out. He released her wrist, and she fell onto the sofa, remaining there for a few minutes before lifting herself.

"How dare you treat your mother this way? I will call the police, and they will put you in jail where you belong."

Jude laughed. "Are you serious, woman? Call the police, please. Let's see what they say about your plots and schemes to injure my future wife."

She lowered her gaze in the most demonic way and sneered. "Future wife. I can't believe you're still going through with marrying this." She flailed her finger at Sofia. She cackled like the sorceress that she was. Coco turned to Michel. "And you are allowing this to happen?"

Michel made his way to his wife. Her demeanor changed—she went from menacing to virtuous in no time.

She truly is a piece of cake, your mother.

Jude coiled his arm around Sofia's waist and held her close while they observed Michel weave his wizardry.

In a commanding voice, Michel said. "Claire, *asseids-toi* (sit down)!"

She did so reluctantly. He sat squarely before her and asked Jude and Sofia to do the same. "Now, we will talk like adults." He peered into his wife's eyes. "I know there's kindness in you somewhere. I would never have married you otherwise. So can you reach deep into your soul and bring her out for the next hour?"

Sofia and Jude marveled at how Michel extracted the decency out of her. She warmed up to his temperate ways and spilled everything to them. She withheld Lennon's status because Gabrielle's mother gave her a choice between Michel and her social standing.

Sofia and Jude spent most of the time having their own mindful conversation.

Evil is as evil does. She is something else, my mother. And to think for a moment, I thought she had found her way back to us. J'suis naze. (I'm an idiot).

She's your mother. Ultimately no one is evil, just misguided. Let's together send her light. That's the best we can do for now.

It's challenging to be so forgiving after a lifetime of emotional ups and downs. Maybe we need to head back to Malta for another getaway.
I'm ready whenever you are!

Coco turned to the twin flames. "What are you two giddy about? Are you enjoying watching me squirm?" She waved her hand toward them and whined to Michel, "Is this respectful to you? Should my son treat me this way?"

Sofia felt Jude's flames ignite and immediately subside.

He replied, "Explain why we should be respectful or forgiving toward you. You chose your country club status over your family. You willingly allowed me to endure years of stalking, putting your son and grandson in danger." He paused and eked out the words, "*Maman, tu m'agaces. Je te comprends pas. (Mother, you're so annoying. I don't understand you).* We are extending an olive branch to you, but you refuse to see the consequences of your actions. Papa has been patient with you for the past forty years, and still, you only see with your eyes and never with your heart."

She scoffed. "See with my heart? What does that mean? I see you have picked up from your father's way of talking." Then she mercilessly added, "I didn't have to adopt Lennon. I did it for you."

Jude relayed to Sofia. *I don't know why we are bothering with her. She's disconnected from us.*

Michel snapped his fingers at his wife. "*Tais-toi! Quelle honte!* (Shut-up! Shameful) You did it for your place at the table. Stop playing the martyr here. We are not going to praise you, nor are we going to give you any accolades. You have wronged your son and your grandson. And you have deceived your husband." He went on to discuss the logistics of how they would proceed. "So this is how it's going to go down. Jude, our son, will get full custody of Lennon."

Coco lamented. "Jude can try, but then I'll remove both his and Lennon's trust funds." She snickered.

Michel sighed heavily. "Oh la la! I believe I speak for both of them. Do as you wish. They don't care about your money. Do it right now." He turned to Jude for approval, and Jude eagerly nodded. He turned back to her. "Do you take me for a fool, woman? Do you think I would leave my kids empty-handed when it was time to leave this earth? Do you believe I trusted you to care for my children?" He let out a bellowing laugh.

He went on, "I have money, my dear. You are not the only one in this family. Jude, Lennon, Etienne, and Xavier are well cared for."

Coco blurted out, "Etienne? He's not even yours. He has a wealthy family to take care of him. And Xavier? You're a foolish old man. Why would you distribute to them?"

Meanwhile, Sofia's and Jude's hearts erupted with love for this selfless man.

Michel ignored her empty words. "After Jude gets custody of his rightful son, I will serve you with divorce papers. And we will be rid of you, once and for all. As Jude said, we tried to reason with you, but you are soulless. And you are no longer allowed to interact with my sons or daughter-in-law."

Coco glared at Sofia.

Michel leaned across the coffee table and looked fixedly into Coco's gaze, "And that goes for your precious Gabrielle. If she for one second harasses either of the people I've mentioned, I will have you and her thrown into jail so fast you won't know what hit you. *Basta! Ça suffit.* (Enough). You will no longer wreak havoc on this family again."

Now I see where you get your fire from, my dragon. He just slayed her.

Michel stood and escorted her out the door. She did not turn around to say goodbye. Their exchange did not end at the couch but continued by the elevator as their voices raised and lowered.

Jude turned to Sofia. "And now we go to war. Are you ready, mon amour? You were privileged to get a firsthand taste of my "doting" mother. She will come back much fiercer once she regains her strength. I can guarantee you that."

Sofia cupped his face and softly kissed his lips. Then whispered, "Oh, I was born ready. This is why we have connected, my dear, to bring our powerful force up against the storm. Little does she know, we are the storm."

****

Sofia snapped out of her dream state and into a pool of emotions. It felt like someone was tugging at her heartstrings. When she turned to talk to Jude, he wasn't beside her. She lay in the stillness with one hand on her heart, and with the other, she performed their symbols in the air. With every outline and gesture, the anguish subsided.

What magic are you using on me, my love? Whatever it is, it's working. I'm lying on Etienne's bed, and we're talking. Yes, I can hear you laughing! Come, if you want.

I will leave you to your brotherly bonding.

It was a good time for Sofia to commune with her higher self. Wrapping the comforter around her, she dragged her body out of bed and set herself up on the carpet with her crystals and paraphernalia. She lit a candle and breathed in and out until she fully grounded in the earth. Her higher self was a chatterbox forewarning her of rocky times ahead. *Take some time to rest because you will be integrating with Jude soon.* She still had no idea what that meant but was looking forward to the unknown.

For fun, she pulled some cards from her tarot deck—the Devil, the Queen of Swords in reverse, and the 2 of Cups. The bottom of the deck was the King of Wands in reverse. She didn't have time to analyze the cards when she felt Jude worm his way under the blanket. She loosely stacked them back in the box.

"Are you hiding something from me? Is it a bad omen?" he asked as he fluttered her with kisses.

She ignored his question and welcomed the closeness. As she lay her head on his chest, she asked, "Did you sleep well, my love?"

"I did, but...do you remember your dream last night?"

"I woke up from what felt like a deep sleep. Why?"

He fidgeted with the dry sage leaves of the smudge stick lying in the porcelain bowl. He had a hard time putting into words what he wanted to relay. "Uhmm...I'm pretty sure we were both in front of a light being, maybe your mother, I don't remember, but they were teaching us how to integrate our souls."

Sofia felt the warmth of his words in her heart. "I wonder what's next for us."

Jude coiled his arms around her and lifted her onto the plush carpet. "Whatever it is, we are ready for it. I love you so much. As long as we are together, we are stronger, right?"

They lay in each other's arms in the sweet contemplation of their present and their future. When electrical currents traversed through their bodies, a tingling sensation soothed them. And when their lips brushed up against each other, a heavenly aroma danced around them. And when their bodies curved perfectly into each other, rapturous flames united the twin flames.

42

Jude's role in the plan had been set in motion. They had to move fast to secure their positions in the chess game. He nervously dressed while Sofia watched him decide which shirt to wear with his slate gray pants. Only this time, he was getting ready to confront Gabrielle alone.

It was Sofia's idea—the only way Gabrielle would accept to move forward. They all knew that. It had to come from Sofia, or Jude would never have gone ahead. She jumped up to help him with the buttons on his shirt. With every button, she reassured him that she was okay. "I trust you completely." Button number 2. "It's a genius plan." Button number 3. "I love you." Button number 4. "I will be with you every second." Button number 5. "We got this."

She looped her arms around him and laid her cheek against his chest as he shimmied into his Merino wool sweater. He tried to convince her he was calm, but she could hear and feel his heart racing at a supersonic speed. He kissed her on the top of the head. "Okay, my love, I have to go."

She turned to Etienne in the kitchen when he jumped into the car with Xavier. "So, are we going to follow them or what?"

Etienne winked at her. "I'm way ahead of you. Sit down and have a bite with me. Xavier will return for us as soon as he drops him off."

It gave Etienne and Sofia time to catch up as they reviewed last night's details. He told her that Lennon was getting curious and asking many questions.

"Don't worry. I'm not saying anything." He placed his hand onto hers, and a shock drilled through them. "Ouch. Did you feel that? Is this because we are soul mates?"

"I have other soul mates, and it doesn't happen with them. I will look into it, which reminds me, I need to prepare a new video soon. I miss my research and my online community."

"Take your time. I still have a lot of videos to watch now that I've started from the beginning. I find it amazing how much power we all have dormant in our souls." He cut two slices of focaccia and handed one to Sofia. "Freshly made by ours truly. It's so good."

She wasn't in the mood to eat, especially since she had just tapped into Jude and Gabrielle's conversation. She felt sick to her stomach. "The dragon has landed."

43

A few minutes into their espionage work, Lennon secretly opened the car door and slid in next to Sofia and Etienne. Sofia leered at Etienne. He lifted his palms in the air. "Don't look at me."

Lennon put a finger to his lips. "Shhh…Pretend I'm not here."

Sofia shook her head. "First of all, how did you know we were here?"

Lennon confessed, "I walked by the restaurant and saw Jude with Gabrielle and said for sure someone from my family is keeping an eye out, and as I expected, here you are."

Jude expressed concern but said, *Go ahead and fill him in with the plan. She's just as narcissistic as my mother. I can't deal anymore.*

You're doing fine. I would think you were having a great first date if I didn't know you.

Sofia! It's all a game, remember.

Etienne tugged at her arm. "What are they talking about?"

"Gabrielle is quite the chatty cat."

When Lennon remarked on Gabrielle's beauty, Etienne slapped him. "What? It's true."

Sofia turned to Etienne. "He's right. She is gorgeous. I'm not worried about her stealing his heart from me."

IT'S NEVER GOING TO HAPPEN, EVER, was Jude's response.

Sofia chuckled but also felt a tinge of jealousy wash over her.

While Gabrielle prattled on and on about their childhood and teenage years, Etienne and Lennon babbled on about girls. Listening in had its perks but also its downfalls.

Sofia jumped in her seat and shrieked, "Oh my God. Oh my God." She had to breathe in and out a few times before divulging to Etienne and Lennon, who just showed up. "Coco has just arrived. Gabrielle invited her."

Jude was freaking out. Sofia had to appease him, and quickly. *Remember why you are doing this. It's to rid both psychopaths from our lives. Stay level-headed. Your mother wants nothing more than to rile you up.*

Etienne and Lennon hammered into Sofia. "What are they talking about? What's happening?"

Lennon suggested he go and help his brother, Etienne, and Sofia shouted, "NO!" They startled Xavier, too.

When Lennon attempted to open the door, Etienne grabbed his arm and stopped him. He asked Xavier to lock the doors.

Lennon shifted his eyes from Sofia to Etienne and asked, "What's going on? Why are you being so shady with me?"

Fuck, fuck, fuck!

It was now Jude's turn to calm Sofia down. *Take a deep breath in. Just tell him it's part of the plan.*

Collecting herself, she white-lied about the plan and told him it was essential to follow it to a tee, or they'd have to start all over again. He complied, but his expression resembled his father's when Jude didn't believe in a lie.

Etienne quickly veered the topic back to girls—it was an easy transition for a sixteen-year-old to focus on.

Jude swooshed in again and said, *You guys need to get out of the car and hide somewhere. The witch is on her broom, and she's headed your way.*

The trio exited the car and ran to the side of one of the buildings. She was too fast. Coco knocked on Xavier's window; he opened it halfway. "Are you alone?"

He politely nodded. But she was insistent that he open the window to the back seat. Seeing no one was there, she groaned and left.

Jude advised them that the coast was clear. *I see you all made it in time. She's headed back this way.*

The secret agents headed back to the car.

When Sofia checked her social media, Gabrielle had already posted multiple pics of her and Jude. The comments flooded in. "Your boyfriend is so cute."— "You look so happy together."— "Is he the one?" Sofia chucked her phone on the seat in front of her. Etienne picked up her phone and scanned the photos. "*Bah* (Come on), Sofia, don't tell me you're jealous. She's got nothing on you."

It didn't help that Sofia tapped into Coco, concocting wedding plans for Jude and Gabrielle. *Don't for one-second pay attention to my mother. It's a farce. I'm so close to losing it. She's so delusional. The encounter we had with her never happened in her mind. She's back to her old self.*

Lennon then made another inane remark. "They do make a cute couple. They would probably make some beautiful children."

Sofia did not dare look over at Etienne. He nervously laughed and told Lennon, "*Quoi? C'est une blague?* (What? You're joking?) *Mec* (Dude), why would you say stupidities like that in front of Sofia?"

Lennon innocently replied, "Sofia and Jude are the ultimate couple. But I'm just being honest."

Sofia narrowed her eyes at Lennon, then spoke to Jude. *I think Lennon is onto something. He's hinting at many things that don't sound like coincidences.*

Sofia texted Etienne asking him if he had disclosed any information from the exchange. The answer was,

—No, absolutely not. But if his mother is Gabi, he will be as cunning as she is.—

Jude came in. *I guess the time has come to talk to Lennon. Let's do it as a family, please. I'm almost done here. These two are driving me nuts.*

****

Lennon bravely digested the information. Jude did not hold back. He revealed it all—Gabrielle was his mother, that it was a one-night affair, that he had sole custody of him, and that Coco lied. But he gave his mother props for having the decency to adopt him. Lennon didn't say a word. The only angst felt in the room hovered over Michel and Etienne.

Lennon turned to Sofia. "Did you know about this when we spent the day in the park together?"

She shook her head. "We found out right before going to Malta. Your father," —she lovingly looked over at Jude— "needed time to absorb the revelation."

Lennon remained quiet.

"But you already knew something was up." Sofia prodded. "When did you put things together?"

Lennon enthusiastically jumped up from the couch. "Yessss!!! After the telephone conversation between Gabrielle and my mother....er....grandmother, I had a feeling something was up." He looked over at Sofia. "You know, the one I told you about."

Jude arched his eyebrows. *Is there anything I need to know about this conversation?*

No, my dragon. It's not important. What is important is Lennon's keen sense of himself. He's so very much like you, my love. It's such a pleasure to watch.

He looked over at Jude, Michel, and Etienne. "And it's undeniable that they are my parents. I look exactly like my father. And I love the limelight like my mother." And then he primped his hair and joked, "And I'm handsome, like my parents."

That prompted Jude to leap off the sofa and encircle his arms around Lennon. Lennon crumpled into his father's embrace. A downpour of tears cascaded down his cheeks, Jude's cheeks, and Michel's cheeks. The cry fest was real. Etienne joined in, as well. Meanwhile, Sofia got up and made herself at home. She boiled some water in the kettle and put the coffee machine on.

You are part of our family, too, Sofia.

I know, but this moment has been in the works way before me, so I want you to enjoy it.

They spent the rest of the day reminiscing about their past. Sofia listened for the most part until an incoming call from Lola interrupted the love fest. She stepped away and enclosed herself in the dining area. Lola cried joyfully when she disclosed the basics on speaker, while Emma responded with concern. "How's Jude? What about Lennon? Are they in shock?"

Sofia filled them in with the essentials. She chose not to dive too much into the Coco story—that required a face-to-face conversation. She broke the news about Malta. More excitement from Lola. Less excitement from Emma. Same story, different day.

Sofia heard her twin flame chime in, *My love, I was just about to talk to Lennon about Malta, too. Join us, please.*

She spent a few more minutes with her best friends and then arranged a FaceTime call later in the week. When she returned to the boys, the mood had one-hundred-percent changed from low-key to glee. Even Michel casually reclined on the sofa while he listened to the animated stories from the designated narrators: Etienne and Lennon.

Lennon quipped, "So, what do I call you now? Maman, or are you my evil stepmother?"

Jude dotingly looked over at Sofia. She smiled. "Just call me Sofia for now. I think you have enough mothers on your list."

"If I may, she will be your mother as soon as I do the legal work. She's going on paper as so."

That was news to Sofia and everyone else. Jude was adamant—there was no changing his mind. There was no one opposing his decision either.

"You heard the man," Michel added. "So, Maman, it is!"

Sofia had been stoic until she realized her vision of a child was materializing. She buried her face in her hands to hide the pool of tears welling up in her eyes.

The first person to hug her was Lennon. "I don't care what I have to call you as long as you're with my broth...er...father, I know that I will be safe. And also," he snickered, "I look forward to making your life a living hell!"

Jude laughed but then glared at Lennon."You'll have me to deal with if you cause too much havoc, my son." Jude's face gleamed when saying that word out loud.

The atmosphere was upbeat until it wasn't—until Coco made her way into the apartment.

Jude looked over at his father. "How is she freely walking into our home?"

Coco swung the electronic tag in her finger and howled, "Your father and I are still married, my boy. This is still my home."

Michel quietly got up from the couch, swiped the tag from her finger, and growled back, "Not anymore. Get out. We are in a family meeting."

Sofia wiped her tears, turned to Lennon, and whispered, "You don't know anything, okay? Play dumb if she tells you anything." She made a last-minute decision according to their plan.

Good call, Sofia. She'd be stupid to even say a word to him.

Coco stomped her feet like a child. "What's the meeting about? I'm still part of the family. Are we talking about what I think we're talking about?"

Jude shouted a believable, "No!"

Michel caught on and repeated the same to her. "Okay, I'll walk you out again. This time, if you come back, I will call the police. And then both Christofle men will have two restraining orders on women."

Mic drop. Your father has been on the ball lately. I love these exchanges.

Where do you think I learned my quick-wittedness?

Coco was not going to leave that quickly. She twisted her head and looked straight at Etienne. "What is he doing here? He's not part of the family." And she further added fuel to the fire and pointed at Sofia. "And her, who is she?" She grumbled and swooshed past Michel. She sat on the sofa with crossed arms. "So, what are we talking about?"

Etienne rolled his eyes and was about to get up, but Michel pushed him back down. "Where are you going, son? Do not listen to the rhetoric of a crazy woman. You are my son. You know that. Stay put, please."

Etienne blushed and nestled back into the chair, much to the dismay of Coco. She sneered at him and then casually asked again what the topic of conversation was. Everyone fell silent. She then, surprisingly, brought up her plans for the upcoming wedding.

Jude ordered her to shut it down. She ignored him, of course, and went on. "Lennon, did you know your brother is getting married?"

Is she going there? Is she for real? People did not generally shock Sofia, but his mother was a unique species.

The best option right now is to go ahead with her delusion. Let's give the floor to Michel. He'll have a field day with this one. Jude slung his arm around Sofia and brought her closer to his body.

It never went away; the electrical shocks between them. In times of heightened emotions, the currents were more potent than ever.

Coco did not appreciate the closeness of the twin flames and began regurgitating her stupidities, further infuriating Michel.

"What are you talking about, woman? Jude and Sofia are getting married, no one else. Do you hear me? Now, why would he marry his stalker? Have you lost your mind? Where do you come up with these ideas? Have you forgotten to take your country club meds today?"

The avid onlookers found the confrontation very entertaining. Michel was the fierce gladiator, and Coco was the worn-down feline. Their bickering was non-stop. Lennon and Etienne were even counting points.

Did this often happen when you guys were young?

Yup, this was a typical day when she graced us with her presence. And these two —he pointed to Etienne and Lennon— *usually had cards with numbers (like in the Olympics). It was funny but not, if you know what I mean.*

Jude had had enough of the fiasco. He kissed Sofia on the cheek, got up, and went over to his mother. He extended a hand out to her. She furrowed her brows and slowly placed her hand in his. Everyone else continued watching the show. He forcefully lifted her to her feet and said, "*Allez hop!* (Let's go) *Maman*." He escorted her toward the door. She held herself back, trying to sit down, but he wrapped his arm around her waist and kept her standing.

"*Mais, voyons donc.* (Come on). How old are you, Mother? You're acting like a two-year-old." Jude strengthened his grip on her.

She relented. "Okay, okay. I'll go. Please, let go of me."

He released her from his grasp. She fixed her blouse and patted down her ash-blonde hair. Then she stared straight into Jude's eyes. "You shouldn't have done that, my son." And she turned to Lennon and blurted out, "Jude is your father."

Lennon jerked his body upward and skillfully acted shocked. Coco acted almighty. Jude feigned fury. Michel conveyed anger. It was a masterful scene from The Art of War. Sofia and Etienne pretended to be equally appalled. She had no idea she was the pawn. The theatrical piece did not end there.

She also eked out, "And your mother is Gabrielle."

Lennon played an Oscar-worthy role. Jude and Michel dragged her out. The last words spoken to her were from Jude. He said sternly and concisely, "We gave you many chances to uphold your role as a mother in this household, but you have given it away. Papa will go down to the police station and file a restraining order. I will do the same for both of you. The next time I see you, we will be in front of a lawyer or a judge. You no longer control my life, Lennon's, or anyone in this household. Are we clear?" He paused, inched his face closer to hers, and raised his voice, "If you tell Gabrielle, your reputation is on the line. Pierre is waiting for my call. Are. We. Clear?"

Coco snorted like the bull that she was. She pounded her fists on Jude's chest and hollered. "Everything I have done was for you, Jude—you and your brother. Why can't you see that? One day, you will understand that this was not only for my status. But, if you take that from me, I will have nothing left."

Jude shook his head. *She's outta control.* He gripped her fists and asked again, "Are we clear?"

She stopped wailing at him and simmered down. She nodded, eyes menacingly narrowed with anger.

He released her. "Now, go. You are no longer welcome here. You are not my mother. You are not Lennon's grandmother. You are not Michel's wife. You are nothing." He sighed heavily. "Oh, but you are still a country club member."

He headed back to his family. Michel remained there with her and parted ways with his wife. Sofia felt the torment rise in Jude's body. The flames consumed him. When he turned the corner, she was waiting for him. He fell into her arms. Lennon assumed his position as son and wrapped his arms around both of them. Etienne did the same. No one was going to tear them apart. No was going to come between them. No one was going to quash their unbreakable bond. No one.

****

Michel was in charge of police duty. He knew someone in the task force that could help with restraining orders. Jude went straight to Pierre for the changeover of custody and his father's divorce proceedings. Coco would never cross Pierre, not even as an afterthought. Gabrielle's father was their best bet. He gladly took their case on even though he wasn't vigorously practicing.

Pierre invited Sofia and Jude to convene at his home. He preferred discussing a slight glitch in the proceedings face-to-face. He set them up in his study—it was not a typical all-wooden square room. Instead, it was a 2-story circular room with a cascade of natural light flooding in from both floors. The slight odor of cigars lingered in the air.

Now that's an odor we don't often smell anymore, Sofia remarked.

Jude rolled his eyes. *It depends on which circles you keep, my love.*

One of Pierre's assistants ushered them onto a butterscotch-colored leather loveseat. The Persian carpet under their feet screamed luxury. Law books lined the dome-shaped bookshelves. Classic reading lamps and tropical plants littered the room. His massive oak desk was barren, with only one lone picture frame, donning a photo of Gabrielle as a child. When he walked in, both Sofia and Jude stood to their feet.

He waved them down. "We are friends. No need for pompous ways. I'm an old man tired of these silly politically correct gestures."

They smiled and sat back down. Another assistant helped him in his leather chair. As he propped the cane against the sidearm, Pierre politely asked the girl to get the papers in his desk drawer. He searched for his glasses for a few seconds. Sofia wanted to tell him they were on top of his head. Jude shushed her.

It will irritate him. Let's have him in the best of moods.

Jude's nervousness was back. Pierre, after all, was his nemesis' father. Pierre seemed more than willing to help in the matter. He expressed to Jude, "Your call made this old man smile. I could imagine this decision not being an easy one. We probably have Sofia to thank."

Jude nodded and then relayed to Sofia. *He is a very observant man. That's what makes him a good lawyer.*

Sofia laced her fingers into Jude's as he leafed through the papers. *My dragon, breathe in and breathe out. Pierre is a good man. He will help us through this.*

"Ah yes, here it is!" Pierre exclaimed. "The contract stipulates that you are the lone parent because the mother relinquished parental control. But we both know that she did not. In good conscience, we cannot continue with this lie."

Sofia interrupted and, jokingly, said, "But lawyers don't have a conscience."

Pierre bent his head and peered through his glasses at her. He then looked at Jude and let out a boisterous laugh. "Now I know you are the right woman for Jude. And the right woman to be Lennon's mother!" He went back to his papers, all the while chuckling to himself.

Close call, Sofia. You almost gave me a heart attack.

Relax, Jude. He's not going to do you wrong. He's doing exactly what you would do.

He went over the semantics. "I will document that my daughter was incapacitated at the time but that Jude would still be the sole custody because she is unfit to be a mother." Pierre squinted his eyes and looked at the couple. "This process could be easier if you were both married." He grinned. "By any chance, would you be interested in tying the knot tomorrow?"

Jude winced and blurted out, "Tomorrow? Why so fast?"

Pierre laughed. "Because I will see my judge friend in a few days, and if we can get the papers done pronto, you can rid your mother sooner." He leaned in and whispered, "I heard through the grapevine that she's hired a young lawyer to fight you in court."

Jude rolled his eyes. "Why am I not surprised?"

Pierre agreed, saying, "It's in our best interests to move on this as fast as possible. We know how primitive the French legal system is. If there is a maternal presence in your plea, they will be more favorable toward you."

Sofia squeezed in a request, "Can your judge friend marry us?"

Pierre removed his glasses and pointed them at Jude. "A woman with a mission. If you want, I can get you in front of the mayor in the next few hours. Sofia, I would need a copy of your birth certificate."

"I'll get right on it." She then looked over at Jude. "What do you say? You know how I feel about these silly legalities that mean nothing, but if it's for Lennon, I'm willing to do it."

Jude had to take a moment. *Are you sure, my love? You don't want to exchange vows in front of our friends?*

Sofia confirmed with Pierre that they were ready whenever.

Pierre summoned his assistant and broke down the list of actions he needed from her. He was proficient when he spoke. She promptly jotted down everything with precision.

Meanwhile, Jude was relaying non-stop messages to Sofia. *Are you sure this is how you want to go about this?*

We will have an intimate gathering in a few days with our friends. I will call Emma and Lola, and they can come if they wish, and that's it.

She twisted her body and whispered, "A wedding is not necessary, you know that. I am yours, and you are mine. It's set in stone already."

Pierre interrupted the lovers. "In the meantime, my clerk will amend the document, and you can sign all the papers. So, when the marriage certificate comes in, you won't need to come back. I will take care of everything."

Jude then looked Pierre steadfastly in the eyes and asked, "So you are okay with all of this? You are fine that Gabrielle does not have custody over your grandson?"

Pierre leaned back, observed Jude and Sofia briefly, and affirmed, "You have known me, Jude, for a long time. My word is gold. I truly believe you and Sofia have much to offer this boy." He sighed. "My daughter, I fear, will never be mentally or emotionally stable enough to care for her son. But, if you promise she will play a role in his life much later, that would make me happy."

Should we tell him that Lennon knows?

Jude opted in and told Pierre the whole truth. Pierre's response was priceless, "This is why we need to get rid of this monster, and the sooner, the better."

He expressed his disgust for Coco's poor decision-making. "This decision is so much easier for me now. We will speed up this process so she can be out of the picture. And hopefully, she can get her claws out of my daughter too."

Jude added, "We can speed up the process, but your daughter remains a constant force of nature in my life. Is there something you can do to help with this?"

Pierre looked off into the distance in contemplation. He looked back at Jude. "I will take care of my daughter. I will invite her to return home or take a trip with her to a foreign land for a few months. It's time this father bonds with his daughter again."

Before he could sail away into nostalgia, one of his assistants rushed in, squatted down to his level, and softly spoke in his ear. He continuously nodded his head, then thanked the girl. She left hurriedly.

He turned to them. "Ok. Back to business." He informed them that the only date available for the wedding was in three days. "It seems everyone wants to get married in February. I booked for the 17th." He gazed at Jude. "Isn't that your birthday?"

Jude nodded. "It's meant to be." He lovingly kissed Sofia on the cheek.

Three days was enough time for Lola and Emma to fly over. Three days was enough time for Jude and Sofia to collect themselves. Three days was enough time to organize an intimate event amongst family and friends.

****

Jude and Sofia summoned Etienne, Lennon, and Michel to the dining area. They called in Lola and Emma on Zoom as well. The emotions ran high as Sofia and Jude reclined in their chairs and observed their lively family at play.

Then Jude took the initiative and stood up from the chair. The room silenced, and all eyes landed on the dragon. He first mentioned their meeting with Pierre and how everything was set in motion. He glanced at Michel and said, "Expect a call from Pierre's assistant, Nathalie, this week. The divorce proceedings have begun."

Michel sat back with his hands in a prayer position. He thanked his son.

Jude turned to Lennon. "We are in the process of finalizing custody, but," —he paused and stole a look at Sofia, then back at everyone else— "to speed things up, we need…"

The bystanders waited anxiously for his next words. Etienne yelled out, "Yes! You're killing us, Jude. What do you need?"

Sofia rose to her feet and declared, "We need to get married ASAP for the ball to roll faster. We are going to tie the knot in three days."

Lennon bounced out of his seat in excitement. Etienne rubbed his hands together, psyching himself for the next steps. Michel clapped his hands together. Lola joined the high-vibe train. Emma eked out a smile but remained silent.

Jude placed his fiery claws onto the table and asserted, "We know it's fast, and if I leave it up to Sofia, we will do a quick signing at city hall. So," —he slyly twisted his head toward Sofia, blew her a kiss, and then eyed his family— "we have some work to do because I am not just signing a certificate with this woman. I want it to be a touching moment. Got it?"

Sofia slipped her arm around his waist and leaned her head onto his shoulder. *You're so hyper-romantic.*

He planted a kiss on her forehead. *We're going to do things right for once, my love. So, maybe not a wedding in Malta but a honeymoon for sure.*

"We're booking a flight pronto," Lola exclaimed. "Jude, let me know if you need anything from this side of the world. And, Sofia, let me know if you want a specific outfit from your wardrobe. I'll text you. Okay, bye, everyone. We'll see you hopefully tomorrow!" The Zoom call ended.

"It's imperative that Coco not get wind of this," Jude said. "She already has wolves sniffing around and getting ready to attack. Please, be as discreet as possible. Pierre is graciously stepping up for this family and preparing for battle alongside us."

"Why would Pierre care about us?" Lennon asked.

Jude first glanced at his father for approval, and Michel gave it. He then answered, "Pierre is your grandfather."

"Oh yeah? Cool!" Lennon then thoughtfully ran to Michel, hugged him, and said, "You will always be my favorite one, though!"

Michel heartily laughed and returned the affection. As Lennon hung on to Michel, he looked over at Sofia. "Will that mean that your dad will be my grandfather too?"

That was one way of creating joy in an awkward situation.

Lennon made his way next to Jude. "What happens to Gabrielle? Does she ever get told about me?"

Etienne and Michel fidgeted in their seats while Jude and Sofia remained calm.

"When the time is right, your mother will know, but for now, we must keep our lips zipped for everyone's safety." He informed Lennon that one day they would drive together to Pierre's house when he was ready. Lennon seemed receptive, always ensuring not to step on anyone's toes.

As Lennon talked, Sofia gently twirled the hairs on Jude's head and combed her fingers along his scalp. When Etienne snapped his fingers in front of their faces, they only then realized how easily they got lost in each other. They moved forward with the designation of tasks. They moved forward with the plans. They moved forward with the Art of War.

ART OF SOUL

HONOR

Honor your soul.
Honor your feelings.
Honor your thoughts.
Honor your light.
Honor your now.

44

Sofia set herself up before the altar and connected with her higher self. Her whole spirit team was with her, sending her messages and protection energy. So tangled up in all the drama, she hadn't realized how in-tuned she was getting with the surrounding energies. She spent most of the morning reaching out to her followers, replying to their messages, and sending her loving energy to them. She even went on a short "live" to appease their requests.

Jude and Sofia spent some hours apart to prepare for their big day in their unique way. When Lola burst into the room, Emma berated her for intruding on Sofia's quiet time. Her best friends flew two thousand miles to be part of her quickie wedding—she was okay with the intrusion. Sofia opened her arms and welcomed her eccentric friend into her embrace. As they fell backward on the carpet, she listened to the funny airport and airplane encounters as Emma sat on one of the chairs.

Etienne joined the wild bunch. He sat on the bed and chit-chatted with Emma. When Sofia peeled herself off the floor, she got woozy and almost tumbled. Etienne instinctively leaped off the bed and caught her.

"What would you do without me?" He exclaimed. And when their energies met, a surge of electricity seared through their arms. They both let go.

What was that? I felt that right into my bones. Did you just shock yourself, my love?

She assured Jude it was nothing. But it was something. And her mind was abuzz with all the scenarios. When she tapped into her higher self, she only received. *You will soon understand. Don't worry about it. It will all make sense.*

Meanwhile, Emma had opened her suitcase and laid out Sofia's wedding options on the bed. While she coordinated the outfits, she turned to Sofia. "I picked out the clothes I know you love the most. Wanna try them on?"

Sofia spent the next few hours parading all the outfits with her friends. They yayed, they nayed, they laughed, and they bonded.

Are you having the wedding party without me?
Are you done with your things?
Not yet. I have one or two things left. I will see you soon.

"Okay, people, I need some time to write my vows. Also," —she turned to Etienne— "It's Jude's birthday, and I want to do something special."

"We ordered a cake for him," Etienne said. "It's all set up. Don't worry. He's not fussy about things like that. But we've got it covered."

She turned to Lola. "Did you get the painting for me?"

Lola pulled out a tube and handed it to her. Sofia had called her trusted artist friend and commissioned a painting of their sacred Malta spot.

Once alone, she cleared her mind, calming her senses, when a vision popped forth—Gabrielle dressed in a black wedding gown and Jude by her side. Sofia quickly tapped in, and her higher self reassured her it was only her ego making a play.

Then she heard Jude. *Hey, are you sure you're okay? I feel a tightening in your chest. I can come over right now.*

No, no, no. I just had a bad dream. No worries. Please get out of my head for the next thirty minutes. I love you.

She sat by the desk with paper and pen and plugged herself into her headphones to not get so distracted by the merrymaking happening downstairs. She tapped into her heart and composed her love story.

****

Lola and Emma accepted an invitation from Etienne to explore the Parisian nightlife.

Meanwhile, Jude and Sofia retired earlier than usual. Their higher selves instructed them to do so to get ready for integration. When they researched it, they came empty-handed in the process.

While the twin flames lay facing each other, a resonance of energy vibrated between their bodies. And in one graceful move, Jude hoisted himself up, simultaneously lifting Sofia. He then positioned himself in a lotus pose. Sofia mimicked him. He lay his palms facing upward and welcomed Sofia's hands in his. "Let's do this again, my love. We don't know what is going to happen tomorrow."

As Sofia slid her hands onto his, a sweeping wildfire of emotions erupted, sending glints of love, sadness, ecstasy, and anger through their energy centers. A crescendo of heat engulfed their bodies. They couldn't unclench themselves even if they wanted to. There was a unification occurring that was both foreign and natural to them. The never-ending surge surfed along the high-frequency waves in their bodies.

And when Sofia's higher self came in, she was told to relinquish all control to Jude. She was told the same directive was given to him. She lost all connection with him for a few moments and again was guided to calm down. *This is normal. We are reformatting and upgrading your DNA.*

Sofia momentarily lost her cool. *And I shouldn't be freaked out right now?* Her higher self had a sense of humor like Sofia. She heard heartwarming laughter and consoling words of affirmation.

When the electromagnetic currents abruptly stopped, she snapped open her eyelids. Jude was still consumed in his process, separate from hers. They advised her to stay locked in, no matter what emotions were to emerge from him. And when the deluge of tears rolled down his cheeks, she was advised. *Hold back and let him resolve them on his own.* Excruciating cries of pain echoed out of his lips as the energies ripped through his body. His eyes remained closed. Sofia felt helpless as she gripped on tight. Usually, she felt the pain but was feeling nothing. She panicked. *Sofia, we need you to breathe. He is fine. It's just his body. His soul is not feeling the pain. All will be well in a few minutes.*

She drew their symbols in her mind's eye. *Do the dragon and phoenix symbol over and over, my child.* And after nine drawings, he flipped open his eyelids. When they locked eyes, the sensation was remarkably familiar. Their souls fused as one, tears tumbling from his face.

Eventually, they were able to set themselves free. Jude bent forward, grabbed Sofia's face in his hands, and fastened his lips onto hers. She tasted the saltiness of his tears and the sweetness of his love.

He removed her nightgown and undressed as well. He delicately laid her on the bed and caressed every inch of her as if memorizing her body. His touch was spine-tingling but not overly erotic. His kiss was passionate but not carnal. His words were sentimental but not corny. His movement was vigorous but not erratic.

He took his time with her, drinking in every taste of her body, listening to every lyric of her mind, and reveling in every sensation of her soul.

****

When they woke, she gifted him his painting—a new set of tears streamed down his cheeks. He held on to her all morning, expressing his undying love for her. He filled her in on the acquisition of the home in Malta. All was going to plan except for the withholding of his trust fund. But Jude had enough money to put a down payment. He mentioned to her over and over that she needn't ever worry about money. "Malta will be our haven when we need to connect. It will be ours, always and forever. I can't wait to get the keys in hand."

It was hard not to be suspicious of his ramblings, but her higher self assured her that everything was running smoothly. And that he was just nervous about the big day. As he talked, she noticed the faded tattoo was no longer on his finger. She caught his finger in mid-air and brought it to his attention. "What the eff is happening here? Where did it go?"

He inspected it closer and said, "I didn't notice." He brushed it off and whispered, "It doesn't matter. It's probably the alkaline in my body that's affecting it."

Sofia made a face but chose not to dive into that one. She was getting nothing from her higher self, so she dropped it. He mapped out the day. When he told her what time Pierre set up their wedding, they both smiled. "Do you think he knows about angel numbers?"

"He must know something. Who else would book the ceremony at 4:44?"

When they went downstairs for breakfast, a feast of chocolate chip pancakes, fruits, and chocolate croissants was laid out for the birthday boy. They sang, he blew out the candles, they ate, and they enjoyed each other's company. Jude was outwardly affectionate with Etienne. And equally so with Lola and Emma. When Yolande bustled in, he invited her to join the love fest.

*****

Sofia admired her reflection in the mirror as Lola and Emma helped her dress on her wedding day. Last night, something unprecedented happened between her and Jude, yet she had no words to convey her feelings about it to her friends. Instead, she regaled in the light-heartedness that they brought to her life.

When Emma helped slip on the jewel-toned green lace dress over Sofia's head, Emma was careful not to snag it with her jewelry. Their initial thought was to coil her hair into a bun on her head, but Jude requested only one thing from her—to keep her hair down with its natural waves. They rifled through Sofia's jewelry pouch for the right pieces when, at the corner of her eye, she noticed Lola tap Emma on her arm and mouth something to her. Emma nodded her head and turned to Sofia. "I believe Jude has something for you."

Another gift from my beloved.

Jude walked in, right on queue. The girls scurried off to their rooms. He eyed his future wife and softly purred, "Oh la la, you look radiant," as he grazed his hand down her backside.

Dressed in military blue fitted pants and a crisp white shirt, he always looked sublime in Sofia's eyes. He whispered in her ear, "Close your eyes, my love."

He took one of her hands and gently fanned each finger out, and then she felt a pointed object settle at the base of her palm. It was slightly cold to the touch. When she snapped open her eyes, there sat her mother's pendulum. She encased her treasure with the other hand and brought it to her heart. Staring wide-eyed at Jude, Sofia fought back the tears, but they won.

"How? Where?" were the only words she was able to eke out.

Jude wiped her cheeks and disclosed that Gabrielle had texted him a photo of the pendulum a few days after the incident with Sofia and Lennon. He met up with her in private to retrieve it.

"Is this wedding morning confession time? Should I be worried?"

Jude lifted her chin and peered into her eyes. "Seriously? You don't know how hard it was for me to do that, especially when your injury was fresh in my mind. I had to bite the bullet for you, Sofia." He rolled his eyes and let out a heavy sigh. "I didn't want anything more than retaliating, but my focus was the pendulum, and I did what I had to do."

Slinking her arms around his waist, she drew his body closer. His heart was heavy; she felt it in the depth of her soul. "Thank you. Thank you. Thank you. I know how difficult that must have been for you, my love. I owe you the world."

He stepped back and shook his head. "No. You owe me nothing. If anything, I owe you for putting up with all the terror she has put you through. Never say that. Do you hear me?"

He unclenched her fingers and pulled out the pendulum. "May I have the honors?" He fastened it around her neck and let the pendulum hang down her open back.

As they stood in front of the mirror, she noticed changes in their appearance. Her hair was lighter. His eyes were more transparent. Her skin was flawless. His complexion was getting paler. They acknowledged the changes in their minds but didn't have a chance to delve deeper into them when a knock at the door interrupted them.

Etienne stood there staring at them. His lips were moving, but she couldn't make out his words. They seemed to be fading further and further away. She squeezed Jude's hand and asked, *Can you hear him?*

No. I thought I was going crazy. But he is standing in front of us, right?

Meanwhile, Etienne snapped his fingers in front of the telepathic couple. It took a few minutes for both of them to hear the snapping. When Jude came to, he pointed his finger at his friend and twisted his head toward Sofia. "What the heck was that?"

She was just as dumbfounded as her husband-to-be.

Etienne furrowed his brows. "You guys are getting crazier by the day. It kinda makes me feel too normal now!"

Jude rested his hand on Etienne's shoulder. "Normal, you will never be, my friend! So, what can we do for you?"

Etienne stood there looking very refined with burgundy fitted pants and a white shirt. "I picked something up for you guys in Malta, knowing you would marry one day. I didn't think so soon because I would probably have expanded on the gift, but I found it in the market. It spoke to me. And I liked the vendor's energy as well."

From behind his back, he pulled out the metal box the older man had shown them made by his daughter Esmerelda. Sofia stumbled backward, and Jude caught her. He held on to her as they collected themselves. Their reaction stupefied Etienne. "Am I missing something here?"

Jude explained the story to him. Etienne, too, had to take a moment to gather his composure. He then looked into Sofia's eyes. "Nothing is a coincidence, right, Sofia?" He thought a little more about his interaction with the man. "You know, I should have known it was you he was talking about. He had mentioned that he hoped the couple he served earlier would have bought it. But, he then peered into my eyes and said, 'I have a feeling they will get it anyway.' Of course, I was clueless, and my German friend also distracted me. " He snickered and handed over the box to them. "I thought this would be nice to keep your rings in for the ceremony."

LOVE YOU. LOVE ME.

I love you. You love me. I love you. You love me.
You love me. I love you. You love me. I love you.
I love you. You love me. I love you. You love me.
You love me. I love you. You love me. I love you.
I love you. You love me. I love you. You love me.
You love me. I love you. You love me. I love you.
I love you. You love me. I love you. You love me.
You love me. I love you. You love me. I love you.
I love you. You love me. I love you. You love me.

45

The I-do's declared—the rings exchanged—the *Livret de Famille* (Family Booklet) issued. Jude and Sofia were "official" under the guise of the Matrix. No more Coco. No more Gabrielle. No more war.

The ceremony was conventional and systematic. Rows of couples lined the seats, waiting their turn for their 'happily ever after.' But there was nothing mediocre about Jude and Sofia. Their soul-level vows rendered applause from the other couples. Their energies outshined any banalities emerging from the mayor's lips. Their union forged a deeper connection between the twin flames.

The car ride to Guillaume's bistro overflowed with laughter and merriment. Jude, Etienne, and Lennon luxuriated in the festive moment by drinking bubbles and gossiping about the other couples and the officiants. The rest of the crew worked hard to set up the room and finalize the last-minute tasks. Sofia sat back and enjoyed them in their element. In the meantime, she sent her family some of the pictures from the civil ceremony. While she was online, notifications popped on her feed from Gabrielle. She debated whether to open them or not. Before going down that rabbit hole, Jude slipped his arm around her and said, *My love, join us as we celebrate our coming together.*

It wasn't hard to be swayed by his beguiling ways. A steady stream of vibrational waves replaced their electrical currents.

She rested her head on his shoulder. *I adore you. I'm so excited to spend the rest of my life with you. You are my everything.*

Me and you, it's forever. It is written in the stars, no matter how we end up together.

She lifted her head; something remarkable happened when she met his eyes. She transiently found herself in his body, looking out at the boys and herself. She immediately shut her eyes and called in her higher self. *Breathe, my child. All is well. Enjoy the festivities today. You are ready.*

46

Guillaume's welcoming embrace greeted them. Etienne and Lennon rushed past them, but Jude and Sofia were held back. Guillaume whispered, "You will be amazed at what this wonderful family has organized for you. You are much loved, and that is the best gift anyone could have in this life." He paused for a moment and then motioned them to the bar. "Come, sit, and have a drink with me. Let them prepare their finishing touches in peace."

The restaurant brimmed with locals and tourists alike. He opened a bottle of his finest champagne for the couple and shared it with his staff. As they clinked their glasses and rejoiced, Sofia noticed one of the servers give a side-eye to Guillaume. And when Guillaume turned to face them, he landed on Sofia's gaze. She raised her eyebrows and was about to inquire when he leaned in and, in a hushed voice, said, "I wasn't going to tell you, but it's best that I do before things get out of hand."

Jude didn't seem fazed by his declaration. Sofia, on the other hand, was not in the mood for any surprises. *Don't worry, my phoenix, whatever he has to tell us. There is nothing we can't handle.*

"Two days ago, the Queen of the French Riviera blessed us with a visit," Guillaume began. "I hadn't seen her in quite a while. So, we got to drinking and talking about the past when one of my servers made the mistake of mentioning your wedding party to Coco." He roughly wiped his face and continued, "She jumped right on that one, asking for all the details."

Jude and Sofia glared at him.

"No, don't worry, I didn't say a word. I denied everything. But we all know how clever she is. I just wanted you to know that Coco is privy to this feast. God knows what she will try to concoct but rest assured, we will not let her in."

Jude placed his hand on Guillaume's shoulder and consoled him. "No worries, my friend. My mother had been too quiet these past few days. I knew she was up to something. Today, my only concern is eating good food by yours truly, enjoying the company of my friends and," — he draped his arm around Sofia— "showing this woman how much I treasure her."

Sofia felt her cheeks redden. Guillaume raised a glass to Jude and shared a moment with his longtime friend. Meanwhile, Sofia delved into her own bout of concern. But Jude quickly swooped in and reassured her, *There's nothing she can do to tear us apart. We are married now. We are one.*

And just like that, an influx of loving energy traversed through her body. She remained in that state for the length of time with Guillaume.

Guillaume received the approval by text and beckoned the twin flames to follow him. "Come, I will take you up there myself. I'm curious to see what they have designed. They had some unusual requests." He snuck his head past the kitchen's swinging doors and shouted orders at his staff. Guillaume then escorted them outside and around to the back of the restaurant. "It's easier from here." The narrow alleyway led them to a back door.

Once the door was unlocked and opened, a tsunami of white starry lighting lit up the darkness. The abundance of lights flabbergasted Guillaume. Jude and Sofia felt right at home. With each step upward, they basked in the downpour of illumination. When Sofia turned back to look at Jude, she saw a sphere of glowing light.

"Are you sure our family is here? It's too quiet."

Both Guillaume and Jude chuckled. Jude added, "It won't take them long. Wait for it." As the words spilled from his lips, they heard Etienne shushing Lennon. "Like I said."

Guillaume held them back again. "One second, let me just check."

While he did, Sofia held out her hands to Jude. "It's so surreal, my love, that we find ourselves here—married by law and soon to be integrated by soul."

He swept her in his arms. "Always and forever, my phoenix." He planted a passionate kiss on her lips. "I am you. You are me. Don't ever forget that."

Jude and Sofia entered a magical wonderland. The glass-encased room built on the restaurant's rooftop burned light through the night sky. Orange and red fairy lighting coiled around tall, grassy shrubs. Long-stemmed dark orange and red roses hung from the ceiling and over the table in the center of the room. The left-over dragon-themed accessories from New Year's appeared as accents throughout. "Eternal Flame" by the Bangles streamed out of the speakers.

Lennon ran over to his newly appointed parents, repeating, "This is all for you! Do you like it?"

Etienne made his way through and hugged them. "You deserve every inch of this lighting because you are the light." He winked at Sofia.

Michel was next to congratulate the two. As poised and humble as ever, he took them in their arms and whispered, "There is no amount of decor or celebration to describe how much I love you both." He then waved Etienne and Lennon into the embrace and exclaimed, "You are the joys of my life."

And the tears began so early on in the night. Jude responded reverently and remained in his father's embrace longer than usual. She snuck away and found her way toward Lola and Emma, anxiously waiting by the sideline. While she hugged them and thanked them for their exquisite attention to detail, she waved to Yolande and Xavier; they were both accompanied by their partners.

As the twin flames mingled with everyone, servers rolled in with plates of food, setting them down on the golden charger plates. Guillaume summoned the guests to their seats and directed the servers to stand by him. He parted heartfelt words to the couple. He then thanked Lola and Emma for turning his place into a fairytale. While the servers popped a few champagne bottles and poured the bubbly, he wished them all a pleasant evening.

The first plate was a yin and yang shaped soup, one side tomato red, the other side pumpkin orange. Sofia turned to Emma, "Did you help with the menu?"

"You betcha I did. Perfection is my middle name. Speaking of which, would you like to indulge the table with details of your ceremony?"

Sofia gladly chronicled their experience. Etienne and Lennon didn't take long to jump in and elaborate. Jude remained silent as he relished in their storytelling ways. When he wasn't eating, he was flattering Sofia with affection.

The medley of personalities at the table kept them entertained all night long. Jude and Sofia sat back and cherished every moment.

We have the most amazing family and friends, mon amour. He looked over at Sofia and eyeballed her. *Can you please stop thinking about her? Whatever she does can never take away this unforgettable evening from us.*

Sofia nodded.

When we integrate, will he still listen to my thoughts? She tried to tap into her higher self but got nothing.

They rolled in the wedding cake—a simple three-tier cake with an impressive hand-painted phoenix and dragon entwined around the cake.

Lennon teased, "If you're a dragon and she's a phoenix, what does that make me?"

Jude reached over and patted his blond curls. "Whatever you want to be, my son."

They cut the cake. They took the photos. Joy abounded.

And then they heard a loud stomping noise climbing the stairs. Jude immediately said, *And so it begins.*

Sofia was not going to have his mother ruin this night for Jude. She rushed to the door and whipped it open, only to come face to face with a winded Pierre. Leaning on his cane, he managed to eke out a smile. Jude appeared behind her and exclaimed, "Do what do we owe this pleasure?"

Jude reached over to help him, but Pierre kindly waved him away and handed over his briefcase. "Thank you, but I need to try to walk more. This is a good lesson for me." He patted down his hair and adjusted his tie.

They accompanied him into the room. Michel swiftly came to his feet, rushed over, and greeted his old friend. Once settled in his chair, he scanned the table. When his gaze landed on Lennon, Pierre's demeanor changed from grumpy to contentment. He smiled at Lennon and militarily saluted him. Lennon returned the salute. And when he turned to Jude for approval, he was met by the eyes of a proud father.

Pierre then reached into his briefcase and pulled out a stack of documents. He said, "I hope you don't mind me intruding, but I wanted to personally deliver these papers to you as a wedding gift from me to you." He handed over a pen to each Sofia and Jude and said, "Once you sign, it will be official."

They signed the papers. Thanks to Pierre's connections, Sofia and Jude married and became parents in one day. The festivities continued. They fed Pierre and welcomed him into the family. There was a tender moment between him and Lennon, which happened organically.

Life was falling into place for Jude and Sofia.

It was all great until it wasn't.

DRAGON

One love. Two flames.
One soul. Two flames.
One breath. Two flames.

47

Their efforts to ignore the commotion outside the door were futile. When Michel recognized the voice, he leaped off his chair.

Jude stretched his hand in the air and sneered. "Papa, let me handle her. It's my wedding 'Thank you' to the family." He turned to face Sofia. He feathered his fingers through her waves and whispered, "You are the best thing that has happened to this family and me. This ends here." He endearingly kissed her, then stood up from his chair and announced to the table, "Thank you to everyone for making this day extraordinary for both me and my love. You all truly hold a special place in our hearts. I apologize for the raucous ensuing in the next few minutes." He then turned to Pierre. "Your daughter will accompany her. Would you like to exit from the other door?"

Pierre shook his head. "Thank you for thinking of me. I need to see this with my own eyes to understand better all your family has endured." He winked at Michel. "It will help your case."

As Jude marched to the door, Sofia trailed him, but he appealed to her to stay put. "Please, my love. It's between my mother and me."

Relenting, she stood behind Lennon's seat. Guillaume was the first person at the door. In self-defeat, he apologized to Jude and the table for the interruption. Jude whispered in his ear and then heartwarmingly waved him away, just in time for Coco to make her grand entrance. Jude stood squarely in front of her. He did not say a word; he just stared. Sofia felt a squeezing in her chest.

Coco began her rant. "Why wasn't I invited? I am your mother. This is my family, too. You should not have gone behind my back. Things will get worse for you and your beloved wife. You take my power for granted, my son. But I have the money to crush you and ruin your future." And it went on and on. She didn't stop. Jude remained quiet. When she tried to get around him, he blocked her. She cried out for help to the very people that she shunned. No one moved.

Gabrielle lingered in the background, stuck between the doorway and the staircase. When Sofia caught her eyes, she seemed frightened and out of sorts. Etienne waved his hand before Sofia and warned her, "Remember who you're dealing with. Do not fall for their deceit." She acknowledged Etienne.

Coco carried on for a few minutes until she threw her arms around Jude. "*Je t'aime, mon fils* (I love you, my son). Everything I do is because you mean the world to me." When he did not respond, she pumped her fists against his chest and scolded him for being an ungrateful son. Still, Jude remained silent.

He spoke to Sofia. *Can you have Pierre call one of his police friends or someone to scare her off, please?*

She went over to Pierre and relayed the request. He patted her on the arm. "Already done. He's on his way."

She gripped his hand and whispered, "You are a good man, M. Lavigne."

He winked. "Pierre, to you. We are friends, remember?"

Sofia returned and wrapped her phoenix wings around the table to protect them from the lower vibrational energy leaking in. Then, Gabrielle made her move. Pierre perched his hand on his cane and tried to lift himself, but Sofia ensured that Xavier halted his movement.

The last battle was at play.

Dressed in an elegant black gown, Gabrielle slinked in front of Coco and coiled her arm around Jude. He peeled her arm off him and asked, "What are you doing?"

She pouted. "What do you mean what am I doing? Aren't we getting married today?" Confused, she looked back at Coco and then at Jude.

Crazy is as crazy does. These two are mad.

"It's too late. I'm already married to my only true love. You can go home now." She whined and wailed like a child. When she turned to Coco for validation, Jude smirked. "This woman cannot love anyone, especially not you." He leaned into Gabrielle's face and asked, "Is this how you want to live your life? Playing into the hands of this insane woman?" He shook his head. "You are a beautiful woman. You are smart. You have much to offer but are not mentally and emotionally well. It's time to take care of yourself. And I know who will help you—your father will."

His sensitivity and caring nature knocked her for a loop. Sofia was in awe of her dragon. Pierre shed a tear or two. Coco was not having it and twisted his words around to instigate Gabrielle. "He is a liar, just like his father, just like his wife. They are all liars, Gabrielle. The only person you can trust is me. I will take care of you. Your mother never loved you. And your father doesn't even know you're alive. I am the only one who loves you."

"*Ça soffit!* (Enough)," was the voice that echoed from the back of the room. It was the voice that silenced Coco. It was the voice that stunned Gabrielle. It was the voice that commandeered the subsequent few happenings.

Jude stepped aside for Coco and Gabrielle to witness the man now standing up with the help of his cane. Pierre hobbled over to his daughter. "First, I need to apologize to you, Gabri, for leaving you alone to contend with this woman." He sneered at Jude's mother. He returned to face his daughter. "I promise to devote the rest of my life to you. I will try to make up for all the years we lost." It didn't take much convincing for Gabrielle to fall into her father's arms.

Coco could not speak, for her status remained suspended with every word after that. But she tried anyway. "Pierre, I did everything I could to care for your daughter. Your wife rejected her, so I stepped in like any mother." She paused. Her devilish side flared. "Ever since Jude and Sofia befriended her, she's begun to act up."

He shook his head and pointed his cane at Coco. "Begone, woman. You are done. Are you blaming my late wife, your son, and daughter-in-law, too? The word will be out by morning that you are a home wrecker and an unstable woman. You can kiss your status goodbye."

She looked to Michel for help, but he kept his arms crossed and said, "I have saved you so many times, woman. I'm done with you. You are a disgrace to this family."

Meanwhile, Sofia found her way to Jude's side. The moment she slipped her hand into his, a flaming energy blazed right through them. They both acknowledged the sensation but remained still.

As Coco searched for someone to help her, she fell on vacant eyes. The scent of victory wafted in the air for a split second until she spotted another victim in her game. When she leered at Jude and darted toward Lennon, Jude let go of Sofia's hand and immediately pounced on her. Her mouth was already running off, "Yoohoo! Gabrielle, you want to guess who…"

She had nothing to lose, but Jude had so much to lose.

When he reached his mother, he grabbed her jacket, leaned in, and fixedly stared into her eyes. "Why must you be so evil? Do you have any ounce of love in your heart?"

She blankly stared at him. "No. You have taken my chance away from living the life of my dreams. And for what? So you could be married to a nobody?" She removed his grip on her and threatened him. "No more. Do you hear me? I will tell all, and you will continue to live a life of hell like you deserve."

Lennon slammed his fork on the table, startling everyone. He violently pushed out of his chair, stomped forward, and stood before his grandmother. As he towered over her, his resemblance to his father was uncanny. The Christofle's were men of few words when angered, but their actions spoke volumes. Jude kept a protective barrier around his son. Before she could make a sound, Lennon slapped her. The whole table gasped. Jude wasn't sure if he should reprimand him or laugh.

Sofia chuckled. *Well, that's one way to shut her up.*

Michel jolted from his chair but did not interfere. Instead, he journeyed right by Sofia. They were ready for whatever she had to say. But no one expected her to slap him back and screech, "You are just like your father—insolent and foolish."

Fury roared through the dragon. His eyes blazing with rage, Jude's temperament was deafening.

Etienne rose from his chair and tried to seize Coco in his arms, but she wormed her body out of his hold and shouted, "Do not touch me, you poor excuse of a man. Your mother was right to shun you. You have no spine, just like your father."

Etienne stood motionless—his eyes instantly welled up, and cheeks flushed beet red. She managed to silence everyone at the table with her vile words.

Coco didn't care and continued, "Just because my husband took you in doesn't mean you are part of my family. Now, sit down and leave this matter to us."

Jude swooped in. "*Tu es nul, maman. Nul.* (You are nothing, mother. Nothing). Etienne has shown more love to our family than you ever did."

Yolande thundered toward Coco. "Do not talk to him like that. You have no idea what it is to be a mother."

Coco shot right back, "And you do? You don't know love until you have children."

Jude clapped his hands and howled, "Bravo. And the Oscar goes to…Coco! You have no idea what that word is. Do not insult us."

She tightened her fists and pressed her lips together. She spoke under her breath.

"What did you say, Maman? Please share with us."

She struggled against her anger as she glared into her son's eyes. "You were not easy to love. You never listened to me. If you did, you would be married to Gabrielle, and we would have our place in society. But no, you had to make my life difficult. You made me work hard to keep my status. What kind of son does that to their mother?"

Jude's expression was priceless. As was everyone else's at the table. Jude rolled his eyes and waved her away. "I give up. From this day forward, you will never have any access to this family again, do you hear me? We are cutting you off, effective immediately." He glanced over at Pierre. "And thanks to Pierre, you will also have no dignity left in your precious community."

The last words struck fear into her heart. She panicked and grabbed whatever she could find on the table. When she waved the sharp wedding knife at her son, Sofia fearlessly stood in front of her.

"Put that down."

Coco sliced the air around Sofia. "Why are you not afraid of me, my dear? Do you deem yourself invincible? You would die in the place of my son?"

"Yes, I would." She narrowed her eyes at Coco. "This is love."

Sofia, can you step away from her? I don't trust her, my fiery phoenix.

Coco did not take too well to that comment and lashed out by grazing Sofia on the arm with the tip of the blade. She didn't react because the adrenaline was rushing through her body. But Jude did, and he charged toward his mother.

No one expected Coco to drive the knife into his body. No one expected to witness a fountain of red blood canvas Jude's white shirt. No one expected Jude's fiery dragon energy to extinguish so abruptly.

His last cry reverberated in the air, "Maman."

Coco dropped the knife and fell to the floor, "*Oh, mon Dieu.*" (Oh my God)

Sofia dropped to her knees, frantically called out for napkins, and applied pressure to the wound, but the bleeding was continuous. The harrowing wails and erratic movements all around her became a blur. She could no longer hear, see or feel anyone or anything. She became acutely aware of the brightness of the blood, the velvety sensation of it as it trickled down her fingers, and the fragrant aroma as it lingered under her nose. The muffled cries behind her fluttered in the background. Jude's heart raced at lightning speed, and then, as the rhythm slowed down, she felt his strong fingers clench her wrist. He eked out, "It's time. This is it, my love."

Her higher self kicked in. *He's right. Get ready. It will be beautiful, you will see.*

Beautiful? This is not what I signed up for. Jude, you cannot leave me. Please, my love. You are my everything. No, you cannot go this way.

I can't live without you. No!!! No!!! No!!! I can't do this alone. Please, don't leave me. I'm not ready. This is not fair.

She held on to him and wailed, "No. Jude. Not this way. How am I supposed to live without you by my side?"

Sofia escaped her inner torment when she heard Lennon echo the exact words to his father, "No. No. No. It was not supposed to be this way." He rocked back and forth while holding onto Jude. "I love you. You can't leave me now. I need you now more than ever." Jude managed to relay his love by feebly squeezing Lennon's hand.

Etienne had no words. His expression was lifeless. He could only watch as he lay one hand on his best friend's leg. Michel howled as he wiped away any blood on Jude's face. He bent over and kissed his son's forehead. Gabrielle found her way and knelt in a prayer position with her head in her hands. She apologized over and over again. Lola and Emma whimpered in the background. Xavier wept, holding onto Michel.

And then it happened. A glowing light swelled out of Jude's body. Yolande rushed over and said, "I'm here for you. I've been waiting."

Sofia flashed her eyes between tears at Yolande in bewilderment, but she didn't have time to ponder her words when the warm glow descended around her and encompassed her in a bubble of pure ecstasy. And then Jude appeared before her eyes. He wasn't hurt or bleeding. Jude was luminous. He was sitting cross-legged with his palms facing her as he had done the night before. He asked, *Are you ready for our souls to merge, my love? It's how we planned it all along. We will forever be one. Now repeat after me, I will accept his heart and soul as my own. We merge as one.*

When she repeated the words, a flaming dragon and phoenix swirled around them and through them. The two mythical creatures chased each other until they eventually fused into one infernal beam of energy. Then a reel of images from their past, current, and future lives scrolled through her mind in a flash. His life experiences were now her life experiences. His memories were now her memories. His emotions were now her emotions. And when the final moments of integration occurred, she felt compelled to chant, "I call to the Divine in Jude to merge with the Divine in me. I call to the Divine in me to fuse with the Divine in Jude. I call to the Divine to protect us. I call to the Divine to heal us. I call to myself as I am the Divine. And so it is."

When she came to, she was holding Jude's lifeless body in her arms, and then she heard, *I'm still here, mon amour. You will have me in your head and your heart, always and forever.*

She placed a gentle kiss on his glacial lips. *What happened to all the fire inside you, my dragon?*

It's inside you now, my love.

She laid his head on the ground and lifted herself from the floor. Still, she was in a daze. Still, she was in a bubble of light. Still, she felt him blazing inside her.

When she feasted her eyes on the tragedy before her, she felt a profound sadness emanating from everyone else. She didn't have much time to gather her emotions when Lola and Emma embraced her in their arms. Emma took great care to wipe Sofia's blood-stained hands as much as possible. She instructed Sofia to lift her arms as Emma removed the lace part of the dress over her head. Sofia clutched onto her friend's arm and insisted she not discard the dress.

Why am I not feeling grief-stricken? Why am I feeling profound love? Can someone explain this to me?

Jude popped in. *It's my love for you that you are feeling. And it will forever be part of you. I will do my best to engulf you with my burning love every day.*

Two paramedics knelt beside his body and finally covered him with a sheet. Seated in the far corner with an oxygen mask, Coco acted out her final role as the drama queen. Pierre chatted with police officers. Yolande comforted Etienne. Michel comforted Lennon. Gabrielle lay in a fetal position on the ground.

Sofia felt Gabrielle's suffering and remorse in the depths of her soul, so she pried herself out of her friend's arms and made her way to Gabrielle. She lay beside her on the floor. Sofia placed her hand over Gabrielle's and whispered, "This is not your fault. Get the help you need. Your father is a good man. Jude always cared about you."

Gabrielle's lips trembled. "It makes sense now why Jude picked you. I'm sorry for all the hurt I have caused him and you."

Etienne knelt beside Sofia. "Come with me." He helped her up and motioned to Lennon to do the same. The three of them went onto the rooftop and huddled on a wooden crate. When she looked up, the Sirius blue star shone brightly in the night sky. And as she stared upward, flecks of cottony white snow sprinkled onto her cheeks, making for a magical wedding night.

"He is home now." She enveloped Lennon in her arms as he wept. Etienne draped his arm around the two of them. Looking into Etienne's eyes, she whispered, "This was the plan all along. Jude is still with me. He's still with us."

Etienne sobbed but grumbled, "Well, can you tell him it wasn't cool to leave this way? But his dramatic death outshined Coco any day of the week."

Etienne masking sadness with humor was expected. Sofia, he will need you in the next few weeks. Be patient with him, my love.

Etienne continued, "And when all this is over, you must tell us what happened between you because it freaked us out. As you can imagine, Coco yelled, 'I knew she was a witch. What is she doing to my boy?' Thankfully, Yolande was there to calm everyone else down as she gave us a briefing of what was occurring in a '3D' kind of way, as you would say. Was that the integration you had been talking about?"

Sofia nodded and then relayed a message from Jude to Etienne. "Jude says, 'Ti Ti, keep your mind open, and you will be amazed at what Sofia will share with you. And now that I have left you with the best prize, treat her well."

Etienne's face went completely blank. "That's what he used to call me back when I first met him." He wiped his nose and eyes with his sleeve. "Jude truly is with us." He combed through Lennon's curls and said, "Did you hear that? He's still here but in a better-looking package."

Etienne managed to get a smile out of Lennon, but it was understandable that the grieving process would take time. After all, he witnessed his father die at his grandmother's hands. Their job would be delicate, but Sofia was well prepared for it. She volunteered on earth to assist her fellow souls through the transition phases, and that's precisely what she would do.

When they were getting ready to wheel the love of her life away, it hit her—she would never see him again. She asked Lennon if he wanted to say goodbye one last time to his father. He stared blankly at her with tears plastered all over his cheeks. She looked at Etienne; he shrugged his shoulders. She grabbed them by the hands and urged them to follow.

She uncovered the sheet and canvassed Jude with kisses, having the privilege of hearing him exchange sweet nothings with her. She removed his necklace and wedding ring. Lennon lay on his father for one last time, uncontrollably sobbing and mumbling words to himself. Etienne knelt, his pale face staring at Jude. Michel rushed over, kissed his boy, and then reluctantly covered him with the sheet. Lennon would not have it and yelled at his grandfather for doing that. When Michel wrapped his arms around Lennon, he punched, kicked his way out of the embrace, and resumed his position. The paramedics were getting antsy, but Etienne and Sofia blocked them to allow Lennon the appropriate time he needed. The energies were dense with a fluctuation of highs and lows.

There were tears, there were wails, but mostly there was disbelief. The silence of death hung over their heads.

When the paramedics finally wheeled him away, Sofia collapsed on the floor in tears.

I am here, my love. I am here. Do not cry. I am here with you. I will be with you until the end of time.

Still, she cried because she would never have the chance to feel his touch again. Still, she cried because she would never have the chance to kiss him again. Still, she cried because she would never have the chance to look into his mesmerizing sea-greens again.

Michel mourned the loss by stepping outside onto the rooftop and wailing into the wintery night. Both Lennon and Etienne joined him. As they huddled outdoors, Sofia collected herself indoors with the help of her best friends.

When they heard Guillaume's cries from the bottom of the stairs, tears flowed once more down everyone's faces.

When Michel made his way back in, he barrelled right to his wife, who was being cared for by a paramedic. He yelled at the top of his lungs, "Can you remove this insane woman from our sight? She murdered my son. Why is she still here? If you don't take her away, I will throw her off the roof myself."

Coco pleaded with him and begged him for forgiveness. As Sofia observed her, she felt her malevolent energy rise in her soul. And when Coco caught sight of Sofia, she reverted to her maniacal self. "It's her. She's the one who killed him with her spells. It's not me; it's her."

Try not to listen to her, my love. She will pay for her crime. She will have many years of silence ahead of her. And she will come back into her heart.

Michel raised his hand to slap her, but Pierre stopped him in mid-air. "She's not worth it. She will get what she deserves, old friend." Michel reluctantly pulled back but incessantly yelled to have her removed from the scene.

Pierre ordered one of the cops to take her out of the room. Her lawyer was already on the scene pleading self-defense and trying to find a way to implicate Sofia, but Pierre did not have it.

When Guillaume made it up the stairs, he stood in the doorway and stared at the blood-stained spot where Jude took his last breaths. His face streaked with tears; he fell into Michel's arms and wept for the loss of his dear friend.

Once the police, lawyers, and paramedics left the scene, they all sat around the table and shared a few moments in sweet reverie of the man, the brother, the father, the friend, the son, and the husband they lost.

As for Sofia, the integration process was still in its final stages. She could feel the last fusions settling into her body. She may have lost Jude, but she gained the other half of her soul.

PHOENIX

One flame. Two loves.
One flame. Two souls.
One flame. Two breaths.

48

Every morning, Sofia stretched her arm out in search of Jude but came empty-handed. Every morning, she silently wept, missing the sound of his breathing. Every morning, she yearned for his sweet kisses.

That morning, she woke up with the glorious sun rays cascading throughout the room. She hopped out of bed and lingered by the window overlooking the turquoise sea. As they chattered away, Etienne and Lennon were piling logs and rocks near the fire pit below.

Jude chimed in. *Lennon is exactly like Etienne. They love hanging around and talking about nothing.*

Sofia looked at her watch. Lola and Emma were flying in from Portugal in the next hour. She went to her closet and stood before her clothes for a minute. She had been living in the same yoga pants and hoodie for nearly three months; it was time to look half decent. As her fingers grazed along the hangers, she fell on the dress she wore at the wedding. Still wrapped in the dry cleaners' plastic, it hung next to Jude's suit jacket made from the finest Vicuna.

Jude's faded tattoo miraculously appeared on Sofia's finger the night he died. There was too much fuss that night for anyone to notice. His dragon tattoo also cropped up on the side of her torso. Later, she told everyone that she got both tattoos in honor of him—a white lie seemed easiest at the time.

She slipped on her black jeans with her off-the-shoulder teal knit sweater that Jude loved. And then she wrapped one of his cashmere scarves around her neck.

Mornings in May were still coolish. Sofia prepared hot tea and warmed up the pastizzi for the boys. She filled in her role as a mother quite naturally. She and Etienne remained the bestest of friends. He lived in the tower, while Sofia, Lennon, and Michel lived in the main house.

After Coco's conviction of involuntary manslaughter, Michel performed his last act of benevolence toward his wife. Instead of sending her to prison, they sent her to a detention center for the wealthy, where she would live out her days confined to a room with a comfortable bed and private bathroom. She wasn't allowed visitors for the first five years. No one intended to visit her, anyway. Her house was sold in a record-breaking time due to her notoriety. Coco finally got her wish—she was the talk of the town, even if it was in a sick and twisted way. She never had time to finalize the termination of the trust funds to her sons, so Jude took care of the house in Malta.

Sofia met with Pierre and secured Lennon's trust fund under his name. Any leftover money from Jude's trust fund would also go to Lennon. He informed her that Jude had included Sofia in his last testament the day they had gone for Lennon's custody. She remembered getting into a conversation with Jude:

You are a sneaky one, my dragon.

Did you think I was going to leave you high and dry? I know you have your own money. But if you are me now, you must get used to living as I did.

At that meeting, Pierre presented her with handwritten letters from Jude for Michel, Lennon, Etienne, and Yolande. He then handed Sofia two more letters, one for her eyes only and the other for everyone. Pierre told her that Jude had also left him a letter, as well as his daughter. If she wished to read Gabrielle's letter, she could do so. But Sofia refused.

Much to Etienne's dismay, she stayed in touch with Gabrielle after the loss. She reached out to Pierre once a week, and when Gabrielle wasn't depressed, Sofia made an effort to talk to her. It's what Jude would have done.

Before leaving France, Sofia met up with Yolande to hand her letter in person and to better understand her role in their integration. Yolande explained that she had received messages about the twin flame integration years before. She didn't know it was going to be Jude and Sofia.

Sofia asked, "Were you given any other instructions?"

"Only that I would be needed to facilitate it—it was part of my mission. But we still have much work to do." She reached over and laid her hand on Sofia's shoulder. "We have been working together for lifetimes, my dear. It's not over yet."

Sofia planned to hand over the letters to all of them later that night. It hadn't been an easy ride for anyone. Jude was the leader of the pack, and with him gone, they looked to her to take on the leadership role. And she took on her part very seriously, too.

She relied on Pierre for all the legalities. She relied on Michel for the bureaucratic nonsense she had no patience for in France and Malta. She relied on Etienne to help her with the day-to-day. Sofia made sure Lennon lived as everyday a life as any teenager. She was her usual self, but when she had to put her foot down, she did it in a way that would make her mother proud.

"Where is your grandfather?" she asked Lennon.

"He's out and about, looking for rocks and shells, old man stuff!" He rocked his head back and let out a laugh. It had been weeks since he smiled, let alone laughed.

Their transition to Malta was smoother than she had expected. Lennon willingly left Paris behind. Jude always said he would adapt well to island life—his father knew best. He had already made a group of friends, and there were already a few love interests to keep his mind busy from the tragic loss of his father. There were highs and many lows, but Sofia was well-trained in dealing with tragedy. She made sure to keep the communication lines open at all times.

They decided to commemorate Jude every 17th of the month—this being the third one since his departure from the Earth plane. It felt like forever, and sometimes it felt like yesterday. Often, Etienne would talk vicariously to Jude through Sofia. Lennon was not ready for that part just yet. Michel would ask a few questions here and there, but he, too, was heavily grieving the loss of his son and preferred to spend his days alone trekking in the Maltese terrain.

She hadn't spoken to Lola and Emma in over a month. It worked out well that they were on their bi-annual buying trip.

She always talked to Jude; it felt like they were in a long-distance relationship. But she innately knew she would see him one day. The veils were thinning around her, and the time was nearing when they would all one day see their passed-on loved ones. It could have been wishful thinking on her part. But she always retained her keen sense of intuition. It only intensified since the merge.

A few days ago, while she sat on their "spot," they had a serious conversation about her relationship with Etienne. Jude told her that one day she would be romantically involved with him. She didn't want to hear about it, but he told her their combined role as twin flames was to show Etienne the utmost love in this lifetime. He took care of the first half, and it was up to Sofia to take care of the second half.

She wasn't ready to contemplate it. Jude teased her about it in a loving way. Still, she let it go, knowing it would be so.

49

Sofia woke in complete darkness to a low whimpering outside her door. She rose and quietly stepped outside. Lennon lay in one of the hammocks with his hands behind his head. He was playing with Jude's pendant between his teeth. His teary eyes glistened amidst the orange and red hues of the sunset. She knelt by him and held one of his hands.

"It's the colors," he whispered, "They remind me of you and him, the dragon and the phoenix." He turned to Sofia."I've decided to take on the role of the dragon if you don't mind."

She got up and kissed him on the forehead. "He is very pleased with you taking over his role. His only request is that you don't make the phoenix too angry."

He smiled and asked, "Is it weird that he's always in your head?"

"He was always there even when he was alive." The word alive hit her hard, and she turned her head toward the sunset as a lone tear rolled down her face.

It was Lennon's turn to land on his feet and drape his arm around Sofia, much like his dad used to do. "We'll get through this together."

The bonfire party was getting started with Etienne and Lola weaving the funniest of tales. She grabbed Lennon's hand. "Shall we join the wild bunch?"

When Emma caught sight of Sofia, she squeezed her tightly. "How are you, my friend? I've been thinking a lot about you. I remembered what a trooper you were when your mom died, but this time, you know, you can rely on us a lot more, right?"

Sofia appreciated the tender words from her longtime friend. "Lola tells me you've met someone. When were you going to tell me about him?"

"She has such a big mouth, that girl!" She briefed her that he was a client who had just moved to Montreal from South Africa.

Sofia giggled. "So, not a Latin man?"

Emma's eyes twinkled. She smiled and blushed, "Nope. He's handsome and so worldly. I think you will like him. Maybe I can bring him the next time I come."

Lola interrupted and gave Sofia a big teddy-bear hug. She whispered, "I can't stop thinking about that night. How is everyone doing? How are you doing? I often dream about him. Does it mean he's trying to give me a message?"

What are you doing in her dreams, my dragon?

Are you jealous of a dead man? Lol! I go into her dreams to remind her to call you. I know when you are missing her.

Sofia relayed in her ear what he told her so Emma wouldn't get jealous. Lola smiled. "Tell him I love him. Next time, I will pay more attention and maybe talk back."

They sat around the blazing bonfire, watching the flames spark and pop. Michel joined them as well.

She commemorated this momentous day by sharing a message from Jude. "He wishes to simply say that he loves you dearly. And that he's always with you."

It didn't take much to render them all to tears. Sofia pulled out the letters tucked under her sleeve. "I kept this a secret from all of you, but when I finalized some papers with Pierre, he handed me over these letters that Jude wrote to all of us in the early morning before the wedding."

Lennon asked, "How did he know that he was going to di..leave us." They were all still struggling with the word "die" and "death."

"Well, do you remember the night he passed away and the light that shone all around him and me?"

He enthusiastically nodded.

"The night before our wedding, Jude and I had a moment where he went into a trance, and I believe at that moment, he was told about the fateful night. He didn't even tell me. And, I feel that it was not about the wedding, but his birthday played an important role in it."

I knew you would have figured it out, my love, so I didn't tell you.

"So, he knew he was going to leave us?" Lennon asked, having a hard time wrapping his head around this information.

Sofia reiterated from Jude, "Yes, he knew it was on his birthday. This is why he wrote these letters." She turned to face Michel. "He wants me to tell you that he chose not to tell you because it would have ruined the whole evening."

Michel replied, "It was ruined anyway. But he has a point. He was always a forward thinker, my son." The tears liberally gushed down his face.

She distributed the letters with instructions for each of them from her beloved.

Still giving me orders even from the other side. Sofia giggled.

You love it. Admit it.

Sofia remained standing and cleared her throat. "Ahem. There is one letter that he wants to be read aloud to us all." She turned to Emma. "And he wants you to read it. Because you will be the most eloquent of them all."

Flattered, she obliged and gently pulled it out of its envelope. When she unfolded it, she became teary-eyed but composed herself in the most Emma way and began:

To my crazy, loving family!

I have been sitting with pen in hand for about an hour. I do not share the same proclivities as Sofia does when expressing myself. But I need to recount the mind-blowing experience Sofia and I shared last night. Because not only will it change my life, but it will also significantly impact all of your lives.

When I sat facing my gorgeous phoenix, they revealed my physical death. I know it will be at the hands of my mother or Gabrielle. I know it will happen on my 37th birthday: 3+7=10, 1+0=1. As Sofia always explains in her videos, 1 is a new beginning.

At the moment of the epiphany, my body went into shock. I experienced a whirlwind of emotions, from heartbreak to sadness to disbelief. But, it was quickly replaced with abundant love and euphoria. All my lifetimes with you and Sofia scrolled through my mind and heart, and I absorbed all the emotions and events of millions of years in seconds. Next time Papa talks to you about Quantum anything, please listen.

Lennon proudly touched his grandfather's shoulder as Michel fought back more tears.

I was privy to a team of light-bodied beings surrounding me and Sofia. Sofia, your mother is indeed around you all the time. She has assisted me greatly in this transition.

Lola, Sofia, and Emma fought back the tears, but Emma forged on.

Everything just made sense. I learned that we all share parts of one soul. You heard right, my beloved. That is why we are so familiar with each other. We are all from the future. We've come to right the wrongs we've made in this past that we are reliving. That is why we love each other so dearly and sometimes painstakingly.

I am not dead, for I am a part of everyone listening to this letter—even Coco. God bless her soul. Like my beloved twin flame has always said, 'That is a 3D construct.' The only thing that has died is my physical vessel. My burning soul has merged with Sofia and fused with all of you. I am very much alive. Sofia is now my vehicle. Please, speak to her as you would me, for she will respond as me, for she is me.

Etienne, this message is for you: Please listen to her videos. Because then you can understand when we speak. Thank you for being my bestest friend. I love you, brother.

Etienne burst out into laughter amidst his tears.

The moment I clicked into my God-self, it was then that I realized how truly powerful we are and how we have forgotten that we are the light of this planet. We are the reason Gaia has ascended. We are the creators, the builders, and the innovators. We are everything.

Sofia, in that instance, I was transported back to when we would say, 'I am you, and you are me.' It was from remembrance because I am you, my love.

Hearing Jude's words from Emma's lips made his death more real for Sofia. She lifted her knees into her chest, hid her face in her crossed arms, and sobbed.

Lennon, I know you think you are more clever than us. But please pay close attention to Sofia, Etienne, and Michel. They are wise, and their decisions will always be in your best interest. I wish I had more time to spend with you as father and son, but we had plenty of quality time as brothers. I love you.

Lennon blushed, smiled, and cried in a matter of seconds.

Michel, my patient and caring father, I love you so much.

It didn't take long for Michel to break down again.

I look forward to watching you and Sofia dive into research together. You two will come up with excellent content for her viewers. You two will become the best of friends you have been in your past lifetimes. One day, we will discuss it. Love you, Papa. I'm so grateful for all your unconditional love.

This message is to Lola and Emma.

Emma choked back some tears. She took her eyes off the letter for a moment. When she collected herself, she continued:

You are Sofia's pillars. The three of you all need each other. Please find a way to put away the bickering because you are more potent together. Lola, you are a bright shining star, and I am blessed to have met you. You are a loyal friend; in my books, that is the best trait any friend could have. Continue being that bright light. It will serve you well in the future. Emma, I love your quiet and contemplative demeanor. Please do not change who you are. Sofia and Lola may take up more space than you, but your presence is just as far-reaching. Thank you for holding Sofia up when she is down. Thank you for showing her the love that she deserves. Thank you both for joining our family. We love you and appreciate you.

Etienne, Lennon, and Michel clapped and shouted, "Yes. We agree." Lola got up and curtsied. Emma smiled.

And finally, Sofia. Two things: 1. Please continue your videos. Once we integrate, I will have plenty of insight for you to share with everyone. 2. You will be hard on yourself for not being the best you can be for Etienne, Michel, and Lennon but know that just being there is enough for them. All they need is your devotion, your love (and much of your guidance).

This is not a coincidence that you find yourselves altogether in this way. It is all part of your blueprint. We will get through this as we've gotten through our past lifetimes. Plus, I am here for all of you. As long as Sofia is on the Earth plane, so am I.

P.S. Lennon, when the day comes that you choose to take on the role of the dragon, I will stand by you proudly, my son.

Lennon shouted out, "I just told Sofia this right now." His giddiness put a smile on everyone's faces.

Emma cleared her throat. "Wait, there's more."

You are quite the letter writer, my dragon, Sofia conveyed to Jude.

Oh, and one last thing! In the coming days, you should receive the final book with the meaning of our last symbol. I was told what it meant last night. Are you ready? Sit down if you are standing, my love. Sacred Union.

And sacred, it is indeed. When my Divine Masculine merged with your Divine Feminine, Sofia, we made a choice as souls because we knew that humanity would experience the miraculous shift of Ages. The Divine Masculine ruled the Age of Pisces. But, now that the Golden Age of Aquarius is upon us, it is time to honor the Divine Feminine as she is the full embodiment of the New Earth.

50

Every morning at 7:17 am, Sofia made her way to their spot and sat at the cliff's edge. She breathed in the salty morning air. She welcomed the luminous embrace of the sun. And she listened to the stillness of her heart.

Every morning, Jude and Sofia shared a tender moment as she read a page from one of his many journals. He was her advisor when she sought counsel. He was her light when the darkness settled in. He was her one true love, and he was there for her, always and forever.

Every morning, Etienne joined her. He brought her a hot cup of water with lemon and honey. He brought her the extra blanket she always forgot. He brought her the physical comfort she cherished.

> I am light. You are light.
> I am one. You are one.
> I am you. You are me.

About the Author

Meet Sabrina Dinucci: A Montreal-Based Tarot Card Reader, Akashic Records Reader, and Spiritual Advisor known for her unfiltered guidance. She works as a Content Creator by day, but in Quantum time, she connects with her higher self, dragons, and soul family. When she's not admiring sunsets, singing out loud and out of tune to her favorite music, storytelling and traveling the world, she is just BEING. Her soul journey led her to write her first book, *I Am You. You are Me.*

Connect with her:
www.sabrinadinucci.com
IG: iam.you__youare.me
YT: We Love Divine Tarot
E: sabrinadinucciauthor@gmail.com

Printed in Great Britain
by Amazon